SWEET LEMONS

SWEET LEMONS

FIDELMA KELLY

POOLBEG

This book is a work of fiction. The names, characters, places, businesses, organisations and incidents portrayed in it are either the product of the author's imagination or are used fictitiously. Any resemblance to actual persons, living or dead, events or locales is entirely coincidental.

Published 2021 by Poolbeg Press Ltd
123 Grange Hill, Baldoyle
Dublin 13, Ireland
www.poolbeg.com
Email: info@poolbeg.com

© Fidelma Kelly 2021

The moral right of the author has been asserted.

© Poolbeg Press Ltd. 2021, copyright for editing, typesetting, layout, design, ebook

A catalogue record for this book is available from the British Library.

ISBN 978178199-722-2

All rights reserved. No part of this publication may be reproduced or transmitted in any form or by any means, electronic or mechanical, including photography, recording, or any information storage or retrieval system, without permission in writing from the publisher. The book is sold subject to the condition that it shall not, by way of trade or otherwise, be lent, resold or otherwise circulated without the publisher's prior consent in any form of binding or cover other than that in which it is published and without a similar condition, including this condition, being imposed on the subsequent purchaser.

www.poolbeg.com

About the Author

Fidelma Kelly is from Dublin. An English Literature & M.Phil. graduate of Trinity College, Dublin, she has worked in education, opera, PR and property. A fluent French and Italian speaker, she has spent extended periods in both countries, particularly in her beloved Sicily. In 2017, she was one of twelve finalists in the Irish Writers' Centre Novel Fair. Previous work has been shortlisted for the RTÉ Radio 1 Francis MacManus Short Story Award competition and she has contributed features to the *Irish Times* and the *Sunday Business Post Magazine*.

Sweet Lemons is her first novel.

Acknowledgements

To my publisher Paula Campbell for having faith in me, and the team at Poolbeg Press, particularly Gaye Shortland for her forensic editing.

I have been writing a long time. Thank you to those who offered invaluable insights in workshops or read material along the way: Ita Daly, Patricia O'Reilly, Jonathan Williams, Susan Elderkin, Sheila O'Flanagan, Hugo Hamilton, Conor Kostick, Catherine Dunne and Lisa Harding.

To my friends in the opera world, for the opportunity of working alongside you and the privilege of watching you work: David Collopy, Majella Cullagh, Marco Guidarini and Dieter Kaegi.

To my personal circle – writers and non-writers – who listened to yet another plot idea, offered feedback and encouragement, linguistic, IT and word-processing advice, or just practical help with printing off submissions when I was out of the country: Daniela Crowe, Ethel Dwyer, Una Kelly, Margaret Meehan, Anna Noone, Ciara O'Shea, Sîan Quill, Ester Tossi and Karen Whelan.

To the communities in Blackrock, Rosslare and Nice who afforded me the time and space to write, not forgetting the wonderful, rich location of Cefalù, Sicily, which inspired me to write this book.

Finally, to my parents, John and Maura, who in their ninety-fifth year, are not fully aware of the joy of this publication, but who always had my back on the journey.

For John P & Maura

Chapter 1

Hotel Panoramico, Cefalù, Sicily

This was not the way it was supposed to be. The impulsive decision to pack several bags and take two flights southwards to a sunnier clime had promised a healing balm for her battered ego. Away from the familiarity of Dublin she would blossom, and her novelty value as a foreigner was sure to guarantee an incessant stream of exotic cocktails delivered to her table by mysterious strangers in search of an introduction, a mild flirtation, an easy lay. That, at least, was the theory.

Instead, she had in the main been left to her own devices. Despite the polite but politically correct friendliness of the hotel staff, Isabelle had scarcely shared more than a couple of sentences with anybody since her arrival.

'You're depressed,' the GP had said. 'It's like a bereavement, only with no dead body. Take a break – as far away as possible. Challenge yourself to something different.

You'll use up so much energy trying to cope that you won't have time to feel sad.'

She had taken his advice. Now, following a third day spent sunbathing in an old man's deckchair on the hotel's concrete bathing platform, she was standing in this Sicilian bathroom, examining the results of her labours. The white stripes which punctuated her pink stomach surely suggested the presence of unwanted rolls of flab. Or maybe it was the fault of the deckchairs? Why couldn't they have regular sunbeds like other civilised resorts? At least, stretched out, she could *pretend* to have a flat stomach and it would minimise the resultant stripey tan.

She never used to be hypercritical about her appearance. She knew she was carrying surplus weight – it wasn't anything to panic about. But recently she had begun to scrutinise herself with others' eyes, startled by the realisation that while she was busy living, somehow one year had lurched into the next and now – suddenly – she was freewheeling downhill towards her thirty-third birthday. From the evidence of this bathroom mirror, the first flush of sensuous girly youth had well and truly passed.

Perhaps she was just being over-critical since she felt so exposed – flying solo in a hotel teeming with happy couples. This was not her first holiday alone. Once – between men – and on an occasion when her female friends were *with* men – she had ventured abroad among the odd consortium of waifs and strays which populate a Group Holiday. The formula, though safe and economic, had something so intrinsically depressing about it that despite the beauty of the picturesque lakeside towns of Garda, she had returned home subdued.

Yet following her experience, she wondered if she had been too quick to sneer at those former travelling companions. It no longer seemed fair to consider them 'en masse', ignoring the personal histories that had brought them together.

Identifiable types began to emerge:

Type 1: Solitary virginal female – perhaps

Type 2: Separated half of wedded bliss

Type 3: Solitary male homosexual: not out

Type 4: Young female: victim of bitter estrangement/divorce/abandonment

Type 5: Single and proud

Isabelle wondered, as she adjusted the temperamental taps of the shower, to which category her current holidaymakers had assigned *her*. The invigorating cascade of cold water made her feel animated, and despite the ever so un-Italian ripples of flesh, less lethargic.

Through the open patio doors wafted the scent of cocoa butter, a popular soother for over-enthusiastic sunbathing. Isabelle breathed in the familiar fragrance. Her heart began a nervous, juddering pound. A tightening seized her chest and crept up her throat, causing her teeth to clench.

Her hands, covered in cream, were soothing the broad scorched shoulders stretched across the modest double bed. The intermittent whine of a man in pain, imploring a double balm for his burning body and his bruised emotions. A man straddling the threshold between the duty love for the first woman in his life, and the pulsating urges of sexual love for her younger replacement. One at the expense of the other, it seemed. No room for both mother and lover.

They were on holiday in Scotland, in a small country hotel at the foothills of the Trossachs, where the conservative proprietor appeased her beliefs by pretending they were married.

When they had not shown up for their restaurant table, she'd phoned the room to enquire if they needed anything. Her emphatic stress on *'Mrs* Murray' was designed to let Isabelle know what she truly thought of their marital status. Isabelle recalled her excuse.

'Thank you for calling, but there's been a change of plan – unfortunately, my *husband* has taken a little too much sun and is feeling unwell. We won't be coming down to dinner.'

Her 'husband' lay face down, blocking her out of his sight and temporarily out of his life. Not even the suggestive massaging of his shoulders could provoke a reaction. Dinner was not the only thing off the menu.

He hadn't taken Isabelle's advice about the sun cream, nor about calling his mother to see how her tests had gone. As he suffered the consequences of his inaction, Isabelle tried to kiss away the pain, but he shrugged her off, determined to find someone responsible for his own shortcomings.

His brown-red face turned towards her. The curl of his upper lip, which she had always found attractive, looked petulant and childlike. An adult child who, scolded by the primary female in his life, now lay limp and emotionally exhausted, incapable of the passion he had until recently been all too willing to express.

Past and present fusing and confusing, Isabelle's current hotel phone rang.

'*Mi scusi, signora*, a call for you.' Salvatore Nicolosi, the receptionist, connected the caller.

'Hello,' a well-spoken woman with an English accent began. 'You don't know us, but my husband Robert and I have seen you in the dining room, and we wondered, since we all speak the same language, which is a bit of a novelty over here – if you'd like to join us for dinner tonight. I'm Helen, by the way.'

'Thanks ... Helen. How will I know who you are?' Isabelle remembered seeing an elderly couple, returning hot and sweaty from an excursion – they were probably Helen and Robert. The invitation was a kind and friendly gesture but what if they pitied her?

(Type 1: Solitary virginal female)

'Oh, you can't miss Bobby and me. We're at one of the

window tables – the only Brits on the German side of the restaurant! We'll have to see about that for next week.' She laughed. 'OK, dear, see you later.'

I was right, Isabelle groaned, they feel sorry for me. OK, *dear*. All the way to the Med to have dinner with my grandparents. Never mind, as long as they don't make a habit of it. This would be her third evening to dine alone, and there was a limit to how much one's own company was satisfying.

Appraising herself in the mirror, she smoothed the creases in her silk blouse and felt for a moment the dreaded insecure pang of being alone. She doused herself with a second compensatory spray of Issey Miyake and picked up her bag and key.

Despite Mr Miyake's best efforts, the oily fragrance of cocoa butter clung with a vengeance to the room.

Chapter 2

Rome

Rico studied the email. '**Your address in Sicily –** *Hotel Panoramico, Via della Baia, 2, Cefalù.*' This just would not do. He couldn't be expected to work and live normally in a *hotel* at the height of Sicilian holiday season. What was the agency thinking of?

His long, manicured fingers groped for a concessionary box of Marlboro. He had given up ten months previously but, somehow, being back in Italy had its own stresses. In Pavlovian fashion, the mere sight of a blue T outside the tobacconist's or a vending machine on a corner had him searching his trouser pockets for the appropriate coins.

His London agent's phone rang several times before the recorded message engaged; he was probably in a lunch meeting. Rico waited for the beep and cleared his throat.

'*Ciao*, Ernest. It's about the Sicilian job – particularly the *hotel* part of it?' He spoke without much politeness. 'Can you call me? It's Rico. I'm in Rome.'

He swiped the phone silent and strolled to the window, where there wasn't a breath of air. The surrounding palazzi were absorbing and radiating back the 36 degrees of the city-centre in mid-July. He wondered if he should just give up on the day, shutter out the glare, and take refuge in the darkened, cooler bedroom.

In the street below, all human noise had abated. There was a tangible feeling of life having been suspended. Rico thought how desolate the city seemed amidst the heat shimmer of the afternoon sun. The normally raucous shouts of ambulant fishmongers and fresh-produce vendors were absent. As the sun approached its highest point in the sky, they carefully packed away their goods and returned home to eat and sleep, leaving behind an eerie silence.

Rico was reminded of that same unnatural hush in the streets below his childhood apartment in the central market district of Florence. Although north of the great Italian north-south line, his parents were still southern in the taking of their afternoon siesta – mostly because on the Via Sant'Antonio where they lived, it was impossible to sleep well during the night. A district with many hotels and budget pensioni, backpackers 'doing' Europe were determined to eke out every last minute of Florence's night life and often returned home noisily, in time to meet the market-traders setting up. Neither group believed in curtailing their natural exuberance, so Rico learned to sleep almost anywhere, despite the noise.

Even now, during the hectic conducting schedule that took him across all continents, he seldom lost out on sleep. No 'settling in' night of tossing and turning for him! To lose the first night in every new place would have meant too much lost sleep, and you had to be sharp on the first day of rehearsal.

Along with his accommodation details, Ernest had sent through other bad news. The original Tosca – an Italian soprano well-known and experienced – had cried off and been replaced by someone Rico had never heard of. An American – Beverly Millar – was the new soprano.

Great, thought Rico, *Tosca* with an unknown in the title role. He scrolled through the biography Ernest had attached. Actually, Beverly had done quite a lot, though in small to medium-sized houses. Besides, he could usually draw out the best from his leading ladies. Temperamental tenors, now – they were another story.

This Sicilian contract had come in at much shorter notice than his usual engagements. He had originally planned to take August off, knowing by his schedule that he would be in Europe. It still amused him that he only felt in holiday mood once within the sight and sound of the Mediterranean. The Italian obligation to kick back in August, as the summer heat built to intense levels, meant that years of conditioning had not left him unscathed, but it did amuse him that when in North America he would happily rehearse through the whole month without feeling he had missed out on anything. Pavlov again!

Usually by this time in July, his brother and family would have moved their parents out to the jointly owned summerhouse in Viareggio. Rico should be up there now, spending time with his mother, but this year he couldn't face it. His father, Giuseppe, had slipped out of their lives in May, dying unexpectedly when Rico was in the middle of a run of *Madama Butterfly* in Sydney.

In life, he hadn't had much time for his eldest son, and dying he wasn't able to hang on so they could salvage some semblance of a relationship. Rico had hauled the assistant conductor back from holiday and got out on the first available flight but, still, that wasn't good enough. Giuseppe Mauro Parisi had breathed his last, flanked by his wife of forty-five years and his younger son, while Rico redirected his nervous energy into annotating a score of *La Traviata* 15,000 feet over Greece.

His death had hit Rico hard, harder than he had thought possible. Giuseppe had never approved of Rico's work and showed no understanding of how a son of his could have such an extraordinary talent, when no one in the immediate family could hold a tune. He had resented the 'unmanly' traits in his eldest son, who preferred to hang around the tiny apartment listening to crackling broadcasts of the Radio Orchestra, while his contemporaries were punishing a battered football down in the market square. He thought that if he ignored Rico's fantasy life it would go away.

But it didn't. His father's opposition made Rico more determined to work longer and harder at his music, availing of any free tuition he was offered, even shadowing senior students in their lessons at the local music school.

Giuseppe Parisi did not understand the world of the music school. A Sicilian who had migrated north to Florence, he had worked as a labourer on post-war construction jobs, until he was chosen to apply for a clerical position in the city council's headquarters. Once appointed to the *Comune di Firenze*, he threw his dungarees in a heap on the floor and donned a jacket and tie, his days as a manual labourer over. A State employee with a pensionable position, he had finally arrived. No longer the downtrodden Sicilian peasant, Giuseppe's feelings of pride in his work grew as he made token progress up the ranks of bureaucracy. When seventeen-year-old Rico was due to finish school, Giuseppe had persuaded one of the managers to consider him, and he arrived home triumphantly waving the headed notepaper confirming Rico's interview.

Rico had laughed in disbelief. He had, he said, no intention of curtailing his young life by joining a clutch of dusty fossils who whiled away each day, worrying and weighing the cost of water and refuse collections.

When offered a scholarship to study violin in Siena's Musical Academy, Rico left home, to the protestations and tears of his mother, and the stony silence of a father who dismissed him from his affections the day he laughed at the office of *Comune di Firenze*.

In his early professional engagements, he would send two guest tickets to the Parisi household. Religiously, his mother would open the envelope and prop the tickets behind the clock, and equally as religiously she would return a couple of hours later, to find one face down. Giuseppe had resolved never to cross the threshold of any theatre or auditorium where his son was playing.

Twenty years later and somewhere over Greece, Rico lost his father again. Was this why he had impulsively decided to accept the Sicilian job? Despite the negative aspects of the contract, somehow it was easier for Rico to escape and work, than face the house by the sea, listening to the recriminations of his brother and sister-in-law, and witness the light extinguished in his mother's eyes. At least in Sicily, he might have some sense of his father as a living entity. The names of the villages which peppered Giuseppe's tales of childhood floated in and out of Rico's subconscious like a soothing mantra. In Sicily, these places would be real. He would make this half-rate festival *Tosca* his best ever. More than that, he would make it Giuseppe Mauro Parisi's *Tosca*.

The electronic bleating of the phone was insistent. Rico reached out to the nightstand.

'*Pronto?*'

'Rico? Ernest. How's Rome?'

'*Ciao*, Ernest – hot and humid, but nice to be back. *Senti*, this thing about the hotel in Sicily. You know I hate hotels. What happened? I thought we agreed about an apartment.'

'That's what I suggested, but the festival organisers insist that you would have much more difficulty getting any sort of peace in a central apartment during the summer. They are all in the old town, apparently, where, of course, the young people congregate till all hours.'

'Noise isn't the problem. I am Italian – I am used to Italian noise. But it's the inconvenience of the hotel – I cannot sleep late when I need to. Either someone is wanting to clean the room or change the towels – plus, the restaurant hours don't suit our rehearsal times.'

'Well, the only option left was a house-share near the venue in Pianetti, with some minor artists and Stephen the director but, frankly, Rico, I don't think these communal arrangements work when *you* are conducting operations – in all senses of the word. You need to keep a bit of distance from the cast, to have their full respect.'

'Oh, Ernest, how English! But no, you're right. I am not prepared to share. Is there no other choice? Further out? I could get a car.'

'No. There's some international sports thing on and they've block-booked the self-catering places long-stay, while they are in training. However, I have spoken to the hotel manager and he suggests you take one of the small "villas" in the grounds of the hotel. They look tiny – but more private, with their own garden. I suggested the same for Beverly.'

'Are you trying to be mischievous, Ernest – putting no one but me and my leading lady in the hotel?'

'No, but if you are a non-hotel person, Beverly is definitely anti-self-catering, and threatened to set her contract alight if she had to share. I convinced her that what the hotel lacked in stars, it made up for in charm.'

'This job is sounding more and more like one big headache. Can you tell me anything good to cheer me up?'

'Well, the scenery is great and the food in the hotel is supposed to be marvellous. Look, Rico, enjoy it. Treat it like a holiday with a little Puccini thrown in. You have had a long, tough year so far.'

Rico frowned at the suggestion that he would ever 'play' at Puccini, but he had to admit he was tired. A change of scene might lift his mood.

'*Allora,* I know I'll regret it, but Hotel Panoramico it is.'

'Wonderful! I'll confirm the villa at the hotel. If anything comes in, I'll send it on. And, Rico? Thanks for being so co-operative.'

'That's OK. I hope this trip is worth it.'

'It will be. You'll see. It'll be well worth it.'

Chapter 3

Hotel Panoramico

Isabelle awoke to the sounds of the hotel stirring for the day. Because her room was a garden studio off the hotel avenue, she had begun to recognise the noisy early-morning arrival – in sequence – of the refuse collection, the breakfast staff and the fresh-produce deliveries.

Not usually an early riser, here there was no merit in lolling around in the rather stuffy little bedroom, once she was awake. At home, she would stress her already tight schedule by stealing an extra fifteen minutes in bed, only to join the queueing morning commuters *just* about on time. She enjoyed the adrenalin rush this gave her, which she was sure others with a more tranquil routine did not enjoy. *Why* did she do it? On the one hand, there was the incontrovertible evidence that it took her 44 minutes to shower, dress, eat and make-up, and yet she whittled this down, revelling in the challenge of beating the clock.

It seemed to Isabelle this habit was a metaphor for her life. If there was an easy or a difficult way to do something, inevitably she chose the latter. Take her current position. One would have imagined that by thirty-two years of age, she could enjoy the comfort of drifting off on a fortnight's holiday with a lover or husband – or, failing that, at least with a female companion. Instead, she had chosen to subject her emotionally fragile self to the obstacle course of a long-stay stint in a small Sicilian hotel, where she knew nobody and where, with not much Italian, she was hardly likely to be able to unburden herself in deep and meaningful conversation.

Despite her initial reservations, she had been glad of the company of Helen and Bobby the previous night. It was a relief to be able to chat while enjoying her meal.

Their solicitous questions, however, had bothered her.

'And had you no one to come away with, dear?' Helen poured more wine. 'It seems so sad, to go on your holidays on your own.'

'No, Helen. It wasn't like that. I wanted an extended break and either my friends couldn't afford it or weren't willing to leave their other halves for over a month. I've taken out a loan – and unpaid leave from work – to top up my holidays.'

'Won't you find it a bit *too* long?'

'Probably, because I've found the first three days have

really dragged. But I have to stick it out. Returning to Ireland just now is not an option.'

'Isabelle, have a limoncello with me. That will sort you out.' Bobby ran his tongue along his lower lip in anticipation of the liquid he was about to imbibe.

'Maybe I will, though I tried one the first night and I thought it too sweet – almost cloying.'

'It's that all right. But there's no harm in having a bit of sweetness in your life!' He raised the shot glass of the complimentary greenish-lemon liqueur that the waiter had placed before each diner. 'Cheers!'

Isabelle knew that was part of it – not accepting sweetness in her life. A line-up of all the 'sweet' men she had known materialised along the restaurant wall. She could hear her rejection speech each time: 'We want different things.' 'It's not you, it's me.' Surely *the* most unkind line. Well, she could hardly have said: 'Your chemistry and mine don't interact positively/You make a sucking noise with your teeth when you drink/I can't bear the way the crotch of your trousers finishes up nearly halfway down your thighs.'

And yes, they *were* sweet. They had good jobs. They would have married her. (*Ay, there's the rub.*) Instead, she was attracted to the one irascible, difficult man among them. The more he treated her badly, the more she hoped he would reform – soften, melt into the adoring lover she knew he could be. And, in the interim, there was always the challenge of winning him around, living on that knife-edge of suspense wondering if a meet-up would happen or be cancelled at the last minute. Mind-wrecking behaviour, but exciting! Exciting, where all the Mister Sweets had lulled her to sleep with their predictable, polite courtships.

If she was honest, even as a teenager she had been like this. The safe, reliable lads on whom her friends practised held no appeal. She just couldn't be bothered wasting time with dullards.

'You've invited *who?*' Her mother's voice had shrilled around the tiled kitchen in their home, south of Dublin.

'Ricky Shaw.'

Her late mother was a woman who when confronted by emotional crises, cleaned to exorcise her feelings. On that occasion, it was to the advantage of a rather greasy oven.

'*Ricky Shaw*, no less! Well, Miss High and Mighty, the local Brothers' lads not good enough for you?' The pink, frothy soap from her Brillo pad dripped down the oven door.

Ricky Shaw was older and worked in Dublin. A flamboyant young man, with a badge-emblazoned leather jacket, he drove around Wicklow town atop his 500cc motorbike, russet locks streaming out from under the crash helmet. The mothers did not approve. They huddled in defensive groups, arms firmly folded across their ample bosoms and prayed he held no appeal for their daughters. Ricky Shaw was a Protestant.

'Over my dead body will you bring that long-haired

private-school la-di-dah to the convent Debs! Haven't you loads of boys to choose from, without resorting to the likes of him?'

But Isabelle held firm. She was the only sixth-year to arrive at the Arklow hotel with her long white dress hitched up around her knees and the careful hair-do squashed under a motorbike helmet. How they had laughed at the disapproving glances of well-wishing parents waving them off from the school!

Had Isabelle known then that it would be the only white dress her mother would live to see her in, she might have been a bit kinder.

Was that when the rot set in? Maybe Ricky Shaw was the start of her predilection for bad choices. But, she thought, as she pushed the air-con slider into the 'on' position, bad choices according to whose norms? Her natural inclination had been to spend time with men who made her *laugh*, who were physically attractive. She wasn't on the trail of a trainee husband, whom she had to put through a series of tests to see if he responded appropriately.

When she started work in the public-relations firm in Dublin, she remembered how the young women with whom she socialised were firmly divided into two types: those who were out for a series of fun relationships and those who were looking, looking, looking – almost with a tinge of desperation — for a life partner. They criticised Isabelle's 'living in the moment' philosophy, and sometimes she broke her own rules and gave the sweet, steady types a whirl.

But it always ended, and at Isabelle's instigation.

That's what had made Con suitable. He was a dash of excitement, diluted by a large dose of mystery. He made her laugh. She hadn't laughed much in those early Dublin years — (her mother's unexpected diagnosis, the rapid decline, her sudden death) — followed by the numb, aimless drifting that accompanies post-bereavement grief. And then, along came this subversive, intelligent, good-looking man, with whom she began to laugh again. Once the obsessive, passionate phase abated, they had drifted along together, avoiding the pitfalls of the dull and steady twosomes, exiting and entering the dancefloor in an elaborate minuet — sometimes holding each other at arm's length, other times admitting no one else into their private room.

Isabelle wiped sweat from her brow. Either the thought of past romance was having an overheating effect on her internal thermostat, or the air-conditioning was set to 'hot'. Dressed in only a silk nightdress, perspiration streamed down her neck and onto her chest as she studied the switch-panel again. What was *wrong* with it? The control was at the cold setting, but the motor lay silent. She would have to complain to Reception. She flung open the veranda doors, in the hope of a breath of air.

It was on occasions like these that doubts niggled at her staunch conviction that she was perfectly happy to be away on her own. Not that on a scale of world events complaining about malfunctioning air-conditioning was up there as one of life's major stressors, but it would have been nice to 'dispatch' someone else to complain. If you had a husband, that's what you'd do: send him over to deal with it.

But she had no husband and although people all around her hurtled unquestioningly onto Noah's Ark – and then demanded a life-raft when they wanted out – she was not afraid to admit she *liked* having a part-time lover. When she had put up with – maybe even welcomed – Con's lack of dependability, perhaps it was because she was no more enthusiastic about marriage than he was.

Yet why had his marriage sent her fleeing to this faraway bolthole, to recover her equilibrium?

Because *he* had defected. When Con had said he didn't want to marry, what he really meant was he didn't want to marry *her*.

Seated in a triangle of shade on her Sicilian terrace, Isabelle stared at the azure sea, wondering if it might hold a balm for her bruised ego. Over the dividing lavender hedge, two chambermaids energetically beat dust out of cushions in anticipation of setting up the room for a new arrival. She was about to have a neighbour.

Chapter 4

'*Sì, signore,* we'll send someone over immediately. Yes, within the hour.' Salvatore noted yet another room with no air-conditioning. That made eleven complaints and it was only breakfast-time. July was always hot, but not constantly in the mid-thirties. The latest heatwave drifting in from North Africa had seen the thermometer climb steadily – a degree a day – until the mercury had hit 36 that morning.

'Salvo, can you email the drivers' pick-ups – and please stop chatting on the phone.' Giorgio, the manager, hung his jacket on a hook behind Reception.

Salvatore pulled a face behind his back. Did Giorgio actually believe he had *time* to take personal calls in the middle of high-season mayhem at the Panoramico? Besides, the emails were already sent. He scanned that evening's arrivals: nothing too exciting. A couple of Germans from

Catania at four o'clock. Another elderly couple requesting to be met at the port. They were driving, but wanted a car to lead them in case they'd lose their way. An escort – were those days not over for Sicily? The O'Rourkes at Palermo for eight. The Irish couple were booked in for a long stay. He'd send Vincenzo – he was chatty and had some English. The Irish were sociable and liked to be made welcome from the start.

'Roberto? The air-conditioning has gone down in a whole series of rooms. Can you come around immediately? What do you mean *tomorrow*? These people are cremating in their rooms and screeching into my ear at half-hourly intervals. And I might add, the fault seems to be in the rooms where you recently "upgraded" the system! You need to get your ass around here and within the hour!'

The hotel phone vibrated with the Sicilian dialect oath that Roberto unleashed. Salvatore decided he'd better cool his attitude if he expected to see the electrician ever again.

'OK, Roberto, but as soon as you can.' He put down the phone with as much restraint as he could muster. 'Signora, can I help?'

It was the nice English lady. She and her husband had arrived on the late flight from Gatwick on Saturday.

'Yes, I hope so. You are the one who speaks very good English. Am I right?

'Well, I like to think so. What can I do for you?'

'We want to book an excursion to the temples at Agrigento. Remind me again what day it goes?'

'Every Wednesday – so there's one tomorrow. It's an early start – six forty-five.'

'Oh, that *is* early. Do we have an English-speaking guide?'

'Yes, Gianni is taking it. He speaks everything, so you should be all right.'

'Fine. Book me and my husband in then. Do I pay you now?'

'I can charge it to the room.' The phone rang. 'Excuse me, signora – Hotel Panoramico? *Si*, yes, I have your reservation. *Si*. We'll see you soon.' He replaced the phone. 'Sorry, signora, would you like a wake-up call for tomorrow?'

'I think we'd better! I know Bobby has the travel clock but, with your ever so good Sicilian wine and then that limoncello, I'm afraid we sleep a little too heavily for our own good! You'd better set the alarm thing for six o'clock.'

'Done. Anything else?'

'No, only it's a pity *you* aren't coming as our guide tomorrow. You speak such lovely English, and it would be nice for you to get out for a while.'

Salvatore thought about this after she left. The lady was right. After all, he was as qualified as the guide who would take the tour to Agrigento. He had studied English, German and Art History at Palermo University, and spent his childhood in New York, where his family had emigrated. All his early education had been in that city. So why was he only the glorified receptionist-cum-general-dogsbody in the hotel? Like most things on the island, it had to do with politics: the politics of the haves and the have-nots. Salvatore's family were decidedly in the latter category. It didn't matter what individual merits their son had acquired or how many degrees *cum laude* he had clocked up. He was still the son of a peasant worker, and therefore had his place in the social order. His role was to serve, and be grateful for *any* employment on an island populated by thirty-something sons still living at home and receiving pocket money in lieu of a salary. Knowing this did not stop Salvatore feeling resentful of the young language teachers who came to the hotel to give lessons to the tourists. *He* could have done that, had anyone bothered to offer him the hours. But no, in the eyes of Giorgio and the management he would always be dear obliging Salvatore at Reception, dishing out keys and doling out sympathy. Why upset the hierarchy by allowing him access to the middle-classes?

'Salvo, a moment. About the Vazzana wedding party.' Signor Bruno, the banqueting manager, had appeared from behind a potted palm. 'Can you tell Housekeeping to have rooms 204, 309 and the wedding suite ready by one o'clock? Apparently the family want to change between the church and the banquet. It's a very monied union, and the bride's family will not be outdone by their new in-laws who, rumour has it, are wearing formal dress for the dinner. See what you can do.'

'Signor Bruno, be reasonable! None of those rooms are free. We are fully booked.'

'Look, Salvo, I don't care what you do with your foreign tourists. Tell them the view is better from another side of the building. Or the rooms are infested with ants. I don't care *what* you tell them, but *move them* or else the Panoramico will never do a high-society wedding again. Do you *know* whose wedding this is? It's only the daughter of the mayor of Messina. Use your charm, and those multilingual skills that you are always showing off, and get them out of there!'

Salvatore hated situations like this. Every egalitarian bone in his body groaned at complicity in such a scam. Besides, it didn't make good business sense. On the one hand, he knew about the prestige associated with hosting the wedding of the mayor's daughter, but the foreign tourists were the backbone of the hotel's business. To shunt them into inferior accommodation went against his better judgement – all to look good in the local press and drive the rival hoteliers into an envious rage. He really wished Bruno wouldn't put him in this position, or that Giorgio didn't endorse it. They were either running a tourist hotel or a banqueting service. Would somebody please decide?

This was only one aspect of the job that was bothering Salvatore. He knew his family depended on the money he sent home every week; yet he was convinced he could do more, achieve more elsewhere.

'*Scusi.*' A foreign accent interrupted his thoughts.

Frowning, Salvatore looked up from his screen. It was the blonde Irish lady.

'*Scusi, signora.* How can I help you?'

'It's the air-conditioning in my room – *Lipari*. No matter what I do, it doesn't seem to work.'

'Let me look. Yes, *Lipari*, Signora Ryan. Was it working before?'

'Well, yes, it was working normally yesterday. It's just this morning that nothing is happening.'

'Leave it with me, signora. The electrician is already called. It should be fixed soon.

She didn't move from the desk.

'Was there anything else, signora?'

'I saw your notice about Italian lessons. How do I go about booking one?'

'Just turn up at the time on the noticeboard and have a chat with one of the teachers directly. But you already speak a little Italian, Signora Ryan?'

'Please – Isabelle. I hate all this "*signora*" business. I find it so strange – so *old,* to tell you the truth. I'm afraid my Italian's long forgotten. I did it in school, but that's a few years ago.'

'But you must practise! Every day a few words, OK?'

'*Va bene,* Salvatore. I'll try a few words with you, every so often.'

'Do! Oh, I almost forgot. More Irish come this evening – a couple – O'Rourke. Maybe you will find some friends?'

'I doubt it, Salvatore. Couples on holidays only fraternise with other couples. They wouldn't become too friendly with a lone female! Far too dangerous.'

'I don't understand. If they're Irish, they might like to meet one of their compatriots?'

'Probably that'll make them run even farther away! Ireland is a small place and they won't want to get stuck with me. It would mess up all their romantic, hand-holding dinners.'

'I do not believe this is true. Irish people are so friendly.'

'Yes, Salvatore, they are, to foreigners abroad and to others for whom they feel no responsibility. But they would probably prefer not to encourage me, in case I attached myself to them!'

'It's not like this in Italy. If people are friendly people, they don't care if it's with a single or a couple or an old person or a young person. They like the person for what he is.'

'Lucky Italy!'

'Sometime we must have coffee and you can explain this to me a little more. Now, *purtroppo*, I must work, so if you can excuse me —'

'Of course, I'm sorry. It has been lovely chatting to you. *A fra poco.*'

'*Si! A fra poco.* Till soon.'

Flashing lights indicated both external and internal calls. Salvatore picked up.

'Hotel Panoramico. Oh, it's you, Mamma. No, this isn't a great time. Here's Signor Bruno, I'll have to go. Can I call you later?' Ending the call, he said, 'Signor Bruno, I haven't had a chance. I'm looking to see if there are any late arrivals – maybe we can put the wedding guests into those rooms to change? They don't want rooms for the night?'

'Not *now* they don't, but who knows, Totò? After an eight-course wedding banquet, they might decide to stay. In any case, if we give them a room to change in, they'll scatter their belongings all over it. It would be hard to turn it around fast.'

'Well, that idea won't work.'

'What happened with 309 and 204 which I promised them?'

'Signor Bruno! You know those clients are in the middle of a two-week stay. It would be ridiculous to move them out for a night. Anyway, *I* won't tell them. If you want to move them, stop being Mr Nice and *you* tell them.'

'Salvatore, you are becoming even more impossible! OK, OK, they don't get the good rooms – we'll run with the courtesy-room idea. Which rooms are they anyway?

'Numbers 106 and 245.'

'You're suggesting *245* for the Mayor of Messina's wife? Are you crazy? Back to your reservations page. Find other late arrivals to put into cold storage – ones booked into a decent room. I'll need them till eight.'

'Till *eight*? What if the guests arrive on schedule?'

'Use your initiative. Tell them they must have dinner immediately. Problem sorted, understood?'

'Understood.'

He really had to leave this place. Today wasn't even a particularly demanding day, but this elastic-band routine, stretching in all directions to accommodate whichever member of senior staff clicked his fingers loudest, was exhausting, and most of the time ended up irritating other colleagues who vented their anger on *him*, the first in the chain of communication and always accessible.

The loud klaxon of several cars announced the advance party of the Messina wedding. Five twenty-something males in dark designer suits hopped out of two sports cars and swaggered through the hotel foyer, looking for the drinks' reception.

Yes, the party was on its way. ETA thirty minutes. Salvatore gave them directions to the terrace where the champagne was set up. Their superior attitude irritated him. It was one thing being spoken down to by foreigners, but by your own peers? Professional courtesy necessitated that he bit his lip, but it was just another in a series of revelations which seemed to be saying *Go, Go, Go*.

Chapter 5

Rome

Didi leaned across her mother and tried to claim a little space at the tiny hub window. From the quick glimpse, she recognised the familiar granite buildings of Rome unravelling elegantly along the meanders of the Tiber. She could almost feel the intensity of the afternoon sun, and a promise of reliable, constant heat.

'That's the second time we've passed over St Peter's, Didi. I hope everything's all right. Why are we hovering for so long?'

'Relax, Mother. We're just holding – waiting for clearance – so he can make an approach and land. Rome's a busy airport, so there's bound to be congestion.'

'I told you we should have flown direct. All this hanging around. We'll miss our connection.'

On cue, wide flat fields gave way to long ribbons of concrete and the plane bumped its way to earth, to the loud applause of all the Italians on board. Pauline's eyes flashed triumphantly.

'See what I mean? Even *they* are relieved we're down.'

Didi suppressed a smile as the aircraft rolled at a more leisurely pace towards the terminal building.

It was three years since she had first landed at Fiumicino airport, and she noticed a new glassy pier had been added. Wonderful! An extra kilometre to hoof to domestic departures, and guess who'd have to lug all the carry-on bags? Her mother had insisted on packing about three days' supply of clothes and toiletries into hand-luggage, working on the principle that since they weren't flying with the carrier whose planes are named after saints, the baggage-handlers would probably lose their luggage.

A waft of heat hit Didi as she emerged from the plane. This time, it was the genuine thing.

'That's very hot,' Pauline panted, as she negotiated the steps. 'What temperature would you say it is?'

'Mid-thirties, or near enough. There'll be a rolling weather forecast on the tellies in the terminal – we'll find out then.'

'*Televisions,* Deirdre. Honestly, for a university graduate you have a very casual way of expressing yourself.'

'Telly, TV, television, what does it matter? You know what I mean.'

'No need to take that tone with me. We're on holiday – and remember how it is you come to be here at all.'

Before Didi could retort, the automatic doors of the first

bus shut in her face, stranding her on the tarmac whilst whizzing her mother off to the terminal building. It was probably just as well they were separated, because Didi could feel her fuse beginning to shorten. Once again, she began to question the foolhardiness of agreeing to this holiday. Her mother – or Pauline as she preferred Didi to call her – had offered the trip as a treat for finishing her music degree, but a month, just the two of them? Was she nuts?

On her bus, everyone except Didi seemed to fish out their mobiles, switch them on and coo to their beloved – though mostly they seemed to be calling their mothers if '*Ciao, Mamma*' was anything to go by. Middle-aged men, with dark locks or none, babbled as excitedly as fourteen-year-olds returning from their first student exchange. The practice wasn't sex-specific. Females of all ages were at it as well. Didi felt a little puzzled by her own ambiguous feelings towards her mother and wondered would the time ever come when she would feel the need to call her the minute she alighted from a plane.

'*There* you are!' Pauline was waiting inside the automatic doors of the terminal. 'The bus taking off like that gave me quite a fright. I didn't realise there was another one behind, but this nice young couple on honeymoon got chatting to me and pointed it out. The girl reminded me of Jan, in all her excitement. *Now* where do we go?'

Well done, Mother, Didi thought. You have managed to make it through four hours twenty minutes without mentioning Jan's name.

'Let's see, we just follow the signs for *Voli Nazionali* – domestic flights. It's quite a trot. I think I'll collar one of these mini-trolley yokes. Do you want one?'

'Oh yes, please.' After some hesitation, Pauline caught her up. '"*Collar*"? What sort of a colloquialism is that? I suppose that's one of your flatmates' little gems. It sounds more west of Ireland to me – it must be Imelda.'

Didi shared a small house in a bohemian quarter of Dublin, with Tony, a percussionist, and Imelda, a medical intern. Pauline approved of neither of them. On the few occasions when they had met, she had declared Tony 'badly groomed' and 'an awful flirt'. As for Imelda, she was never in with a chance, as she was one of those large women whom Didi's mother instinctively disliked. In Pauline's world, anyone over a Size 10 had let themselves go, and she blamed Imelda for Didi's own 'sloppy look'.

'My trolley has a wonky leg. It keeps veering to the left.'

'*Wonky*? Now, Pauline, what sort of an adjective is that? Would we find it in the O.E.D., do you think? Or maybe your trolley is made of chocolate – you know, Willy Wonka!'

'Deirdre, what sort of rubbish are you talking? What's chocolate got to do with anything?'

'Relax! I'm just teasing since you were upset about me and my "telly"!'

'Sometimes, Deirdre, even when you *are* speaking properly, I can't make head or tail of what you're on about. I never have this problem with Jan. She speaks like I do *and* she's not always making silly jokes.'

Ah, Reference Two. Five hours, ten minutes. Jan, the Queen of Perfect Daughters. Of *course* she speaks like you, Mother. She *is you*. Thirty-five years younger she may be, but she flashes the same smile. She glitters and glints like a gaudy piece of crystal in a shop window and, although you sing her praises on the hour, you'll never know – *no one* will ever know – if she cares deeply for us at all.

'Here we are. Gate A12. Grab a seat, it's a while before we board. Do you fancy a coffee?'

'No, Deirdre. But a nice cup of tea would go down a treat.'

'They're not great on tea here. Have a cappuccino.'

'Oh, get what you want. Just don't leave me here on my own too long, with all those queer dark-looking fellows hanging around.'

She's hilarious, thought Didi. She books this marathon trip and boasts to everyone in the bridge club about her adventurousness, and then as soon as she spots a tanned face, she panics.

Didi was looking forward to her own first real coffee, and that curious Italian mixture of cold sophistication and earthy friendliness, as she queued for the thimbleful of potent treacle. It made her smirk the way people, sharp in business suits and designer sunglasses, lined up in a detached and orderly fashion to acquire their receipt – and then, once armed with their caffeine permit, elbowed their way chummily to the counter, with a familiar '*Scusa*' and a broad grin, Armani suits rubbing shoulders with chain-store inferiors. She could see it now, a new advertising slogan – '*Lavazza the Leveller*'.

'Here you are. One cappuccino. The queue was very slow.'

'Did you forget the sugar?'

Didi retrieved the sachets from her pocket. 'The guy behind me got chatting and asked where I was going on holiday, and when I said "Sicily", he put his finger to the side of his nose and said: "*Attenta! Mafia!*"'

'Oh, that's all over and done with now. I was reading an article about it in a magazine at the doctor's surgery.' Pauline popped the sugar into her coffee. 'Apparently the ordinary people have turned them in – you know, made confidential phone-calls to the police and had them all arrested.'

Didi noticed that a man sitting opposite, studying a music score, emitted a snort when her mother said this. His long musician's fingers flicked back and forth over several pages, making notes with a chewed-off pencil. He was extremely handsome, with tousled dark curls long enough to sweep back behind his ears. His brows arched upwards, from a central point over his nose, giving him a puzzled look.

'Something's happening. We must be about to board. Have you got your stuff?'

'Deirdre, don't talk to me as if I'm a two-year-old. *Yes*, I have all my bags *and* my boarding pass. You know, it's not the first time I've travelled!'

Yeah, Didi thought, but it's the first time without Dad. Although a quiet, unassuming man, her father had been one of those traditionalists who held the two passports, the two boarding passes, and anything else of an important nature. It had always irritated Didi the way he treated his wife like an unaccompanied minor.

It wasn't a problem her mother had to contend with any longer. Harry O'Rourke had stepped out one evening the previous November to adjust the heater in his glasshouse and collapsed between trays of fledgling Granny's Bonnets and a sack of John Innes potting compost. When they found him, he was already cold, and the screeching, whining ambulance only went through the motions, to make the family feel they had done their best to save him.

Didi missed her father like crazy. He had died in her final year at Trinity College and she was already under pressure. Although they had always barked at each other, rather than enjoying the cosy, affectionate relationship he had with Jan, his dying had thrown her into a panic. He had always been there – someone to bounce ideas or scrounge a few euro off, as the need arose. She had never really thought of him as a safety net, but now that he was no longer around, she felt scared. It was different for her sister. Jan was a serial girlfriend, and the emotional detachment from her parents had begun around seventeen, wrapped up as she always was in some Romeo or other. When Didi moved out in second year she never brought any guys home to her parents, so they presumed she didn't have boyfriends. Jan was forever traipsing her current incumbent in for tea or to make chitchat with their dad about whatever sporting fixture was on at the time. Because Harry O'Rourke had never seen his Deirdre in the arms of another man, she remained his little girl for longer.

'At last. I thought our row was never going to be called.' Pauline shuffled along beside her.

Didi noticed the musician in a heated exchange with the airline steward who had his hand on the passenger's carry-on bag. Although they couldn't hear the conversation, it had evidently failed the dimensions test and was being taken away from him. The musician insisted on opening it on the threshold of the plane, successfully blocking anyone from boarding until he had secreted his cache of treasure into the various pockets of his linen jacket.

'You'd wonder what could be that important to make such a fuss.' Now on board, Pauline was fumbling with her seat belt, trying to tighten the receiver part of Didi's.

'Maybe he has work to do on the flight … I think that's my bit you have.'

'Oh, work! That's all you young people ever think of. Couldn't he just sit back and relax and look out at the view?'

Didi smiled, as her mother, eyes shut tight, had no intentions of taking her own advice. She snuggled back in the seat, profiting from the lull in Pauline's demands. This trip mightn't be too bad. She loved Italy and Italians, and although she would miss being among locals like when she worked in that Roman bar, there could be advantages in being free to enjoy it all. The tour of Sicily sounded interesting. The travel agent had suggested this, fearing four weeks in the one town might push them over the boredom threshold. Didi nudged the camera bag between her feet. She had always been a serious photographer, but hadn't done much in recent years. This trip would provide a great focus – and if she were honest, an ideal activity to create some space away from Pauline.

'*Signori, signore,* Ladies and Gentlemen, shortly we will land at Palermo Airport.'

Didi woke with a start.

Pauline was already sitting bolt upright, looking cross. 'Another horrible landing to get through. Can you see the airport yet?'

Didi scratched at the grime on the porthole, but as the plane made its final approach it tilted to a 45-degree angle and her over-wing seat revealed very little except an expanse of murky-looking water. 'Nah, we're still out over the sea.' Then suddenly she saw it: an enormous mountainous headland looming right in front of her window, its slopes barren of any vegetation, save scorched russet-coloured straw. The plane was fast descending towards this mountain and, although normally a very relaxed flyer, Didi held her breath until the narrow strip of runway separating mountain and sea became visible. The pilot timed his landing expertly and they taxied towards the terminal building, making their final turn with metres to spare before the end of the apron.

'What was that bump? I thought you said we were over the sea.' Pauline had her eyes open but her head pointed rigidly at the headrest of the seat in front. 'Are we down?'

'Yeah. That's some mountain, isn't it?'

'Stop. Don't tell me things like that. That's why I don't like looking out the window. Oh, there's that fusspot again, demanding his big wheelie case.'

Didi had also spotted the dark-locked musician.

'Don't exaggerate. It's not that big.' Still, if all Sicilian men looked like him, well, maybe she was in for an interesting month.

Once through the baggage hall, they saw their driver, a low-sized, rotund man, with glasses and a tanned bald head. He was clutching a sign with '*Hotel Panoramico*' and in smaller letters underneath '*Signor Orourke*'.

Didi went straight over and introduced herself.

'Hotel Panoramico? Signora O'Rourke.' She pointed to her mother, standing with the trolley.

'Ah, Signora Orourke. I expected man. And you? The lovely Signorina Orourke?'

'Eh, yes.'

'Come. I take the signora's ... *carrello*. We go.'

As the driver loaded the luggage, Didi noticed the dishy musician shaking hands with several people boarding a rather rundown yellow minibus. When it pulled out, a green-

and-gold sign in the rear window caught her attention. It read: *Gibilmanna: Festa di Musica*, with the dates underneath in a print too small to be read from a fast-disappearing vehicle.

Regretful that they were probably being whisked off to opposite sides of the island, Didi wished the handsome musician a silent goodbye, and smiled at her uncharacteristically romantic thoughts about a stranger. This wild, passionate country had a lot to answer for.

'Are you comfortable?' Didi noticed how the long day's travelling was beginning to take its toll on her mother, who looked decidedly bushed.

'Oh, let's just get to the hotel. I'd never have chosen Sicily if I'd known it took a full day to get here.'

'*Aria condizionata?*' the driver was asking from the front.

'*Sì.*'

'*Allora, andiam.*'

With that, the silver Peugeot pulled straight out into the fast lane, and Didi and Pauline hurtled towards the impressive Monte Pellegrino and their home for the next month.

Chapter 6

Hotel Panoramico

Salvatore flicked through the documents of the previous evening's arrivals. The Germans on the Catania flight had been very late checking in – just as well, since their room was awash with bridesmaids changing and redoing their make-up. Vincenzo had left his claim-form for the Palermo pick-up. Apparently, the O'Rourke couple turned out to be '*due signore*' – the passports suggested a mother and daughter. How had he imagined they were a couple? The daughter was pretty – typically Irish – with reddish hair and pale skin. He checked her date of birth: she was twenty-two. Her mother was attractive – tanned and well-groomed in a French sort of way – with smartly cut dark hair, greying a little. She bore no resemblance to her fair-haired, fair-skinned daughter. Salvatore wondered if they had been caught up in the wedding chaos, but the register indicated they were in *Vulcano,* so that should have been available on time.

'Good morning, Salvatore. My newspaper, please.'

It was Signor Russo. He had stayed at the Panoramico every July for as long as Salvatore had worked there. Exactly one calendar month, full board. His table in the restaurant – the same every year – was strategically placed to allow him to survey all the other diners, or if he was feeling anti-social to escape their attention by looking out the window to sea. So associated with Signor Russo had the table become, it continued to be called after him during the other eleven months of the year. On the beach, his name was unofficially on the red-and-yellow-striped deckchair in the best spot at the water's edge, and any other guileless tourist having the audacity to park themselves in it immediately incurred the wrath of Federico who managed the beach.

'Here, Signor Russo,' said Salvatore, handing him the newspaper. 'Any special plans for today?'

'My usual, Salvatore, with an even longer sleep after lunch, since I have been awoken shortly after seven this morning by someone playing Callas out in the garden!'

'Oh, that must be our resident *live* diva, Signora Beverly Millar from the US. I can't believe you could hear her from your room! I thought we had put her out in *Salina*, one of the villas.'

'A *diva*? Staying here? Is she going to perform for us?'

'No, Signor Russo. She's here as part of the Music Festival in Gibilmanna. I think she's the Tosca.'

'Wonderful! When is it on?'

'August.'

'A pity. I will already be back in the heat and humidity of Milano.'

Salvatore became aware of an agitation in the young woman standing at the information carousel. From her appearance, he thought her the newly arrived Irish girl, though it was difficult to tell, since her distinctive hair was tucked up under a broad-brimmed straw hat.

'*Buongiorno, signora*. Can I help you?'

'Oh, *buongiorno*. I was just looking for some leaflets on what's happening around here. Have you a programme of cultural events, or of music anywhere?'

'The list of trips and excursions, you have already. Individual concerts are advertised as they arise. There's a jazz night in the Piazza this Friday. Here's the flyer.'

'Did I hear you mention there's going to be a performance of *Tosca* soon?'

'Yes, but not soon. Not till mid-August, I think. Some of the performers are staying in the hotel.'

'I didn't know there's an opera house in this town.'

'Oh no! It's an outdoor festival, in the hills above here. In Gibilmanna. You should visit Gibilmanna sometime – there's a lovely church with a spectacular view.'

'And the *Tosca* dates – do you have them?'

'The publicity material is not here yet, but I could ask the diva the next time I see her. She's sure to know.'

'Yeah, thanks. If I'm still here, I'd like to go. Oh, the shuttle bus. Into town. Is there a timetable?'

'The times are written on the noticeboard.'

'Great. Thanks.'

As the Irish girl jotted down the times of the buses, Salvatore heard the *whoosh* of the revolving door, accelerated by the day's strong *scirocco* wind. The door ejected a tall blond man in cycling attire. He looked the girl up and down and, considering her worthy of notice, nodded a perfunctory greeting.

'Salvo, how are things?'

Salvatore lowered his head and tapped furiously on the keyboard.

'Any chance of service?'

'Just a moment ... Christoph, how can I help you?'

'My new guests – already they are on my mobile at eight this morning, complaining that their room was not clean when they arrived last night.'

'Room number?'

'305. This is not good.'

Salvatore recognised the room as one of those Signor Bruno had hijacked. 'I'll contact Housekeeping immediately and ask them to do a check before they begin their rounds.'

'I want to know *why* it happened. My guests are going to complain to the agency.'

'Look, Christoph, I am dealing with the problem. If the guests complain, they complain.'

'But it reflects badly on me!'

Salvatore fought hard to restrain himself from commenting that Christoph wasn't always so worried about his reputation.

'Tell them you have resolved the problem. Anything else? I have a lot of work to do.'

'No, for the moment, that is all.'

Salvatore watched as the Lycra-sheathed body disappeared down the steps to the terrace. He wondered what the German group leader was about to ask. Salvatore knew it was his own exhaustion – he hadn't had a day off in ten – but he found Christoph most unpleasant. What he needed was a distraction, some pleasant company away from this infernal hotel! The Irish passports seemed to wink out from their cubbyhole at him. That Deirdre O'Rourke looked nice … if only …

Out on the avenue, the glare of the morning sunshine caused Didi to squint. She had forgotten her sunglasses, and even her large hat wasn't sufficient to protect her eyes. Already, shortly after nine, the thermometer at the pool entrance showed 34 degrees. New tarmacadam bubbled and blistered under the relentless rays. Didi trod carefully, not wanting to step into the viscous goo and ruin her espadrilles. She really couldn't cope with heat like this. Unlike Pauline who was a sunworshipper, Didi had to retreat to a shady corner with a book. If she *had* to move around, she preferred to cover up in loose-fitting layers like she was currently wearing. What she *really* wanted was her first plunge into the salt-laden Mediterranean below. Just to float on the surface of the balmy water and let the cool breeze wash over her. She'd have to get Pauline into the habit of moving a bit earlier – at least until she found her feet and knew her way to the beach on her own. Then she could follow Didi down at a more leisurely pace.

As she opened the front veranda door, Didi was surprised to hear Pauline's tinkling laugh drift in from the rear patio. Who was she talking to at this hour? Maybe it was Jan, on the phone, availing of her work perks.

Her mother, dressed in an olive, yellow-and red-striped sarong and co-ordinating turban, was smoking a cigarette as she chatted over the boundary hedge. As the door slid open, she swung round.

'Deir – goodness! Deirdre, it *is* you under all that get-up?'

Didi blushed at the slight, but the blush became deeper when she discovered to whom her mother was chatting. Across the lavender hedge stood the Dishy Musician, not a trolley-bag in sight, looking extremely self-possessed in crisp khaki-coloured shorts and a luminous white T-shirt. He too was smoking. Didi suspected her mother had probably asked him for a light, to initiate a conversation.

'Deirdre, this is Rico, our neighbour. Rico, my daughter Deirdre – she is also a musician, by the way.'

'*Buongiorno*, Deirdre.'

'Hello. I recognise you! I think we were on the same flight from Rome yesterday.'

'Were we? I cannot say, Deirdre.'

'Please – *Didi*. Nobody calls me Deirdre.'

'Only her own mother.' Pauline threw her eyes up to heaven.

'Mom, I thought we might make tracks to the beach. It really is hot out there, and I could do with a swim.'

'Oh, there's no rush! I'm on holidays. It's not as if we're programmed for ballroom dancing at midday, followed by lunchtime bingo! I mean, this isn't a tacky holiday camp. Breath-taking views like these should be savoured slowly, don't you agree, Rico?'

'Well, the view really is spectacular. You can see almost twenty kilometres up the coast. It is supposed to be the best view on the northern side of the island – that is why the hotel is so popular for weddings. It is a photographer's dream. Were you out on the terrace last night?'

'No, we were too tired after our journey.'

'It is so beautiful. The lights flicker from the houses, and then you can see this curious effect as the pulsing car beams keep appearing and disappearing around the bends on the road beneath. Then, of course, there is the moon and the stars twinkling away, above it all.'

'I look forward to seeing it tonight.'

'*Mo-ther!* The beach. Leave Rico in peace.'

'Oh, I suppose I should. But if you're thinking of heading down to the sea, will you go and put on some more suitable clothes? You'll never get a tan, dressed in the Turin Shroud.'

Didi fled through the patio doors, her cheeks burning with embarrassment. *Why* was her mother doing this? Did she have to humiliate her in front of that man? For one mad moment, she had thought Pauline was *flirting* with Rico, but then she had done her 'this is Deirdre-my-daughter-the-musician' routine. This was usually followed by a litany of Didi's diplomas, awards and successes. Didi didn't know which was worse – the praise or the put-downs.

Still, her mother might be right about the clothes. She really was *very* hot. The layers were becoming oppressive – maybe she'd be more comfortable with a good dose of Factor 50 and a light dress over her bikini.

Outside, Pauline's voice was bouncing through the truncated version of their family history.

'Of course, Deirdre didn't get my good skin. She takes after my late husband. Harry – God be good to him – was fair-skinned and freckled, obviously descended from the Vikings, whereas my lot came in with the Spanish Armada. We're all olive-skinned and tan easily.'

A peek through the muslin curtain revealed that Rico and Pauline had settled themselves quite comfortably in deckchairs on either side of the lavender divide and seemed in no hurry to go anywhere.

'Now my other daughter – she *does* take after me. She has such exquisite skin.'

Oh, no, thought Didi, the Jan story. She really must hurry, otherwise poor Rico would be bored out of his mind.

'Recently she was on honeymoon in St Lucia and, goodness, she came back looking almost native!'

Didi emerged wearing a lime-green cotton sundress, her

straw hat in place, and her retrieved sunglasses now on her nose. 'Well, will I do?'

'*Si, molta bella*, Didi.'

'Yes. Well, it's a big improvement. Though why the enormous hat?'

'OK. Do you have your beach bag?'

'*I've* been ready since before you went over to breakfast. It's you who's been holding us up, with all this clothes-changing.'

Pauline really was impossible, thought Didi. The previous day, she was all clingy and dependent but, within a couple of hours, she dismissed Didi as if *she* were the one out of touch.

'Enjoy your swim, Didi!'

'*Grazie*, Rico. See you around!'

'Oh yes, we'll see you soon. Don't work too hard!'

As Didi slid the door to, Rico waved goodbye and, with Pauline firmly out of sight, added a broad wink of complicity.

Chapter 7

Cefalù

Rico sat at the last remaining table outside Caffè Duomo. He quite enjoyed having an aperitif in the touristy places where the locals wouldn't dream of paying the inflated prices. He sipped his drink slowly, early for his dinner appointment nearby with Stephen, the *Tosca* director.

It was impossible to ignore the posing all around him. On this his third visit, Rico recognised the same elderly character lurking in the square. About seventy, he obviously continued to colour his hair – its reddish-brown hue typical of a badly applied home tint. He was taller than most Sicilian men, but shabby. The well-worn shirts with their loud floral patterns recalled previous decades. On each occasion Rico had spotted him he was wearing white trainers – unpopular with his contemporaries. They gave him an American-on-tour look. He had piercing, bulbous blue eyes, and Rico wondered which particular race of invaders were his ancestors.

His game was a simple but ancient one. He was on the prowl for susceptible lone women who might pay him some attention, listen to his stories, and then buy him a drink or a coffee or, if he had really impressed, invite him out to their hotel for a very welcome dinner. When Rico became aware of the ritual, he was greatly surprised by the elegant, attractive women this prowler targeted. He wasn't one of life's more presentable specimens, yet the women welcomed his attention and accepted the offer to be shown around. Shortly after his own arrival earlier, a fifty-something German tourist – following what seemed to Rico a perfunctory courtship – had hopped onto the back of the man's beat-up moped and sped off down a dusty side street.

The episodes with the Prowler disturbed him. What degree of loneliness motivated these women to entertain the overtures of such an odious man, when before his arrival they had seemed so in control and happy in their own company? Was the nature of loneliness such – that people grasped at *any* attention even from an old waster like this – rather than stand out in the crowd as the one alone?

Yet Rico was on his own and quite happy to be so. He never felt lonely. So much of his professional life involved motivating, encouraging and soothing the egos of disparate personalities that he found silence was indeed sweet.

That morning's rehearsal had gone badly. Beverly Millar was proving to be a bit of a prima-donna – in the worst sense. She had sung the role many times, but in small opera houses, and was having problems in the open-air setting. The latest blow-up had been over the director's idea to use the porch of the beautiful Gibilmanna Church as part of the set constructed on the top level of the steps. Rico and the orchestra would be on the second level down, with the audience seated in a tiered semicircle behind them.

Beverly was to begin her duet with Cavaradossi from inside, visible to the audience only through the arch.

It was impossible to hear her. Rico had relented and she was fitted with a discreet pick-up mike, tucked into the folds of her dress, but this did not solve the problem. She had complained in frustration.

'Rico, you *can't* expect me to begin the aria from inside! I can neither see you – nor hear the orchestra cue. The wind is blowing the sound all over the place – and that was *before* Einstein over there decided to stash me away in the vault.'

'Einstein' was not overly impressed. A tall gangly man, Stephen the director had cropped fair hair and wore horn-rimmed spectacles, which made him appear more bookish than musical. He usually worked in theatre, and this was his first time directing an opera. Rico understood that he was excited by *Tosca*. He had recounted in minute detail his extensive research – the visit to Castel Sant'Angelo in Rome, the original setting in Puccini's libretto – to see what he could adapt to the Sicilian space.

But what Stephen failed to understand was that in opera, the drama sprang from the music – and in order to succeed, the production must work with what was musically feasible.

This was why Rico had suggested meeting for dinner, to try and soften the blow of changes he was going to request.

'You really are a traditionalist, Rico.' Stephen gulped down a large mouthful of Corvo, the local red. 'You have single-handedly denuded my production of anything original and exciting. Why won't all my brilliant ideas work?'

'Stephen, *caro mio*, it's not that these things will not work. It is that they will not work in *Tosca* on top of a hill. You know I am not happy with the acoustics of this crazy place, but this is where we play it, so we do our best. If it were the Massimo – *Teatro Massimo* – in Palermo – then we could be innovative.'

'But it is the *first* year of the festival. I want to make an impression, and I want the *festival* to make an impression. I don't want people to think that we have a less committed approach to *Tosca* in Gibilmanna than elsewhere.'

Light from the ambient candle caught the lens of Stephen's glasses, creating a curious effect in which the flicker of candlelight was reflected on the lens, but irradiated the enthusiastic spark in the eyes they protected.

Rico smiled at Stephen's passion; he was warming to him.

'And, of course' – Stephen dangled a piece of spaghetti on his fork – 'the sub-plot between our Cavaradossi and that Ornella girl in the chorus is not helping. Paolo really should know better. His attentions are so obvious that Beverly feels ignored, which makes their love scenes on stage unconvincing.

He looks bored! Whereas any time the chorus comes into range, our Cavaradossi lights up like a beacon!'

'He's a tenor, *caro*. It's obligatory,' chuckled Rico. 'The tenor has to be in love with someone. *And*, by rights, I should be in the throes of passion with Tosca!"

'*What!* You and Beverly? I couldn't begin to countenance that.'

'Don't look so startled. It is an assumption in opera that the conductor is always sleeping with his leading lady. Think back to Puccini and how proud he was of the long list of sopranos he bedded. He even had their photos lined up on the piano in his villa at Torre del Lago! Or there are more recent partnerships – Sutherland and Bonynge – even between singers – Roberto Alagna and Angela Gheorghiu, for example. Sometimes the emotion in producing an opera, coupled with proximity, releases the only aphrodisiac needed to fall in love.'

'And did that happen to you? Sorry. *Sorry*. I shouldn't pry. I'm being personal.'

Rico observed the embarrassment and was touched by it. 'There is nothing wrong in trying to know me as a man as well as a conductor. For me, no, it wasn't a singer or a musician. Four – no, nearly five – years ago, I was the assistant conductor on *Carmen*, at Rouen. If you know the opera, you will remember that there is a very exciting ballet sequence in the tavern of Lillas Pastia. During the rehearsal period, one of the dancers received the bad news that her young brother had been killed in a car crash. I was very sad for her and tried to comfort or help in any practical way. Her name was Monique. We were married two years ago.'

'Oh! I didn't think you were married – you somehow don't *look* married!'

'And what does married look like?' Rico was interested. Monique had often expressed the same concern.

'I don't know. You're very sociable – and charming – around women. Not in a flirtatious way, but you're not afraid to get close to them. In England, if you're a married man, you convey this immediately, by the presence of a large gold band and repeated references to your spouse's name. And through an aloofness which conveys your unavailability – even for conversational purposes.'

'*Che strano!*' Rico rested his chin on his clasped hands, his naked left hand reinforcing Stephen's point. 'So married English people don't have friends?'

'Well, yes, I suppose. Same-sex friends, or other couples with whom they socialise, but generally "spare" friends are not encouraged. Perhaps it's the fear of that proximity thing you were talking about earlier. They're not taking any chances!'

'You know, Monique is my wife, but one of my closest friends is Irena, a woman I studied with in Vienna. We meet up every time our schedules permit and, when we do, it is like no time has passed since we last saw each other. That is friendship, Italian-style. I do not ask for Monique's approval, nor do I need it. I love both of these women, but in very different ways. They do not threaten each other.'

'And why does Monique not travel with you when you work?'

'She's a dancer, with her own schedule. She's currently taking part in the annual Festival in her native Montpellier. Do you know Montpellier? It's a wonderful city.'

'No. I did Avignon Festival once. That part of France appeals to me.'

'Go to Montpellier if you get the chance. It's young and vibrant – because of the university faculties – yet it hasn't sacrificed anything of its classical appeal just because it has great modern development.'

The waiter placed two espressos and the bill on their table and Rico pulled out his cigarettes, taking the opportunity to turn the conversation back to the business of *Tosca*.

'Do you find it strange that some of the singers smoke?' Rico shook his box of Marlboro at Stephen, who plucked one and lit it from the dwindling candle.

'Absolutely! *And*, opera singers are not quite as temperamental as I had expected them to be.'

'It's a job, like any other. You throw histrionics, you earn a reputation, you don't work. Despite the romantic notion, most artists don't want to live in a garret, burning their paintings for central heating!'

'Do you think we'll ever resolve the tension between Wolfgang and his ex-wife? It really is bad luck that she's in the orchestra.'

'Oh, Maria-Elena is a very fine cellist. I have worked with

her before. Wolfgang is difficult, but' – at this Rico's face spread into a mischievous grin – 'all this friction will surely only fine-tune his performance as a thoroughly nasty and aggressive Scarpia.'

'I don't know. I think touring Oscar Wilde plays around British heritage houses was an awful lot easier. At least, you didn't have to deal with the offstage drama.'

Rico excused himself to go the bathroom, discreetly taking the bill with him. As he stood up from the table, he observed with a sigh that the Prowler had reappeared on the restaurant street, dressed in a tatty yachting blazer.

When he returned, Stephen was stubbing out his cigarette.

'*Andiamo?*' Rico placed his hand in the small of his colleague's back and ushered him in the direction of the Piazza.

'Are you getting a taxi?' Stephen tried to catch the attention of a nearby driver. 'He can drop you out at the hotel?'

'*No, grazie.* I feel like the walk. It helps me think things through. *Buonasera, caro.*'

'*Buonasera,* Rico.'

The sea crashed against the rocks as Rico headed along the windy cliff road towards the hotel. Stephen's taxi sped past, heading for the hills of Gibilmanna. Rico waved at the silhouette framed in the back window and wondered what the subsequent days would bring.

Chapter 8

Hotel Panoramico

Isabelle watched as Helen and Bobby negotiated their way down the 105 steps to the beach. She knew there were 105 steps – she had counted them as she struggled to climb back up one midday – a feat she was not likely to repeat any time soon at that time of day.

Her shared dinner with the English couple had only succeeded in making her more self-conscious at being alone. Ever-so-polite questions had punctuated each morsel of food. Like John the Baptist, she had laid her life if not her head, on the platter.

Her holiday escape was not proving as complete as originally envisaged. In moments least expected, her senses were assaulted by echoes of their shared music, things as mundane as an old hit-song piped into the hotel restaurant, or a good *pasta alla carbonara* – the only Italian meal he could cook. Then there was that cursed cocoa butter, so favoured by many sun creams.

The unthinkable had even happened. Tucked into the back of a holiday novel lurked a photo of a youthful Con. She thought she had dumped them all in her Christmas Eve bonfire – eleven years' letters and birthday cards and all the usual female memorabilia – but this one had survived.

Isabelle studied the picture. It had been taken on a daytrip to the seaside town of Tramore, where they had gone with his sister and her young baby. The outing had been a disaster.

'He hasn't been sick *again,* has he?' Con's irritated voice barked, eyeing the baby in the rear-view mirror.

'Oh, I'm sorry for the inconvenience,' Fiona had retaliated, 'but yes, that's what they do a lot of at this age. Don't worry, his aim was directed solely at my new shirt. Your precious car has escaped unscathed.'

Once there, Tramore was cold and breezy but, with the false summer optimism of the Irish, they strolled the beach, in shorts and T-shirts, their increasingly goose-bumped arms turning blue.

'Jaysus, I need a pub, preferably one with a big fire and a hot whiskey!'

Con had rubbed his hands, partly to revive the circulation, but mostly in a gesture of triumph. The walk was over, and now they could adjourn to the real business of the day.

'I don't think a pub atmosphere in the middle of the afternoon is a healthy environment for Charles.'

Isabelle could still see his sister's pinched face, set in a weary expression of dissatisfaction.

'And you think this ball-breaking cold east-wind *is* healthy?' he snapped back.

'Well, it's a bit cool all right, but at least he's not subjected to all sorts of germs.' Fiona looked tired.

'Oh, excuse me, I didn't know you were a microbiologist now!' Con pulled a packet of cigarettes from his shorts and lit up.

The smell of baby-sick mingled with salt spray; Charles had thrown up again. This time his aim was more accurate, and Con's Ralph Lauren polo shirt had some interesting spots competing with its logo.

'Christ, look what he's done now! Hon, have you a scarf or anything in that haversack you call a handbag?'

Isabelle smirked as she recalled the unselfconscious vanity of a man who could allow himself use *her* scarf to mop vomit from his shirt.

His cocky grin continued to stare up at her from the terrace table, the colours of the photo somewhat diminished in the Sicilian light. That grin had never changed, nor lost its cockiness, even on the last day she had seen it.

Everybody had said it was a bad idea. She would only be embarrassed and upset and, goodness, they might think she had come to stand up and cause a scene when they got to the bit about any reason why those two before the priest might not wed. What her friends had failed to understand was that was *exactly* what she had in mind. To jump up at the crucial moment and burst into song with '*It Should Have Been Me!*'. In her more inebriate moments, she had even anticipated the congregation's reaction to a loudspeaker rendition of '*Don't Marry Her, Have Me*' played loudly from the church grounds. Her firm handled a political party's PR account and she could easily have organised a campaign car.

Eventually, responsible, dignified Isabelle won the day. No point making a 'show' of yourself.

Isabelle looked around at the animated faces of the Sicilian women on the terrace and felt quite sure they would have done it. They had the emotional freedom to be temperamental, and nobody would stop them 'making a show of themselves'. What's more, they probably would have arrived with a posse of brothers, uncles and any male relative available on the day.

What nobody had understood was *her* need to face the wedding – to witness the self-professed commitment-phobe demonstrate his change of heart – and to make sure he would actually go through with it.

On the wedding day, she thought carefully about how to dress, afraid that if she made too much of an effort, people might take her for a guest. In the end, she opted for something business-like and dark – work clothes – to give the impression that she had just 'dropped in' as she rushed from one appointment to another.

Her cheeks still burned when she remembered the concern her boss had shown as she excused herself for a fictitious afternoon appointment with a gastroenterologist. There had been too many questions about her symptoms, the likelihood of intervention, the stresses and strains of modern living on the digestive system (he had a peptic ulcer and this was a subject close to his heart). Her impulsive decision to cut work had backfired slightly in her choice of pretext – she had forgotten the peptic ulcer. She really should have concentrated on a tubal ligation or an ovarian cyst, in the hope that he hadn't had one of those.

Isabelle could see her now – the real rival for Con's affections – tall and erect, with a suitably over-the-top mother-of-the-groom's hat. Nothing was going to spoil Annie Murray's big moment. The omnipotent matriarch looked happy with the match. From what Isabelle had heard, someone like Janice didn't present a threat; Janice would never take Con away from his mother.

Not like Isabelle. From the outset, Annie Murray had never really liked her. Con was so full of her – talking endlessly about her friends, her talents, her DIY skills – that his mother felt demoted. In a moment of pique during that winter Annie was taking French classes, she had once referred to their relationship as a *'grande passion'*. Over the years, she grew to accept Isabelle and welcome her into her home, because she knew if she presented obstacles, Con would only become more smitten.

On the terrace of Hotel Panoramico, Isabelle felt a heat

rash engulf her neck when she thought of the family's expressions at the recent June wedding. She didn't know how she had the courage to break from a clutch of congratulators and make her way towards Con.

Absorbed in the camaraderie and introductions to family and friends of Janice's he hadn't previously met, Con was basking in the attention visited upon his new role.

Cocooned in his moment of glory, he didn't see her approach.

The photographer had just lined up the Murray family and Isabelle watched as domino-like, their artificially bright smiles reset in various expressions of discomfort and anxiety.

The younger members reacted immediately, but the change in Annie Murray's expression was only that of controlled recognition. Annie had looked on as Isabelle engaged Conor and Janice in conversation.

'Con, what a lovely day for it! Congratulations on finally taking the plunge.' Isabelle had extended her hand. Her voice cut through the incessant babbling of social niceties.

For once, he had nothing to say.

Then, recovering his decorum, he finally spoke.

'Izzie! Isabelle – what a surprise. What brings you here?'

'Oh, I wouldn't have missed it … for the world. Aren't you going to introduce me to your lovely bride?'

'*Uh*, Janice, this is Isabelle … a family friend. We've known each other … forever.'

Janice extended a dainty French-manicured hand and Isabelle's fingers closed on a sharp diamond.

'Delighted you could make it, Isabelle. I don't seem to remember your name on the guest list, but then, the Murray clan does go on forever – it's hard to keep track of you all.'

'Oh, I'm not *related* to Con – goodness, no! I think there's a law against that sort of thing.'

Isabelle thought she saw a flicker of comprehension in Janice's eyes before she took her new husband away by the arm.

'Darling, there's Uncle George. Isabelle, will you excuse us? See you at the hotel.'

'Oh, Isabelle's not coming.' Con's usual high colour flooded his cheeks.

'Bye, Con … good luck.'

'Izzie —'

'Don't.'

That was it. Those were the last words they exchanged, and Isabelle knew that in all likelihood they were the last words she would ever exchange with him. Not that Con mightn't try to get in contact – a casual call, first lunch, maybe a drink after work, still good friends – she could hear it now, all the usual crap.

Only this time he had gone too far. This time he had well and truly nailed his colours to the mast and she had no intention of playing second fiddle to his perfect wife. Never again would she make herself vulnerable by falling for such an empty charmer.

'Signora, the ashtray – may I take it?'

Isabelle's sun was blocked by a body leaning across the table. She recognised the intruder as her musical neighbour from the adjacent garden.

'Yes, of course. *Prego.*'

'Ah, you speak a little Italian?' He pointed to the hotel's free copy of *La Sicilia* nestling beside her coffee. 'Then, I can introduce myself in Italian. *Mi chiamo Rico*, Rico Parisi.'

'Isabelle Ryan.' Isabelle took the offered hand and he shook hers firmly. 'I think I have seen you from my terrace – you are in *Stromboli*, aren't you?'

All the garden studios were called after each of the Aeolian Islands. Isabelle had been cast up on *Lipari*.

Rico put his jacket on the back of the chair and sat.

'Yes, *Stromboli*, that's me. Just like the volcano. I hope there's nothing sinister in that! Are you Canadian – that is not an English accent?'

'No, I'm Irish. From Dublin.'

'*Che bello!* I have never been, but I want to go sometime. I have a lot of friends who have worked in Ireland, and really enjoyed themselves there.'

'You're a musician, aren't you? I noticed you with that lady who sang after dinner last night – the American?'

'Yes, I'm a musician, more particularly a conductor. I am working on *Tosca* – you know, Puccini's opera?'

Isabelle nodded.

'We have some performances next month in Gibilmanna. It's only the first week of rehearsals, so there are a lot of problems.'

The waiter excused himself, cleared the used ashtray, replacing it with a fresh one, and swiftly removed Isabelle's espresso cup.

'*Un altro caffè*? Another? No? A *digestivo*?'

Isabelle shook her head. Rico, who appeared to have abandoned his original table, was now ordering a grappa. 'Do you like opera?'

'Yes. Well, the popular ones where I know the tunes. I work in a PR agency in Dublin, and one of our clients organises cultural trips for his corporate customers. I handle that account, so I've been to quite a few shows – eh, concerts.'

'It's a pity you will not be here for our *Tosca*. Though, if the problems continue – maybe it's better that you hear this beautiful opera in perfect conditions.'

'When did you say it was?'

'The twelfth, fourteenth and sixteenth of August, around the Ferragosto holiday.'

'*What* holiday?'

'Ferragosto. The fifteenth of August, the big Italian holiday weekend.'

'I *will* still be here – that's my last week.'

'*Come mai*? Why do you stay so long? Do you like Sicily so much that you stay more than a month?'

'It's a long story. I needed a – break – away from my life

in Dublin, and I thought, why not Sicily? Somebody at work recommended this hotel, which does a good rate for longer stays. So, here I am!'

'*Bene!* So, you will come to my *Tosca*?'

'Yours, is it? I thought Puccini wrote it.'

'Ah, you tease my vanity, *bella irlandese*! Of course, it first was Puccini's – now I feel it is a little mine.'

'Well, yes, I'll come. What are all these problems you keep talking about?'

'My dear Isabelle, in life there is only one problem: sex. Unfortunately, my opera is experiencing a lot of it at the moment, and it's messing with the music.'

Isabelle laughed at Rico's worried expression. His previous cavalier charm had dissipated.

'You mock me! Am I not right? Is there not really in this world ever only one problem? *In fondo*, right in the centre of everything, there is always sex. If I were not a gentleman, I would say that a beautiful young woman like you – here, alone, for a month far from home, has escaped because of this same problem. *Non è vero, cara*? I am right, yes?'

Isabelle found herself about to reply, to unload her problems onto the table between herself and this stranger until she realised she wasn't on a long-haul flight, where with two G & Ts down, you could share intimacies, safe in the knowledge that at baggage reclaim, social politeness would necessitate a casual salutation and a 'Bye, have a great trip', but shared secrets would die anonymously once the travelling companion had cleared customs. This was different. This guy was *Stromboli* – he was her next-door neighbour, and would be, it seemed, for the next month. Caution reasserted itself.

'Oh, as I said before, it's a long story – too long to spoil this beautiful afternoon, and to keep me and my suntan apart! If you don't mind ...'

'*No, no! Mi dispiace.* Sorry, I have been impolite. How do you say – nosey? And anyway, I also must go – alas, not to the sea and the sun, but to study for an hour, before my five o'clock rehearsal. *Senta*, to show that I am sorry for my nosey, will you have a drink with me after dinner tonight? It might be late – eleven even – but I could meet you here on the *terrazza* when I come back from rehearsal?'

Isabelle hesitated. Some company would be pleasant, but she was not in the frame of mind for anything other than a friendly drink. Still, it was either take a chance with smoothie Rico, or be subjected to another grilling from doe-eyed Helen and 'poor-poppet' Bobby. (He had called her this so frequently in the previous three days that it was beginning to irritate.)

'All right, I don't see why not. You can tell me how all the sex in *Tosca* got on this evening!'

'*Madonna*, I hope that they have all tired themselves of that during siesta, and we can do three hours' good work. So, *Isabella, a più tardi!* Till later.' With that, he swept his cigarettes from the table, draped a sand-coloured linen jacket around his shoulders and without a backward glance strode purposefully across the terrace.

I must be mad, thought Isabelle, agreeing to meet the

archetypal Latin lover *even* for a drink. What was that I was saying about falling for charmers? Yet, Rico seemed respectable and there was nothing intrinsically threatening in the arrangement.

She hated the way she felt nervous when confronted by such unsolicited attention. It wasn't that long since she would have been flattered by a handsome man like Rico, but Con had ruined all that. When he marched up the aisle of that south Dublin church, he had taken her self-esteem with him, eviscerating it in front of the congregation, as he casually declared for another team. It wasn't as if she wanted to be up on the altar with him; it was just that she had never expected to see him up on *any* altar, ever. She had been publicly passed over, and she felt humiliated.

No matter how hard she tried to forget, it was a scene that refused to leave her mind.

Chapter 9

Gibilmanna

Members of the *Tosca* cast rambled into the monastery chapel, leaving the searing July sunlight outside. The stage manager had arranged a semicircle of chairs for the soloists, in front of the large wooden table. Graduated steps were positioned closely behind the soloists' chairs. As the chorus of thirty seated themselves on the narrow and uncomfortable tiers, they chatted and pulled music from their folders.

The principals, who had already arrived, were scattered around the chapel, each passing the time before rehearsal in a different way. Beverly was behind the altar, warbling her way through a series of warm-up exercises, her back turned on her assembling colleagues. Paolo, the leading man, was busy pulling on the last dregs of his cigarette, half in, half outside the doorway, much to the annoyance of the stage manager. Stephen was already seated at the scrubbed table, studying notes.

Rico swept past Paolo, consulting his watch, and appraised those present. Greeting Stephen, he placed his jacket on the back of the chair and flipped open his dog-eared score.

'*Buonasera*, ladies and gentlemen.' He tapped the table. 'Thank you – most of you – for arriving punctually.'

The heavy door groaned as it swung inwards, admitting Wolfgang, the cast's Scarpia.

'Let's make a start, now we seem to have everybody. I want to work on Act I again, since we encountered difficulties yesterday with the acoustic in the outdoor setting. For this reason, I propose to run all the music indoors, until we are secure in what we are doing. Then, following the *pausa caffè,* we will try it outside on the set.'

There were general nods of approval from the soloists, complete indifference from the orchestra, and audible mutterings of dissent from the chorus, who had their representative primed to ask the maestro to rehearse their scenes first, guaranteeing an early finish. So confident in this plan were they, that their spokesperson, a vivacious red-haired soprano, had already booked a table at the Pescatore for nine-thirty, a full hour before the rehearsal was due to end.

The proposal of running Act I in sequence – twice – effectively put paid to any premature chorus escape, since they were needed for the Finale. Rico, aware of the huffing and puffing, addressed himself to their rep.

'Rosalba, is there a problem?'

'No, maestro, we – we had hoped you might work our scenes first and then let us go.'

'This is only the third rehearsal and already you want to leave me! Do you not enjoy our work?'

Rosalba coloured as Rico launched his high-wattage charm in her direction.

'It is not that at all, maestro. Your rehearsals are ... fascinating. It's just we have so little ... and there's all this waiting around. We had hoped you might do the chorus music in a block, and we could finish early.'

Rico no longer felt like entertaining this woman. Everywhere he worked, he was offered a variation on this chorus theme, and he found it most disturbing that professional singers could not understand his reasons for working a piece in the order in which the composer had ordained.

'Ladies and gentlemen of the chorus, I am sorry to disappoint about your early finish, but there is a well-known expression of which I am very fond, about the merits of apparent inaction. Waiting to add your voice to the culmination of the drama constitutes a most definite action, for out of context the climax would not happen. So, please, do not ask me to cause Puccini any more unnecessary discomfort in his grave, by bastardising his music out of its intended sequence. Enough.' With a sharp flick of the wrist, he opened his score at the appropriate page. 'Orchestra, I give you two free bars for my *tempi,* and then you're in.'

For Rico, one of the trials of *Tosca* was the inclusion of

a boys' chorus. It ranked up there with *Aida* when it came to disaster opportunities. At least in *Aida* the elephants came with full-time handlers, equipped with stun guns if the need arose. Hardly the recommended line of action if the twenty young exuberant choirboys should misbehave. Luckily, they featured early in the running order.

'Right, boys' chorus and main chorus, take your places for the entry. Where's the boys' chorusmaster?'

'Here, maestro.'

'Have the boys ready for a speedy entry. When we're outside, you'll have a monitor inside the church and the boys start singing as they run out onto the steps. Am I right in this, Stephen?'

Stephen was busily scribbling his own notes. '*Mmm* ... Rico, *scusa*?'

'The choirboys' entry: they sing stage-left and then come forward through the church porch?'

'Yes, that's what I had thought, but if there's a problem ...'

'*Nessun problema*. But we'll need a monitor on both sides of the porch, Stage Manager – can you note that? One for Beverly and the other for the boys. OK. Is everyone ready? Let's have this chorus. *Tutti,* Bar 180.'

The orchestra struck up several chords and, miraculously, the boys made their entrance on cue and in tempo, their sweet boy-soprano voices counterbalanced by the resonance of the adult chorus.

Wolfgang, the sadistic Scarpia, was about ten bars into his opening music when the atonal, electronic beeping of a mobile phone permeated the melodic tones of the string section.

Rico threw the pencil he was using as baton onto his score.

'*Ma che imbecille!* What have I *told* you about mobiles in the rehearsal room? *All off, off, off!* Whose is that? Will he please *turn it off now*!' Rico glowered from orchestra to singers.

Paolo involuntarily patted the tiny handset in his breast pocket. Beverly didn't believe in cell-phones. Wolfgang knew his own efficiency couldn't possibly let him down, so he didn't bother to verify his three-year-old instrument was in the 'off' position.

As the beeping persisted, Beverly, nearest to the desk, was trying to make eye contact with Rico, as the noise seemed to be emanating from his battered leather briefcase. Enraged by the insult to his rehearsal in leaving one of these contraptions in a live condition, he was too busy scanning the orchestra to see who the guilty party was, to notice her grimacing.

'Maestro, *maestro*! I think it's yours!' Beverly hissed in a throaty whisper.

Realisation dawning, Rico went cold with embarrassment as he was forced to rummage under the table for the phone in his bag. Monique's number flashed up at him. What should he do? Switching it off immediately was of course what was required, but he knew Monique. He would suffer the consequences for several hours later that evening if he didn't speak to her.

Speaking softly in French so his close colleagues might

not catch it, Rico answered the call. 'This is not a good time. I am rehearsing. I will call you later, OK?'

Even though he made to switch the phone off promptly, those in the immediate vicinity could hear screaming down the line from a woman clearly displeased. The screeching cheered Beverly up no end.

Rico readdressed his score, flicking forwards, then back a few pages.

'*Scusatami*. Again, let us take it from 180. *Pronti?*'

Whether because of his own preoccupations, or through a lingering feeling of embarrassment, Rico started the final chorus with a marked increase in tempo. Chorister Ornella, in a dream world on the steps, failed to pick up on the conductor's change in pace, and soared in with an unscheduled solo.

'*Ma che fai?* Please pay attention to your score. Bar 200 *again.*'

Ornella burst into tears and ran towards the altar-boys' vestry, much to the amusement of those in the company not party to her romantic see-saw relationship with Paolo, the tenor.

Rico glanced at his watch. He really should deal with Ornella's unscheduled departure – his cast couldn't run off at will, just because they produced a few tears. Although they had repeated the choirboys' scene several times and polished some scrappy orchestral playing, he felt they'd achieved very little and it was already ten minutes to coffee break. Maybe he should pause at this point; all the interruptions were disturbing his concentration, but he knew the precise argument he had earlier offered the chorus meant he should rehearse to the Finale in the context of what had been building in the preceding scenes. No, let emotions run high, he would finish out Act I.

Ornella's outburst had upset him more than it should have done. Volatile young sopranos were forever breaking down, but somehow her tears recalled Monique's anger on the phone, and he wondered just exactly what he was supposed to have done – or not done – to have elicited such a tirade of confused emotions from his wife. They had been apart now for over two weeks, by which time Monique always imagined him captivated by some new love. No matter how often they travelled apart, she repeatedly worked herself up into a frenzy of insecurity, constantly envisaging him in the throes of an affair.

He found it exhausting, knowing that he was never trusted, that he was constantly under suspicion of playing around. The irony was that despite opportunities presenting themselves on a daily basis, he rarely felt tempted. His emotional energy was consumed by the work, and while he frequently sought the company of both sexes, he had in the two years of their marriage never been unfaithful to his wife. Recently, a more sinister element had insinuated itself into Monique's insecure ramblings: she now blamed his absence for rendering her ready quarry for any unscrupulous dancer or director who wanted to sleep with her. Phone communication was unsatisfactory for conversations like these. He really would have to speak to her seriously the next time they were together. But when would that be? After Montpellier, her company was touring Canada and he was due in Berlin. Were there a couple of days' hiatus between finishing in Sicily and his first rehearsal in Germany? He'd have to check the contract again.

'*Maestro*? So, would that be OK?'

Rico, jolted from his reverie, was aware that Marilena, the principal cellist, seemed to have asked him a question.

'What is it, Marilena?'

'The sectional rehearsal? It's all right then if we take the first ten minutes after the break to tighten up some sloppy passages?'

'Yes, of course. In fact, it's almost coffee time – let's stop now and you can call your rehearsal ahead of the company resuming.'

Paolo, cigarettes stuffed into his pocket, was already halfway across the chapel, making for the tiny sacristy, which despite its meagre dimensions was serving as a temporary canteen for the duration of the rehearsal period.

Wolfgang, seated next to him, didn't move. 'Maestro! Because Marilena cannot discipline her section, we start our outdoor rehearsal late. We must use *all* our time for this difficult place. We cannot lose even ten minutes with the *Orchester*. I do not agree to begin later than the schedule. It is not right if *celli* make a rehearsal alone. I want full O*rchester* for my music.'

'Wolfgang, it's only a short sectional. Take a walk, have another coffee. It is better for them to rehearse and have it perfect, than to have them misplaying your music, no?'

'She is incompetent, that stupid little bitch!' This last insult was flung directly at the cellists led by Marilena, who were filing past.

What was *wrong* with everyone, Rico wondered. This sort of tension usually erupted nearer performances – not in the first week of rehearsals. Admittedly, the unrelenting heat was a contributory factor, but it was more than the heat. It seemed as if the choice of opera was forcing the cast to resort to type. Paolo was overdoing the romantic suitor. Beverly, obsessed with her fading looks and jealous of everyone – was determined to prove herself attractive – to anyone – himself included, he suspected. Wolfgang's latest verbal assault on Marilena bore all the hallmarks of Scarpia's cruelty.

He took his box of cigarettes from his breast pocket, only to find it empty. *Damn!* He was really in need of a short sharp fix of nicotine. Stephen would be sure to have some. He wandered outside towards the church steps, to find the director busy marking the ground with tape.

'Stephen, *una sigaretta, per favore*. I've had it with all the fraught emotions this evening. I feel like taking off for the second half.'

'And leave me to the lions? Don't even think of it. Look, I'm resorting to fluorescent tape, because no matter what position I give her, Beverly upstages everyone, even when she's far from central to the action. Maybe if I mark all their finishing positions with a big X and letters B, W and P, that will keep her under control.'

'Some chance! But at least, with the tape there, you'll

draw everyone's attention to her vanity – that might go some way to curtailing it.'

'That was rather a blow-up between Wolfgang and Marilena. How long have they been divorced now?'

'I'm not even sure they *are* divorced, but they are apart five – maybe six – years?'

'I'm beginning to dislike him even more. Though why is she so passive? She never rises to the bait.'

'Probably wise. And with Wolfgang, I'd say she has seen similar blow-ups – and worse – before. She knows he's only looking for a reaction.'

'Well, he can certainly be very sarcastic.'

Vitriolic exchanges with Monique flashed into Rico's mind. She always said their rows were what kept the passion fuelled – once all the insults had been traded, they invariably fell upon each other, mouth latching on to mouth in a different kind of fury. Yet he wondered about the long-term effect of such constant rowing. They never resolved any argument; they just consummated it in the only way they knew how. But the differences between them remained, unspoken, unexplored, until the next blow-up, usually initiated by Monique, and usually concluded in the only manner she understood.

'Shall we call them?' Stephen said. 'It's gone quarter past, and I need all the time here I can get.'

'*Va bene.* I'll go and hunt them out. What are you particularly anxious to rehearse?'

'Beverly and Paolo's duet is looking unconvincing. I

know she's probably method-acting, but her jealous routine is so over the top she's reducing the scene to farce. And the *Te Deum* chorus again – mostly for logistical reasons, because I need to see how quickly we can get all sixty bodies, including those kids, out from the arches and onto the church steps.'

Rico was glad that Stephen was in charge for the second session. He felt inexplicably weary. Why, oh why had he promised to meet that Isabelle after rehearsal? He was definitely going to be back at the hotel later than expected, and he had to deal with Monique on the phone first, which could run into half an hour or more. Maybe he should just ring ahead and offer his excuses, but he was so wound up he knew he wouldn't sleep, and he *did* fancy sharing a bottle of wine with someone and chatting a while. The wine he could have either way but, if he wandered down to the terrace alone, it would only be a matter of time before Beverly drifted out and attached herself to him, which would mean work talk again, or deflecting her come-ons, and he hadn't the energy for either. Besides, it would do him good to listen to someone else talking for a change. Isabelle had struck him as an independent, interesting woman, with a story to tell. And the best part of it? She cared very little about opera, singers or the complications of estranged partners with artistic temperaments! No, he wouldn't cancel.

He'd ring the hotel to say he'd be late.

'Stephen, *sei pronto*? Orchestra, on two. Company – director's call. We'll run until Stephen calls a halt. OK?'

'Ladies and gentlemen, opening Act I positions. All other cast members on standby for your entry.'

When Stephen nodded that he was ready to proceed, Rico raised his baton, intending to change the tempo slightly from earlier and keeping his movements small in order to extract the maximum concentration from his players and singers.

'Ready? Bar 5.'

Chapter 10

Hotel Panoramico

Very few deckchairs were free when Isabelle descended the final few steps to the bathing platform. Greased bodies lay stretched on the bumpy concrete, wedged between towel-bedecked chairs, the territory of absent conquerors. She was later than usual, having slept heavily following her midnight drink with Rico. This was ridiculous – where was she to go?

Federico, the *bagnino*, spotted her dilemma. '*Buongiorno, signora*. Where I put you today? Not much place, I think.' His eyes darted around, looking for a spot to squeeze a third chair into his Noah's Ark configuration.

Great, thought Isabelle. Even the deckchairs come in twos. Yet another stress on the lone traveller! One week into the holiday and dining alone continued to be trying. When she analysed why, it was mostly other people's reactions that were making her uncomfortable. In the restaurant, it seemed all eyes were upon her when she took her assigned table. Then there was all that silly business with removing the cutlery. Why did the waiters set for two and make a big production of clearing everything away, with a sympathetic *'Da sola?'* Of course she was bloody well on her own! Hadn't she been sitting at the same table for the entire week?

She could have cut and run into the old town to eat, but the Panoramico, like most out-of-the way Sicilian hotels, offered only a half-board rate in high season – making their profit on the wine they served to a captive audience. She had already paid for her meal: why should she have to pay again? Besides, it was too lonely a road to walk and too expensive a taxi each evening home.

If it wasn't sympathetic but inquisitive glances – (was she a young widow or a divorcee perhaps, or maybe just a lonely woman with psychotic tendencies and no friends?) – it was a kind of 'how-dare-you' stare. Strangely, this was delivered by the female of the couple – age immaterial, but the younger the woman the more indignant the stare. Isabelle thought she was imagining it at first – the near hostility wafting in her direction – but as the week progressed, she realised she wasn't mistaken. She definitely was getting funny looks. When Helen and Bobby had invited her to join them that evening, she was acutely aware of the *absence* of such glances. In fact, she was wholeheartedly ignored by the neighbouring tables, because now in company she was invisible, not the lone blonde by the window, who, despite being alone, seemed to enjoy engaging the waiters in chat and was receiving, in return, far too much attention.

The table beside hers was occupied by an elderly Italian gentleman. Isabelle had heard the waiters address him as *Signor Russo*. Judging by the way they scurried back and forth with his various courses, and attentively checked that everything was all right, she thought he must be important. What Isabelle enjoyed most about Signor Russo was the relish he took in the meals placed before him, his slow consideration of which wine to choose. This was a man not about to apologise for eating alone. Politely at first – and more warmly as the week progressed – he would greet Isabelle, enquire about her day, and wish her a lovely meal. Some evenings he complimented her on her appearance with an enthusiastic '*Che bella!*' in a friendly gesture of solidarity, not in flirtation. The man was at least seventy-five.

But was it different for men alone, Isabelle wondered? Maybe, in a smalltown, traditional hotel like this, a woman of marriageable age alone on holidays was sending out an 'available' signal. Nothing could be further from the truth. She had come away to restore body and soul from the perils of sexual relationships. The last thing on her mind was seduction.

'*Signora! Here, a place for you!*'

It was Federico, descending from the most northerly tip of the promontory, where, perched precariously between two scary-looking rocks, was now a deckchair – hers obviously – if his frantic gesticulating was anything to go by.

'You like?'

Well, actually, no, she didn't bloody like, but did she have a choice?

'*Si, va bene,* Federico. I'm on my way.'

What she really wanted was to stretch out flat and sunbathe, but it wasn't that kind of a beach. As she clambered up to the Panoramico's version of Hanging Rock, she spotted Bobby and Helen under a large parasol, he in the company of John Connolly, she engrossed in the latest Katie Fforde.

'Hiya, Bobby, Helen. Not too hot for you?'

'Oh, Isabelle dear! No. Not too bad under the umbrella. We'll head back up to the room before it gets really hot. Otherwise, I worry about him climbing those heart-attack steps.'

''Ello, love. My, you're taking a bit of colour. I saw you with your nice young man last night. Very dashing, if I may say so.'

'*Oh yes!* I forgot about that.' Helen put down her book. 'He's one of those musical people from the festival, isn't he?'

'Yes. Actually, he's the conductor. He's in the villa beside mine – that's how we got talking. And sorry to disappoint you, Bobby, he's not my "young man".'

'Not yet, love. Not yet!'

God, what was it with everybody! Isabelle had encountered nothing but winks, knowing looks and encouraging smiles since she had received the call from Reception the night before to say Signor Parisi had been delayed, but would join her shortly. On her second crème de menthe, she was ready to head for bed, when he arrived fast on the heels of his message.

She didn't know what to make of Rico. He was all charm, but it seemed forced, as if he was consciously trying to impress. Full of probing questions, he tried to draw her on why she had fled to Sicily for so long. She had been on the point of telling him when the raven-haired diva attempted to pull up a chair, and Rico – although perfectly polite – most definitely conveyed to Beverly (that was her name), that he wanted to talk to his friend alone. She backed off, visibly shaken, and begrudgingly wished them a pleasant night. Isabelle didn't know whether to be flattered or offended but, without a trace of vanity, Rico had explained that the soprano fancied him and it was beginning to be a bit of a nuisance.

Isabelle, slumped in her look-out deckchair, was dreamily reliving the conversation when she became aware of a commotion below. She sat up.

A young man, standing at the water's edge, was waving his arms wildly and calling to Federico. '*Bagnino, bagnino*! Help! Help! Help! Help! My friend – in the kayak!*'

It was the German with the distinctive dreadlocks, from the sporty Aktiv group, who was doing the shouting.

Federico immediately launched his red lifeboat and started rowing in the direction of the kayak. The waves had become choppy and, though strong and muscular, he was making slow progress towards the struggling canoeist whose bald head dipped and ducked under the swelling water.

Somebody on the platform roared '*Elicottero!*'. Mobiles were pulled from beach bags and then there was a dispute as to who would actually dial the emergency coastguard number. The head surfaced one more time, the man raised both arms and then was sucked from vision.

The happy holiday noise of the horrified onlookers was silenced. Many people were on phones. All watched anxiously as Federico reached the kayak and made an exploratory dive into the waves. Several minutes later, the *tac-tac-tac* of the coastguard helicopter, which circled the bay regularly during the busy high season, announced its arrival. It circled lower and lower until a frogman entered the water near the capsized kayak.

Federico, who had fruitlessly continued to dive, surfaced for air as the frogman made his first dive.

People of all nationalities fell into conversation on shore, united by the terrible circumstance. Isabelle was talking to Bobby and Helen when she heard what she thought was an Irish accent. Behind her, a willowy, sandy-haired girl wrapped in a toga-like garment, was talking in a low voice to a diminutive, tanned lady with dark hair. Isabelle had seen them in the dining room, but thought they were foreign because of the older woman's colouring.

'It's awful, isn't it?' the willowy girl said to Isabelle. 'I hope he's all right.'

Isabelle grimaced. 'I'm always respectful of water. It's so unpredictable.'

'That's an Irish accent, anyway!'

'Yes. I'm Isabelle. When did you arrive?'

'Wednesday. I'm Didi. And this is my mother, Pauline.'

'Oh, you must be the Irish "couple" Salvatore at Reception was telling me about.'

'Yeah, the driver who collected us thought that as well. He was looking for *Signor* O'Rourke.'

'Oh look! The frogman has come up.' The tanned lady squinted in the direction of the lifeboat.

'Federico has gone back down again.' Isabelle noticed a motor launch rounding the headland. 'Here's the coast guard boat.'

'Oh, dear God, now Federico is up and he has a body. Is he dead, do you think?'

'Moth*er!*' Didi coloured as her mother articulated what everyone was thinking, but no one dared say.

Isabelle threw her a sympathetic glance. Even on first meeting, she reckoned that Pauline was a bit of a handful for the pale-skinned daughter.

A hush descended on the waiting crowd. A young uniformed coastguard, who had disembarked from the motorboat, was now inspecting the banana boats, kayaks and *pedalos* on the shingle beach, while the helicopter paramedic worked on the inert body of the canoeist on the jetty.

Federico couldn't bear to watch and, drying himself in a borrowed towel, he wandered over to the boat hut to rummage through his selection of lifejackets, to find one without a puncture to show the officer.

The official's phone rang.

'*Si. Niente? Va bene.*'

Following a quick consultation with Federico, the officer was pointed in the direction of the dreadlocked German, now distraught.

The young man put his head in his hands and wept.

'*Annegato! Annegato!*' The phrase rippled through the Italians, who crossed themselves and hugged one another, some of them wrapping towels around their shoulders, for it suddenly felt chilly.

'What does that mean?' Pauline asked the younger women.

'I think it's the word for "drowned". He didn't make it.'

'Oh Lord, no!'

Didi looked shaken. 'Christ! One minute you're worrying if your shoulders are getting a bit red, and the next you see someone's life expire before your eyes.'

Pauline blew her nose in the corner of her sarong. '"*You know not the day nor the hour …*"'

'Are you OK, Mom? That was terrible.'

'Maybe we should go up and have a little brandy? I feel quite wobbly all of a sudden. That stupid *bagnino* only has beer in the snack bar.'

'It's too early for me,' said Didi. 'But I'll keep you company if you want one. You must be bad, if you're going to head up those steps again now.'

Pauline acknowledged the kindness, with an acquiescent nod to her daughter. 'Isabelle, would you like to join us?'

'No, thanks, Mrs O'Rourke.'

'*Pauline*, please!'

'Pauline. Another time? I think I'd prefer to be on my own —'

'Of course. It's been an awful shock. Not that you knew him or anything, but in a hotel like this, you *feel* as if you know everyone, and for someone to die before your eyes, well, it shakes us all.'

'Yes, that's exactly how I feel. Were they a couple do you think, Didi?'

'I'd say so. The poor drowned fellow wasn't much older than the other guy – he was a competitive cyclist – hence the trendy bald head.'

'Well, if you're eating in this evening, Isabelle, I insist that you join us at our table. We'd love to have you.'

'Thank you, Pauline. I'd like that. What time do you usually eat?'

'Say quarter to nine? Or is that too late for you?'

'No, that's perfect.'

'It's a date! See you then.'

'Yeah, we'll look forward to it, Isabelle.' Didi seemed pleased with the arrangement.

No wonder, thought Isabelle. It couldn't be much fun being away with your mother. She must be – what, twenty-two, twenty-three? She'd probably prefer to be living it up in Ibiza with a gang of girls than in sedate Sicily with her mother.

Isabelle wasn't being anti-social when she had declined the brandy, but her emotions were all over the place. Part of her was horrified at the speed with which the holidaymakers resumed their normal activities. Were people that heartless? Could they so easily resume applying Factor 30 when someone had just died in front of them? She felt sick. The drowning incident had shaken her, recalling watery mishaps from her former life.

She had been paying Con's mother a visit. She often did this, to remind her she was still around, even if they were officially having one of their 'off' periods. It was early September and the kettle had just boiled. Annie was about to make the most awful instant coffee which she persisted in serving, despite Isabelle having selfishly bought her a cafetière one Christmas, in the hope that real coffee might threaten the bastion of the Murray household. No such luck. Annie said it was 'too good' to use on an everyday basis, and she'd save it for special occasions. While Isabelle toyed with the insipid liquid, Annie went out to answer the house phone.

It was Con. He was calling from Cork University Hospital where he had been admitted following a sailing 'accident'. He had slipped off the gangplank and ended up banging his head on the jetty. He had mild concussion but was otherwise fine. Annie had succumbed to paroxysms of anxiety, easily provoked when anything to do with her Conor was concerned. To calm her nerves, she had delved under the sink for a pack of Silk Cut Blue hidden behind the Domestos, since Matt, the fifteen-year-old, was smoking and she was supposed to be taking a firm 'anti' stance.

Something did not ring true. Con was an experienced sailor and banging his head on jetties was not usually part of his act. There was only one way to find out. She would have to get into the car and drive to Cork. He'd only lie if she phoned him.

Many years later, sitting in her stripey deckchair on Hanging Rock, Isabelle wondered what had possessed her to drive a round-trip of over 500kms just to reassure herself he wasn't half-dead, when they'd been barely speaking at the time.

But her suspicions had been right. In that Cork hospital, if Isabelle hadn't asked at the nurse's station, she would have walked straight past the bed. His head swathed in bandages, and his face a vicious purple, he was unrecognisable. He'd had a substantial quantity of painkillers, the nurse said, and they were making him dozy, but she was assured he was conscious.

Two teenagers were hovering around his bed, the girl sitting on the small piece of unoccupied space beside his raised and plastered left leg, while her male companion glared from under a baseball cap, muttering something about needing a smoke.

'Con, what on earth!'

Isabelle bent to kiss him, instinctively aiming for his swollen mouth but, inhibited by the two young strangers, settled instead for a sisterly peck on the only piece of bandage-free forehead.

Through a drug-induced haze, he turned his face towards her, the dilated pupils trying and failing to register pleasure.

'How are ya, hon? How did you know I was here?'

'Your mother. She thinks you "slipped" while getting off the boat. I hope she doesn't pay you a surprise visit. What *did* happen?'

Signalling that the teenage couple were following every word, Con didn't answer. 'Hey, could you two get a Coke or something? Izzie's come a long way and—'

'Sure, Con. We should have copped on. See you again tomorrow, OK? Com'*on*, Mick.' And with that, the girl had slid off the bed and left, dragging Baseball Cap behind her.

'Friends? A bit young, even for you.'

'Ah no. We're doing an "outreach" project: sailing lessons for kids from a socially "challenged" area. This pair stuck to me. Kinda hero-worship. Heard on the grapevine I was crocked and have called in since.'

'That's kind of them. So, the real story?'

'Nothing much. Linked up with some guys from the club. Out on this fella's yacht, had a few bevvies too many, you know the way. An argument started over something, and we were throwing punches on deck and he flung me against a steel door. I lost my balance and fell overboard. I must have been concussed before I went over. Anyway, hon, I might have spent the rest of my days with the little fishies. Luckily, I half-came round when I hit the water, but not enough to stop me glugging down an awful lot of it first.'

'You stupid, stupid man! You could have drowned!'

'One of the lads hauled me up, but I took a few knocks on the way – managed to break two bones in my foot.'

This was so typically irresponsible Con that Isabelle had been torn between feeling sorry for the bruised mess of his body and angry at his stupidity. She was better off out of it. Such behaviour would just have kept happening through their lives together!

Or would it? Was it possible that he might become domesticated – the harder to train, finally the most obedient pet in the house?

The question was now academic.

But the pain she had felt when she left that hospital! After what seemed a brief visit, he had perfunctorily dismissed her. The current girlfriend from the club – Melissa or Melanie or someone – was on her way in, and Con, never one to enjoy head-on collisions between his various women, requested that she sling her hook. What's more, she had done so, retreating quietly.

It was one of those defining moments in which she began to question if he felt anything for her at all. Because she was so attracted to him, she repeatedly chose to ignore aspects of his character that she didn't like. His vanity and lack of dependability had become so much part of her life that she physically didn't know how to excavate it from deep inside.

She had got back into her car, her vision obscured by streaming tears, and driven erratically back to Dublin.

He could have drowned that day; maybe he should have. Instead, some poor innocent German on a fortnight's holiday had ventured out in a canoe, encountered a swell he couldn't cope with, and had his life extinguished in front of his fellow holidaymakers. It was all so unfair.

'*Signora Isabella! Telefono!*' Federico was waving the portable phone over his head.

Who could it be? Nobody from home would ring at this

hour. A curious quiver of expectation brought Rico to mind. Maybe he was ringing to say how much he had enjoyed their drink last night.

'Hello?'

'*Pronto – Isabella?*'

It was a male, Italian voice. She was right! It *was* Rico ringing between rehearsals.

'Isabelle, it's Salvatore at Reception. I understand you've made friends with the other Irish, and I thought we might go with Didi to the cinema some night – maybe Tuesday? There's an English film on. What do you think?'

'Oh … Salvatore. Well, yes, that would be nice. Where's the cinema?'

'Just outside town, the open-air one. So, keep Tuesday free, *d'accordo?*'

'Yes. *D'accordo*. Thanks for asking.'

'See you later.'

Isabelle handed the phone back to the still-shaken Federico. '*Va bene, Federico?*'

He pulled a face.

'He drown. On my beach. Never a person he drown on Panoramico beach.'

'I know. But it's not your fault, Federico.'

Then Federico, trying to put the trauma behind him, assumed the role of a pastiche Sicilian tease. '*Allora, Signora Isabella!* Two admirers in two nights, what a woman!'

'Federico, stop. You'll get me a reputation.'

'*Una bella donna* like you should be *proud* of a reputation.'

Isabelle laughed. 'And how did *you* know about last night?'

'Signora Isabella, in this hotel nothing moves that we don't know about. Remember!' He tapped the side of his nose with his index finger.

'I certainly will. No secrets in Sicily then, Federico.'

'No, Signora Isabella, no secrets.'

Chapter 11

Salvatore turned the key in the ignition for the third time. Nothing. A few encouraging splutters, and then the deafening sound of silence. It had to be the starter-motor. His ten-year-old Fiat was mirroring its owner's mood – weary of constantly putting in the effort for a paucity of praise at its performance. The car park was full of sleeker, newer models owned by the younger members of staff who seemed to be able to afford them, while he was still struggling with his temperamental dinosaur. One final attempt yielded nothing. Why did it have to happen when he had finally managed to get time off and was on his way to Bagheria? He'd just have to hitch a lift into town and catch the train.

'*Ciao*, Totò! Off to the beach on your free day?'

It was the breakfast waiters who, now finished, were heading back to the staff quarters in the grounds of the sister budget hotel for a couple of hours' sleep before the demands of lunchtime.

'*Ciao!* No, no beach today. I'm going to Bagheria.'

'Say hello to Maria-Pia from us.'

Salvatore took his knapsack from the boot, locked the car and dropped the keys at Reception in the hope that the mechanic might be able to collect it during the day.

Out on the main road, he soon caught up with the waiters.

'Taking the train, Totò?'

'Yes. Car won't budge. I think the starter-motor has had it.'

'You need a new car.'

'A new car? I need a *new life*.'

The train speeded up considerably once it cleared the periphery of the town. The trip to Bagheria took around forty minutes. Salvatore was preparing himself for whatever he might meet at home. He wished his parents wouldn't do this – call him in as if he were the cavalry. He wasn't all that worldly wise, and it placed him in a superior position to his sister who always clammed up once she realised he had been asked to intervene. What if whatever was bothering her was something beyond his experience?

His dad was waiting outside the station. Salvatore had phoned ahead.

'*Ciao, Babbo!* Thanks for coming for me.'

'It's a short enough visit so I thought I'd better pick you up. I suppose you know your mother wants you to talk to Maria-Pia and see what has her so down again.'

'Yes. Has she split up with this new boyfriend?'

'Massimo. No, he's around the apartment all the time. I don't think it's him. Who knows? Women are complicated. I have been married to your mother for thirty years, and I still don't understand her.'

The car slowed and pulled into a space, outside a pink-fronted terraced building, three streets in from the sea.

'*Here he is!*'

As Salvatore heard his mother's voice, he looked up to the balcony, where she and his sister were watching out for his arrival.

'*Ciao, Mamma!* Eh, Maria-Pia, how tanned you are!'

His sister was mahogany-brown from her days on the beach. His mother was as white as a pale-skinned Scandinavian tourist. She took no pleasure in summer – it only meant oppressive heat and the increased bother of keeping fresh produce from deteriorating into an inedible mess before she got a chance to transform it into a sauce or a preserve for the slim times in winter. Sometimes, Salvatore wished she would just stop the muling for his father and sister – all the compulsive sweeping, cleaning and cooking. She should just shutter up the apartment, take a book down to the beach and do nothing for the afternoon. He had never known his mother to bathe in the sea. When they had returned from New York, he and Maria-Pia exploited the easy access to the beach and had practically lived there during the long summers, their father joining them late in the afternoon for a refreshing swim. Their mother frequently sent down a snack, but never came in person. Her life had changed so little with their return to Sicily – she had just swapped one make of cooker for another and accumulated an array of cleaning products whose instructions at least she could now understand.

'*Mamma!*' Salvatore held his mother in a warm hug. 'How *are* you?'

'*Insomma.*'

This was a word Salvatore hated. It meant nothing, yet it conveyed a mood more forcefully than a whole string of transparent adjectives. When he tried to translate it for his English-speaking friends, he joked that it normally signalled the launch into a litany of woes. When his mother used it, she meant things were as well as could be expected *under the circumstances*, circumstances she refused to disclose.

He knew today's usage stemmed from her worries about Maria-Pia. What was going on in that girl's head? She looked great, bronzed and relaxed. Salvatore was always disturbed by her lack of interest in finding work. Everybody knew the employment situation was difficult in Sicily, but Maria-Pia was an attractive, personable eighteen-year-old, and there were lots of seasonal tourist positions in the resorts near Palermo which she could have availed of. For some reason, she preferred to hang around Bagheria, helping her mother occasionally with the washing-up or making the odd bit of sauce, but showing no sign of wishing to join the adult workforce. Salvatore found this puzzling. She wanted to be treated like an adult, yet she persisted in behaving like a child, the dutiful daughter helping with the chores at home, waiting for her prince to ride into town. Salvatore thought of all the friends he had made through the hotel – the foreign women single, married, divorced or widowed – who if not in possession of their ideal, interesting career, had at least jobs and some means of paying their own bills. Sometimes he felt a bit ashamed of Maria-Pia's lack of ambition. She couldn't have it both ways. Either she should grow up and partake of the adult world and its associated responsibilities, or else accept that she had no right to claim the freedoms she vociferously demanded, while living under the parental roof.

Later, following a respectable interval after their meal, Salvatore asked Maria to join him for a walk through their old haunts, gesticulating that he was in desperate need of a cigarette – his parents hated him smoking in the apartment.

'Let's head up towards the square, OK?'

'OK.'

They set out.

'A cigarette, please?' she said.

'I didn't know you smoked. Since when?'

'Since I feel like it.'

'You're not in great form. I mean, you *look great,* but there's something wrong. Mamma was saying you've been feeling depressed again. Do you want to talk about it?'

'No.'

'Well, can you even give me a hint as to what's bothering you?'

'To fuck or not to fuck, that is the question.'

'Since when did you pick up such colourful language?'

'Colourful? There's nothing colourful about it – it's Shakespeare – adapted admittedly – but you recognise it.'

'Massimo putting on the pressure? I thought you liked him. I don't see the problem.'

'You wouldn't. You're a man.'

'Even so, maybe if you explained to me what's worrying you, I could offer an opinion.'

'It's very simple really. Massimo insists on referring to me as his "*fidanzata*".'

'But don't you consider yourselves "exclusive" as it is?'

'Oh yes, but in the absence of sex that counts for nothing. However, Massimo is happily pursuing that aspect, certain that when he sleeps with his eighteen-year-old "*fidanzata*" he is going to go where no man has gone before. In other words, he expects to sleep with a virginal Maria-Pia.'

'And he's not going to?'

'No.'

This was not something that Salvatore had ever given much thought to. As an only Sicilian daughter, Maria-Pia had been over-protected since they had escaped the loose morals and promiscuity of New York and moved back to the island. Even though he no longer lived at home, he had always considered his sister shy where boyfriends were concerned. Evidently, he had misread the signals.

'Well, I am sure even Massimo can stretch to the notion of women having more than one sexual partner.'

'Massimo is very traditional. And I'm so much younger than him – probably one of the reasons he's with me. He wouldn't like to think of me having been with someone else. I've heard him refer to girls who have had a lot of men as "used goods".'

Salvatore flushed with anger at this small-town, sanctimonious idiot calling any girl 'used goods'! 'And if we were to hold the same judgemental candle up to him, what would the light reveal? A blemish-free record? Will Massimo grace *your* bed in all his pearly innocence?'

'Of course not. And anyway, I wouldn't want him to. I need him to be experienced.'

'Listen to yourself, Maria! What rubbish you talk! You're worrying yourself silly over being sexually experienced but lauding *his* many liaisons as a positive for a successful relationship. Talk about double standards!'

'There's something else. It's not – it's not only that it's obvious I'm not a virgin. It's … it's that I don't have very *positive* feelings about sex.'

'I'm not being inquisitive, but if your other time was the first time, well, it's always a bit awkward … and embarrassing and … uncomfortable. You probably didn't have much time to think about enjoying yourself when you were trying to work on all those other feelings.'

'No. You don't think about enjoying yourself when you're being raped.'

Salvatore thought he heard his sister say she'd been raped, but blood was rushing around his head and, although he heard her voice stammer on, it was at a distance, as if he had held his head underwater too long, and his ears were refusing to 'pop' back.

'*Maria!* What are you saying?'

'I'm telling you I was raped. It was last July, when I came up to stay with you. I had a great time with your friends and the waiters, dancing till four in the morning, drinking beer down on the beach. It was at one of the beach parties that I met Christoph – the German guide. I knew him to see from the hotel, but at that beach party he brought me over a beer and introduced himself. I thought he was gorgeous. That first night, nothing really happened. He suggested we go for a quiet walk and we headed into the secluded area around the swimming pool. We kissed – and you know, the usual sort of stuff. It was fine. I really fancied him. He drove me back to your place after.'

'And where was I during all this? Was I already in the flat?' Salvatore tried desperately to recall why he had left his young sister so much to her own devices when she was supposed to be in his care. Last July? That was around the time he was chasing that silly Dutch travel rep. Feelings of guilt engulfed him when he thought of what his selfish behaviour had brought about.

'But when and where did he attack you?'

"Patience. I'll get to that. And he wasn't that sort of rapist. I mean, no attack in a lonely lane on a dark night. No, he built up my trust. We went for several walks, he took me up to Isnello one night for an ice cream, another evening for a cocktail to one of the bars on the seafront. When we were alone together, I was just as passionate with him. Until –'

'Until what?'

'Until the night he promised to cook me dinner up at his studio. I remember I brought fruit – grapes and half a watermelon. We had some wine and watched a funny film – in German – while the dinner was cooking. I couldn't understand much of it, but he thought it was very funny. I was really relaxed with him, enjoying his company, kissing and, well, the rest. This is what I don't understand. One minute it was fine, all cosy, and the next, he was standing over me, with the most obvious erection protruding from his shorts. He was pulling at my clothes, clothes I didn't want him to touch or open, and although I asked him to stop, and told him we'd better see to dinner, he seemed to think this was funny.'

At this point Salvatore sat down on the boundary wall of the Town Hall and looked over the roofs below and out beyond to the Mediterranean. There was a long pause in the narrative. A hiccough alerted him to the fact that she was sobbing. Her breath came in gulping waves, and the remainder of the story rushed out in intermittent bursts of clarity and incoherence.

'He kept smiling, muttering things in German … he was

on top of me. I tried to slow it down – just to hold him, like I had enjoyed doing before, but he was impatient with this, pulling at my underwear, manoeuvring me into a position where ... he could bear down on me.'

Salvatore reached for another cigarette, but his lighter failed to make contact, the flame held by his shaking hands missing every time. By Christ, when he got his hands on that bastard Christoph!

'He said I wanted to, but I was being typically Sicilian – pretending that I didn't. This was half-true. I did want to have sex but not that night, and not in that way. I wasn't ready. I told him that. I tried to take his hands off my underwear, but he become more insistent. I asked him to stop – several times – but he laughed and just kept going – until he had penetrated me.'

'For heaven's sake, why didn't you tell someone right away? Why didn't you come back to me and we could have made a complaint to the police?'

'Because half of what he says is true. I *did* want to sleep with him. I had been alone with him and allowed him to be intimate in the preceding days. I knew he would say that, if we went to the police station.'

'But listen, Maria. On that particular night, in his studio, you said "*no*" and he didn't accept that. It doesn't matter if you were going to say *"yes"* two days later, or a week later, or never. You said "*no*" on that night in July, and he raped you!'

At this, Maria-Pia shuddered, and covered her eyes with her hands as if to block out an image she could still see.

'There were so many things that made me doubt if it *had* really happened. He kept insisting that I had gone with him voluntarily, that there was no force. He said we were from different cultures and this sort of misunderstanding often happened. I knew the way it would appear at the police station. He would be the mature German tour guide, a valuable member of the community, responsible for bringing in a lot of money to the nearby hotels. And me, the little innocent Sicilian virgin, dying to have an exciting experience, but too aware of the damage to my reputation to risk it with a local man.' Maria-Pia took another cigarette from the packet, lit it, inhaled deeply, expelling the smoke with unnecessary force. 'If you were the police, who would *you* have believed?'

Salvatore knew she didn't want an answer. His instincts told him that Christoph was quite capable of what she had related, but he also understood her hesitation in making an allegation. Christoph was a smooth talker. He had resources behind him and the means to hire a top lawyer from Palermo. She had let too much time pass. She had not seen a doctor. There was no evidence.

'It wasn't your fault, you know. *You* shouldn't feel guilty.'

'But I didn't fight and scream! Maybe he thought I *meant* yes, although I said no.'

'*Maria,* stop this! No, *nein, no,* it all means the same thing. You said *no,* he ignored you. How many times do we have to go over this?'

'That's right. You lose patience with me as well, why

don't you! This is the *first — the only* time — I have gone over it.'

'Maria — Christ, I'm so useless at all this — I'm sorry, love. Truly sorry.'

Salvatore looked at his younger sister. Her nearly-adult eighteen years didn't show in the childish, trusting face that looked back at him. Suddenly he was seventeen again, and she only seven. They were returning home on the subway when a group of local thugs tried to frighten them. He had placed her behind him and edged closer and closer to the doors, ready to jump off at a station, long before their usual one. She had laced her little arms around his waist, under his winter anorak. Her arms were so short that they couldn't meet, so she clung to the two pockets of the jacket, ripping one seam completely, such was the force she applied in holding on.

He wished it were that simple now. He wished that they could just jump off at an earlier station, and he could protect her from the Christophs of this world.

'*Totò?*'

'Yes?'

'Hug me.'

Salvatore wrapped his arms around his sister's frail body and held her.

'It will all be OK. You can talk to me about this *anytime*. There are also professionals who can help you through this.'

'No, I don't want to talk to strangers about it.'

'Not now maybe, but when you feel able you know they are there.'

'I want this to stay between us. I don't want Mamma and Babbo to know. It would kill them.'

'OK, but they know there is something wrong with you. They have noticed that you are unhappy. What will we say?'

'Oh, I don't know. Maybe that I'm having doubts about Massimo – which is true. Something simple. They are better with simple answers.'

'All right. Massimo is getting too serious and you're not ready for marriage, kids, the whole blissful deal. Do I sound convincing?'

'Very! But do you think it's likely that "used goods" like me would be *allowed* to marry and have the children of a good upright citizen of Bagheria like Massimo Glorioso? I do not think this is possible!' A glimmer of a smile crossed Maria's face.

Responding to a hint of levity in his sister's tone, Salvatore leapt from the wall, dragging her with him and, linking arms, they half-ran, half-stumbled back down the road.

'Totò, you really have to stop treating me like a child.'

'So I see.'

'What time's your train?'

'I should get the five-ten. I have a double date this evening.'

'*What?*'

'No. I'm joking. But I'm taking *two* women to the cinema – two Irish girls from the hotel – to an English film, at the Arena.'

'Knowing you, that means you fancy one of them, and the other is there as camouflage. Am I right?'

'Little sister, you know too much. Yes, I like the younger one – Didi she calls herself. You'd like her. Studies music.'

'What a weird name!'

'Short for Deirdre, I think.'

'You go for it! And, Totò, thanks for listening.'

'My only regret is that I didn't drag this out of you a lot earlier.'

'Well, now that you know, don't do anything foolish with Christoph. You still have to work with him. I don't want you putting your job at risk over me, understood?'

'Don't worry. I won't. We'd better hurry – I need to say my goodbyes before I head for the station.'

Maria-Pia cupped her brother's face in her hands and kissed him on the forehead.

'You really are the best brother in the world.'

Chapter 12

Hotel Panoramico

Isabelle wound her long hair into a French pleat and pinned it up. Even at seven in the evening, the heat was unbearable and although she had intended to wear it loose, practical considerations triumphed. As she was crossing Reception on her way to meet Didi, the manager called after her.

'*Signora Isabella?* There is a message for you.'

'*Buonasera, Signor Giorgio. Come sta?*'

'Now you speak Italian, Signora Isabella! *Complimenti!* Salvatore phoned. He asked if you and the signorina could meet him at the Caffè Duomo at nine. He sends his apologies. He has a problem with his car. Will I book a taxi for you for eight-thirty?'

'No, thanks. We'll probably walk – the exercise would do us good.'

'*Va bene.* Do you have Salvatore's *cellulare*, in case you miss him?'

'His *what?* Oh, his mobile. No, I don't as it happens.'
'Here. I'll write it down for you.'
'*Grazie.*'
'*Buona serata.*'

The terrace space that evening was restricted because of a drinks reception for an incoming wedding. Only four tables on the upper level were set for the casual drinker, and those with the best view had already been hijacked by early wedding guests.

Didi was nowhere to be seen. Isabelle ordered a Campari-soda and settled herself at a table, good for admiring the stylish guests as they arrived. It had taken her less than a week to deduce that weddings in Sicily were just as snobbish, if not more so, than in Ireland. Here, it centred on what *time* your wedding took place. Late evening was the prestigious slot. If you had your church and civil ceremony around six, you slowly wound your way to the hotel following the picturesque sunset photo-shoot in the old town. Noise from the previous week's weddings had floated on into the early hours, as course after gastronomic course was served. Tasteful musical accompaniment was provided by paid entertainers – no opportunity here for maudlin Uncle Joe to seize the mike and inflict an emotional rendition of 'The Fields of Athenry' on the gathered assembly. Isabelle thoroughly approved.

Sipping her Campari, she couldn't help but muse on the irony in her choice of hotel. Escaping everything to do with marriage, she had only booked herself into the most popular location on the island for showy weddings. Rough justice or what?

'Hiya. Sorry I'm late. Pauline made me blow-dry her hair before I left. Can I get you another?'

'No, thanks. This has just arrived. Get whatever you fancy – we're not in any rush. Salvatore can't come out for us. We have to meet him in town at nine.'

'Oh good! I'll have that cocktail the barman made me the other evening.' And with that, Didi clicked up the steps to order.

She looks different, Isabelle thought. The floaty skirts had been abandoned for a tight-fitting pair of orange cut-offs and an attractive gauze top. Her hair was plaited and hung across her left shoulder. This was a far sexier look. Though not conventionally good-looking, Didi was attractive, though it was hard to imagine she was Pauline's daughter. Her mother was so diminutive, with her bird-like features and olive skin, that when you saw them together you'd be convinced Didi had been adopted.

'God, that Luigi is a bit of fun!' Didi said on her return. 'I was about to order my cocktail when his coffee machine blew up, scattering coffee grains all over his lovely white shirt and making a mess of the bar counter. He let rip a few expletives and then I happened to notice it was exactly the same model machine I had in Bar Guglielmo in Rome. I sorted it out for him, so, *cara Isabella*, my cocktail is on the house, and I think he said that when I wanted a second, to give him the nod.'

'Hey, steady on! You *do* want to be awake for this film, don't you?'

'Yeah, I'm only joking. Anyway, with another fuckin' wedding on its way in, I need a bit of fortification.'

'Why? Don't you like weddings?' Isabelle had taken Didi for a romantic. It was all those floaty, peasant clothes.

'Weddings are fine – as long as they're of people you don't know and with whom you have no personal connection. I'm off them at the moment, having just escaped the pre, present and post-plotting phases of the Wedding of the Year.'

'Meaning?'

'My beloved sister decided to get hitched in June. No. Let me rephrase that: she decided to get hitched at about eight years of age – a master-plan awaiting execution – but she finally pulled it off in June. For months I had to suffer the boredom of being dragged around shops to pick out bridesmaid dresses. I spent hour upon braindead hour flicking through back issues of *Brides* magazine in search of her perfect design. I have even been known to field phonecalls at eleven-thirty at night over seating-plans. Believe me, I'm off weddings for good!'

'Ah. A recent, painful experience then.'

'Sorry, Isabelle. I probably come across as a complete bitch, but if you knew my sister you'd understand how self-obsessed she is. She never considered that it might not *interest* me what colour the decorative flower on the place-setting cards should be. She just took it for granted that I *had* to be interested. I couldn't even express how I felt, because her trump card was to call me jealous of her having *"made something of her life".*'

'She sounds like she'd fit in perfectly in Sicily! I didn't think Irishwomen with that sort of mentality still existed.'

'Are you for real? Of course they exist! My sister has a good job and will probably keep it for a year or two, until she decides to become pregnant. Then she'll tighten the domestication noose around your man's neck by staying at home, having maxed out the maternity and parental leave, helpless and dependent on him. That way, he'll feel so *needed,* so indispensable, that his straying will only ever be temporary and never lead to him abandoning her.'

'You paint a rather pretty picture of marriage. And this guy your sister married – is he given to straying?'

'They're *all* given to straying. Monogamy is a bit of a swizz. Take the world of nature. The simplest creatures – an amoeba, an earthworm – replicate themselves without a partner. As you travel up the chain of complexity, you encounter animals who mate, procreate and then feck off, yet we humans – supposed to be the highest ranked and most sophisticated in the hierarchy – have created a socially acceptable system whereby one human expects to meet and mate with another – and stay with them forever. Fine if you're an amoeba, but it doesn't satisfy highly tuned men and women.'

'So young and so cynical! Though you have a point about monogamy. We cause our own problems by setting unattainable targets. If one or other partner wants to be really honest, then the relationship usually crumbles, because a lot of marriages are based on anything *but* honesty.'

'Exactly! Now take Jan – that's my sister – and *her* husband. He's a real lad-about-town who's had loads of women. But she won't even acknowledge that some of them were important to him. It's as if she believes her married state is a protective igloo into which no harm can ever come. Sometimes, I think she doesn't care if he *is* misbehaving, as long as she doesn't get to hear about it. "Being married" is all that matters to her. She'll accept his dishonesty as long as they don't discuss it and he doesn't humiliate her publicly.'

'*Finito?*' The barman had taken away the two very definitely empty glasses. '*Altro?*'

'Have we time for another?' Isabelle checked her watch. 'It'll take us about twenty minutes to walk in.'

'Or we could get the bus at ten to nine.'

'I'd forgotten the bus. Same again?'

'Yes. Luigi, how's the coffee machine? *Perfetto?* OK. Another Campari-soda and one of your delightful cocktails for me.'

'*Si, Didi, subito.*'

'I think you have a fan there.'

'What, Luigi? Ah, he's harmless. I just enjoy the flirt. No, the hotel is pretty thin on fanciable men, apart from that dishy musician in *Stromboli*. Have you met him yet?'

'Rico? He seems very nice, though it must be hard trying to work when everyone is on holidays.'

'I'd love to sit in on a rehearsal. I'm going to ask if he'll take me some day. Spin him a yarn about being a music graduate and big into Puccini. That should do it!'

Luigi interrupted Didi's plotting by depositing their drinks onto the table. '*Eccoci.*'

'*Grazie, Luigi.*' Isabelle tucked the bill under the ashtray and, after Luigi departed, asked, 'So, do you think Rico's that attractive?'

'Have you eyes in your head? He's sex-on-wheels!'

Isabelle was quiet. She hadn't considered Rico in this light before. Didi's obvious fascination made her re-evaluate their drink together. She supposed he was an interesting man – a little vain – but which of them weren't?

'What about yourself, Isabelle? Any jaunts up the aisle planned?'

'No. Sometimes that decision is taken out of your hands.'

'Were you engaged to someone and it broke up?'

'Nothing as conventional as that. I had an on/off relationship with this guy for a long time. People kept saying we'd end up together and, when you hear that often enough, you begin to believe it.'

'So, what happened?'

'He married someone else, without letting me know what he was planning.'

'The bastard! Sorry, Isabelle, but he sounds like a creep.'

'Judged by his final action, yes, I suppose he does, but

there was – is – a very funny, loving, man, buried under the layers of arrogance.'

'Well, I don't think I'd have the patience to unwrap the layers.'

'Probably wise where my ex is concerned! Now, I hate to break up the soul-searching, but drink that up fast, if we're to catch this bus.'

'OK, OK! *And* I need the bathroom.'

Isabelle waved the docket at Luigi, who brought his machine to the table.

'Cash or room?'

'Cash.'

'Going to town?'

'Yes, the cinema. There's Didi at the top of the steps. I'd better go.'

'*A domani.* Have a good evening.'

Salvatore was glad of the cinema arrangement with Didi and Isabelle. It had given him an excuse to escape dinner with his parents and leave Bagheria early. On the return journey, the magnitude of his sister's revelation had hit him, and he alternately felt very low and very angry. He hadn't even suspected Maria-Pia was interested in Christoph, let alone that the relationship had got physical. He should have been attentive – more protective of her. Christoph was a womaniser. It was a standing joke among the cycling instructors – how many days it took him to bed one of his newly arrived guests.

His sister wasn't like the foreign tourists. She had never been away from home on her own. If she even wanted to go for a walk, she would ring around until she found a friend or one of her cousins free to accompany her. If nobody were free, she just wouldn't go. Being alone didn't seem to present a similar problem to foreign women.

'Salvatore! *Ciao!* Here we are at last.'

Salvatore swallowed the dregs of his coffee as Didi, looking hot and flushed, and particularly nice in some orange combination, approached the Caffè Duomo.

'Sorry we're late, but you'll never believe what happened. We took the nine o'clock bus, which arrived bang on time, but this little old lady got on at the Pescatore and asked the bus driver about the route. I couldn't follow it, but Isabelle reckoned she wanted to go up the higher road – the road the bus *doesn't take*. Well, the driver checked with everyone if it was OK, and when he got a sufficient number of nods and "*va bene*s", we detoured up through all those apartment blocks, until we dropped the old lady at her son's place! It added nearly twenty minutes on to the journey.'

'*Cara Didi*, this is Sicily. Personal service! Where's Isabelle?'

'At the cash machine. She'll be here in a minute. I was really impressed the way the other passengers were so agreeable. Nobody complained or said they were in a hurry.'

'One of the good things about living in a small community. Ah, *eccola*! Hi, Isabelle. Now, *al cinema*! It's a pity your friendly bus driver isn't around – he could detour the next bus up the hill and save our legs.'

The Cinema sotto le Stelle – Cinema under the Stars – was just that, an idyllic open-air arena, under the natural, iridescent stars overhead. The screen was framed against the rocky headland of the town. Confused bats made desperate lunges at the lights, which regular cinemagoers nonchalantly ignored as they studied the rolling intro for *The Proposal*.

'I'm terrified of bats,' Isabelle admitted to Salvatore, patting her firmly pinned-up hair with relief. 'What if their radar goes wrong? I don't fancy one of them swooping down on me, when I'm concentrating on Ryan Reynolds.'

'You're OK. They're more terrified of you.'

Although it was a short film, it was the cinema's practice to break for a revenue-generating interval and, after no time at all, the screen went dark.

'I'll go get some drinks,' offered Salvatore. 'Any popcorn?'

'We'll come with you. See if there's any talent around!' Didi bounced out of the row ahead of him.

Salvatore frowned. He didn't really understand her humour. He hoped this reference to 'talent' didn't mean she was like the other foreign women, hunting down any man to amuse her for the duration of the holiday. He had thought her a little more discerning.

At the kiosk, Isabelle ordered two bottles of Moretti and

a Coke, while Didi eyed the popcorn selection.

Suddenly, Salvatore saw him. Lounging against a crash barrier, a can of Heineken in one hand and his elbow propped on top of the metal divider, was Christoph, in the company of one of his young guests – female, of course.

The sound of a good-humoured laugh appeared to Salvatore as a leer, as if he was recounting the fun to be had toying with the natives. His long, sinuous arms escaped lecherously from the blue denim shirt. Salvatore could see those arms, imagine those hands—

As Didi turned to share her chosen tub of popcorn, she saw Salvatore advancing on the railings.

Concentrating his efforts into a sharp uppercut, Salvatore made one, clean contact. Christoph reeled from the surprise blow and watched as blood dripped onto his denim shirt. The girl shrieked in horror, and impugned Salvatore's sanity in a string of explosive German, before tending to her wounded soldier with a cotton bandana.

Isabelle and Didi clutched their drinks and observed in shock.

'What the hell!' Didi rested the cardboard popcorn tub on a nearby table.

'He's the last person I would have suspected of having a violent streak – quiet-spoken, gentle Salvatore. Why the unprovoked attack?'

'Don't ask me. Though your man looks familiar.'

When Salvatore returned, he wiped his hands on a clean hanky and asked for his beer. Isabelle handed it to him, as if nothing out of the ordinary had happened. She offered him some popcorn, which he duly accepted. The lights flickered two or three times, alerting the audience to the imminent start of Part 2 and, without a word, all three trailed back to their seats. On the way, they passed the afflicted victim, who had evidently decided to forego the second half of the film, as he and his companion were heading for the exit.

The onscreen story was predictable and clichéd, when compared to the intermission drama. Isabelle found her mind wandering to the image of Salvatore thumping the tall, blond man. She would have loved Didi's speculative opinion on the matter but, with Salvatore seated between them, that was impossible. One thing she thought strange was the man's passivity in the light of Salvatore's blow. He hadn't raised an arm to protect himself, let alone actively fight back. The rest of the film passed in a blur and when the final credits rolled, she was relieved that it was time to go.

'Will we go for a drink somewhere?' Salvatore suggested.

'Thanks, but it's late,' Isabelle responded quickly. 'I think I'd like to head back.'

'Me too.' Didi accumulated her rubbish for the bin. 'Swim planned for the crack of dawn.'

'OK. We have to detour a bit to the mechanic's. He's left my car parked outside.'

The walk to the garage was punctuated by a mixture of gibberish conversation and a tension-ridden silence. Salvatore made no reference as to why out of the blue he had executed an uppercut worthy of any professional boxer on a fellow cinema-goer, and returned afterwards to sip beer and share popcorn as if nothing had happened.

The newly overhauled Fiat hummed like a two-year old and took the bends on the way out to the Panoramico with added verve. Salvatore concentrated on his driving, making the odd comment at the girls' exaggeratedly jolly conversation.

'So, you enjoyed the cinema. We do it again?'

After a second or two of silence, both responded in unison:

'*Love to.*'

'*Of course.*'

'*Eccoci.*' The car swung left at the green hotel sign. 'Do you have your keys? We don't need to pass by the Reception?'

'No – well, I have mine anyway. Didi?'

'Pauline's probably in.'

'OK, then I'll say goodnight, and thank you for your lovely company this evening. *Alla prossima!*'

'Thanks, Salvatore, for the lift back.'

'*Niente. A domani.*'

Didi and Isabelle waved as Salvatore did an unorthodox U-turn outside the villas. Isabelle noticed that Rico's light was on; he must be home.

'Christ! Weird or what?' Didi, animated by Salvatore's new air of mystique, said at once. 'I haven't a clue what that was about. Most strange. The blond guy works here. I've seen him before.'

'And then, not to refer to it *at all* afterwards.' Isabelle took out her key.

'Not that we know him well or anything, but I'd have thought Salvatore was the type to agonise over his every move, and yet he does something impulsive like that and offers no explanation.'

'Anyway, the incident certainly livened up that ancient Rom-Com.'

'Oh look, Lover-Boy is home.' Didi nodded towards *Stromboli*. 'Hey, no music tonight. Maybe he has Black Beauty in for some "private" tuition.'

Although it was meant as a joke, Isabelle was annoyed by Didi's comment. She suddenly felt weary of the sparring and the matchmaking – *exactly* what she had come to Sicily to escape.

'Didi, I'll say goodnight. I'm going to Palermo tomorrow, and I've an early start.' Without waiting for her new friend to reply, Isabelle turned and made her way up the dimly lit garden path to *Lipari*.

Puzzled by Isabelle's abrupt departure, Didi rapped gently on the window of *Vulcano*, hoping her mother was still awake.

Chapter 13

Dawn was so spectacular that Isabelle frequently set the clock early so she could lie in bed and watch the sun rise across the silver sea. The sights and sounds of the hotel were so different early in the morning that the thought of breakfast on a nearly empty terrace appealed greatly. Having avoided the organised excursion to Palermo, she planned to visit by train and be free to leave whenever she felt like it.

As she draped her towel on the patio chair to dry, she noticed that Rico's shutters were firmly closed. Maybe Didi had been right about Beverly. It certainly would explain why the singer had been so offended when Rico gave her the brush-off that night at the hotel bar. They had crossed paths on only one occasion since and, although Isabelle had greeted her in a friendly manner, the American had stared through her.

Isabelle checked her watch. If she were to catch the bus

to the train station, she had better grab breakfast quickly. She was looking forward to the trip. Despite all she had said about feeling conspicuous alone, she wasn't yet at the stage where she wanted to team up with a 'buddy' and do everything together. She had enjoyed the outing with Didi the previous night, and it certainly was more relaxing to know that she could sit with her and Pauline at dinner if she felt like it, but something within her resisted it becoming a regular arrangement. The maître d' had been a bit presumptuous in trying to reclaim her lovely window table beside the gentlemanly Signor Russo. In her sharpest professional tone, Isabelle had informed Signor Bruno that she most definitely *would* still have need of her own table. Didi and Pauline were nice people, but they were staying nearly as long as she was, and it was too much to impose an intimacy on both parties just because they happened to live in the same city.

At Cefalù station, Isabelle noticed that the 8.45 to Palermo read '*in ritardo*', but it was only late by a matter of minutes, so wouldn't upset her plans unduly. When the train eventually pulled in, she saw that it had come from Venice. She climbed into an empty-looking compartment – empty, except for a young couple. Nods were exchanged and Isabelle settled herself by the window.

The youngsters had a lot of luggage and seemed tired.

Obviously, they had come the full journey from the north. They looked about eighteen or nineteen. Their sexual chemistry ricocheted around the compartment. They were holding hands, varying this as their need required, embracing or kissing or caressing some part of the other's body. Isabelle felt like an intruder, yet if she got up to leave she would appear like a disapproving prude. The couple were so unselfconscious in their affection that they frequently included Isabelle with a conspiratorial nod or laugh, or by making an occasional comment.

She tried to recall what it was like to be so young and so uncritical in your loving. She was like that, in the early Con days. She remembered how selfish they had been. Their relationship had no need of anyone else, even to the exclusion of his family. When he was still studying down south, she remembered the stolen Sundays of day-return tickets spent in her bed between trains, holding him with her eyes, believing that if she blinked he would disappear.

She wondered at what point the passion had faded and the drudgery had begun. For although she considered their relationship to have lasted on and off for eleven years, latterly there was no joy. There were plenty of recriminations and apologies, plenty of urgent, clinical couplings, but couplings without closeness, without intimacy.

'*Biscotto?*' The hazel-eyed girl opposite extended the packet.

'*Grazie.*'

Isabelle watched as the young girl ate her own biscuit,

leaving a crumb rest on her lower lip. It was too much of a temptation for her companion. Quick as lightning, he leaned across and with a swift lick of a practised tongue, swept the crumb into his mouth. This sent both of them into childish giggles, which in turn ceded to something more adult, and they kissed hungrily for several minutes.

'Palermo Centrale, Palermo Centrale. Terminus.'

The young lovers gathered their copious bags and said a warm goodbye to Isabelle. She envied them not only their happiness, but where they were at in their lives. It was easy, when you were eighteen. The only thing driving you was hormones. When you introduced careers and compromise and diverse lifestyles, on top of all the problems that the hormones continued to produce, then loving became difficult.

Once out of the station, the early-morning sunshine favoured the right side of Via Roma. The pavements on the shady left had a disproportionate number of pedestrians. Sun-starved Hibernian Isabelle started her ramble on the sunny side, conceding after two blocks that the natives had the correct idea. Senses assaulted on all sides by various stimuli, it was her hearing that suffered the greatest offensive. Although she knew Palermo in the 21st century was a much safer place to be, the constant klaxon of carabinieri cars made her feel anything but secure. Native

Palermitani tripped past in cool linen suits, never rushing yet covering considerable ground, apparently unperturbed by the security noise.

Isabelle checked her map to establish at exactly what point the Via Vittorio Emanuele intersected Via Roma. She wanted to see the Fontana Pretoria which looked amazing in her guidebook, and she needed to check what hours the cathedral was open to sightseers. She might leave it till the hotter part of the day, if she could visit in the afternoon. Her plan was to walk up Via Maqueda to Piazza Verdi and the Teatro Massimo. Before leaving work, one of their opera-mad clients had convinced her she had to visit the theatre. He had eulogised to such an extent on its renaissance from fire, war and Mafia manipulation, that she really hadn't the heart to look him in the eye on her return and lie. It would be far simpler just to go and see what all the fuss was about. She would take a quick run around before having lunch.

She had no idea the opera house was going to be enormous. Thinking of theatres back home or venues in which she had seen the occasional opera, she imagined something more modest. Instead, this elaborate pillared monument announced its presence the minute she emerged from Via Maqueda. Surrounded by railings, majestic steps led to the Ionic-columned entrance. Palm trees flanked two enormous statues inside the gates. Despite her reluctance, Isabelle was overwhelmed.

Meekly, she made her way up the steps to the door.

A small uniformed usher greeted her.

'*Visita?*'

'*Sì.*'

'*OK. Ma silenzio. Prova.*' At this, the usher made a '*shishing*' sound, and placed an index finger on his pursed lips.

The door to the parterre was open. Even Isabelle's cynicism faded when she saw the extent of the auditorium before her. Row upon row of red-velvet chairs led to the stage and orchestra pit. Stacked on all sides, five tiers of gilt-painted, upholstered boxes extended vertically. Leaning backwards to appreciate how high they went, she gasped at the ceiling – a flower-like wheel of petals, painted with elaborate scenes.

'*Shhh! Il maestro.*' It was her guide again.

The previously empty pit was now replete with musicians, dressed in cotton dresses, Bermudas and T-shirts. The conductor muttered something and they flicked forward in their music. Onstage, a thin young woman addressed him and was joined by two men – a young one, and a debonair fifty-something man. A group of people wandered in behind.

'*Allora, OK. Act 2 conclusion. Prima del "Di sprezzo degno". Alfredo, Barone, Germont, Violetta, tutti!*'

The usher gestured to her to sit. Isabelle crept quietly into a row. The chorus seemed very angry with the younger man, pointing and singing in his direction. Suddenly, the crowd parted, and the older character appeared. His low voice cut through their anger with a quiet dignity and, although Isabelle didn't recognise the opera or understand the story, she knew the older man was pleading with the younger – perhaps chastising him – like a parent correcting an errant child, in angry tones, but tones imbued with love.

The music moved her in a way she had never before been moved by opera. It felt different to see it in rehearsal – with the performers in their ordinary clothes – just to listen to this powerful music sung so passionately. Apart from one other couple, she and the usher were the only audience, and yet the cast performed as if the house were full.

At the end of the Act, the usher brushed his eyes with the back of his hand.

'*Traviata*. Every time, I cry.'

Isabelle's visit to the Teatro Massimo was humbling. She was beginning to understand why opera generated such an emotional response from its fans, a reaction she had previously ridiculed. She wanted to sit and hear the music out to the end, but the official tapped his watch. She thought of Rico and his work as a conductor. No wonder he was so absorbed by it, if he was responsible for putting together something as momentous as that which she had just witnessed. She longed to discuss it with him, to seek an explanation as to *why* this music had brought her to tears, sitting alone in one of the biggest opera houses in Europe.

Tipping the usher over-generously, she headed out into the real world of screaming sirens, carrying customers to the nearby courthouse. The conductor she had just seen in action was old and balding, but she kept imagining Rico in his place – baton raised, the entire orchestra and cast in thrall. She remembered Didi's plan to sit in on a *Tosca* rehearsal. It did not fill her with joy.

What was happening? She didn't have any feelings for Rico, so why be irritated because Didi fancied him? Or did she just want Rico to want her? Was that what this was about?

As she waited for her lunch order to arrive, Isabelle wondered how the festival rehearsals were going. Rico had kept a low profile since their drink together. She had seen him coming and going from the villa but, as he didn't observe hotel mealtimes, she had never had the opportunity to invite him to join her. They had greeted each other over the boundary hedge but, apart from small talk about the increasingly oppressive heat, their conversation had been impersonal.

Once lunch was finished, the shops were shut. There wasn't a breath. The electronic thermometer on a nearby building pulsed forty-one degrees. She knew this was probably an exaggerated reading because of the concentration of tightly packed buildings but, still, it was too hot for wandering around. The prudent thing would be to take the shady Via Maqueda back towards the station and relax in the cool of the cathedral on the way. She'd catch a return train before the working commuters converged later. Shopping would have to wait for another day.

Back in Cefalù, the town shops were buzzing with post-siesta activity. Isabelle appreciated the cooling sea breeze, following its absence in Palermo. She was thirsty and fancied a drink in her favourite spot, the Bar del Molo, down at the tiny harbour.

There were few customers – it was too early. She chose a table on the perimeter, overlooking the sea. The waiter had just taken her order when someone walked towards her. Rico! What was he doing there at this hour? Shouldn't he be working?

'*Ciao, Isabella.* Here you are!'

'*Ciao, Rico.* No rehearsals?'

'*Grazie a Dio,* free day. No, we had all reached the point of – how do you say – no return? It is always wise in such a moment to take a *pausa*. Nothing is gained by making people work when they are tired and – *demoralizzati*?'

'Demoralised. What has them demoralised?'

'Oh, many things. Frustration at the work. Tiredness. The heat. Maybe they are pissed off with me!'

'I doubt that very much!'

'You flatter. It's not really an admiration society, you know, working with all those artists and musicians.'

'Maybe not. I saw a rehearsal at the Massimo in Palermo today. *Traviata.* I get it now – how powerful the conductor is. I had never thought of that aspect of it before – you are really in control of the whole thing.'

'Musically yes, but artistically no. That depends on the director.'

'And in your production? Do you work well with the director?'

'Oh yes, Stephen is fine – naïve, but fine. No, I am lucky. He consults with me and we agree on things, rather than it being a battle of wills. *Allora*, you were in the city today? You should have told me you were going. I would have gone with you – with your permission, of course. I like Palermo, but I don't know it well.'

'I just fancied a day on my own. Don't you ever get like that?'

'*Cara Isabella*, *every* day I feel like that. Listen, since for once I am free to eat at a normal hour, would you like to stay in town and we'll try one of these amazing small restaurants?'

'Oh Rico, that would be lovely, but I couldn't survive until dinner. I'll have to go back to the hotel for a rest, a shower and change of clothes. After that, I'll be ready to hit any restaurant you should choose.'

'*Ha!* You are becoming Sicilian. All this sleeping in the middle of the day.'

'It's hardly the middle of the day – and I have been up since seven this morning.'

'So, why don't we both go back after our drink and we can eat in town about nine. Would that suit?'

'That's fine. *Signore, il conto!*'

'*Prego!* Let me! I'm afraid we Italian men are very traditional. We have a difficulty in letting women pay. Where are you going?'

'To the bus stop.'

'We take a taxi. It's simpler. We can pick one up at the Duomo. *Va bene?*'

'*Si, benissimo.*'

'I am looking forward to tonight.'

'Me too.'

'I think you are a very beautiful, very complicated lady, Isabella, and I plan to find out more tonight!'

'Maybe. No promises.'

'OK. As long as you are honest.'

'I am *always* honest. Are you?'

'*Dipende!*'

The taxi pulled up, and they got in. The driver, taking the direct route, delivered his passengers to the hotel in five minutes. Isabelle felt good driving up the avenue with Rico by her side. When the car stopped directly outside *Vulcano,* she silently prayed that Didi would be taking the evening rays out on her veranda.

Childish or what?

Chapter 14

Cefalù

Il Pirata, a new seafood restaurant, was a fifteen-minute taxi ride the other side of town and the only one with an unreserved table at short notice for the popular late-evening slot. Isabelle watched Rico as he leaned forward to pay the driver. He really was very handsome, but seemed unconscious of it. His hair was receding, but because he wore it long and swept behind his ears, it looked artistic rather than just a clumsy effort to disguise incipient hair loss. He was the sort of man who would become the centre of your world if you let him, his intensity radiating ever-increasing circles to suck you in. As soon as you understood him on one level, he would unravel another and yet another, until you were enmeshed in the various layers of his life.

'You are dreaming of faraway places, I think!' Rico looked over his menu at her.

'Sorry? No, I was just studying people around us – wondering who they were, why they're together.'

'Such philosophy on an empty stomach! I think we'd better order some wine. Can I recommend the Colombo Platino? It will go well with seafood or fish.'

'I don't think I've tried it before.'

The waiter took the drinks order and left.

'*Allora*, you are interested in our fellow diners?'

'Not *interested* in a personal way, but it always intrigues me to watch groups or pairs of people and to imagine their interrelationship.'

'You know, if *you* are looking at them and thinking these things, it's quite possible some of them are looking at *us* and wondering about our relationship.'

'More than likely. Human curiosity – a prerequisite for life to move forward. If we weren't curious about anything, we wouldn't travel or make new friends or stumble into relationships with different people. We'd clock up a limited set of experiences, have a controllable circle of friends by a certain age, and then just repeat the same exchanges over and over, till we die.'

'So how do you account for two people falling in love – let's say at twenty – and living together with *no* other experiences until they are – eighty years old?'

'Either they're two very lucky people, or they don't necessarily *stop* seeking new experiences, new friends – just *because* they're married or together. Each keeps growing, keeps their curiosity alive, with the partner they love alongside. They don't see their life as lived out, just because their relationship is a "fait accompli". Do you use that expression in Italian?'

'Oh, I am well familiar with it. Remember, I have a French wife!'

This piece of information hovered in the air over Isabelle's head. It wasn't as if she presumed Rico was *available* in any conventional sense – no one that attractive and personable could free-float through life without having a serious attachment in tow. But married? This she had not suspected.

'You seem surprised. Did you think I was gay?'

'No, not at all. I just didn't think you were married – to either sex.'

'Again, this happens! First Stephen and now you. Do I appear that unattached?'

'Not in the sense of someone *without* deep attachments, but the overriding impression you give is one of independence – of someone who marches to the beat of his own drum.'

Rico groaned. 'No, please! Don't mention the word "drum" – if you heard how the percussionist in the Orchestra della Madonie plays, you would never frighten me in my leisure time by mentioning this instrument.'

Isabelle smiled across the candlelit table, glad of the levity and the change of topic. Talk of his marriage was bringing her into a territory where she didn't want to go. She wanted to enjoy the moment, not think of absent people. But between mouthfuls of *pasta alle cozze*, she couldn't resist, and slipped in the inevitable question. 'Your wife – what's her name?'

'Monique. She's a ballet dancer, with a company based in France.'

'Oh, not a singer then.'

'Definitely not. She's difficult enough as a dancer. What's your spaghetti like?'

'A bit salty, but otherwise fine.'

'So, *mia bella Isabella,* what about you? Have you abandoned some angry husband back in Dublin?'

Isabelle looked sharply at Rico to check if he were making fun of her. His expression was open, the question innocent.

'No. No husband, abandoned or otherwise. I am escaping from a man who for a long time I thought I wanted to be with. Now, I'm not so sure.'

'Why the change of heart?'

'He married somebody else.'

'No! *Come mai?*'

'Afraid so. Now, I guess that's not the only reason. Certainly, at the beginning it was – wounded pride at being publicly passed over. As a man, Rico, you won't identify with this, because most men set the agenda where marriage is concerned: they usually do the asking. I know the occasional woman proposes, but if she does she keeps it to herself.'

'Monique proposed to me. *Opéra de Marseille* on a warm

June evening. Emotions were running high after a performance of *Carmen*. I was caught up in the moment – I said yes.'

Isabelle felt her cheeks tingle. 'Oh. I didn't mean any offence when I said—'

'Don't worry! How could you have known? So, continue your story. Why is it different for men when someone they love marries another person? Don't you think we hurt too?'

'I'm sure you do, but you don't have to convince people that you might have had a choice and opted out. I mean, when's the last time you heard a man described as *jilted*?'

'*Jilted*? This is not a word I know. What does it mean?'

'One of my Granny's favourites! Used to describe someone in a serious relationship – usually a woman – who was let-down, abandoned – maybe left for someone else.'

In a rich baritone, Rico began to sing: '*Sola, perduta e abbandonata!*'

'*Excuse* me?'

'It's from *Manon Lescaut*, another Puccini opera, a very beautiful one. The heroine awakes to find her lover missing. They are on the run from the authorities, in the wilds of Louisiana, and he has gone to look for drinking water, but she believes he has left her and, losing the will to live, she sings this aria, before dying of exposure and exhaustion.'

'God, Rico, are there any *happy* operas? That's nearly as bad as *Romeo and Juliet*.'

'Well, yes. It *is* like *Romeo and Juliet*, because Des Grieux – that's Manon's lover – comes back. He hasn't abandoned her at all, but she was so tired and ill that she believed he had. Unfortunately, she awakes only for a moment, then expires in his arms.'

'So, it was all just a big misunderstanding?'

'Sadly, yes.' Rico moved the *pesce spada* around his plate, adding a little oil. 'A lot of important decisions are made on the strength of misunderstandings.' He squeezed a little lemon over the fish. 'For people who never stop talking, it's amazing how little we listen to what is being said.'

Isabelle sensed that Rico was no longer referring to events in *Manon Lescaut* but alluding to his own story. His distracted look was replaced by an expression of melancholy. After a few minutes, he raised a newly recovered bright face and refilled both their glasses.

'So, the former lover, does he have a name?'

'Con. Short for Conor – it's a popular Irish name. Con by name, and con by nature.'

'You mean like in American – a conman?'

'I mean exactly that, Rico.'

'*Scusami, Isabella*, but if you say this about him, how can you have loved him?'

'Have you never been attracted to someone even though you knew she was bad for you? And Con, well, he wasn't always bad. Particularly in the early years, he was great.'

'This Con, he's been around for many years?'

'Nearly eleven, give or take. The first time I saw him, I thought he was the most conceited man I had ever met.'

'How did it begin?'

'In unusual circumstances – Rico, if I start on this, we'll be here all night!'

'I have all the time in the world to listen to you, c*ara*, though we might need to order more drinks—' As Rico turned to signal to the mature waiter, he noticed him seating a couple at the table just two behind his own. '*Merda*! It's Beverly and Wolfgang – from the cast. What are they doing all the way out here?'

The waiter, now free to attend to Rico's request, added second bottles of water and wine to the docket.

'*Mi dispiace, Isabella*, but I really will have to go and greet them.'

'I'll just stay and wave from here.'

Rico grinned and, removing the linen napkin from his lap, got up to greet his colleagues at the nearby table.

'*Maestro*, what a surprise! Enjoying your meal?' Beverly raised a heavily powdered cheek to Rico's descending lips.

'*Si, grazie*. Wolfgang, *buonasera*. Enjoying your free day?'

Wolfgang studied the German translation of his menu and didn't reply.

'Well, *maestro*,' said Beverly. 'What did *you* find tasty this evening? Would you recommend anything in particular? Say, isn't that your little colleen from the hotel?'

'Yes, Isabelle also likes seafood, so we decided to come and try this new out-of-town restaurant. Everything we had was excellent. The swordfish is particularly good.'

'Rico, why don't you and your little friend join us later for coffee and a *digestivo*?'

'*Grazie, Beverly,* but we are so advanced in our meal that I think we will be gone before you reach the point of caffè. Now, I see our drinks have arrived, so I must return to my friend. *Allora, buon appetito.*'

Rico sighed as he resumed his seat.

'It wasn't all that bad, was it?' Isabelle asked.

'No, but anybody from the cast other than those two. He is most difficult, and she – well, you know her already. It's unfair, when I am here to relax with you, that they should turn up to spy on us.'

'Maybe they just like seafood! Do you want to go?'

'No! We will enjoy our wine and return to your wonderful story of the conman.'

Not for the first time, Isabelle suspected Rico was making fun of her. It was so hard to interpret gestures and facial expressions across cultures and, although his English was excellent, sometimes he sounded sarcastic, perhaps without intending to. Yet her need to talk about Con was becoming increasingly pressing and, besides, Rico had honest eyes.

'I was twenty-one and had just started my first job in a new public relations firm in Dublin. My boss was crazy – a really exuberant, energetic type – very young to head up his own agency. He had a staff of ten or so, all from different backgrounds, but most firmly established on the PR career path. One of his "team-building" exercises was to take us away to an adventure centre, where we had to indulge in outdoor pursuits – abseiling, canoeing, mountaineering – you know the sort of thing.'

'I hate it already.'

'Well, I wasn't too crazy about the idea either, not being madly sporty, but there was no way out. Only, the location was fabulous – the centre was set on a lake in the heart of Connemara, and it ended up being one of those freak weekends you occasionally get in Ireland in April, when the temperature outstrips anything you could expect in the so-called summer. Despite my apprehension, I relaxed and opted for the less challenging activities. We were divided into teams with an instructor each. Ours was a tall, muscular fellow from Dublin. His name was Conor.'

'The famous Con.'

'He was so full of himself. I was mesmerised, watching the capacity his ego had to expand in any given direction. The other girls hung on his every word, practically drooling over him.'

'Was he very beautiful?'

'That's the funny thing. He wasn't conventionally handsome. Yes, he had a good, well-built physique, but he had a pretty face which didn't seem to match the very masculine body. For the first two days I gave him a wide berth – do you know what that means?'

Rico nodded. 'I feel a biblical "on the third day" coming!'

Isabelle laughed. 'Well, there's nothing terribly biblical about it, but it *was* the third day. We were white-water canoeing on a fastmoving river. We had previously paddled around a calm lake and I had enjoyed it thoroughly, but the river was different. You really had to judge the current and paddle fast through the difficult stretches, or you went nowhere. One of my workmates had a bet with the others as to how long it would take me to get through this sluice thing. Everybody was laughing and egging me on. I got to the weir and paddled like mad, but the boat seemed to spin around. Greg, the smart-aleck colleague, whooped with laughter, counting the seconds aloud as his stopwatch ticked on. I was really scared. The water was rushing all around and buffeting this fragile piece of fibreglass with me in it! Everyone thought I was enjoying it, but I was terrified. Suddenly, Con brought his boat as close to mine as he could and steadied it with his outstretched paddle. He urged me to grip the two paddles and to mimic his movements. With a couple of swift strokes, we were through the tanks and back out onto the relative calm of the river.'

'So, you fell for your rescuer!'

'You make it sound dramatic. It wasn't like that. I was impressed by the way he could tell my bravado was just that. He had known me only a couple of days, yet the people I had been working with every day for over six months couldn't see how frightened I was. I came off that river with a new respect for him.'

'Did you get together that weekend?'

'God, no! Besides, I think the adventure centre had all sorts of rules about fraternising with the clients. But when I was leaving, I thanked him particularly for the canoe episode, and he said he'd call into the office someday, if only to protect me from maniacs like Greg.'

'Did he?'

'He took his time – I can't remember – maybe three weeks later. What I didn't realise was that he was a student, doing a sports-management degree in Cork – a couple of hours' drive south of Dublin. The adventure centre job was a casual thing, a chance to make some cash during the Easter holidays.'

'*Scusatami, signori. Dessert? Caffè?*' The rather hassled-looking waiter had materialised at their table.

Isabelle became conscious of a long queue near the entrance.

'*Isabella?* Yes? No. OK. I'll just get the bill, and we can head into town, away from the Spanish Inquisition!'

'Leaving us already, *maestro*? Well, have fun!' Beverly looked up from dissecting her fish and directed this at Isabelle, who smiled graciously in return, and resisted the temptation to laugh at the American's perfectly executed dentistry, ruined by the presence of a small rocket leaf wedged between one of her incisors.

'*Arrivederci, Beverly, Wolfgang.*'

'*Buona notte!*'

'*A domani, maestro!*'

The taxi was waiting and Isabelle and Rico climbed in, giggling like teenagers.

'I'm glad we've escaped that pair,' Isabelle said with a laugh. 'I thought Beverly was bad but, beside that guy Wolfgang, she seems positively normal. What's his story?'

'Oh, nothing very interesting. Bitter, having split up from

his wife, who happens to be the principal cellist in the orchestra. See? I told you that there were all sorts of tensions in my *Tosca*.'

Out of sympathetic solidarity for the misfortune that had placed Wolfgang and his ex-wife in the same production, Isabelle gave Rico a quick, friendly hug, and found her hug reciprocated. Initially, she tensed, but it felt so good to feel the strong arms around her. He smelt appealing – his scent a mixture of faint, residual smoke and a citrus-based cologne. The easy thing would be to stay in his arms, but that couldn't be right. First, she wasn't ready and, secondly, he had very clearly stated that he was married.

Yet she was excited. His touch, his smell – the feel of someone new – reawakened in her feelings that had been dormant for too long. She had almost forgotten the thrill of those first hesitant kisses, the awkwardness of two ill-adapted bodies, noses nudging, hearts pounding, neither knowing exactly what to do, what to say. She allowed herself to relax into the comfort of his warmth, registering acutely the lack of affection she had been suffering since she was alone.

'*Va bene?*'

'*Si. Va bene.*'

The taxi dropped them at the promenade and they walked, arms linked, towards the port.

Isabelle breathed in the night air. 'I prefer walking by the sea when it's quiet, like this. Fewer people around.'

'When I can't work things out, I always go to the sea. The

perpetual motion is comforting – a guarantee that no matter what I decide, life will go on.'

'What would *you* have to "work out"?' Isabelle gave him a friendly punch on the chest. 'Handsome. Talented. A successful musical career, a wife who loves you and the opportunity to travel the world and get paid for it.'

'It all seems so wonderful, doesn't it?'

'Pretty much!'

'I ... it's just not always as clear-cut as it may seem.'

Cushioned as she was against his left side, Isabelle could feel the vibration in his shirt pocket communicating an incoming call. Rico eyed the caller display, promptly rejected it, and powered off the phone.

'Not in the mood for talking?'

'Not to Monique.'

'You just turned off the phone on your *wife*? Won't she be annoyed?'

'She'll be as mad as hell.'

'Then why did you do it?'

'Look, Isabelle, I have already had over an hour of argument on this phone tonight. I have no desire for any more. Now my phone, it will stay *spento*. Off.'

Feeling the discussion was also 'off', Isabelle was glad when they had reached the *gelateria*. She hid her face behind the list of ice creams, eliminating the combinations one by one until it was a final showdown between *pistachio/vaniglia* and *cioccolata/panna*.

Rico interrupted her selection. 'I want a baby.'

Isabelle checked the menu. No, she hadn't misheard. There wasn't any exotic cocktail on the drinks list that could approximate to what he had just said.

As if to restore faith in her sense of hearing, Rico repeated: 'I want a baby. Monique will not hear of it.'

'Oh, I'm sorry.'

'Do *you* think I'm being unreasonable? We have been married two years now, and I am nearly forty. I don't want to wait much longer, or else I will be too old to play with and enjoy my child.'

'And Monique – what age is she?'

'Younger. Thirty. But it is not an age thing. She doesn't want a baby for professional reasons. She's at the peak of her career and it's not possible now. Monique says that if a dancer disappears for a year, she disappears forever.'

'I suppose that's probably true. It's not like it's an ordinary job – being a ballerina.'

'Yes, but creating a baby is the single most important thing anyone can do. I would have no problem taking one, two, *three* years off work to care for it. But I can't actually have it – since I am a man.'

Isabelle didn't know what to say. Despite their many years together, Con and she had never discussed children or their feelings about having them. She had observed his lack of tolerance with Charles – his nephew – and had avoided the subject in case he thought she was getting broody, particularly in their later years, when she knew he was likely to flit if anything challenging was mentioned.

'Don't *you* want children?' Rico asked.

'My, all the difficult questions tonight! I *have* thought about it, but it would depend on the type of father I could offer the child. I don't want a child just for the sake of having one.'

'Are you suggesting that's why *I* want a baby?'

'No, I couldn't possibly make that judgement. I am talking strictly from a personal point of view. I don't want a child just because I feel I *should* have one – like people want a state-of-the-art kitchen or a neat iPad. I guess the ideal scenario is to have a baby born out of the love of two people who will see it through to its adult life, though I know that's not always possible.'

'Beneath that independent feminist beats a traditional heart!'

'No – I just have strong feelings about people having babies for the wrong reasons.'

'Believe me, Isabella, I want a baby for *all* the right reasons.'

'*I* believe you, but it's Monique you need to convince, not me.'

The ice creams finished, there were no longer distractions preventing them from focusing on each other. Rico took Isabelle's left hand in both his. The marble bistro table was small, and it wasn't long before their heads inclined, forehead touching forehead. Each mouth tentatively sought its opposite number, in a languid, careless way.

Isabelle's first proper taste of Rico sent a rush of emotion coursing through her body. The wet, thrusting tongue smacked of light, filtered cigarettes and his cleanly shaven cheeks rubbed their perfumed presence over her face.

A different taste, a different scent, a different man, but she was taken aback at how she stirred to his touch, the touch of this new stranger. Her mourning body involuntarily reacted to the pleasurable sensations.

When he took her hand and they strolled up the Corso to the taxi rank, the only emotion she felt was one of satisfaction at having attracted a loving, sensual man like Rico Parisi. Cocooned in a glow of shared happiness, had anyone at that moment mentioned the name Con, she would have said: 'Con who?'

Chapter 15

Didi woke to the sound of drilling. At least, it sounded like someone drilling. More fully alert, she realised that it was the pounding of several wheeled suitcases rolling in the direction of a transfer coach at the end of the avenue. The circuitous layout of the hotel's driveway prevented the larger coaches from accessing its carpark, and departing clients were asked to meet their buses outside the gates.

She wondered who was leaving. Was it that group of French tourists? The elderly English tour customers? No, Pauline had mentioned they would fly home on the Saturday-night Gatwick connection, so it couldn't be the English, since it was only Thursday. Whoever it was, Didi contemplated how they must feel now that their two weeks in the sun were over.

She had just managed to survive one week, closeted with her mother, and was proud that she hadn't succumbed to the temptation of strangling her. She had come pretty close – particularly on that first morning with the ritual humiliation in front of Rico – but the more Pauline found and made friends of her own, the freer both of them were to enjoy themselves. Didi had watched, amused, as her mother played to the gallery with new friends Helen and Bobby and an extended circle of bridge-players. She had seen a side of Pauline's personality that had never been evident in her domestic setting. There was definitely a free spirit lurking behind the societally conditioned "perfect-wife-perfect-mother paragon". For the first time in years, Didi realised her mother was good fun.

Kicking off the bedsheet, she giggled when she thought of how her sister would disapprove if she had seen Pauline dance the tarantella around the swimming pool with the maître d' or knock back the limoncello before a singalong in the hotel bar. It shocked her to realise that Pauline and she had more in common than either had with the idolised Jan. Yet sometimes her mother dominated the show so much that Didi couldn't help wishing that she would become more Mammy-like, ask for a Britvic 55 and sit quietly in a corner, letting the wild young things hog the limelight. It was almost as if the generations were out of sync. Didi felt like the sensible protector of her wayward elder parent, the chaperone ensuring that three brandies were quite sufficient, thank you, and pointing disapprovingly at the clock when it was time to go to bed. Pauline drew admirers: old and not so old Sicilian gentlemen cornered her and tried in broken English or she in pidgin Spanish, to conduct a conversation, offering drinks, cocktails, coffees, whatever she desired. Pauline was in her element.

Didi didn't envy her mother her fun. She'd had a terrible year. Despite the oddities of their relationship, her mum and dad had loved each other, and his being snatched away suddenly inserted a bleak full stop into her mother's life. In a way, had it not been for the cursed Wedding of the Year, Pauline would probably have fallen to pieces. Yet, if it wasn't irreverent to suggest it, the unexpected death had unleashed upon the world another Pauline. This new Pauline laughed a lot and certainly indulged herself much more than Mrs Harry O'Rourke had ever been known to do.

'Are you going to get up at all today? The sun is splitting the stones and there are people in the sea already. *Deirdre,* are you awake?'

Didi turned over, faking a protracted yawn, to see her mother, fully dressed, standing over the living-room sofabed. 'What time is it?'

'Just nine. Did you go into town last night? I didn't hear you come in.'

'No, there was no one around. I thought I'd see Isabelle, but she must have stayed in Palermo to eat. Even Salvatore wasn't working. In fact, I haven't seen either of them since the cinema outing.'

'You never told me how that went. Could you follow the film in Italian?'

'It was the original English version, with Italian subtitles.'

Disarmed by the new Pauline, Didi found herself relating the interval episode of Salvatore punching the familiar-looking stranger.

'I don't believe you! Was he provoked? I mean, did they have words beforehand?'

'No, that's just it. There was absolutely no communication between them. One minute he was sipping beer, the next knocking this guy for six.'

'Well, you must have missed something – otherwise, it doesn't add up. As the French would say, *"Cherchez la femme!"*'

Didi supposed there could be something in this, but she had never seen Salvatore with a girlfriend, or even heard the others in the hotel tease him about anyone. Besides, not wishing to be big-headed, but she had got the distinct impression that he was making overtures in her own direction. Before the punch-up, Didi had thought him sweet but a little boring. This tinge of controversy gave him hidden depths. Maybe she shouldn't be so hasty in dismissing his attentions. After all, three more weeks could drag a little, and it would be nice to have someone to take her to the local haunts.

'Deirdre, I've had breakfast. In case you nod off again, don't forget I won't be here all day. I'm going on the "Unknown Sicily" tour with Helen, so don't fret and think I've been kidnapped!' Pauline collected her day-bag and banged the door behind her.

When had she planned that? Really, she was becoming more secretive by the minute. Didi wondered what she would do until dinnertime, now that she was a free agent. Maybe this would be a good opportunity to ask Rico if she could accompany him to a rehearsal. That was a good plan. She would order room-service breakfast, like he did most mornings, and take it out on the patio. That way he couldn't escape without her seeing him and they'd have to make small talk.

A series of bumps and bangs next door alerted her to the arrival of the maestro's breakfast. Damn, she was going to miss him! She hadn't even phoned in her order yet. What was the number for Reception?'

'*Pronto?*'

'Reception? It's Didi O'Rourke in Vulcano. I want to order breakfast in my room.'

'*Didi!* It's Salvatore. *Buongiorno!* Are you tired? You don't usually have breakfast in your room.'

'Well, I'm in a hurry this morning and I don't have time to go over to the terrace. Can you have them send it over soon, please, Salvatore?'

'*Certo!* What hot drink do you want with it?'

'Oh, a cappuccino will be fine.'

'OK. Oh, by the way, Didi, when do you go on your *giro* – your tour of the island?'

'The fourth, whenever that is – Tuesday?'

'We must have another night out before you go away.'

'Yeah. Whatever. I'll see when Isabelle is free. So, my breakfast?'

'*Sì, sì.* On its way.'

After her shower, Didi peeped out to see if Rico was on

his patio. With the *Repubblica* spread before him, he was carefully cutting a croissant into manageable morsels. He didn't appear at all rushed.

Good, Didi thought. Strike while the iron is hot! Grabbing a floaty cotton dress, she fished out rust-coloured espadrilles from under the bed. The orange floral number toned with rather than matched them, but they would have to do. She hoped she would cut enough of a dash for Signor Rico and his operatic friends up in Gibilmanna.

'*Buongiorno, Rico. Come stai?*'

'*Didi!* How are you?'

'*Bene, grazie.*'

'On your own? *La mamma,* where is she?'

'She's gone on an excursion to Hidden Sicily or something. God knows where they'll end up.'

Rico laughed. 'Probably Corleone or San Giuseppe Jato!'

'Why? What's so special about those places?'

'Don't you remember *The Godfather*? Corleone and San Giuseppe Jato are where the famous Mafia bosses hung out.'

'Oh, according to my mother, the Mafia has been wiped out.'

'Only half true. Ordinary Sicilians have turned against them, but wiped out? I don't think so.'

'Well, she'll just have to find out for herself. Anyway, how's *Tosca* coming along?'

'You know the way it is with music – good days, bad days. We had a free day yesterday, so I'm hoping to do a great rehearsal later.'

'Since I have time to myself, I was wondering – if you didn't mind – if I could sit in on a rehearsal? Puccini is one of my favourites, and I'd love to see you work.'

Rico crumpled the newspaper noisily. 'That is a lovely idea, Didi, but unfortunately my cast would not be happy if I brought a stranger to their rehearsal. *Mi dispiace,* but it's not possible.'

Didi felt the colour rise from beneath the tasteful tucks of the bodice of her orange dress. She imagined it engulfing her neck and finishing with a dramatic flourish on her cheeks.

'Oh. OK ... I understand ... you couldn't upset your singers. I'd feel awful if it messed up the rehearsal.'

'But you will come to the performances? The 12th, 14th and 16th of August.'

'We'll see. It depends on what I'm doing.' Attending a public performance as a paying customer was all that Rico's offer amounted to? Didi was not going to appear over-enthusiastic. The room doorbell rang. '*Scusa*, Rico. I think that's my breakfast. Have a good rehearsal.'

Didi fled the patio, her heart pounding and her awkward, gangly body shaking all over with foolishness. How could she have made an idiot of herself, to such a cool, self-contained character like Rico? Maybe he *was* telling the truth – maybe it was just the accepted protocol, keeping outsiders out of rehearsals – but he could have been more apologetic about it.

The doorbell rang insistently the second time. Standing

on the front veranda with a breakfast tray was Salvatore.

'Goodness! I didn't expect you to personally bring me my breakfast, Salvatore.'

'It was my break, and I know how slow they are in the mornings. Anyway, for the room orders, you do really need to book the breakfast the night before.'

'Oh, sorry, I didn't know.'

'*Fa niente.* But that is why I bring it. Otherwise, it would be ten before you see your breakfast.'

Didi noticed that, as well as her cappuccino, there was an espresso coffee on the tray.

'Are you joining me?'

'If I may, I will have my coffee on your *bella terrazza.*'

Conscious of Rico's recent slight, Didi effusively welcomed Salvatore out onto the patio, fervently hoping the maestro was still in the company of his newspaper. Salvatore, unsuspecting and delighted by the gesture, followed her through the sliding doors, where Rico, alas, was nowhere to be seen.

They sat and Didi noticed Salvatore suddenly looked very uncomfortable.

'It is true that I am having my coffee break," he said, "but I also wanted to have an opportunity to talk with you in private.'

Didi hoped he wasn't going to declare undying passion. One awkward drama was sufficient for a morning.

'It is about the night at the cinema. I … I do not want you to think I am a violent man. The guy I punched – there is a reason why I am angry with him. When I saw him, I lost my patience, and I am sorry that you – and Isabelle – must witness such unpleasantness.'

'Apology accepted. It's none of our business. You live here. We just come on a couple of weeks' holiday. We cannot possibly understand what happens in a place like this throughout the year.'

'So, what are your plans for today?'

'I think I'll go for a swim and maybe into town to shoot some film up on the hill – the Rocca.'

'No Isabelle today?'

'No. I haven't seen Isabelle since the cinema.'

'She has been busy all right." He swallowed his espresso in one gulp. "Didi, I really must go or else Signor Giorgio will be screaming. Have a lovely day, whatever you do.'

'You too. Well, don't work too hard. And Salvatore? Thanks for bringing over my breakfast – you really are very considerate.'

With everyone gone, Didi found the room uncomfortably quiet. She changed out of the dress, packed the beach bag, and threw in her phone and earbuds. She would carefully avoid any Puccini downloads she happened to have. She thought of her mother – probably whizzing along on the coach tour – and she could imagine her regaling her new friends with funny anecdotes, her tinkling laugh, bouncing around the confined space of the bus. If Didi had known today would work out this way, she would seriously have considered accompanying her. She wasn't such a bad old girl, particularly when they were away from the restricting pressures of their respective lives in Ireland.

When Pauline got back that evening, they could have a special meal together. She would ask the maître d' to give them one of the balcony tables, and to have a bottle of that expensive rosé chilling. Didi disliked rosé, but never mind – if it was to be her mother's night, she'd grin and bear it. She would pay the 10-per-cent charge for the outdoor service directly to Reception, and her mother need never know about the extra cost involved.

Eager to firm up the plans for her treat, Didi checked the bus timetable and saw that she could make the arrangements comfortably before the shuttle's next departure. Placing her camera bag on her shoulder, she left *Vulcano* and walked in the direction of the main hotel building.

Footsore and still a little tipsy from the elaborate five-course lunch, Pauline turned her key in the door. It was after six. She didn't expect to find Deirdre in. Good! She could have a long shower and then sleep for an hour before dinner. As she undressed, an envelope on her pillow caught her eye. It was Deirdre's writing.

'Hi, Mom. Hope you enjoyed your trip. Put on your gladdest glad rags tonight, because we're celebrating over a week away together. I've even managed to get us a table on the balcony, reserved for 8.30. See you later, D.'

Pauline wondered why Deirdre was being so thoughtful. Had she done something terrible that she needed to break to her? If there was no ulterior motive, well, it was a very nice gesture indeed, and she'd dress to kill, to show Deirdre that she was entering wholeheartedly into the mood of the evening.

The orange shuttle-bus disgorged its passengers at the Panoramico, the driver saying a personal goodbye as each one alighted.

There were new towels hanging over the veranda rail. Pauline must be home.

'Mom, are you in the bathroom?'

A voice came back from the bedroom. 'No, I'm just lying down for a bit. It was a long enough trip.'

Didi opened the door to her mother's room.

'Did you get my note?'

'Yes, pet. I'm looking forward to it. What time again did you say you'd booked the table for? Eight?'

'Half past. What if we have an aperitif on the terrace before?'

'Perfect. You have your shower, and I'll get all dolled up in a while!'

Mother and daughter entered the restaurant and were ushered onto the balcony by Signor Bruno.

'*Buonasera, signore.* It is a lovely evening, and I hope you enjoy your meal at this the best table, not only in the Panoramico, but in the whole of *Sicilia*!'

The maître d' seated Pauline first. 'May I pour you some wine, Signora O'Rourke?

'Oh look! My favourite – rosé! How did you know, Signor Bruno?'

'It was ordered for you by the *bella signorina.*'

Scribbling their chosen courses on his notepad, he turned on his highly polished heels and glided effortlessly back indoors to another group of diners.

'You look nice. Isn't that the Monsoon dress I bought you a few years ago? I thought you didn't like it.' Pauline sipped her wine, eyeing Didi. 'You've gone to a lot of trouble to organise this. Is there any special reason?'

'Do we need a special reason to spoil ourselves?' Didi concentrated on cutting a piece of bread. 'I suppose, in a way, I wanted to show my appreciation – to let you know that I *am* glad to be on holidays with you. I know sometimes we don't always get on, but this year – so many things have changed, that … well, maybe we could look on this holiday as a new phase in our mother-daughter relationship.'

'Deirdre, we *do* get on. It's just that I don't always under—'

Signor Bruno was hovering with a phone in his hand.

'*Scusatami, signore. Telefono per la Signora O'Rourke.*'

Didi had seen this happen before. Obviously, if calls came for clients during mealtimes, the receptionist transferred it into the restaurant, where it could be taken on the portable phone.

Nervously, Pauline pressed the button to connect the call. Didi watched as her mother's anxious expression relaxed into a beaming smile.

'Jan, darling!'

And as if Didi were deaf, Pauline covered the microphone and repeated this piece of information. 'It's Jan, God love her.' She uncovered the phone. 'What are you doing calling me at this hour from home? It'll cost you a fortune! You should have waited till the morning and phoned from the office.'

At this point, a young waiter had arrived with their first course – *spaghetti alla marinara* for Didi and *rigatoni alla Norma* for Pauline. Didi signalled to him to hold both dishes, but then indicated a change of mind, extending her hand outwards for her own dish.

Jan. As usual, perfect timing. Trust her to make a call on the *one* evening she might finally have got her mother's attention! Didi covered the pasta in *parmigiano* and plunged her fork into it.

'I had a lovely day. We were all over the place, in little villages off the beaten track ... Well, no dear, we're not Siamese twins, you know! We like to go our separate ways. Anyway, what about you? How's that gorgeous husband of yours?'

Although she couldn't make out exactly what was being said, Didi could hear Jan's voice reply more animatedly than usual.

'Men need their space, love. This climbing weekend – it'll do him good to be away with the lads. Haven't you your own things to do? The house, the garden—'

Jan's shriek was audible.

'Would you like a word with Deirdre? We're sitting out on the restaurant terrace waiting for our dinner. There's the most magnificent view. Well, when I say waiting, Deirdre has started hers already, but Davide took mine back, since I was on the phone … *Davide,* our waiter … OK, I'll tell her that. Mind yourself, love, and remember, no sulks when he gets back. OK. Bye bye!' She stared at the phone. 'How do I turn this thing off?'

She handed the phone to Didi, who hit the red button. Ever attentive, Davide returned with the *rigatoni*. Pauline gave him a warmer than usual smile.

'Can you take this back to Signor Bruno?' she said, handing him the phone. 'It was my daughter, phoning from Ireland.'

'*Vero?* How nice!'

'Yes, it wasn't only nice – it was *wonderful* to hear from her.'

Nice, thought Didi. How exactly do you define *nice*? Sitting at the reputedly best table in Sicily, dining well, downing overpriced rosé in the company of your pleasant, if a little plain, second daughter, now that was considered 'nice'. But taking a two-minute phone-call from your beloved Jan, that was said to be *wonderful*. Didi pushed the plate with the rest of her pasta to one side.

'So, was Jan on an economy drive? She didn't have enough coins for the call-box to talk to me?'

'Call-box? What are you on about, Deirdre? Oh, I get it. You're being sarcastic. No, she didn't want to disturb you when I said you'd started your meal.'

Didi wished her mother wouldn't lie. Both of them knew that she and Jan had very little to say to one another face to face, let alone on a long-distance call.

Pauline tucked into her rigatoni with vigour, positively exuding contentment. Didi's appetite was gone. Try though she might, she could not banish the thought that her mother's glow was more attributable to the phone call than to the special meal.

'Did I detect trouble in paradise? Is the Reluctant Bridegroom stretching his legs?'

'Why ask me, if you already heard our conversation? And I wish you wouldn't call him that. He's just ... more independent than Jan. Gone off on some mountaineering trip to the west.'

'And Jan has to spend a whole weekend on her own. Isn't that awful?'

'I wish you and Jan could like each other a bit more.'

And I wish you could like her a bit less, thought Didi, but she lacked the courage to actually say it. Despite all the efforts with her appearance and the meal, she and her mother were back to square one. Didi would never make Pauline's eyes dance with pleasure like Jan could. Maybe it was chemistry. Maybe it was a first-born thing, but no matter how hard she worked at pleasing her, she would never succeed. It was as simple as that.

The meal over, Pauline had excused herself and gone to the bathroom. Descending the steps to the bar, Didi ordered a grappa, trusting in local knowledge about the benefits of a *digestivo*. All the terrace tables were occupied, so as she watched out for her mother returning, she leaned over the balcony railing and sipped her drink.

'I wouldn't, if I were you. Jump.'

Didi turned to find a blond man standing beside her. Even in the dim light, she noticed he had a blackened eye. The man extended his hand.

'Christoph.'

'Didi. What happened to your eye?'

'Oh, it is nothing. A disagreement with a colleague.'

Suddenly, Didi recognised him — Salvatore's victim from the cinema debacle!

'Would you like to join me for a drink? You seem sad here, looking at the moon.'

'Thank you, but I'm OK. I'm just waiting for my mother.'

'Another time?'

'Yes, why not?'

'*Wiedersehen, Didi.*'

The grappa was beginning to kick in. Didi was surprised at how much she had gulped. Uncharacteristically, she felt like a second. As she crossed through the bar, who should she see ensconced in a group of four or five, a large brandy in hand and a deck of cards about to be dealt, but her beloved mother.

There really was no point in hanging around, cramping Pauline's style. She would skip the grappa. Didi scanned the terrace, in a last childish attempt to see if she could level the score by finding Christoph to drink with, but she had lost her opportunity. Christoph was gone.

The whole night had been a disaster and, besides, she looked like an extra from *Little House on the Prairie* in that fucking flowery dress. So much for new beginnings! Feeling ever so fragile, Didi waved at her mother's party and headed for the comfort of *Vulcano*.

Chapter 16

Isabelle got out of the car and looked at the three tiers of steps leading to a sandstone church: the 'Sanctuary Chapel of Gibilmanna', or so the plain wooden board at the gates declared it. On the highest level, there was a cream canvas awning and some additional partitions, which she presumed were the outline structure of the set. Several people with instruments were making their way towards the monastery on the right.

Rico, visible only from the waist down, was rummaging on the back seat of the car, gathering his papers and briefcase, and chatting with the driver. Isabelle smiled as he emerged into the sunlight.

'So, what will I do? Just walk in with you?'

'*Aspetta!* Wait until I have a quick word with Stephen. You could always go in and have a look around the church. It really is beautiful.'

'OK, but come back for me. I'm not going to flounce in on my own.'

Having climbed to the uppermost tier of steps, Isabelle was puzzled by the various fluorescent stripes of sticky tape zig-zagging across the improvised stage. She turned to admire the view but was not expecting the panorama that lay below. At nine-thirty, the temperature hadn't built to the level where a blanket heat haze obscured visibility and, although she had registered that they must be quite high since the car had climbed steadily from the town, she still was not expecting the view to extend so far. Forested areas gave way to the occasional tilled field, their various hues culminating in the vivid blue of the sea, now swirling beneath a tiny concrete blob that was the Rocca, no longer the imposing headland when seen from the town.

Once indoors, the dominance of the location was soon forgotten. Isabelle entered a narrow, intimate chapel, its centre aisle flanked by a series of ornate side altars, decorated in gilt or elaborate silver. Serenity enveloped her as she sat in the silence, not praying, but letting her thoughts float in whichever direction they would, more comfortable in this smaller, less threatening, version of the Sanctuary of Gibilmanna.

When she came back out and her eyes had readjusted from the dimness of the church, she climbed down several steps and sat on the cool stone of the second tier. She noticed that the stream of people going into the monastery had ceased.

Rico appeared at the big brown door and beckoned.

Isabelle ran down the steps. 'It's OK?'

'Yes, of *course*! I am the conductor – why wouldn't it be OK?'

'It's magnificent up here.' Isabelle half-turned to indicate the view. 'Most inspiring!'

'Well, I hope when you hear the music, you will still find it equally inspiring.'

'I'm sure it will be fantastic.'

'Wait until the orchestra begins to play, then come and sit at the back of the chapel. No one will notice you that way. I will not close the door fully as I go in, so it won't make noise. *Allora, a più tardi.*'

Planting a swift kiss on her lips, Rico turned, crunching the gravel in his suede moccasins. Isabelle hovered outside, feeling ill at ease. The whole point of having delayed her entrance was to accompany Rico into the rehearsal. Now she still had to sneak in like a nosey tourist, infiltrating the privacy of these people's workplace.

After several bars of orchestral music, a male voice began to sing. He continued for some time and, as the orchestra grew louder, Isabelle pushed the wooden door open and crept in to the third row from the back.

The music stopped.

'No! Wolfgang, no. The phrasing at the end of 42 is not right. Can we take it again from, say, 30. Orchestra?'

Rico pivoted from his players to his soloists and Wolfgang – the man they had met in the restaurant the previous evening – began again, singing and pacing. Wolfgang was joined by two other singers, the smaller, thinner one dragging a well-built handsome man behind him.

'Beverly. *Bev-er-ly*. We can't hear you if you mark that softly. We want to enjoy your offstage concert piece, before Cavaradossi and Spoletta come in.'

'Rico – *maestro*, I told you! I am not well today. I cannot sing out.'

'Stage manager, where is the understudy? Did you not call her half an hour ago?'

'*Si, maestro. Sta arrivando.*'

'*Sta arrivando, sta arrivando.* Christmas is also coming, but it is a long time away! Ring her again, please.'

Isabelle had never imagined Rico could be so acerbic. It was the same tone he had used when she had admonished him about turning the phone off on Monique.

The chapel door reopened with energy, and the stage manager returned in the company of a pretty, dark-haired woman in her twenties. She was wearing a flimsy muslin dress with a soft leafy pattern and was clutching a score to her chest.

'*Finalmente!*' Rico gestured to her to join the other soloists. 'Ornella, Beverly has a throat infection, so could you sing her role, please – beginning at the offstage aria and continuing to where you join Scarpia in his quarters. *D'accordo?*'

Swathed in a Hispanic shawl clutched dramatically to her throat, Beverly interrupted. '*Wait* a minute. Maestro, don't make me laugh and tell me that *she* is my understudy. Is that all the budget could rise to, in this godforsaken backwater of a festival?'

The local company members tut-tutted their disapproval at her double insult – to the festival and their promising young soprano.

'Beverly, *per favore*. Ornella knows the role perfectly and, since you are feeling so unwell today, it would be better if you sat out rehearsal. Let Ornella walk it through, as much for the others as anything.'

'I never heard of anything so ridiculous! A local church choir singer replacing *me,* who has sung in top houses in Portland, Salt Lake City, Opera Memphis. Well, honey, all I can say is, I hope I get better *real* quick!'

Was every rehearsal like this, Isabelle wondered, or were they just exceptionally cranky today? Her brief visit to the Teatro Massimo had been tranquillity personified, everyone nodding agreement with everyone else. It certainly was poles apart from the fraught and bitchy atmosphere in Gibilmanna. You'd think the peaceful influence of the location would have had a soothing effect on temperament, but this lot looked as if they were badly in need of a large dose of some herbal remedy for overwrought nerves.

Rico lifted his watch off the table and checked it.

'*Signore, signori*, I have no intention of losing any more time. Since my Tosca is obviously not able to sing her role today, I will continue rehearsing with her understudy. When I last checked my job description, I do believe that this decision is mine. So, let's go back to 48, just before the offstage aria. Ornella, *pronta?* Wolfgang – *tutti?*'

The young Tosca made her entrance and was singing a duet with Wolfgang when a gangly, bespectacled man – Stephen, the director, Isabelle presumed – leapt up from the desk.

'Rico, *scusa* —'

Rico nodded and put down his pencil.

'Wolfgang, you *want* her. You *lech* after her. More than that! We have to feel this is an unseemly admiration — this is no harmless flirtation. There is danger here. You're in a powerful position and you intend to use that position to get your way. We must see that from your body language, instead of looking like a student chatting up a girl in a Kaffeehaus. I need *sinister*! This is far too amiable.'

'Maybe I don't do *sinister* very good.'

A loud snorting noise came from the cello section, where Marilena, Wolfgang's estranged wife, was busily rubbing out notes in her part.

Stephen ran his hands through his hair and expired loudly.

'Sorry, Rico. Can we take that sequence again, and remember, Wolfgang, *menacing?*'

When the music resumed, both Ornella and Wolfgang tried to establish a more believable relationship and were soon joined by the good-looking man, Paolo. Ornella broke away from Wolfgang and embraced him passionately.

Stephen was not happy with this either.

'Paolo! Ornella! *Per* fav-*ore*. Passionate yes, but this is not the privacy of the bedroom. Could you cool it down a little, *please?*'

'Oh Steeven, he is going away!" said Paolo. "He is leaving his beloved Tosca to be tortured at the hands of this – disgraceful man. Cavaradossi is an Italian man, a passionate man, passionate about love and passionate about his cause. He is not going to say goodbye *all'inglese* with a little peck on the cheek, as if *la bella Tosca* were his aunt!'

'I am *au fait* with Cavaradossi's character, thank you, Paolo, but there is passionate and there is *passionate*. What I see has more to do with drama beyond the remit of *either* this rehearsal room or the plot of the opera.'

'Ah, but is it not so authentic when I play this scene with Ornella? Do you not believe that I will love her to the death? Do you not see that she will sacrifice anything, *anything*, for this love?'

Beverly recovered sufficiently to interject. 'Don't make me laugh. All I see is a testosterone-tormented, clapped-out tenor, who will use *any* opportunity to get a bit of action. You're pathetic, Paolo!'

'*Qual miracolo!* It speaks. The diva's beautiful voice is returning.'

'Paolo, Beverly, enough!' said Rico. 'Stephen, shall we take that again, or do you want to move on?'

'Let's move on.'

With the first ten or so chapel benches pushed to the sides, the orchestra was accommodated in the remaining central gap. Sometimes Isabelle found it hard to see Rico over their heads, since he remained seated, conducting from a high stool. The soloists passed in front of him as the action required, further obscuring her view. As the music gave way to a slow, melodic movement, Rico rose and placed his score on an upright music stand, addressing the orchestra at a 45-degree angle, in order to rotate to the two soloists. Now Isabelle had an uninterrupted line of vision, greatly assisted by the sun outside, which had ceased playing peek-a-boo with the clouds, and she no longer had to squint through its dusty rays. Rico's face was earnest, his concentration child-like as he frowned alternately down at his music and nodded encouragingly up at his players. He put his entire body into the act of conducting. His shoulders, arms, wrists, even individual fingers all played their own role. As the pace picked up, his lower body swayed, hips gently undulating with the rhythm of the music.

He appeared rapt. In this absorbed state, Isabelle could see he had no need of a Monique, or of any of his countless admirers. No need either, she thought, of a holiday-romance Isabelle. Was this self-containment exclusive to artists? When the music was as perfect as this work sounded to her unprofessional ear, was that the ultimate high? To create something this beautiful from your own talent and the cooperation of other gifted people? Did self-fulfilment derive from such an elevated emotion, independent of the vagaries of love and its many changing unpredictable moods?

The action on the floor had become more intense. The Paolo-man was making tortured sounds at the side of the altar, and Tosca was reacting in various paroxysms of distress. Wolfgang's character was tantalising her which, judging by the way Ornella placed her hands over her ears, was something she did not want to hear. The offstage shrieks from Paolo continued, until Tosca could bear it no more and broke down to a now triumphant Wolfgang.

Interested in the action though she was, Isabelle wondered when they were going to take a break. She had an urgent need to find a toilet, and she didn't fancy having to clamber through the benches and make her way up to what looked like the sacristy, with the rehearsal still in full swing.

Rico, as if telepathic, looked at his watch and muttered something inaudible to Stephen. Following quite a bit of nodding and score-checking, he announced they would break, and Isabelle sighed with relief.

The orchestra filed out in clutches, the confirmed smokers heading for the open air, while those in need of coffee moved in the opposite direction. Rico was chatting with Stephen, and seemed to ignore her presence, the last remaining soul at the rear of the hall.

Damn you, Rico, thought Isabelle, but I need the bathroom. Taking her handbag, she marched authoritatively up the aisle of the chapel, her sandals clip-clopping on the ceramic tiles. Stephen looked up from his notebook at the approaching figure, just as Rico addressed her.

'Are you enjoying it?'

'Yes, very much, but the cloakrooms?'

'Just go through the sacristy, past where the others are

having coffee, and then you'll see the sign.'

'Thanks. See you later.'

Before Stephen had time to ask a question about the retreating blonde, Rico volunteered.

'*Questa è Isabella.* The lovely Isabelle from Ireland, who has become my friend at Hotel Panoramico. Shall we go and take some coffee?'

'Well, *I* don't mind about her, but you know that we did agree to no outsiders at rehearsal. I hope none of the others object.'

'She's my guest. I don't see the problem.'

Isabelle came back into the poky kitchenette, jammed with cast members talking to each other in clusters. She excused herself as she pushed through, anxiously seeking Rico. Then found herself face to face with Beverly.

'Well, *hello again*. If it isn't the *maestro*'s little friend! Taking an interest in opera, honey?'

'Oh, Beverly. Nice to see you again. Well, yes, Rico invited me along and I was interested to see what a rehearsal was like.'

'Well, you are out of luck, because this rehearsal is *crap*.' This was croaked at a decibel level intended to reach the not-too-distant Paolo and Ornella. 'You should have said you were coming – then I wouldn't have been sick. Unfortunately, you have to suffer the village choir-mistress howling her way through my beautiful arias. What a shameful way to introduce a novice to opera!'

Isabelle wasn't too sure that she fully understood the dynamic between Beverly and the understudy who had sounded perfectly all right to her, but she really wished Rico would spot her dilemma and come and extricate her from the situation. He didn't. In his place, Wolfgang materialised.

'*Hallo!* Why are you at rehearsal?'

The directness of the question surprised her. 'The conductor invited me.'

'It is forbidden, you know, to come to a rehearsal. In my contract it says: "*No persons outside of the cast or the company shall be present at any rehearsals.*"'

Not really comprehending the portent of this statement, Isabelle just nodded politely, but felt confident that if she had been admitted by the man wielding the baton Wolfgang's contract wasn't going to bother her too much.

Finally, Rico had seen her.

'*Cara,* did you find the bathroom OK? Have some coffee. No?'

And then without warning, Rico gave her a protracted kiss, a little too passionate for eleven in the morning.

Isabelle felt decidedly uncomfortable. 'Stop, Rico! This is your workplace. Don't put me in an embarrassing position.'

'I am sorry, but I just had an urge to kiss you. It is natural, no?'

'Yes, I am sure it is very natural, but your colleagues are giving us daggers.'

'Non me ne frego dei miei colleghi!'

Isabelle didn't need a translation. Rico's expression and hand-gesture were self-explanatory. His colleagues could hump off.

Hump off, that was, until she heard one of them corner the director.

'Stephen, do you know that in your rehearsal there comes a stranger, a person who has nothing to do with this production?'

Stephen looked uncomfortably into Wolfgang's solemn face.

'Yes. Signora Isabella. She is a friend of the maestro and … is doing research into opera.'

'*Ach so*? Research into opera?'

'Yes, she is Irish and studying opera in Europe.'

'I think she is just studying the *maestro* on tour. I wish that she is removed from the rehearsal, or I do not sing any more. She is an outsider, and in my contract it states that I do not sing until performance before anyone but company members. Speak to the *maestro*.'

The maestro, however, was checking the Call Schedule on the noticeboard and entering some information into his phone when Stephen sidled up to them. The artists had begun to trickle back into the chapel.

'Rico, a moment.' Stephen caught him gently by the arm. 'Excuse me, Isabelle.'

'OK, *cara,* see you afterwards.' Rico kissed Isabelle on the cheek as she made to go.

'No, wait a moment. This concerns Isabelle. One of the company members has made a complaint about an outsider in the rehearsal and won't sing until she leaves.'

'*Porca miseria!* Who? Is it Paolo? Has Beverly put him up to this? No, it wouldn't be Paolo. He would enjoy the opportunity of impressing another beautiful woman. It has to be that anal-retentive Wolfgang!'

'I'd prefer not to say who it is, but we *had* agreed to closed rehearsals, so what shall we do?'

'I know it's Wolfgang! Just because *he* is incapable of attracting a woman, he is determined to interfere with everyone else's happiness.'

Isabelle, hot and embarrassed by the two men discussing her as if she were invisible, interrupted.

'I'll go. I don't want to be the cause of all this aggravation.'

'No!' Rico flicked some hair behind his right ear. 'You are my guest! I will not be dictated to. This is a once-off. It's not as if I bring in people every day! You can be sure if Isabelle were a talent-scouting agent, Wolfgang would have no problem with a "stranger" in rehearsal.'

'I agree, Rico, but he is refusing to sing, and he *is* crucial to Act Two. What if Isabelle goes up to the organ gallery? Strictly speaking, that's not the rehearsal room, and the monks pass through there to work in their little office. Isabelle would be no different.'

'I just want to go home – back to town.'

'But you can't, love, not until my driver returns. Go up to the gallery. I will sort Wolfgang out.'

The company, curious about the whereabouts of the missing maestro and director, focused on the controversial visitor when the main door into the chapel opened. Wolfgang, in particular, followed Isabelle and the stage manager's progress in the direction of a side exit.

'Wolfgang, a word.'

Wolfgang strode over to Rico, ready to express his feelings, but was not afforded the opportunity by Rico's speedy offensive.

'I understand you're not happy with the presence of my guest. I have asked her to leave the rehearsal room, which she is currently doing. If you have a problem with my actions in future, I would appreciate it if you would mention it to me directly, rather than going behind my back. *Grazie*.'

Although open-mouthed and ready to reiterate his point, the singer hesitated then turned from the desk and resumed his position on the floor.

The momentary excitement over, Rico checked his score, cued the orchestra, and normal business resumed.

Isabelle was installed in the organ loft, seated on the farthest choir bench from the front, terrified that Wolfgang would spot her or that she would make a noise and alert his attention to her presence. Fortunately, the plot dictated that Wolfgang and Ornella were very occupied, and this kept his eyes focused on his singing partner, rather than wandering in her direction.

Stephen was on his feet again. 'No, no, Ornella! You must *show* your fear. This is the Chief of Police! If he wants to sleep with you, and you refuse, it could cause trouble.'

Wolfgang was running the leather of a whip up and down Ornella's bare arm, suggesting something, which evoked a hysterically sung reply and a gesture indicating rejection.

'That's better. Now, even though he repulses you, remember the deal. He is promising to release your beloved Cavaradossi if you sacrifice your body to him.'

With that, Ornella began to sing softly, a melody that Isabelle recognised. During the aria, Rico concentrated fully on his soprano, encouraging and calming the orchestra to a *pianissimo* accompaniment. When Tosca had finished, the string players tapped the wooden spine of their bows ever so gently against their instruments in appreciative applause. Rico dropped his head, and held this position for several minutes, not signalling to either orchestra or Wolfgang to continue. The emotion was tangible and, although she was very far away, Isabelle thought there was something about the movement of Rico's shoulders that suggested that he was quelling a sob.

The director was first in with the praise.

'*Bene, Ornella.* But we need to see more confusion as you come to the close of the "Vissi d'Arte" aria. The audience has to understand this is a 'no-win situation': don't sleep with Scarpia and your lover will be lost; sleep with him and you will be lost.'

Stephen's interruption brought Rico back to earth.

'*Continuamo* – Bar 280. Wolfgang, *pronto?*'

Isabelle's attention drifted in and out of the subsequent

action. Since the blow-up with Wolfgang at the break, she had been jittery. Apart from the poignant aria, very little else had engaged her, and snatches of things Rico had said to Stephen persisted in running through her head. What did his stance over her signify? That he would not be bossed around by an arrogant singer, even if that singer was technically within his rights? Or that she was important to him, and he would not have her humiliated and sent home like a naughty child from a birthday party who has upended the cake over a plush carpet?

Angry singing and loud playing from the orchestra forced her attention back to the drama below, quiet moments alternating with more declarations of passion, until Wolfgang, taking Ornella in his arms, declared her finally his. As Isabelle lowered her head to swat a mosquito about to alight on her leg, she missed a crucial move, in which Tosca lunged at the oppressive Scarpia with a knife plucked from his supper table and stabbed him repeatedly.

The orchestra, awaiting Rico's indication to close out Act Two, had their silence broken by the single, congratulatory tapping of a cello bow. Former wife Marilena applauded Ornella's extinction of Wolfgang.

In agitation, Stephen took off his glasses, cleaned the lenses and replaced them on his nose, communicating something to Rico as he did so.

The orchestra, embarrassed by the ironic applause, were relieved when the conductor checked his score, and picked up his improvised pencil-baton.

'Ornella, *sei pronta*? From where your music takes up after the stabbing—'

Glad of the opportunity to ignore Marilena's insult, the musicians hurled themselves into several minutes of indifferent playing, until Rico brought down his arm to indicate the end of the Act, and subsequently the end of their rehearsal.

'*Grazie tutti, va bene così*. Until this evening's session when we will work outside. The call is for six-thirty. Have a good rest this afternoon and I will see you all later. *Grazie*.'

Isabelle, marooned in the choir gallery, hoped Rico hadn't forgotten her. She was keeping a discreet eye on Wolfgang, not daring to move until he had cleared the chapel, but he was huddled with his fellow soloists, making no attempt to leave. The creaking of a timber beam announced the arrival of Gino the stage manager, who had come to collect her and to lock the door behind them.

'*Andiamo?* The *maestro* will meet you in the car park, where his driver should be. Did you enjoy it?'

'Yes, very much. I enjoyed the rows as well!'

'Oh, that was nothing. You should be at rehearsals in Napoli or Verona. Then you would see *real* drama.'

Isabelle followed Gino down the twisting stone steps to the porch and out into the searing bright light of the lunchtime sun. As her eyes adjusted, she recognised the white Peugeot, emblazoned with the green-and-gold insignia of the Festival, parked in the turnabout bay. Rico was already in the front.

When she saw him back in his personal role as her new love-interest, something changed. She was his ally now, someone with whom he could discuss the excitements of the morning's rehearsal. Perhaps that was really why he had brought her along, to involve her in the thing he cherished most in life. It had worked. Isabelle had so many questions she wanted to ask and was concentrating so much on him that she couldn't remember what she had planned to do that afternoon, or if she had made arrangements to meet anyone. Everything beyond Rico seemed unimportant. The enveloping circles of his life were beginning to enmesh her, and her will to remain on the outside, was growing weaker.

'Lunch? I think we've both earned it.'

'That would be lovely, Rico.'

And with that, Isabelle leaned forward from the back seat and slipped her hand around the headrest, to caress Rico's neck.

Chapter 17

The reception desk was experiencing its usual high-season chaos. As the majority of two-week package customers arrived on the incoming charter flights on Saturdays, pressure to allocate rooms was at its greatest. Giorgio, the elderly manager, was unable to use the computerised booking system, and frequently took reservations from individual clients over the phone but failed to log them.

Salvatore had spent the previous half-hour assigning rooms to incoming guests, only to discover that several current clients had dropped off the keys of those same rooms on their way out. A quick call to Housekeeping confirmed his worst fears. Rooms 214, 220, 316, 322 were all currently occupied by various combinations of Italians, while onscreen they were showing up as free. *Merda!* Even before he did the calculations, Salvatore knew they were overbooked. There just was no space to accommodate people due that night. Perhaps he had underestimated the departures. Two pairs of *Saga* customers were leaving, an individual in a fourth-floor single, and the two-roomed villa *Vulcano* was also due to be vacated. Wait a minute! *Vulcano* – that was the O'Rourkes' villa and he was sure Didi had said they weren't going on tour until the 4th. It was still only the 1st. *Madonna!* That meant the overbooking problem was worse than he had thought.

As he dialled the number of the nearest competitor hotel, Salvatore was interrupted by a very cheerful-looking Signor Bruno sporting his best cream-linen jacket. That could only mean one thing – an important wedding.

'My friend! Have the boys arrived to set up for the early wedding? Or the florist? No? Well, when they do, buzz me. I want the flowers done at the very last minute or they'll wilt in the heat. Have Abdul and Sergio put up the canopies?'

'Signor Bruno, I am not being unhelpful but, as you may have noticed, I am stuck behind this desk. How could I possibly know what's happening on the terrace with canopies or flowers or anything else? As for the extras, I certainly haven't seen any of them pass through, but that isn't to say that they're not already here.'

'OK, calm down! Anyway, just to let you know: there are two weddings, and a family reunion in the conference room in the gardens. That's today's itinerary. You'll need to call Andrea to direct traffic in the car-parking areas, or else there will be confusion!'

This was hopeless. The Excelsior was fully booked, as was the Stella. Where was he going to find six rooms? Had he got it wrong about *Vulcano?* Perhaps he should ask Didi to clarify their first departure date. He would welcome the excuse to talk to her, because, unexpectedly, he had been given the night off on Sunday and he really wanted to take her out somewhere. Before he could dial the room, Christoph was at the desk looking for the keys to the bicycle lock-up. Surprisingly, he greeted Salvatore in civil fashion, took the keys and left. The progress of his injured eye made Salvatore laugh. The bruising had matured beautifully and looked like the colour of chopped cabbage, complemented around the edges by a fringe of bluish parsley.

'You seem pleased with yourself.'

Salvatore was delighted to see Didi in front of him.

'*Ciao*, Didi! I was just about to ring you.'

'Oh?'

'Yes. *When exactly* are you leaving for the week?'

'Tuesday, the fourth. Trying to get rid of me already?'

'Definitely not, only there has been a bit of confusion on the computer. I wanted to check, that's all.'

'We *will* get the same villa back, if we leave for the week? I mean, can you reserve it, for our return on the eleventh?'

'Ah, you particularly like *Vulcano?* The other villas won't do?'

'Preferably *Vulcano*. The view from its terrace is superb.'

'Fine.'

'Thanks.'

'Didi, did you know there is a beach party tonight?'

'Where? On the hotel beach or in town?'

'Here. Everyone is going. Will you be staying around?'

'Yes, I think so.'

'Good! Well, I'll see you there. For once I finish early this afternoon.'

'Have you seen Isabelle? She might enjoy the party. I haven't caught sight of that girl for days. Where has she been hiding?'

Salvatore didn't like to suggest that she was probably hiding out closer to Didi than the latter suspected, but in a professional tone he reassured her that all guests would be notified of the party.

'Great. Oh, I nearly forgot: buses to La Kalura? Do you have a timetable? I'm going on a photography ramble later on.'

'*Eccoci.* They are sometimes a bit late arriving at our stop but be sure to be punctual for the return journey, as it's from the terminus. Enjoy your day, take lots of pictures and I'll see you later.'

Didi gave him a little wave, as she was propelled out of the fast-revolving door.

That was it. Salvatore's mind was made up. He would isolate her from the company at the beach party and invite her out for a pizza on Sunday. She must be bored by now, eating in the stuffy middle-aged dining room every evening. If only for a change of scene, she would probably accept.

The chambermaids were in *Vulcano* when Didi returned, engaged in a replenishment of the toiletries, and evidently doing a more intensive clean than usual.

'*Buongiorno!*'

'*Buongiorno, signora. Parte?*'

Didi knew this was 'depart', so she effusively replied in the negative. The girls checked their clipboard and there was a lot of shaking of heads and worried-looking expressions. She recalled Salvatore's mention of the computer error.

'*Error. No parto.*'

Trying to remember the word for Tuesday, she silently went through the days of the week.

'*Martedì. Martedì ... parto.*'

More shaking of heads ensued, until the senior of the team addressed her.

'*Telefono?*'

Didi nodded assent, and the chambermaid dialled an extension number, following which there was a heated and rapid discussion in dialect. Without finishing the extra-special clean, the girls took their utensils and various potions in plastic bottles, said their goodbyes and left.

How strange! She had better not let her mother know they were at risk of being evicted. It was exactly the sort of thing she would go on about. Didi could hear it already – foreign inefficiency, disreputable travel agents, the unreliability of computers. Wiser to say nothing. This was the type of incident of which her poor father had lived in dread, when he and her mother used to travel together or even when they went out for a meal. Pauline was the more assertive – if she found a chip in her glass or a smudge on her fork, she was forthright in drawing the restaurant manager's attention to it. Harry used to cringe with embarrassment, having been the type of Irish customer who makes excuses for the staff he is paying to serve him. They rowed repeatedly about it.

'But, Pauline, why do you have to make such a scene, girl? They'll think we're after a free meal. And did you see George Dolan from the golf club, listening to every word? Oh, it'll be all around the clubhouse that I put you up to it, too mean to treat my own wife to a night out.'

'Oh bugger, George Dolan! That's what's wrong with the service industry in this country. We all whisper in corners and complain to each other, and when the waiter comes over with his usual platitudes, we gush and say "Yes, thank you, everything's lovely," only short of doffing our cap, and saying "*Yes sir, no sir, three bags full sir*", like in the old days. The Irish put up with shoddy standards, in case it might appear that *they*, the paying customer, are getting uppity.'

And on it went. Didi wondered if her father had *enjoyed* Pauline taking the responsibility for such issues out of his hands. There was no doubt her mother was demanding and if she set difficult standards for herself, she expected them to be met by others. It was this aspect of her character that had led to tension between the family. Her expectations of her two daughters were not always endorsed by Harry, who had a more philosophical approach to life. He had been especially defensive of Didi.

'Ah sure, doesn't she look grand?'

'She is *not* going out of *my* house dressed like some impoverished hippy. The hem of that skirt is all frayed, there are holes – deliberately made, it seems – in that jumper she has over it, and those "bovver" boots — she's like Orphan Annie! Well, my lady, what have you got to say for yourself?'

As usual, Didi would just shrug and say she was only going to a mate's house anyway, which seemed to whip Pauline into more of a frenzy.

'You have no *pride* in your appearance. If you won't do it for me, think about this: you are not the smallest of girls, and you have to play it down, by the way you dress.'

Failing to shock Didi into submission with this amazing observation, Pauline would run a weary hand across her brow and concede victory.

'Oh, go on then. If you want to wander the streets looking like a moving mountain, do, but if you meet anyone, don't say you're *my* daughter.'

Through this and many similar encounters, Didi could see Jan, her neat skinny-jean-clad legs slung over the arm of the chair, silently enjoying the altercation, delighted that her younger sister was a big taste-free zone, and admiring her own neat proportions in her beautifully co-ordinated pink ankle socks and matching polo shirt.

It was easy for Didi to laugh now, when she thought of the endless teenage battles she and Pauline had fought over clothes. Her mother had definitely been harder then, more conservative in her approach to life. These days, Pauline was flamboyant in the way she dressed, almost bohemian in her choice of colours, but still as ruthlessly critical of other people's appearance.

As Didi assembled her camera gear and some drinks to see her through the walk, she noticed one of the hotel's post-it notes stuck to the mirror. In an uncanny echo to her reverie, it read: *'Gone to town with Bobby & Helen for last minute shopping. Heard there's a party on beach tonight. Wear something nice. P.'*

Rico sat under the shade of an elderly olive tree. The walk up the steep road had not been a particularly good idea – the temperature was in the mid-30s – but the view from the slopes of La Kalura in part recompensed for his overheating. He really would have to get his hair cut. It wasn't sufficiently long to tie into a ponytail, yet long enough to cling in a most disagreeable fashion to the back of his neck. With a rehearsal at 4.30, he wondered why he had decided to walk this steep incline. He had often observed the little village perched on the side of the hill when he was having a swim below and, having asked the locals, they had impressed upon him that, as a village, it was nothing exciting, but the views back towards the Rocca and the port-side bay were spectacular. Besides, Rico needed to get away from the somewhat rarefied atmosphere of the Panoramico.

The previous night, he had slept with Isabelle. It wasn't premeditated, but as the evening had drawn to a close it seemed the most natural thing in the world that they should climb into the one bed, rather than prissily kiss and retire to adjacent quarters. That had never happened to him before. Of course, there had been women, women who had often and in the most embarrassing and undignified manner, flung themselves at him, but he had seldom been tempted. This was different. This time, *he* had been the initiator.

There was something about this woman. Isabelle was so *comfortable* to be around that she disarmed him. The degree of ease they shared, mastered in so short a time, was a compliment of the highest order. Following a day of clinging, neurotic people, Rico found spending a couple of hours with someone who wasn't constantly demanding attention unimaginably sexy. Isabelle's company was so attractive because she wasn't always hinting at sex, yet she *was* incredibly sensual. Nor had he the impression that if you didn't give her exactly what she wanted there and then, she would metamorphose into a pouting, sulking child-woman. She might gather her things and silently walk away, but she wouldn't plead, she wouldn't implore or exercise emotional blackmail to get her way. Rico admired this in her and knew it must have been the result of her aversion to similar manipulation from the Conman.

But how should he proceed? He was married to Monique, and Isabelle knew this. He had exercised no deception. It wasn't as if he had met her at a nightclub in Palermo, passed himself off as single and had a one-night stand, with no intention of ever setting eyes on her again.

The great thing – and the difficult thing – was that she was living next door and would continue to do so until both of them resumed their ordinary lives. What was the appropriate behaviour? Would she agree to be open about the relationship – because a relationship was what he wanted – or would she insist on keeping it all cloak and dagger, since he was married? The chambermaids already suspected something – they had been in on top of them this morning before Isabelle had left. Rico had stayed in too many hotels not to know that the most powerful chain of communication is that disseminated by the chambermaids.

The hooting of several horns, on board sleek sailing vessels below in the bay, distracted Rico from his musings. There seemed to be some sort of leisure sailing event in progress. Even at a distance, Rico could distinguish the extended limbs of prone people, soaking up the rays on deck, their greased bodies cooled by the offshore breezes.

Didi had spotted the yachts too. Their presence spiced up the already stunning panorama and made it very picture-postcard-like. With both cameras at the ready, she changed the filter to soften the light for the colour film she was shooting and added a zoom lens. She eyed her composition through the viewfinder. Superb! The yachts were all at angles to each other, giving the photo a three-dimensional perspective. She clicked once, twice – then some damn fool was walking straight up the hill into her shot, obliterating the central part of the scene.

'*Hey!* Could you *stop* for a minute? *Ferma! Un minuto!*'

The figure was evidently hard of hearing as well as obstinate, because he kept walking towards her in a perfectly straight line, thus ensuring his inclusion in whatever she might shoot. Didi scrambled backwards through the leg-scratching maquis, to see if that would help, but from her new position she was picking up a gnarled olive tree and its wide-spanning branches.

'*Ciao, Didi!* It *is* you!'

It was Rico. Annoyed as she was for his having ruined her photo, she still managed a warm greeting.

'Rico, what a surprise! *Where* did you spring from?'

'Oh, I was taking a walk, admiring the view. It is so peaceful up here. I didn't expect to meet anyone.'

'Me neither.'

'I think you are something of an expert with the photography, no?'

'I enjoy it. I used to be very good. I was in the camera club at college and we had lots of opportunity to submit our work to campus publications.'

'And now?'

'Now it's just for interest. Everywhere is so picturesque that if I can't bring home something that reflects the essence of the place, I am a very poor photographer indeed.'

Spotting both a water bottle and some juice protruding from Didi's small knapsack, Rico asked her for a drink.

'Let's sit down a while,' Didi said, taking out a plastic cup, and pouring Rico some water. 'Here. You take that. I have some snacks as well. I think we deserve something after that hike.'

'Yes, it's steeper than it looks. Because I have seen the bus whizz up it, I thought it was easy, but, *purtroppo,* I find out today that it's not.' Rico helped himself to a banana.

'How was your rehearsal yesterday?'

An air of tension crept between them at the mention of the rehearsal.

'Oh, *insomma!* There were some difficulties. My Tosca has a bad throat – she couldn't sing at all yesterday. It makes rehearsal very difficult when you work with the understudy, who in this case is quite good, but since you know that you will not work with her on the night of performance, it is really a lost rehearsal.'

'My father got me into opera.' Didi stuck the small straw into her apple-juice carton and took a drink. 'According to him, there were only three operatic composers: Bellini, Verdi and Puccini.'

'I think he is right – well, I suppose I am biased.'

'*Was* right. He died. Suddenly, last November.'

'*Mi dispiace.* I also lost my father recently. In May. He took ill when I was in Australia, and although I left immediately, he died before I got back to Italy.'

'Oh, that's very sad. I'm really sorry. When had you last seen him?'

'Twenty years ago.'

Didi was about to exclaim surprise, but something in

Rico's demeanour made her hold her tongue. He turned to her.

'Do you miss him, your father?'

'Very much. Pauline and I get on well enough, but we were never really close. I suppose I was always Daddy's girl. My mother is closer to my sister.'

'These things happen in families. It's like me and my father. He worshipped my brother because he approved of his work and his lifestyle. He never respected what I do for a living, thought it somehow less manly. I even think he was suspicious of my musical talent since he had none, as if my mother had been unfaithful to him and I was carrying someone else's genes.'

'Still, now he's gone, I'm sure you feel differently about him.'

'Yes, I do. I feel angry for the lost years. His obstinacy denied me a decent relationship with either him or my mother. He put her in the unenviable position of choosing between us.'

'In what way?'

'He would never come to any of my performances. My mother always tried to, if it was in Italy and near home. He wouldn't object or say anything, but his disapproval lingered around the apartment for weeks afterwards. She would come back from her outing – silent, denied the pleasure of enthusing about the concert or telling him all my news.'

'That was very hard on everyone.'

'Yes. Hard *even* on him, I think. In recent years, he might have changed his mind, but he was too stubborn to acknowledge it, and to try and put things right between us.'

A reflective silence signalled that Rico had divulged enough.

Brushing *panini* crumbs from her dress, Didi jumped up.

'Well, I am going to continue up to the village. Do you want to join me?'

'*No, grazie.* I really should head back to the hotel. I need a rest before the afternoon session. We have a second rehearsal this evening, with a very short break in between, since our schedule is a little disrupted at the weekends, on account of the religious ceremonies at the church and in the monastery.' Remembering his harsh reaction to her the previous morning, Rico tried to make amends. 'What are you doing tomorrow evening? Would you like to go into town for an aperitif? I am free any time after seven.'

Didi could hardly contain her pleasure. Far too enthusiastically, she replied in the affirmative.

'That would be lovely, Rico. Will I meet you in Reception?'

'Eh, no. I will see you directly at the seafront. I will be coming from rehearsal. What if we say the terrace of the Bella Vista – you know where that is?'

'Yes, the big white hotel, I know it.'

'About seven fifteen?'

'OK. That's fine. See you there.' Rico kissed Didi on both cheeks and turned downhill.

She called out after him. '*Don't work too hard! A domani!*'

Her long legs bounded up the remaining stretch of road to the village.

'*Yes!*' she shouted triumphantly at a fenced-in Alsatian in an adjacent villa, regretting it immediately as the animal charged the boundary railings and led his neighbouring canine friends in a *Hound of the Baskerville*-type chorus. '*Yes, yes, yes!*'

Her eye sharpened by the elated mood, Didi saw opportunities for landscapes and still-life studies all around her and zoomed and focused in rapid succession, shooting incessantly.

She *knew* if she persisted with Rico, she'd win him around. He was just so handsome *and* interesting, an unusual combination in a man. *Ha!* If Jan could see her now – in the company of this gorgeous hunk, how jealous she would be! Compared to that show-off husband of hers, Rico was a god.

Pauline kicked off her sandals as she came through the door of *Vulcano*. She had spent a great afternoon in Helen and Bobby's company and was really going to miss them when they left. Didi's knapsack was lying on the sofa in the sitting room, and Pauline spotted something colourful out on the patio, which she discovered to be Didi in a lounger, reading.

'Hi! Are you nice and cool there? It really is still scorching in the sun.'

'Yeah. I was up the hill road taking photos and when I got back I was exhausted. Even here in the shade, it's thirty-four degrees. Look at the thermometer. How was your shopping trip?'

'Fine. We had a great laugh with this old Sicilian man we met at the Caffè Duomo. He's a local guide, apparently – offered to show us all the hidden treasures of the place. He gave us his card – look!'

Didi took the yellow card. *Capitano Giacomo Sassi, guida locale,* followed by a choice of two phone numbers. 'Would you be interested in doing the tour?'

'I might be. He certainly looked the part, all spruced up in a yachting blazer with a regimental crest, *and* he was very knowledgeable.'

Pauline went into the bathroom, continuing the conversation.

'Helen and Bobby's flight tonight has been delayed – already they know it'll be at least two hours late. What about this — goodness! What's been happening in here?'

Pauline re-emerged holding four shower caps, three bottles of shampoo and a bag of little soaps. 'Are we that dirty? They seem to have left about three times the usual allocation of toiletries.'

'I noticed that. I think the girls left down their supplies when cleaning and forgot to take them when they were finished.'

'I saw the flyer about this party tonight – are you going?'

'Yeah, I thought I would.'

'Because I'd like to eat early with Helen and Bobby and I thought we could all eat together.'

'Fine.' Nothing could upset Didi, her imminent date with Rico firmly in sight. 'What time?'

'Is half seven too early? They want time to digest their food before heading off.'

'No problem.'

'Right. I'll just buzz Helen and confirm.'

Didi closed the patio door fully, so as not to overhear her mother's conversation, and from behind the protective screen of her paperback planned her outfit for the next night.

'Ti amo, che strano!' the music blared, and every Italian under fifty and some well over it, joined in with Francesca Chiara's classic hit.

The concrete bathing platform had been transformed for the night – deckchairs and umbrellas banished to the winter-storage shed and multicoloured lanterns hung at strategic points from the rocks, their reflection twinkling and bobbing in the water.

Federico, beach-attendant-cum DJ, had donned a floral shirt, replete with palm trees and setting suns. To impress the younger set, he had borrowed his fourteen-year-old daughter's fluorescent headband, the narrow tube of plastic pulsing alternately green and red LEDs to dizzying effect.

On the small gravel beach, two of the waiters tended the charcoal and driftwood fire, over which was suspended an enormous spit, rotating chicken legs, kebabs and various types of sausages. Luigi had been despatched from the main bar to serve in Federico's grotto, a task made all the more difficult in the confined space by the presence of Federico and his amps.

Salvatore turned the last bend in the stone steps. Already quite a lot of people had arrived. Moving from group to group, he chatted easily with guests of all ages.

'*Federico, una birra, per favore.*'

'*Io? Sono il DJ! Luigi – una birra!*'

Luigi poured Salvatore's beer in silence, throwing his eyes up to heaven in an expression of exasperation as he handed it over. Salvatore grinned in sympathy, and from the vantage point of the bar turned to see if Didi had arrived.

Sitting on a rock at the water's edge was Isabelle, chatting to a group of people, including Didi. Extinguishing his cigarette underfoot, Salvatore weaved through the crowd to where they were.

'*Ciao, ragazze! Tutt'a posto?* Well, Didi, how many photos did you take?'

'Too many. It was a great morning.'

Salvatore noticed that Christoph had insinuated himself into the company and was trying to engage Isabelle in conversation. Blocking him from Didi's view, Salvatore stood directly in front of her and continued chatting.

'I had a crazy afternoon. There was a lunch party out in the garden room, and the guests became very noisy. Some of the people in the villas were trying to have a siesta and they complained. Particularly the American diva – have you met her? – Signora Millar. Apparently, she is sick and was trying to sleep it off. She rang four times, each time more angry. I had to call Signor Bruno to go and ask them to calm down.'

'Is she the Tosca?' Didi accepted a beer from the wandering Luigi. 'Rico mentioned something about her having a bad throat.'

Isabelle's antennae shot up at the sound of Rico's name. Trying to sound casual, she turned towards Didi.

'Oh, were you talking to the lovely maestro today?'

At this, Didi became all girly, whispering to Isabelle. 'More than *talking* to him! I met him out walking and we sat and shared my picnic. Did you know his father died suddenly in May? He seems pretty cut up about it. *Any*way, he ended up by asking me out! I'm meeting him tomorrow night. Isn't that exciting?'

The excitement was Didi's and Didi's alone. A stony silence permeated the little group. Even Christoph on the fringe looked displeased, and turned to another German rep. asking '*Wer ist Rico?*'

'Where is he taking you?' Salvatore said, breaking the silence.

'To the Bella Vista.'

'That will make a nice change.'

'I can't wait. He's such a looker and much more sensitive than I'd originally thought.'

Isabelle felt sick. What was Rico playing at? Was he systematically sleeping his way through the entire hotel? Who would be next – Pauline?

The sparkle had gone out of the night for Salvatore. Didi was still wittering on about how lovely Rico was, and her eyes had the glazed appearance of someone not amenable to hearing sense. Rico's timing was also rotten. How often did Salvatore have an entire evening free? When Signor Giorgio had unexpectedly changed shifts for the Sunday, he could have hugged him, since Didi was leaving on Tuesday for the tour and he was running out of nights on which he could invite her out.

'Are you lot listening to me?'

Isabelle and Salvatore tuned back in to Didi's monologue. Although the discussion was distressing her, Isabelle decided she would glean more information about Rico's bizarre behaviour if she presented a receptive and encouraging ear to Didi's excited tale. Salvatore was too proud to let Didi see that he felt slighted by her accepting Rico's invitation and he was already trying to figure out if he could ask someone to swap the late shift with him on Monday evening.

'So, will we go?'

'Sorry?'

'Federico's outing to the Lido Crystal tomorrow?'

Isabelle hadn't a clue what Didi was talking about. Salvatore filled her in.

'There is a shuttle bus tomorrow to the Lido Crystal, a beach concession at the upper end of the seafront. They have a restaurant on the beach, water-sports, everything. The Panoramico does a deal with them every so often, to take groups of our guests – the beach is lovely up that side, very sandy. You should go. It will be crowded on this beach, since it's the first Sunday in August and a lot of day-trippers will try and pay the entrance fee in here for the day.'

Didi exploded. 'The hotel *charges* entry in here? But the beach and the sunbathing area are already tiny! How can they justify charging outsiders to come in? Anyway, where do you put them?'

'Oh, Federico will work his magic, sticking in a whole lot more deckchairs.'

'Well, that's decided it. I'm definitely going in to the seafront. I mean, this place is like a sardine-tin with just the residents. If we are to be besieged by day-trippers, I can't imagine what it'll be like! Are you on, Isabelle?'

Isabelle, torn between the discomfort of the hotel beach and the irritation of having to listen to Didi talk all day about her date with Rico, opted to play for time.

'If you don't mind,' Didi went on, 'I think I'd better bring Pauline with us as well. Her English friends are leaving tonight and I don't want to abandon her on the first day without them.'

This resolved Isabelle's dilemma.

'Of course. Yes, why not? I'll go with you. What time does the bus leave?'

Salvatore checked his phone diary.

'There are a couple – a very early one, and then one around ten-thirty. There's a return run before lunch, for those guests who want to come back to eat, but if I were you I'd stay there for the whole day.'

'What are the return times? After all, I have to make myself beautiful for Rico!'

'On the hour – one at five, six and seven.'

'Well, I'll grab the early one, since my rendezvous is at seven.'

Isabelle drained the last of the punch from her plastic cup. 'If you don't mind, I think I'll head up to bed. I'd like to aim for the early bus, so I'll see you and Pauline in at the Lido, if you decide to take the ten-thirty.'

'OK. See you tomorrow then.'

Didi thought Isabelle sounded annoyed, but maybe she was just tired. Despite her increasingly golden suntan, she looked quite wan. She would try to be particularly nice to her at the beach. Maybe she was still upset about that awful ex-boyfriend of hers. Yes, that must be it. Of course, she hadn't helped by going on and on about Rico. She'd really make an effort not to talk too much about him at the Lido. Besides, she didn't want to give Pauline ammunition if it all came to nothing.

No. Didi was going to work on mastering the art of silence – beginning the very next day.

Chapter 18

The Lido Crystal

The shuttle bus deposited its charges directly opposite a blue-and-white banner proclaiming '*Benvenuto al Lido Crystal*'. Isabelle went down the steps from the promenade. The cash desk was unattended. One of the French guests caught the attention of a *bagnino* straightening rows of sun loungers, and he signalled that he would be with them shortly. He walked towards the coffee bar, where an elderly grey-haired lady was having her breakfast.

'*Mamma, i clienti del Panoramico.*'

'*Sì. Arrivo subito.*'

Isabelle watched the cheerful old woman take up her position at the makeshift reception – really only a wooden table, on which she had a cashbox and a receipt book. When seated, she had appeared of average stature but, as she walked up the deck, Isabelle realised she was tiny.

The old lady took vouchers from the Panoramico hotel

guests and charged them for any extras, after the basic entry fee and deck chair. Isabelle handed over the supplement for a comfortable sunbed and an umbrella to herself.

'*Stefano, un ombrellone, un lettino per la signora.*'

Installed in the best row at the water's edge, Isabelle asked if she could reserve the adjacent seats for her friends.

'*Certo, signora.*' And with that, Stefano removed the umbrella's blue plastic cover, opened it, indicating the spot was taken.

'*Grazie, Stefano.*'

'*Prego, signora.*'

The welcome of the friendly and courteous *bagnino* restored Isabelle's faith in Italian men. Ever since Didi's disclosure the night before, Isabelle had felt edgy, uncomfortably insecure that she had allowed herself become vulnerable to Rico's charm. *Why* had she tumbled into bed with him? She seldom slept with people on such a short acquaintance. In fact, she hadn't slept with anyone apart from Con in many years. During those months when they were 'officially' apart, every time she would begin to get close to a new man, either through instinct or the rumour-mill Con would time his reappearance with precision, launch a charm assault, until she, unsettled, would fancy him all over again and they would end up in bed.

That's why the night with Rico had been significant. She had felt like making love to someone who *wasn't* Con. Rico hadn't been a substitute; he had attracted her in his own right, and she'd thought he found her appealing on precisely the same grounds. Now she wasn't so sure. What if she were just another notch in his travelling baton? Would she have to sit by and watch him pursue Didi until she in turn capitulated?

She *knew* she should have adhered to the promise made to herself before departing: that her Sicilian adventure should be uncomplicated, devoid of any involvement. She had promised herself an emotional limbo, to expel the negative feelings of the previous months. What she hadn't anticipated was that her isolation would feel all the more acute, surrounded as she was by happy, loving people, and that she would seize on Rico's flattering attention, to counteract this loneliness. But was she about to be made appear foolish again?

Before Didi's prattling, Isabelle had begun to feel her former confidence return. She knew she looked better. She got the odd whistle of admiration from strangers in passing cars as she strode along the seafront, or caught the approving eyes of pedestrians as she wandered through the old town. The hotel staff with whom she had become friendly complimented her, and even if it were part of their job description to flatter the female guests, she thought it sincere, and it boosted her morale. Rico's attention had elevated her into the spotlight and, although it went against everything she believed in, she had to admit that her fragile ego had been fortified by being seen as part of a glamorous couple.

She wasn't willing to take her bow and step into the wings just yet, allowing Didi, the Young Pretender, take over her role. In a bizarre parallel, Isabelle had a momentary understanding of why Beverly had demonstrated such abject annoyance at being replaced by a younger, prettier understudy.

The noise level at the hitherto tranquil Lido Crystal increased by several decibels. Sitting up, Isabelle became aware of a large party of elderly people making their way across the decking and following the *bagnino* down onto the sand.

'Harold, keep your trainers *on*. This here sand will burn the skin off of your feet.'

'It sure is pretty. Look at that castle thing down there.'

'That's the church, stupid.'

The *Costa Crociere* group had arrived. Isabelle had heard Salvatore mention that Palermo was one of the ship's stop-offs and the clients were regularly bussed up to enjoy a nice swim at what was undoubtedly one of the prettiest beaches on the coast. There was a sameness about the American clientele, who were on average in their seventies. Many were overweight and they struggled across the sinking sand. Loud and ebullient, but entirely good-humoured, the group called out to each other, discarding dresses and Bermudas, and cajoling their friends to take the plunge into the pond-like sea.

'*Hey, George, are you coming in?*' a grey-haired lady shouted to her reticent friend at the water's edge. '*It's cold at first, but after a while, you'll warm up!*'

Isabelle hoped they never had occasion to put their toes into the briny deep of the North Atlantic if they called this bubbling cauldron 'cold'. Turning back onto her stomach, she pretended to read a magazine, but through her sunglasses was secretly enjoying the exchanges between the latest Lido arrivals. Suddenly, she felt a scratching sensation between her shoulder blades, as if a large wasp had landed on her. Making a frantic swipe at it, she twisted around to find Didi and Pauline standing over her.

'*Ciao, bella!* Your man the *bagnino* asked us were we the friends of the "*bella bionda*" – I think you're in there.'

'Oh, hiya! Morning, Pauline. No, when I got such a nice spot, I asked him could I reserve the seats beside for you. Look at it now – it's full, apart from those claustrophobic back rows.'

'It's just as well you did, Isabelle. It's lovely to be right at the water's edge.' Pauline put her bag on the lounger. 'The breeze is cooling. *When* is this heat ever going to abate? Signor Bruno was telling me that the fire-service are spraying water from their planes onto the scrubland and the forests, to prevent them from becoming so dry that they'll catch fire.'

'Really? Gosh, I never thought of that.' Isabelle took a sip from her water bottle.

'Have you had a swim yet? I think I'll go in straight away, before I put on all that greasy sun-cream.' Didi had her bikini on under a cheesecloth sundress, and in one swift movement she dropped it off her shoulders. Tying her hair up in an even tighter bun, she ran into the sea.

'Pauline, are you coming?' Isabelle asked.

'I'm a bit self-conscious. What with my varicose veins and all, I'm not keen on displaying myself in my swimsuit.'

'Don't be silly! Look at all those big jolly Americans having a whale of a time. You're like a model compared with some of them!'

'Bless you, darling. I'll run in very quickly then.'

'This is the life!' Didi, fully sun-screened, was enjoying her book.

Isabelle was lying on her back, sunbathing.

'Yes,' Pauline agreed. 'Despite all the people, it's a lot more peaceful than the bathing platform at the Panoramico. Have you noticed how few of the customers are locals? Maybe the entrance charge is a bit steep for them.'

'More likely they have their own umbrellas and chairs at home and can sling them in the car and head off to any beach, whereas we need the shade, but can hardly pack a parasol in our suitcase.'

'How much extra was the sunbed, Deirdre? I didn't quite catch what she — Goodness! What was that?'

A shrill scream had pierced the restful atmosphere.

'Stefano! Rag–a–zzi! Ladro!'

The fragile-looking old lady at reception had some pair of lungs. Her cry was primal, its pitch and urgency striking a chord of fear into the indolent sunbathers, who all sat up, clutching unfastened bikini-tops in vague attempts at modesty.

The screaming continued, accompanied by the sight and sounds of several men in pursuit of a tanned young lad making a break for the steps onto the promenade with the busy Sunday-morning takings under his arm.

'Oh my God, they'll kill him!' Pauline stood up from her lounger.

The thief was going nowhere. The collective maternal love of two waiters, the *bagnino* and several clients had seen to that. Pauline was right to be worried. Their show of strength was excessive and the sound of metal chair-legs scraping the wooden floor as the thief tried to scatter them out of his path was punctuated by cries from his captors of '*Vergogna!*' – shame on you!

'Look!' said Didi. 'Here's the police – that was quick!'

'They must be from the patrol parked permanently on the Prom,' said Isabelle. 'I think your man would be safer with them than with that angry lot.'

The navy-and-white uniformed carabinieri descended the steps. The seriously shaken thief was extricated from the pile of sweating bodies and escorted off the premises in a custodial armlock.

The defence corps of waiters set about clearing the debris, cordoning off the offending area with luminous orange tape, sweeping and collecting every broken utensil and shard of glass, depositing them noisily into a metal bin. New tablecloths were laid – it was business as usual.

Isabelle saw that Stefano, the old lady's son, was tinkering with his lifeboat, a couple of paces from them. She smiled sympathetically in his direction, adding a '*Mi dispiace*'.

'*No, no. Signore, mi dispiace.* It is *I* who am sorry for the disturbance. These thieves come here on the train to rob, to frighten our tourists, to give our little town a bad name. We are proud that in this town a woman can walk with her handbag, not afraid that it will be snatched. I am proud that at this Lido a person can leave his money and go into the *bel mare* for a swim, and when he comes back he finds his things untouched. But today – *che vergogna!*' The large, broad-shouldered man dissolved in tears.

Pauline was moved. 'And your mother, is she all right now? She has had a terrible shock.'

'*Si, signora, grazie*. Signora, this is the thing. We are not wealthy people, but we are honourable people. We work very hard in the *stagione* to make money for the rest of the year. There is much poverty in Sicily and much – how do you say – *disoccupazione* –?'

'Unemployment,' Isabelle said.

'*Si*. Much unemployment. But it is not acceptable' – at this, Stefano paused, filling his lungs with air – 'it is *never* acceptable to rob an old lady. She could be your mother. Today, she *was* my mother.'

Overcome, Stefano strode off to bark orders at the waiters resetting the tables, pausing on his way to reassure clients in the rows closest to the incident that everything was fine now – it was all over.

'They're very emotional about things, aren't they?'

'Well, Deirdre, would you not be, if I were mugged?'

Isabelle screwed up her eyes against the midday sun and noticed that the restaurant was already open.

'Look, everything's back to normal. There's even one of the cruise couples sitting at a table in the middle of where the melée was.'

'Well, they're right! You can't give in to thugs like that. You have to make a stand.'

Didi, always sympathetic to the underdog in arguments with her mother, wondered about the thief. 'Maybe he's an addict or has a family to feed. We know nothing about his circumstances.'

'It still doesn't justify it. You heard what the son said: robbing a vulnerable old lady is despicable.'

There appeared to Isabelle to be something of an edge to this conversation. To distract them, she made a suggestion. 'Anybody hungry? Shall we go up and have a leisurely lunch?'

'*I'd* like to,' Pauline said. 'I'll have to go in under the umbrella now anyway, because it's too hot, even for me. I would be more comfortable up there in the shade. Deirdre, what about you?'

'I want to eat very little, since Rico's taking me out to dinner tonight.'

This piece of news had the desired effect on Pauline.

'*Rico!* You mean conductor Rico from the hotel? When did all this happen?'

'Try and not look so shocked, Mother. Some people *do* find me attractive, you know. He asked me out yesterday.'

'That's great news! Why did you keep it to yourself until now?'

'Oh, it's no big deal: a quiet drink, something to eat. I didn't feel the need to broadcast it over the hotel intercom.'

'No, but your own mother!'

'Well, you *never* approve of the people I see, so I've long since given up telling you about them.'

Isabelle had been right about the tension between mother and daughter. Didi seemed to be using the Rico news to get at Pauline, who went all tight-lipped and seemed diminished by the caustic comment. She dressed slowly, winding the stripey sarong around her little body, and putting a few essentials into her straw bag. Didi, meanwhile, had shaken her long hair loose, and assumed a cocky pose, that Isabelle didn't find all that attractive.

'Right, are we moving?' Didi asked.

'Just a minute, Deirdre.'

'I'll wait for Pauline. You go ahead and get the table.'

Didi caught her Titian hair in her hands, tossed it over her shoulder and strode purposefully towards the restaurant.

It was nearly four o'clock. Isabelle watched her sleeping companions. Pauline was snoozing, her lounger tucked tightly in under Isabelle's umbrella, while Didi was under the second brolly on her sunbed. Not able to fall into a deep sleep, Isabelle had placed her bed behind Pauline's deckchair, catching some shade for her head and most of her body, but allowing her legs to protrude into the sunlight. Her discarded novel lay on the small table by her side.

Didi's date with Rico was bothering her. Underneath the flowing skirts and the wild hair, Didi was self-confident. Isabelle had never really acknowledged this before, seeing her as a naïve recent graduate, sent to Sicily to chaperone her elderly mother. Because of this predicament, Isabelle had pitied her. But earlier, when she had swung that mane of hair in their faces, a fleeting glimpse of a determined, sexy woman had passed before Isabelle's eyes. This must be the Didi that Rico saw.

There was no sign of either Sleeping Beauty waking. Isabelle wondered should she let Didi continue in her comatose state, making her miss the all-important early shuttle bus? Yet a badly-prepared-for date wouldn't prove anything about Rico to Isabelle. It was better that Didi kept her appointment and then, with a bit of luck, if Isabelle hadn't shown her hand too much, she would get to hear afterwards how it had gone.

Telepathic waves must have permeated Didi's subconscious. She stretched out her arm and, finding no watch on it, mumbled sleepily: 'What time is it?'

'Gone four.'

'*What?* How long have I been asleep?'

'An hour or so.'

'Christ, I feel dopey. I'm going into the water to wake myself up properly. Are you coming?'

'No. I was in not so long ago. I'm going to take a bit more sun, now that it's cooled a little.'

Isabelle watched as Didi's long, white legs ambled towards the water. She was definitely quite a few inches taller than Rico. It seemed to be something that turned on Italian men – having women who were taller and who physically dominated them. She thought nostalgically about Con. She loved how he towered above her, her head barely level with his shoulder. Walking together had caused them problems: his long legs always out of sync with her stride.

Didi shook drips on Isabelle, like a dog after his bath. '*Oooh!* That was brilliant – just what I needed. I'm fully awake now and fit to face anything. The old dear still out for the count?'

'I heard that. A lovely way to describe your mother.' Pauline squinted out from under the umbrella. 'I fancy a walk. You shouldn't have let me doze for quite so long. Anyone coming?'

'No, Mom. I'm heading off soon.'

'Isabelle?'

'Yeah, why not?'

Although still cross, Pauline had to ask Didi. 'What are you planning to wear tonight? Something elegant, I hope.'

'My gauzy top and my orange pants.'

'Would you not wear your nice Monsoon dress? The one I bought you. Men like women in dresses.'

'Maybe but, as you know, *I* don't like myself in that particular dress. No, I've decided on my outfit. *You* liked it, Isabelle, didn't you, when I wore it to the cinema?'

This was the last thing Isabelle wanted, to be advising

Didi on how to make an even better impression on Rico.

'I can't say that I recall. What colour was the top?' Isabelle could remember every detail about the gauzy little number – principally that it had a lowcut back and was quasi-transparent.

'Kinda multicoloured. Anyway, it's the only thing I have that's remotely cool, so it has to be it.'

Pauline tutted. 'Well, it's your decision. Will I see you before you leave?'

'Doubt it. I'm back into town for seven, so with a bit of luck I'll see you both tomorrow!'

'Well, have a lovely evening. And Deirdre? Don't do all the talking. Listen to the man some of the time. Men love to be listened to.'

'Thanks, Oprah!'

'Don't be smart.'

'I hope that girl takes things slowly tonight.' Pauline and Isabelle had walked the full length of the beach and were on the pleasant return journey, where they could enjoy the magnificent view of the Norman town, perched below the headland over the sea.

'Didi? She'll be fine. She's only going for a bite to eat, and Rico struck me as the perfect gentleman ... what I know of him, that is.'

'Oh, I didn't mean it that way. No, I have no worries

about her safety. Just that I would like Deirdre to meet someone nice, but she tends to charge at men like a bull in a china shop.'

'You *can't* think that Rico would be a suitable long-term candidate? I mean, a holiday romance, yes, but we're all going home in a couple of weeks.'

'I wouldn't rule it out. Deirdre is not rooted in any one place. I could easily imagine her moving from Dublin. You see, her sister's wedding upset her a lot. Although Deirdre pretends she doesn't care, she must be jealous of how well set up Jan is. There's a tremendous security in finding the right man, and knowing that you can relax, and stop all the looking. Once you have him, you can work on all the things that aren't right.'

Isabelle thought this was a dangerous philosophy. She had many – already separated – friends who had started out married life thinking the same thing.

'What about you, Isabelle? I'm sure you have a lovely boyfriend at home.'

'I'm on a sabbatical, Pauline. Taking time out from all that sort of thing.'

'Well, don't take too long. The body has a funny way of forgetting about pleasure if it doesn't get to practise every so often. Don't look so shocked. I may be over sixty, but I do *remember* what it was like to love Harry.'

'You must miss him dreadfully.'

'I do. The funny thing is, it's only since I have been here that I'm beginning to register the loss of our physical relationship. People assume because you're older, that those needs die. They don't.'

Isabelle had never had such an intimate conversation with her late mother. Nor could she imagine her even *thinking* the things Pauline had just articulated. Didi didn't realise how lucky she was to have a mother with an ability to express her feelings.

'Here we are,' said Pauline. 'Back to base. What time is the next bus?'

'Six o'clock.'

'I don't particularly want to run into Didi on her way out, but I've had enough.'

'I'd say you'll cross her on the way. I'm going to stay, Pauline. I love this time of evening. I'll get the next one.'

'You do that. Will I see you later for a drink?'

'Maybe.'

Isabelle wasn't being deliberately obtuse, but she didn't want to tie herself into any arrangement that might see her and Pauline (and maybe later on, Didi and Rico) linking up. The whole episode was irritating and provoking juvenile feelings of jealousy. If she could be assured of not bumping into them, she would have holed up in town for the evening, but the place was far too small, and they were bound to meet. Her reasons for avoiding the early bus were not solely based on the beauty of setting suns. In all probability, the shuttle wouldn't make it to the Panoramico before the public bus left, but if Vincenzo, the Lewis Hamilton of the hotel drivers, was on duty, they could easily arrive ahead of schedule. If Pauline was happy to see Didi off in all her splendour, Isabelle certainly was not.

One by one, tourists and family groups showered, packed up and wound their way back to their respective transport. Isabelle felt as if she had stepped on to the set of *Death in Venice*, a lone figure waiting for exactly what she did not know.

So much for the perfect escape! What sort of a mess had she got herself into now?

Chapter 19

No matter what Didi did, the gauzy top would not fit. It must have shrunk in its first wash. The previously sexy plunging back was now all bunched together around her shoulder blades and looked terrible. Frantically, she searched the drawers for an alternative that would match her orange pants.

It was at moments like these that she wished interfering Pauline were on hand. Didi considered raiding her mother's wardrobe, though unless she went for a loose over-blouse, Pauline's clothes would be far too small. Christ, this was a disaster! Why hadn't she tried on the bloody thing when it came back from the hotel laundry that morning, instead of prancing around the beach all day?

She pulled out a camel-coloured cotton sweater that might work, but it looked so banal when compared with her original choice. Instead of appearing drop-dead gorgeous, she would now look frumpy and sensible on her exciting date.

The chatter of conversation outside the veranda alerted her to the fact that the six o'clock shuttle bus was in. Her mother and Isabelle were probably on it. She really didn't want to meet either of them in this less than satisfactory outfit.

Taking a deep breath, she tried to calm herself. Why was she in such a state? Was her appearance so important? Did she think that much of Rico? She *did* like him, fancy him even, and what with their shared love of music and everything, well, he was the first interesting man she had met in ages. She was so tired of the Dublin pub and club scene. When she wasn't fending off married men with wedding rings stashed in their back pockets, she had to suffer the ignominy of making conversation with braindead drunkards, who thought that because she was an unaccompanied female, she should be glad of company – *any* company – even that of boorish louts, incapable of stringing together an articulate sentence. Sometimes she wondered if Jan had got it right. Chase, pursue and nab the womaniser – and worry later about taming him into what you want. Her sister had landed a man who was *exactly* the type she met in clubs – wedding ring removed.

Pauline's key was in the door.

'Hel*lo?* Anyone home?'

'Mom, hiya. I'm still here. You wouldn't *believe* what's happened. My nice gauzy top has shrunk in the wash. Look.'

Pauline scrutinised the extended piece of multicoloured rayon.

'*Mmm*, well, obviously, you can't wear that. What were you thinking of instead?'

Sheepishly, Didi held out the camel cable-knit.

'God, no! That looks like the schoolmarm's first-day-of-term outfit. Have you nothing else?'

Tears were springing fast and furious. She had been here before. Didi was fifteen again. She could almost see the Doc Martens on her feet and hear the uneasy coughing of the impatient boyfriend pacing the living-room downstairs.

'Nothing that I feel good in!' she wailed.

'Now, now! There's no need for that. Hold on. I have a nice silk blouse that might fit you. It's always been far too long and baggy on me, so it might do.'

In other circumstances, Didi would have attacked Pauline for the implication, but she remained silent and waited, until a magnificent sheaf of soft ivory was produced.

'Here, try this.'

Didi took it, humbled, and went in to the bathroom mirror. It was perfect. The silk fell in sensuous folds over her figure and the colour complemented her ever-increasing healthy tan.

'Thanks, Mom. It's lovely. I'll take good care of it.'

'You're welcome. Now, hurry up and do your make-up and get out of here, or you'll be late!'

Didi's hair had been allowed to dry naturally into twisting curls, thanks to a heavy-handed application of styling mousse. Although she would expire from the heat, she opted to leave it loose, with two judiciously chosen tendrils, laced behind her ears and pinned softly at the back of her head. A final application of a rich bronze lipstick completed a very satisfactory look. Even Pauline was impressed.

'You look well – less "studenty", more womanly.'

'I hope that isn't mother-speak for "old"!'

'Why do you always have to kick compliments back in my face?'

'Sorry. Thanks. *I* think I look good too – very sexy.'

'*Deir*-dre! Less of that, please. It's only a first date.'

Didi grinned at the warning. This felt normal. When Pauline praised her, she never knew how to react. Years of criticism had conditioned her to expect negativity from her mother. She had become suspicious of anything else.

The Bella Vista was situated on the seafront and was very popular with tour groups, principally the French. The terrace bar was buzzing with clients enjoying a pre-dinner aperitif and admiring the magnificent setting sun, its pink rays striping the now silver ocean below. Didi looked in vain for Rico. There were few tables occupied by one lone drinker, so it was easy to ascertain that he hadn't yet arrived. It was gone seven-thirty. A young waiter, kitted out in traditional Sicilian dress, came over to her.

'*Prego, signora?*'

'*Buonasera. Un tavolo, per favore.*'

'*Certo, signora, venga.*'

Didi accepted the table right on the periphery of the terrace and ordered a white wine. She knew it wasn't cool to arrive before the man, but Rico *had* said seven fifteen. The waiter placed her wine and a bowl of olives on the table. Didi selected a black olive and put the stone into the ashtray.

'*Didi, mi dispiace!*' A very ruffled-looking Rico was making his way towards her table, his hair tousled and evidence of an after-six shadow beginning to sprout from his tanned chin. 'It was the rehearsal. It was so bad. We had to stay and talk with the soloists about the problems.' Suddenly, seeing beyond his own concerns, he acknowledged Didi properly. '*You look different this evening!* I think it is the hair, these colours? *Si, molta bella.*'

'Thanks.' In the full glow of his compliment, Didi felt completely justified in the time spent preparing her look.

'What will you …' Rico began, but then cut short his request. 'Oh, you already have your drink. I will have an *aperitivo* to calm my nerves after my difficult afternoon.'

He signalled to the fancy-dress waiter who swooped on the table immediately and took his order.

'*Allora*, Didi, what did you do that was interesting today?'

Didi recounted an abbreviated version of her day at Lido Crystal with Pauline and Isabelle, concentrating on the near pulverisation of an out-of-town petty thief.

Rico seemed very interested and asked a lot of questions.

'You spent the whole day with Isabelle at the beach? I didn't realise that you and she are such good friends now.'

'Why wouldn't we be? We are both Irish and here alone

… that is, if you don't count my mother. What would prevent us from being friends?'

'*Niente.*'

Rico's drink arrived and the waiter removed the cap of the tonic water.

'You're very quiet,' Didi said. 'Something bothering you?'

'*Io?* No! It's just today's rehearsal. You know, Beverly is *still* saying she is ill and yes, I do think she is unwell, but my problem is Ornella – that's the understudy. She is improving with each rehearsal and I think *she* will be a far better Tosca than Beverly. And yet, it is Beverly who must ultimately sing the performances. But I keep hoping she will remain sick, which is *very* unprofessional of me!'

'Don't be so hard on yourself, Rico. You're only human. If you think this Ornella is better than Beverly, it's only natural that you should feel like that.'

'Yes, but I still feel guilty.'

Observing the nearly empty wineglass, Rico pointed at it. '*Altro?* Would you like another white wine?'

'In a while, thanks. You really drink slowly, Rico. You've hardly taken two sips from your gin and tonic.'

'*Piano, piano*, Didi. Softly, softly. That's my motto – *take things slowly* – about most things in life. Do you mind if I smoke?'

Didi shook her head, but she did mind.

Rico searched his pockets for cigarettes to no avail and excused himself to go and fetch some from the nearby vending machine. During his absence, Didi became aware of an elderly man on the street-side of the fenced-off terrace. She could have sworn she heard him make a tongue-clicking noise in her direction but dismissed it as the fruit of an overactive imagination.

When Rico returned to the table, he reacted to the same individual. 'Oh that old creep!'

'Is it that shabby-looking man?'

'Yes. I call him the Prowler. Everywhere we go, he seems to appear. He preys on the tourists, particularly on women alone.'

'Preys, in what way?'

'Chats them up, hangs around for a drink or dinner, for which, of course, they will have to pay. He probably thinks he's operating a legitimate escort service.'

Both Rico and Didi laughed at the thought of this odd-looking character, with the trainers and the dyed-red hair, masquerading as an escort.

Rico gestured towards her wineglass and said: '*Altro?*'

'Yes, please.'

Didi watched in admiration as Rico, as imperceptibly as an experienced bidder at an auction, caught the waiter's attention and conveyed their new order.

'Oh look! The creep's moving in on that lady,' he said.

'It's amazing that the women fall for it.'

'*Cara Didi*, my thoughts precisely, but you know, loneliness makes people do crazy things.'

Didi fell silent. She remembered her own household in the lightless days of the previous November following her father's death. Each of them had acted crazily, from the sheer loneliness of Harry's sudden disappearance. Pauline had been prescribed tranquillisers to see her through, but they had only succeeded in numbing her into a zombie-like state and when, as frequently happened, she skipped a day or two, the fall to earth was so brutal that on each occasion Harry died all over again.

Didi had returned to the family home, hoping to offer her mother and sister some support, but also in need of sharing her loss with people who understood. Her flatmates Imelda and Tony had been marvellous, but she was so down that it was unfair on them to be constantly gloomy around the place. Yet, even in this gesture, she had found herself excluded, her mother and Jan presuming a monopoly on grief as they cried their way through endless boxes of Kleenex.

Two glasses of wine arrived on a tray, this time with a bowl of nuts.

'*Grazie.*'

Rico paid the waiter for their two rounds of drinks, which Didi thought unusual, since the custom was to run a tab for the duration of the evening, Sicilian hostelries showing greater trust in their customers than the bars at home.

'Rico, when your father died, did everyone in your family begin to behave differently?'

'Yes and no. I think *I* have been different since, but the others? My mother and my brother and his family? No, they just continued on as before. But then, I was the one with whom Papa had a difficult relationship – if you *can* continue to have a relationship with someone who you don't see.' He took a large gulp of his wine.

'It's just that since my dad died, we've all altered our behaviour. My mother is fluctuating between her usual, hypercritical self and a new, confident, more adventurous persona. I don't seem to be able to relate to either version of her, and even less to my sister. I can't tell whether Jan's coldness has to do with Dad's death or is a self-imposed distance, since she no longer has any use for us.'

'Why do you talk in terms of "use"? She's family. Families always need each other.'

'Yes, but Jan has her husband now – *that's* her family, as she never tires of reminding me. And when she has a baby or two, her perfect unit will be complete. The Garden of Eden will have no need of single aunts or ageing grannies!'

Rico frowned. He feared Didi's references were loaded with the bitter tinge of personal history, but he had neither the time nor the inclination to listen to a protracted tale. He had arranged to meet Stephen and the recovering Beverly for dinner at nine, in the hope that a more convivial atmosphere might help ease cast tensions.

'Your mother told me you had a degree in music. What are you planning to do with it?' He reached for his wineglass again.

Didi was surprised by the sudden change of topic and Rico's tone. He sounded paternalistic, or like a distant uncle, about to organise a sensible job for her and discreetly hand over a cheque to cover initial expenses.

'I don't know really. I've a place on the postgraduate diploma course to teach music in schools but, well, I'm not convinced it's me. The interviews were about a month after my father's death and I went through with it only to appease Pauline, who was terrified I'd go abroad.'

Rico visibly winced at this. Memories of what could have become his life's work had he been more appeasing sent a chill of fear through him.

'*Cara Didi*, you must follow your heart. You must think: what will please *Didi*, not Didi's mother.' Knocking back the remainder of his drink, Rico rummaged for change and dropped it onto the tip saucer.

'Yeah, I know you're right. Two roads in a wood and all that. I think I want to take the less usual route.'

'Well, *do*. Speaking of routes, *andiamo*?'

Didi automatically drained her still quarter-full glass of wine before her brain had assimilated Rico's request. They had been in each other's company for exactly one hour and five minutes. Where was dinner? She was starving and had suppressed with difficulty the sound of her gurgling stomach pleading for food.

'Do you not like the restaurant here?'

'I don't know it, Didi. I have never eaten here. And you? Where do you plan to have dinner? I think, *cara*, you are going to be too late for the hotel.'

Through the haze of her embarrassment, Didi tried to recall if at any time in suggesting they meet for an aperitif,

Rico had *actually* mentioned following it up with dinner, but in this heightened emotional state her memory could not be trusted.

'Me? Oh ...' she spotted a large poster on the street beyond the fence divider, 'I'm going to the Arena in Campofelice to see a film. We'll probably have a pizza out there.'

'Are you going with Isabelle?'

'No. I'm meeting a group of the sporty Germans – it's an organised thing. Their rep – Christoph – asked me if I would like to join them.'

'What's the film?'

The title had been in Italian; she hadn't recognised it, but she remembered the actor.

'Something with Bruce Willis.'

They rose and walked outside.

'OK, *cara* Didi. I will leave you to enjoy your night at the Arena. I must meet Stephen and Beverly in the restaurant, which if my sense of direction is right ... is here, Via Spinosa. You take care and remember what I said about following your heart – *you* must make the right choice!'

Thus Rico, oblivious to any irony in his parting speech, caught Didi by the shoulders, gave her a warm hug and was off.

Didi stood at the end of Corso Ruggero, wondering what to do. She couldn't go straight back to the hotel, having blown her date with Rico out of all proportion. Besides, there were practical considerations; she hadn't eaten and the hotel dining room would be closed. However, if she went to eat in any of the small restaurants, she'd meet someone from the hotel, or bump into Beverly and Rico on the way home. There was only one thing she could do: fulfil her fictitious itinerary and go and see the Bruce Willis film. At least, that way, she'd find out which film it was, if Rico should check out her story. There only remained the small matter of food.

To hell with it, Didi thought. I'm not waiting for Rico bloody Parisi's permission to eat – *in* company, *out of* company or anywhere I choose! With that, she strode purposefully to the Piazza kiosk and ordered two large slices of different pizza and a Coke.

The half-cold pizza lodged in her throat as she forced it down at speed, conscious that the film was due to start at nine forty-five and unsure of exactly how far away Campofelice was. The gassy Coke put the finishing touch to incipient indigestion, as she hurried in the direction of the seafront and a taxi.

As she passed 'Peppino's Traditional Restaurant', her reflection bounced off a mirror at the entrance, and Didi was startled by how distracted she looked. What *was* she thinking of, wandering around aimlessly, eating furtively on a park bench, dodging people she knew, all in order to keep up the charade of a hot date with the magical maestro?

The only driver at the taxi-rank was leaning on his car-roof, the pink pages of *Gazetta dello Sport* spread before him. He had seen Didi approach at speed and then decelerate within a couple of metres of his car. He wasn't going to let even a hesitant customer escape.

'*Taxi?*'

'*Si, signore.*'

'*Dove?*'

'I'll give Bruce Willis a miss. Just take me home.'

'*Che?*'

'*Niente.* Hotel Panoramico, *per favore.*'

Chapter 20

Isabelle's head slipped from its uncomfortable canvas pillow, and she banged her elbow on the frame of the deckchair. She was embarrassed to discover she had been asleep for nearly an hour, a mini-siesta that was becoming customary. The problem with falling asleep sitting up was that you started off under the shade of the umbrella but as the sun rotated you ended up scalding some part of your anatomy, no longer protected when the angle changed. Today's victims were her left knee and a fleshy part of her inner thigh, now both rather red.

For some reason, she felt edgy, unsettled. These post-prandial dozes were increasingly peppered with colourful dreams and, by her agitation, she suspected she had just had another one. But could she remember it? No.

She looked around her.

The bathing platform had taken on its late-afternoon

configuration – untidy groupings of three and four deckchairs, all unoccupied, but still strewn with the belongings of their owners. Federico's regimented rows had been stood down, and the erratic clustering of chairs reflected the scene of a good card game or bore witness to a wonderful story shared by four or five friends, who had chatted incessantly all morning. Isabelle looked around, wondering if she was the only one left on the beach.

The deckchair occupants hadn't gone too far. They were huddled around the jetty, an informal swimsuit-clad guard of honour for an alighting pair of newly-weds. Isabelle watched in disbelief as a medium-sized yacht launched a smaller vessel into the water, handing down a Sicilian bride and her five metres of organza train to a shiny-faced new husband already onboard. With the photographer documenting events, the couple completed the last hundred metres of their journey in the noisy little speedboat.

Several onlookers called out 'congratulations' as the couple neared the landing point.

'Auguri!'

'Viva gli sposi!'

An international round of applause rippled through the watching bathers, as the over-dressed man and woman prepared for the tricky transition onto the jetty. Federico supervised the operation and took charge of the bride's landing, no mean feat, considering her high-heeled shoes, and wide crinoline dress. A young waiter in silver-service bib and tucker, offered glasses of champagne.

Isabelle watched, bemused. Something was resonating from her snooze dream, but although it hadn't to do with weddings, she had an inkling it had to do with Con. What was it, and why wouldn't it come back to her?

'They must make a fortune out of those weddings.' Didi, swathed in a sarong, and wearing her straw hat, materialised beside her deckchair.

'Oh hiya. Yeah, very over the top. Can you imagine tackling those steps in a long dress and evening shoes? She must be out of her mind.'

'The photographer's assistant was afraid I would pass them on my way down the steps, and was trying to make me wait in the viewing place, as if a glimpse of a real person would mess up the record of their sweaty climb!'

'It's all about show, isn't it? I thought Irish weddings were bad, but I'm reviewing my opinion.'

'You weren't at my sister's wedding. I'm telling you, Isabelle, she could give these Sicilians a run for their money.'

'Was it a big posh do?'

'Not that posh, but oh, the nonsense that went on. Who to seat, away from whom. How to get the photograph into the paper. How to coax the stingy aunties to buy their gift from the Brown Thomas list. I swear, I aged about ten years in the months before.'

'I suppose we'd be the same if it was our day.' Isabelle searched her bag for some soothing After Sun.

'*I* certainly wouldn't. Would you? Why impose your expectations on other people? I mean, if you're really happy and inviting people to a celebration, well, that's lovely, but you can't dictate how they behave or where they should buy their gift! Or worse, what they should wear – my sister even had a colours' list for the extended party, so they wouldn't clash! She was like the stage manager of an elaborate production, rather than the host of a big party.'

'Grab a chair. Those people beside me have left. You're very late. It's nearly three-thirty.'

'To tell you the truth, I wasn't in the mood for company – or sunlight.'

'Oh. Heavy date with Rico last night? Did we overindulge?'

'Far from it.'

Didi began to unpack her beach things, then paused and sat heavily into the deckchair. 'It was *so* awful. Oh Isabelle, I have to tell someone. I made a complete fool of myself.'

Isabelle perked up. 'In what way?'

'I read all sorts of things into his invitation. I mean, the man was only being polite, but I took it up as if he was asking me out on a date. I can feel myself blushing even recalling it.'

'I'm sure it wasn't that bad. What exactly did you do?'

'*Nothing*. I met him for a drink – 'an aperitif', to quote his exact words. But I had this notion that we were out for the *entire* evening, so when he made moves to join his colleagues for dinner, I was disappointed. I handled it badly. I'm sure he thinks I'm an idiot.'

'Rubbish. He probably took it at face value, as men do: a drink with a friend – and that's what you had. If you go on about it, then he will suspect you have the hots for him. You *do,* don't you?'

'Of course I do. He's gorgeous. But there's an iron ring around our Signor Parisi! He's very definite about what he wants and what he doesn't want. He's not a type you could tempt, if he wasn't willing to be led astray.'

Isabelle had to admit that Didi was perceptive. But if her impressions were right, then Rico's post-copulation behaviour seemed incomprehensible. To have allowed himself to be seduced, he must have wanted to seduce her too. So why the subsequent silence?

'Isabelle, do me a favour, will you? Don't tell Pauline about the date that wasn't. Luckily, she was over in the Excelsior at some Karaoke, so she isn't aware I came home early. When grilled this morning, I said I found him incredibly pompous and, like most musicians, full of himself, and I wouldn't be in a rush to spend an evening in his company again.'

'I won't say a word.'

'Thanks. It's just mothers – you know the way they are – always so willing to see romance for their daughters around every corner, and if you don't pull it off, you have some fatal personality flaw that's ruining your chances!'

'Don't be too hard on your mum – she means well. Though I suppose you being in the spotlight all the time is a bit of a strain.'

'You're telling me! I don't know how we're going to cope on this tour thing. On the one hand, I'm looking forward to having a breather from the hotel – for obvious reasons – but I'm worried how we'll get on, incarcerated in strange places without any of you lot to provide a distraction.'

'Oh, you'll make friends in your tour group and forget all about the Panoramico.'

'I doubt I'll be let, even if I wanted to. Salvatore plans to "keep in touch" during the week. He really is quite sweet. He's invited me out for a pizza tonight, and I'm going, since food *was* actually mentioned this time, not like last night, when I came home half-starved!'

'Go. Forget about Rico.'

'But it's so unfair. I feel no buzz about going anywhere with Salvatore and yet, I know he'll turn up when he says, and if he promises pizza, well, pizza we'll have. Unlike yesterday, when everything was unstated and vague, but I had butterflies all day, in the expectation of something – *anything* pleasurable – once I could be in Rico's company.'

Didi had it bad, Isabelle thought. How could she be in so deep following such a brief acquaintance? It was rather fortunate that she and her mother were taking this round-the-island trip. Isabelle didn't want to have to contend with daily bulletins on the progress of Didi's infatuated heart. 'Tell me about your tour.'

'It goes anti-clockwise around the island from here. When we leave tomorrow, we stay in a resort outside Palermo – Mondello. Then, we go all Greek, and head for the temples of Erice, Selinunte and the biggies at Agrigento which are supposed to be spectacular.'

'Will Pauline be able for all this travelling?'

'Oh, she's a tough old bird – she'll be fine.'

The sun, having hidden its face behind the cliff, transformed the bathing platform into a gloomy grey. Isabelle wasn't impressed.

'Didi, I'm going to chase the sun up to the swimming pool. No point sitting in this depressing greyness – we have enough of that at home. Are you coming?'

'Oh, I quite like it when I can forget about getting burnt. I'll chill here with my book for a while.'

'OK, well, sunworshipper as I am, I'll leave you to it. Will I see you before you go touring?'

'I expect so. Probably tomorrow, I have still to pack and then there's Salvatore and his pizza. But we don't leave till mid-afternoon, so I imagine we'll bump into each other before then.'

'Well, have fun with Salvatore.'

'I think the pizza might be the only thing I can honestly say I'm looking forward to.'

'Don't be like that. You never know!'

Isabelle luxuriated in her pre-dinner pampering. If this holiday had achieved nothing else, it had certainly forced her back in touch with her body. All the fleshy exposure to sun and sea, necessitated daily examinations to ascertain how her fair skin was coping. She didn't feel negative about her image anymore, and paraded naked around the room unselfconsciously, not repulsed or depressed by any glimpse of her passing body in the many well-positioned mirrors. In fact, she quite admired her compact little shape, and when Rico had run his appreciative eyes over her, she felt doubly reassured that Con's critical appraisal no longer mattered.

The amount of head-space her ex occupied was diminishing as the days progressed. She read this as positive. That was why the afternoon's dream had been unsettling. It had finally come back to her why she was upset after her siesta. She had been dreaming of their weekend in Westport, the previous December. What an extraordinary animal the subconscious was, the way it could bury layer upon layer of emotions and then spit them to the surface at will. Nothing in her current environment could be responsible for prompting memories of a cold, windy weekend in a renovated castle, miles from civilisation, yet that dream had replayed every word of their phone conversation.

'Hiya, hon. How's it going?'

Isabelle recognised his voice immediately.

'What are you up to?'

'Busy at work. Where *are* you?' She thought she heard the irregular thrum of a traditional bodhrán in the background.

'Out West. Do you fancy joining me?'

'Con, don't talk rubbish.'

'No, I'm serious. I'm on a work junket – deluxe hotel, state-of-the-art pool. All that's missing is you!'

He really never changed. She hadn't seen him for months. 'How long are you there for?'

'Till Monday. Miss the weekend traffic. I'm not exactly in a rush back.'

'Why?'

'Ah, work's quiet, and well, I'm lying low personally.'

Isabelle knew instinctively he was avoiding some woman or other. She really should have ended the call there and then. But this was Con. He could chisel through her defensive armour and, even though she recognised what he was doing, she somehow couldn't prevent herself from succumbing.

'So, where's the mystery location?'

'Westport. The Abbey Falls. Fab place.'

'There's nothing dodgy about this? I mean, you're not using me to make some little Mayo girl jealous?'

'Izzie, you're some suspicious woman! Would *I* do that? No, if you join me, you'll have my full and very undivided attention. Just like old times.'

'Get real.'

'Have you started packing yet?'

Isabelle struggled to force the dismissive words out of her mouth, but they would not come.

'How long would it take me to drive over?'

'Allow four hours. Give me a bell, hon, when you're on the road into Westport. Stop at the Texaco with the burger joint – it's on the left – I'll drive out to meet you. And Izzie?'

'Yes?'

'I can't wait.'

'Ciao, Beverly, ci vediamo domani!'

Rico's voice. Just outside her veranda. Isabelle ran to peep through the muslin curtain, convinced he would ring her doorbell. She watched as he swung through his own archway, ducking his head under the purple bougainvillea. Four full days had passed since they had been together. The longer they went without even greeting each other, the more uncomfortable the whole thing became. Isabelle wondered should she just buzz his room and say 'hello' but hesitated. After all, he had been free the previous night and spent it split between Didi and Beverly; maybe her call would be unwelcome.

Focusing on herself, she flicked through the wardrobe, choosing an elegant black linen top and a red-and-black silk skirt.

In the hotel restaurant, her companion at the adjacent table had left. Signor Russo's month was up, and on Saturday he had headed north to the hot emptiness of Milan. Isabelle missed him – most of all, his morale-boosting comments on her appearance, which she had grown to expect each evening when she arrived. It was almost too embarrassing to acknowledge that on the occasions, when she felt lazy and disinterested in making an effort, the thought of Signor Russo's disapproving glance had encouraged her into full metal jacket and lifted her mood accordingly. Tonight, she was dressing for herself, needing to feel equal to anything Rico Parisi might throw her way.

The dining room was buzzing when she arrived. Signor Bruno hastened down the aisle in quick pursuit, as she hesitated in front of her usual table, currently occupied by Swedish honeymooners.

'*Signor Bruno!* My table's been hijacked!'

'*Mi dispiace, Isabella* – the new waiter, he knows nothing. Come! I will give you a better table, *sulla terrazza.*'

Isabelle wasn't displeased at the suggestion. Over the previous weeks she had watched as endless romantic couples dined on the ambient terrace, the twinkling northern coast spread before them. She had wanted to eat outside too, but in her early days, had felt intimidated that she would look decidedly odd in such a setting, alone. She had now arrived at the point where only self-satisfaction mattered, and dining in the cool night air seemed like heaven.

'*Eccoci!*' Signor Bruno removed the glass globe from the lantern and lit the candle. '*Bellissima, no?*'

'*Si, molto bella.*'

With a bow, Signor Bruno left.

'*Bella, come te!*' In the dim light of the terrace, a disembodied voice came from the strategically positioned cheese-plant that divided her table privately from the next. '*Da sola?*'

Despite her annoyance over his cool behaviour, Isabelle

had to laugh at Rico's earnest face peeping through the waxy leaves.

'Stop! If you are going to talk to me, come out from behind that jungle!'

Rico didn't need a second invitation. He swept his packet of cigarettes into his trouser pocket and, taking his wineglass, sat down opposite Isabelle.

'Is it okay? You didn't answer my question.'

'Which question?'

'I asked if you were alone, or expecting company.'

'Oh, you mean the "*da sola*" routine? I wouldn't respond to that as a real question. That's what the waiter says every evening – I am immune to it.'

'But are you? Expecting company?'

'Why? Will you not do? Or do we need to look for other guests to boost the numbers?'

The waiter, initially thrown by the table change, left a small tray of *antipasti* and moved Rico's bottles of wine and water to his new spot.

Rico looked confused. 'So it's just us for dinner, then?'

'Yes. I was just teasing you. I want to have dinner with you alone. It's just that since we last spent an evening together, I haven't seen anything of you. I thought you might be avoiding me.'

'Whatever for?'

'Maybe you were embarrassed about what happened.'

'If I thought it was a bad idea, I would say so. I would not be a coward and avoid you. I have had a few difficult days at rehearsal – *you* were there last week – you saw how they can be. I even had to take Stephen and Beverly out to dinner, to see if we could calm the situation.'

'How's Beverly's throat?'

'Better, I think. She's due back tomorrow, but I am still calling Ornella every day, because I fear it's a question of stamina with Beverly. If she's not careful how she paces the voice, she will not survive three performances. Ornella will probably end up having to sing one.'

'She looks a lot better than Beverly.'

Rico half-snorted, half-laughed.

'That's the *other* problem. Beverly is so jealous of Ornella that even if she's *not* fit to sing, she won't relinquish her position to the younger woman.'

'Art imitating life, or the other way around?'

'*Scusa*?'

'Competition between females. It's innate – genetically programmed. Most female-female encounters are tussles for supremacy.'

'Maybe in this case, but in all female relationships? I don't think so.'

'But you accept that males are competitive with each other?'

'Of course. They are constantly trying to outshine their friend, their father, their brother.'

'It's similar for women, only they suppress their feelings under the banner of the "sisterhood", female solidarity against all odds, and particularly united against man the oppressor. Yet, if you were to remove men from the equation and place a group of women on a desert island for a period of time, they would play the same competitive power games to establish a hierarchy every bit as ruthless as that of their male counterparts. The female pecking order is a very tangible entity, just more subtly delineated.'

'I don't know if I will ever feel safe around women again! You paint a picture of powerful Amazons.'

'*You* are perfectly safe. As a man, you will never have to compete in that arena.'

'Does that mean that *you* feel competitive towards the females in your life?'

Isabelle recalled her feelings of resentment towards Didi, when she thought Rico might be interested in her.

'If I'm completely honest, well, yes. I admit that if something or someone was that important to me, I *would* set myself up in competition against another female to get it.'

'*Cara Isabella*, all you are proving to me is that men and women are more alike than we commonly take them to be.'

'Not too alike, I hope. The interest is in the difference.'

'As you and I both know.'

An awkward silence fell, during which Rico took Isabelle's thin hand between his strong musician's fingers, and massaged it silently, gazing intently across the arc of candlelight into her eyes. 'I don't want anything else to eat. What about you?'

'No. I think I'll pass.'

The impatience of their passion astounded and invigorated Isabelle. If they did not leave the terrace immediately, she was going to embarrass them both by some highly inappropriate behaviour. Fortunately, Rico seemed to share her sentiment, and leaving behind half-full bottles of everything, they gathered their belongings and left, Rico then returning to reclaim the bottle of water, which he thought they might shortly need.

Isabelle had never been with a man who was so intent on pleasuring her that his complete focus of attention was her every move and reaction. She was able to lose herself entirely in enjoying these sensations, without pondering where he was at, and what did he want done to him next. It was the most unselfish type of lovemaking and contrasted starkly with what she had previously experienced. Taking his cue from the progress of her passion, Rico responded to the pulsations of her body and allowed his rhythm to increase, intermittently calling out or making a comment, as their rasping, hoarse breathing became louder and louder until, welded together in a sea of perspiration, their passion culminated in the most overwhelming mutual orgasm. Dizzy from a lack of oxygen, Isabelle held on tightly to him – as if by releasing him, the intense moment of pleasure might also pass.

When they finally loosened their grip on each other, Rico lay still for a long time, stroking the curve of her spine, his caressing hand making a U-turn at the nape of her neck, and repeating the performance in contrary motion. She held his precious, vulnerable head in her hands, planting kisses on any inch of exposed flesh she could find. Neither felt the need to say anything.

After what seemed like an hour, he got up and opened the patio doors, now that the noisy enthusiasms of their lovemaking had subsided.

As he resumed his place in the bed, snatches of conversations and multilingual phrases wafted in and out of *Stromboli,* as tired and tipsy hotel guests wound their way across the terrace to their respective rooms.

Isabelle knew this was as near perfection as she would ever get: not a moment in which to question motives, or consider futures. The magic was in *being*, in taking and recording the intangible and appreciating the privilege of sharing something that people who often spend a lifetime together never attain.

Curling into the outline of Rico's back, she pulled the damp sheet over their lower bodies and, relishing the luxury of drifting off to sleep with the rhythm of her breathing in harmony with his, she wished that *Stromboli* could drift off into the ocean like its namesake, a little world with no past, no future, only an endless succession of present moments.

Chapter 21

Cefalù

The buzzer sounded again. Stretching his arm in the direction of the alarm clock, Salvatore hit the 'off' button and rolled back to sleep. The noise continued. *Damn!* There was somebody downstairs trying to get into the apartment.

'Yes?' he croaked into the intercom.

'Are you not going to let me in?' his sister's voice chirped back at him.

'Maria! What a surprise! Come on up.'

Salvatore pulled on a T-shirt, just as Maria-Pia's footsteps sounded on the marble stairs outside.

She came in, a big smile on her face, and they hugged.

'Breakfast. Croissants.' She dropped a paper bag onto the table and crossed to the stove to put on the coffee. It was great to see her so full of life. He hadn't been back to Bagheria since she had taken him into her confidence, but they had chatted regularly on the phone. She was still adamant their parents had no need to know of the incident with Christoph, but conceded she should see a counsellor in Palermo. Perhaps she had already – and this was why she was in such good form.

After a while, the espresso pot whistled. Maria-Pia bit into her croissant, the chocolate sauce dribbling down her chin. 'So, how am I going to spend my day here?'

'I have to work – I start at ten-thirty. Come out to the Panoramico with me – you could always use the pool, if you're afraid of running into Christoph at the beach, though Tuesday is his cycling trek to Caccamo.'

'Yes, I'll come with you, but I'll go to the beach. Now that I'm feeling stronger, I need to confront significant places and make positive associations.'

'If you think so. I'm not taking my break till late, as I absolutely have to be around for the Island Tour departure at four. A friend of mine is leaving on that, and I want to see her off.'

'Would this be a certain *Irish* friend?'

Salvatore grinned. 'Yes, Didi. I told you about her before. Why don't you come up from the beach and I'll introduce you to her?'

'Sure. Do you think she's interested?'

'Hard to tell. We went into town last night and had a great evening. Even walked the seafront afterwards. Very romantic, but, well, I didn't make a move, because she spent a lot of time talking about this guest in the hotel – a conductor from Rome. It didn't seem right, when she was thinking about someone else.'

'That'll never come to anything. Don't you think you should shower and get dressed for work? It's a quarter to ten.'

'Yes, Mamma! Right away!' Salvatore escaped as Maria-Pia hurled a cushion in his direction.

Hotel Panoramico

Didi had never got around to packing the previous evening and was now confronted by two mounds of her belongings – a Bring and a Leave pile – strewn across the floor of *Vulcano*. Her triage system was not going as smoothly as she would have liked, and Salvatore wanted the luggage for storage about midday.

Pauline arrived back from Reception and was unimpressed. 'Goodness, you have nothing done! Giovanni asked if we could be as quick as possible, because they need the room cleaned asap.'

'I can't decide what to leave behind.'

'You have far too many outfits. Just repeat a lot of the lightweight ones for when we're sightseeing. Don't forget sturdy shoes and a warm jumper for going up Mount Etna. It's hard to imagine needing a jumper in this stifling heat, but it's cold at that altitude.'

Didi looked more critically at the Bring pile and discarded

a few items. She shoved the remainder into the smaller of her two suitcases.

'Your friend Salvatore was coming on duty as I was leaving. He arrived with a pretty little dark-haired girl. I hear he's arranged to store our excess luggage. Isn't that very thoughtful of him? They must have a special place in the hotel for that sort of thing.'

Didi suspected that Salvatore was going to take their bags home to his studio apartment, cluttering up what already sounded like a very small space.

A sharp tap on the door, followed by the sound of a key in the lock announced the arrival of the chambermaids.

'Oh no, here are the girls! I wish you had some of your sister's organisational skills – she wouldn't be dithering like this. She'd have packed everything last night, instead of gallivanting around the town till all hours.'

Didi bit her lip. So, she was a bit disorganised; it was hardly a hanging offence! The night before, Pauline had seemed pleased about Salvatore; now it was 'gallivanting' till all hours. Her mother was so inconsistent.

The chambermaids, in happy expectation of a large tip, were all smiles and '*buongiornos*'. They looked at Didi's chaotic packing and decided to start in her mother's bedroom.

'Right. Well, my bags are divided and ready to go.' Pauline got up off her knees slowly. 'I'm going to take the first one to Reception. Will you follow me over?'

'Yeah. Leave the big case. I'll take that.'

'Thanks, Deirdre. Good girl.'

Pauline's petite frame disappeared through the shady garden, her Samsonite bouncing along behind. Didi watched her go and felt anxious about the week ahead. She hoped there would be some like-minded people on the tour with whom Pauline could strike up a rapport. Otherwise, it would be a very long seven days.

Maria-Pia reintroduced herself to Federico, who was looking at her suspiciously as she hovered in search of a place to sunbathe.

'You haven't been here this summer at all.'

Maria-Pia lied about having work up in Bagheria. 'But today I'm free, so I thought I'd come and check on my big brother!'

'Oh, that boy! Always with these foreign women. It is because he speaks English so well. They find him charming.'

Federico set up a chair and umbrella far away from the popular front row, actually in a very uncomfortable place where the through traffic to his grotto bar would have to cross practically over her legs, but Maria-Pia accepted this was the price for being merely the sister of an employee, rather than a paying guest.

'Is this OK?'

'Yes, thanks.'

'Sorry – customers.' Federico nodded to his bar.

Maria-Pia took some carrot oil and rubbed it into her already mahogany skin. She inserted her towel between chair and umbrella, and stretched out flat on the concrete platform, balancing the plastic eye-protectors on the bridge of her nose.

'*Buongiorno, Didi.* You leave today?'

'*Ciao, Federico.* Yeah, this afternoon, for a while.'

On hearing the familiar name, Maria-Pia pulled off her eye-protection to squint at the new arrivals. The girl was tall and red-haired, with milk-white skin, accompanied by an older dark-haired lady. The pair weaved their way through the seats towards a prime position, the older lady stopping every so often to greet or chat to some of the other residents, until they reached a clearly reserved duo of the newest striped deckchairs. Evidently, Federico was also smitten.

Up at Reception, Pauline and Didi's non-touring luggage was becoming a nuisance. Salvatore had already fallen over the large suitcase twice. He would have to fetch his car and dump them in the boot – well, one in the boot, the second wouldn't fit. Signor Giorgio would blow a fuse if he found cases behind the desk when he started his shift.

Didi had delivered them earlier, adding a room request which had surprised him. She now wanted to move into *Filicudi* after the tour, rather than the villa they had been in for their first two weeks. That didn't make a lot of sense.

Vulcano had by far the finer view of the sea, and a much larger terrace.

In many ways, she was a secretive girl. They had spent nearly five hours in each other's company the previous evening but, though she chatted incessantly, she had revealed little. Only when they took their midnight walk along the seafront did the conversation become personal, and then she had persisted in asking *him* if he'd a girlfriend and rambled on about how handsome Rico the conductor was. She must know Rico was married, albeit not very happily, judging by the volume and tenor of phone calls with which this Monique person bombarded him. His wife's obsessive calling had become a standing joke among the staff. Giovanni was running a book on how many phone calls she could make in any one day. Even if Didi didn't know about Monique, was she blind to Rico's obvious infatuation with Isabelle? Whenever Salvatore saw them, they were coming or going somewhere together. Could Didi not see this?

'*Andiamo?*' Maria-Pia, now even more bronzed, was standing in Reception, dressed only in a lime-green bikini top, and a piece of chiffon material tied around her midriff as an improvised skirt.

'*Maria!* You need to dress before you come through the hotel!'

'I *am* dressed. Well, I suppose I could put on my T-shirt as well.'

'Yes, please.'

'I saw your friend – down on the beach earlier – with her mother?'

'Yes, probably. What did you think?'

'Attractive, but no beauty.'

'Thank you, sister dearest! You really know how to make me feel good.'

'Beauty isn't everything. I look forward to meeting her.'

'Well, if we don't hurry up, you won't. Their coach is off at four. Speaking of which, *where* is Giorgio? He's due to take over at four.'

'No Giovanni?'

'Only having his lunch now. I don't like doing it, but I'll have to buzz him to come back and man the desk.' Salvatore dialled the restaurant extension. '*Giovi*? I have to pop out for a couple of minutes. Are you nearly finished eating?'

As she waited, Maria-Pia studied the 'welcome' noticeboards with pictures of the hotel staff and the tour operators' representatives. A chill ran down her spine when she looked into the cold blue eyes of Christoph.

Giovanni strolled out from the dining room, carrying a bowl of pasta.

'That was quick!' Maria-Pia kissed the trainee receptionist with whom she had been to school.

'Sorry about this,' said Salvatore. 'He's late *again*.'

'Privilege of being the boss, Totò. These suitcases. I think we should hide them somewhere.'

'When I'm finished saying goodbye to the guests, I'll put them in my car.'

'No! *I'm* not going to take the rap if Giorgio comes in when you're kissing your girlfriend goodbye. Here's the key of the shop. Throw them in there on your way out.'

Aware of the minutes ticking by, Salvatore moved the cases into the shop and shot out through the revolving doors. A large orange-and-gold bus was already parked in the lay-by, its small dark-haired driver in the hold, loading and rearranging the various bags to maximise space. There was no sign of Didi.

Apart from two other passengers having a final cigarette, everybody had already boarded. Salvatore scanned the faces at the nearside windows, finally alighting on Pauline's sharp features. She tapped on the window and waved out. The adjacent seat was still vacant.

Maria-Pia could hear voices from the other side of the bus. She strolled around the back to see Christoph leaning against his moped, chatting to Didi.

'What's wrong?' On her return, Salvatore noticed a pallor had invaded his sister's suntan.

'It's Christoph. He's here.'

'Where*?*'

Silently, Maria-Pia motioned towards the offside of the bus.

Salvatore rounded it just in time to see Christoph pass a piece of paper to Didi. No! This was the limit! How was he expected to stand by and do nothing, when this dangerous man was plying Didi with charm and probably his phone number?

Maria-Pia, several steps behind her brother, decided more drastic action was required. Suddenly, she made a break towards Didi and snatched the paper out of her hand, tearing it into tiny pieces.

'*You maniac! Leave her alone!*' she yelled in English.

Christoph, aware of his audience, relaxed his facial features into a deliberate, ironic grin, and began to slow-handclap.

'*Brava!* What a wonderful performance! *Wunderbar, Liebchen!*' Turning to Didi, he raised his eyebrows and made an upturned hand gesture. 'All mad. I am sorry, Didi. Here, let me find my agency card, since this – this wildcat, has destroyed the other page I gave you.'

'*Stronzo!* Tell her what you are *really* like!' Maria-Pia continued to harangue.

Christoph put a protective arm around Didi's shoulder. 'You should get on your bus now. The driver is impatient.'

Salvatore insinuated himself between Didi and the bus. 'Not just yet. I have come to say goodbye and wish you a good trip. What my sister says is true. This – person – is not suitable company for you, for any woman. Didi, please, do not ring him.'

'Thanks for the advice, Salvatore, but it may have escaped your notice that I am of the age of reason and will decide *myself* who I would like as a friend. If you'll excuse me, I'm holding everyone up.'

Didi leaned pointedly across Salvatore and kissed Christoph on both cheeks, then made her way around to the steep steps at the front of the bus.

Salvatore put his arm around Maria-Pia's trembling shoulders. He knew she shouldn't have come back to this infernal hotel. So much for confronting her fears.

What had the episode achieved? Nothing, only to confirm to Christoph and an array of witnesses that his sister was unhinged. Maria-Pia's intention had been to raise doubts in Didi's mind but, judging by the latter's parting words, she'd only succeeded in creating a rift between Didi and himself, precisely at the time when he should be staying close.

Christoph, unfazed, hopped on to his moped and sped off. He didn't even wait for the bus to pull away.

The driver coaxed his cumbersome 52-seater up the steep incline onto the main road. Salvatore heard the engine shudder as it adjusted to the challenge and watched until the bus vanished. Disaster! Why did Christoph have to turn up just as he was about to say something memorable to Didi as she left for the week? And how had that sleaze become sufficiently familiar with her to hand over his details?

As Salvatore and the trailing Maria-Pia neared the hotel door, a dark green Alfa Romeo practically forced them into the wisteria climbers, as Signor Giorgio accelerated on the narrow driveway, evidently impatient to start his shift.

Salvatore gave his sister a quick embrace and ran up the steps ahead of his boss, to where a now distraught-looking Giovanni seemed to be holding two phone conversations at once. Relieving the younger member of staff of one of the phones, Salvatore injected a levity he did not feel into his voice.

'*Hotel Panoramico – buonasera!*'

Even the drudgery of his dead-end job was a welcome distraction in moments like these.

Chapter 22

Gibilmanna

Rico was glad of his decision to arrive early, although they weren't scheduled to rehearse until seven-thirty. He knew he needed the intervening time to mull things over and focus on what lay ahead. This was the final run-through before the dress rehearsal. The orchestra had been called for six forty-five, but nobody had arrived yet. A sound of sporadic hammering came from the set.

The cool sandstone steps looked inviting. He sat down and lit a cigarette. The small date on his Tag Heuer watch proclaimed it the eighth day of August; his father had been dead exactly three months.

Rico had found himself thinking more and more about his dad recently and was shocked at how little he knew of his life. Before they fell out, he could recall listening to Giuseppe joke about sliding down the icy roads as a child on his way to school in Polizzi. That could only mean that the family had lived within walking distance of the school. On impulse, he had checked the phone book in Cefalù's post office for any remaining Parisis in Polizzi. Although he had found quite a few, there was no guarantee that they were family – it was quite a common name. The official had suggested he include some neighbouring villages and had written him a list of them.

On the next free day, Rico hired his driver to visit the area. What he expected to find he wasn't sure, but he thought if he could stroll through the streets his father had walked all those decades ago and look at the terrain that had formed the mind and spirit of the man, it might help him understand his own roots.

Polizzi Generosa turned out to be a typical hilltop town in the Madonie mountain region, its closely built rows of houses boasting more accommodation and services than Rico had anticipated.

When he had left the driver, Rico wandered through the labyrinthine shady streets. He passed the primary school where his father must have gone, the gates chained and padlocked, its salmon-coloured walls pockmarked by closed green shutters. He studied the shop signs and the plaques of professional offices, interested to see if any bore his own name.

Somehow, that visit made him feel calmer – less at war with his father's memory and more sympathetic to the culture shock that must have been the family's move from the beautiful wild hills of Sicily to the grimy back streets of Florence.

The technical director passed with a clipboard.

'*Ciao,* maestro!'

'*Ciao*, Marco.' Rico stubbed out his cigarette and placed the dead butt in the packet. The hammering above him ceased; the crew were having a meal break before the call. The master carpenter and his technician son walked across the gravel together. Rico was struck by their identical physique, the similar rhythm of their gait – the son a dark-locked replica of his grey-haired father.

With such evidence of genetics at play before him, Rico thought about man's desire to replicate himself – a desire he felt more urgently since he had stepped back a generation, to examine his own origins. Yet something Isabelle had said continued to niggle at him. Was his desire to have a baby a completely selfish act? And with Monique? Would the relationship last? Or would his child be reared by one or other parent, luxuriating in the joys of two bedrooms and double presents on festive occasions, but lacking the nurture and security that average parents living under the one roof bring?

Even if Monique did accede to his desire to become a father, to introduce a baby into their troubled relationship would be irresponsible. Her demanding phone calls continued day and night, and even when he assured her that he'd ring after rehearsal, she left numerous messages in the intervening time. What worried him most was the increasingly hysterical quality of their conversations. She was forever in a state of anxiety about some contract or other, or yet another choreographer intent on bedding her. It never failed to amaze him that of all the dance directors in the world, Monique only worked with those who were straight, libidinous and all of whom fancied her.

'Rico, you're early!'

'*Ciao*, Stephen.'

'Everything OK? Beverly not ill again?'

'No. I saw her a couple of hours ago at the hotel – she seemed fine.'

'I'm a bit edgy. I'm worried about Act Three and the execution scene.'

'Why?'

'The rampart from which Tosca is supposed to jump. Because we have the cushioned platform for her to land on, I'm worried the audience to the side can see it. It's absurd if Beverly *steps* rather than plunges to her death.'

'Well, the stage-crew have been working away up there. Perhaps you should have a word.'

'I have already. I've asked them to increase the masking so she's not visible.'

Feeling uncharacteristically dismissive of his director, Rico let himself into the small chapel. He had several hours of Stephen ahead of him, and he wanted to maximise his private time before official proceedings began. Musically, Act Three was shaping up nicely. The culminating drama focused the singers' minds, and even cynical Beverly and lecherous Paolo were managing to commit themselves fully to the action – egged on, it seemed to Rico, by the very authentic jealousy of Wolfgang's Scarpia.

Flicking through his score, a stapled bundle of the hotel's phone messages caught his eye. He had stuck them in between the pages when the manager handed over the latest collection. Rico felt dejected when he read the scribbled phrases.

'Monique: 8.30pm. Message: Enjoying dinner? Hope the company is good.' And later: *9.20pm: 'Monique. Message: Whatever happened to early nights before important rehearsals?'* They went on in similar vein, culminating with the latest afternoon missive. *'Monique. 4.30. Message: Don't ring. Resisted long enough. Taking Henri up on his offer.'*

Henri was one of the Montpellier choreographers who worked regularly with the company. As Monique told it, he had been hassling her since the day they met. The veiled threat was intended to send Rico into a fit of jealous pique but, as he reread the note, he found it had quite the opposite effect. Monique's ploy was adolescent. He felt neither anger nor jealousy at the thought of another man making love to his wife. The strongest emotion he felt was relief – relief that Henri might take on the responsibility of her.

Was this to ease his conscience over the developing relationship with Isabelle? Or was he just a coward, hoping if his wife found happiness elsewhere, it would remove the obligation to challenge their future together? After all, if Monique left *him,* they could work out the legal details calmly, without him feeling guilty that she might throw herself off the Pont du Gard at any given moment.

When did it all go wrong? He remembered the early days, when Monique hadn't worked at the same breakneck speed she did now, how he used to enjoy her accompanying him to the opera houses and cities where he was engaged. How he looked forward to seeing her dark, curly locks in the dimly lit auditorium – sometimes taking notes if things were not going well. Now, she was bored with his work and she was passionate about her own. His schedule was an impediment to them spending time together, she said, yet it had become her personal crusade, never to refuse work – even petty, uninteresting work – lest she appear less 'professional' than him. Rico realised that in inviting Isabelle to rehearsal the previous week, he had been desperately trying to recapture the warm feeling of support having your loved one watch you brings.

'Well! That's much better now.' Stephen was back, beaming with satisfaction. 'I don't think the audience should be able to see Beverly's landing-pad now. I made one of the technicians jump off a couple of times, so I could check it from different angles and it's fine. Going over your notes?'

'*Scusa?*'

'Your notes.' Stephen pointed at the Post-its strewn across the open pages of Rico's score.

'*Sì. Sì,* my notes.' Rico shuffled the telephone messages together and shoved them into his briefcase. 'So, are we agreed: a complete run-through? No stopping. I'm going to focus particularly on Act Three, though I have to say I'm not displeased with it.'

Stephen took a sip from his water bottle. 'Me too. Technically, there are a few complicated things that I'm not convinced are as polished as they should be.'

'Don't panic. We still have the dress rehearsal to come.'

'OK. If the *maestro* says don't panic, that's good enough for me.'

Rico managed a watery smile, and followed Stephen onto the set, where one of the choristers was on standby to help test the sound levels.

'*Ciao,* Rico!' Beverly approached, in some black-and-yellow nipped-waist dress, which made her look like an over-sized bee. 'It's so goddamn hot. Wouldn't you think at this time of the evening it would begin to cool? *Maestro*, are you unwell? You look a little pale?'

'*Buonasera*, Beverly. No, I'm just a little tired.'

'*Gee*, is that Irish colleen tiring out poor *Maestro* on this very important week! I'll have to have a word!'

Rico turned to snap but thought making an issue of Beverly's remark would only draw the attention of those who hadn't already heard it.

'*Che caldo!*' Paolo was mopping his brow with a large white table napkin. 'This heat! You know, I speak with my brother on the phone in Positano. He is – *come si dice, isolato?*'

'Cut off.'

'Cutta orff in his house, because of the fires. It is not possible to pass the road to Amalfi in one direction or Sorrento in the other, because the *fuoco* is burning on both sides and at any minute, he leap across the road. Everything is so dry, you *breathe* hot air on it and *whooosh,* it go up in flames!'

'*Gee!* You don't think it could come here?' Beverly fanned herself.

'Do not be so stupid,' said Wolfgang. 'Do you know where is Sorrento? How could the flames cross the sea at Messina?'

'And *buonasera* to you too, Wolfgang! *Of course* I know where Sorrento is. I went there on honeymoon with my second husband. I didn't mean the *Sorrento* fire would come here. I meant that it's so goddamn hot that *fires, Sicilian fires,* might start!'

'It's very possible,' said Rico. 'I read in the paper that they are spraying the land to dampen it and make it less likely to catch fire.'

All heads swivelled in Rico's direction. Stephen, unnerved by this information, moved the discussion back to the imminent rehearsal.

'So, Beverly, nothing to worry about. Have the Executioners arrived yet? I want a word with them and you, Paolo.' Stephen took Paolo off in the direction of the two supers, but Beverly hovered.

'S*ì?* Tell me.'

'*Maestro*, it's about earlier – when you said you were tired. I hope you're OK. You're not *worrying* about anything. You know, you could always talk it over with me, if something was bothering you.'

'*No, grazie*. Everything is now going very well with the production. Nothing is worrying me.' Rico pointedly checked his watch. 'Orchestra? Ten minutes. Time to start tuning.'

As he conducted Act Three, Rico acknowledged that Stephen was right about it still being disjointed. At the last production rehearsal, the singers had seemed distracted by their acting demands, and these anxieties had impacted negatively on their vocal performance. At least Beverly was singing splendidly, and for once co-operating with everybody. Even her remark about Isabelle hadn't been nasty, just a good-humoured tease about the person now recognised as Rico's current paramour.

His initial irritation at the comment was borne out of precisely the notion that the cast – or that *he* – saw Isabelle as some sort of diversion, far from home. His feelings were stronger than that. There was no point in trying to convince the singers that he had been confronted by hundreds of Isabelle situations in his career but succumbed to few. This woman was different. He was really falling for her.

He hadn't shared this with Isabelle. He didn't want to scare her off because he knew she still had feelings for the

Conman, but when he tried to analyse his current emotional state, one thing was sure: it was nothing like his relationship with Monique – all highs and lows and seesaws of point-scoring. With Monique, when he did well, he was on cloud nine, but quickly plummeted to earth if for some unfathomable reason he incurred her wrath. Rico spent their time together hyper-sensitive to the inflexions in her voice that indicated pleasure or annoyance, anticipating what she wanted or trying to read minute changes in her mood. He was permanently on high alert – an invisible Richter scale poised between them, primed to warn of turbulent times.

Since he had met Isabelle, Rico didn't see why he should continue to live on tenterhooks. Here was this interesting, independent woman who did not demand the emotional succour that Monique continually craved. Who seemed complete in herself: he was only an enhancement to that completion. Yes, he hoped he made her feel better – happier, more loved – but he wasn't essential to her existence. With Monique, he regularly felt that he had to give one-hundred-and-twenty per cent or it wasn't enough. She threatened him with her insecurities, her weak constitution, her disturbed childhood – all weapons in an armoury of emotional blackmail that she called up, whenever she didn't receive enough attention.

Rico wanted a lover, not a dependent child. He didn't want to constantly offer therapy or deliver reassurance. He wanted a partner who was an equal, who once in a while could support him. Their marriage had always been a one-sided affair. As long as Monique was kept happy, the marriage was wonderful. When he dared to express his desires or opinions, he was being 'selfish', not prepared to compromise. The only problem with Monique's interpretation of compromise was that it required him to capitulate each time – and her never to see his point of view.

'*Shepherd boy*? Gino, *where is* the shepherd boy?'

Rico jolted to reality with the sound of Stephen's angry voice. It was a cue *he* should have given, and the young boy soprano had missed his entrance.

'Where is the boy?' he said. '*Ah, Antonio, va bene? Allora.* Let's go from 28. OK. After three.'

Young Antonio squawked his few bars and scampered back into the wings. Rico felt Stephen's scrutinising eye on him. He really had better concentrate. The tricky section with the bells was coming up soon, and the percussionist was on another planet. It would be his responsibility to ensure that one of the most poignant moments in the opera was not destroyed.

Paolo, soon to be executed, was playing a blinder. His rendition of '*E Lucevan le Stelle*' moved the cast to tears. The lyrics were appropriate – Rico glanced at the imminent Sicilian night and noted with pleasure the stars lending their approval to the action below.

Beverly, in character, rushed onto the set, clutching the false papers that the double-crossing Scarpia had drafted, and Paolo, with tears of joy and relief, prepared to go through with the mock-execution, promising to fall down, once the fatal shot would sound.

No matter how many times he conducted *Tosca*, it made Rico choke, the moment in which the inert body of the ever-trusting and optimistic Cavaradossi failed to move. To Beverly's credit, she responded slowly, believing the ploy, then revealing her realisation that this execution was no mockery. Rico watched her fall to the ground – then, disturbed by the noise of Scarpia's henchmen coming, decide in a split second that life without Cavaradossi was no life at all.

Stephen need not have worried. Beverly's farewell to her dead lover, and her crazed leap from the parapet of Castel Sant'Angelo, would convince even the most cynical member of the audience. The voluminous skirt of her gown disappeared out of sight, to the tumultuous underpinning of the orchestral score. For once, the percussionist managed to time the repeated and dramatic clashing of his cymbals in the correct place. It was all over. Although it wasn't a performance, Rico's heightened emotions had drained him. He wiped the sweat from his brow with an inelegant, checked handkerchief. The opera had once again worked its magic. He was experiencing a fusion of feelings – torment, sadness, *regret* – as if his life in microcosm were spread out before him.

The orchestra were still. Stephen, overheating through tension and a little emotion, was compelled to remove his glasses and wipe them dry. Rico knew it was the moment to praise.

'*Bravi, bravi, tutti!* Well done, everybody! Ladies and

gentlemen of the orchestra, I have a couple of sections that we need to work on a little, but you have done very well tonight, and I do not see any reason to detain you further. Stephen?'

'Eh, no. I agree. Let's call it a night. Any notes, I'll save for the pre-General call – that's six-fifteen on the tenth. We have a well-deserved day off tomorrow. So, *grazie* and *buona serata*.'

Rico smiled at Stephen, who responded with a sigh of relief. It was easy to forget that this performance was his début as an opera director, and despite it being an out-of-the way festival, Stephen's first foray into the genre mattered desperately to his reputation.

'So, Rico, will you join us for supper?'

'Who's going?'

'The cast, me, of course, and Gino. I think a few from the orchestra.'

Rico thought of the Post-its in his briefcase. He knew Monique expected him to call. Her last message meant anything but what it said. When she clicked her fingers, she stood back and expected him to jump.

But not this time. Rico was tired of jumping through hoops. He would go with his colleagues for dinner, like any normal conductor after a successful rehearsal. Monique could choose to "dance" – or *not* – with Henri.

'*Allora*, where are we going?'

'The Pescatore. That's where they've booked. Are you on?'

'Very much so.'

'Good! Then you can give me a lift, when your driver arrives.'

'He's already here. Tommaso is a Puccini fanatic. I spotted him about forty minutes ago, watching the rehearsal.'

'Oh, don't tell Wolfgang or he'll throw another wobbly!'

Rico in a gesture of genuine affection for the anxious Englishman, threw his arm around Stephen's shoulders as they walked towards where Tommaso was sitting, pretending to read his newspaper.

'*Allora, Tommaso, tutto a posto?*'

'*Si, maestro. Dove andiam'?*'

'*Al Pescatore e subito!*

Chapter 23

Naxos

Didi was fully awake, although it was only half past six. Pauline's snoring was getting louder. There was no point in trying to get any more sleep.

One of the drawbacks of the tour had been the necessity to share a room with her mother and on two occasions even a bed – one of those silly joined-up twins – since two people travelling together with the same surname had been assumed to be a couple. The enforced intimacy was torture.

Appreciating the coolness of the ceramic tiles underfoot, Didi made her way to the balcony, to check if it was bright enough to sit and read. She hadn't thought it possible, but some places they had visited had been more oppressively hot than the Panoramico. Agrigento and Ragusa stood out as locations of extreme discomfort, their proximity to the North African coast rendering conditions arid and desert-like. She had begun to think longingly of soft Irish rain.

In the weak light of dawn, she stumbled over a pair of sturdy walking shoes discarded by Pauline after their Mount Etna trip the previous day. It had been the exhilarating highlight of the week, but a long and tiring outing and, uncharacteristically, her mother had abandoned clothes and boots where she undressed. Today was officially a 'free day', and because most of the tour group had been dissatisfied with the guide's rushed visit to Taormina the previous Saturday, Didi had proposed that she and Pauline go back independently and do it properly.

'What time is it?'

Didi didn't move from the balcony. 'It's not yet seven. Stay where you are.'

'I'll only nod off into a fuggy deep sleep, and you said we were going to spend the whole day up in Taormina.'

'That's just up the road! There's no pressure. We can leave anytime.'

'Still, I want to be on top of everything before we head off.'

Didi sighed at Pauline's pedantic nature.

Apart from the inconvenience of doubling up in the one room, the tour hadn't been as stressful as she had anticipated. Her mother had made some German friends, and a young Dutchman had kept Didi company when she and the Germans became heavy going. Pauline had taken to adding a smattering of Germanic commands to her repertoire of broken Spanish, in a bizarre personal version of Esperanto.

This was their last full day on tour. The following morning, they would take the inland motorway back to Cefalù, and although she had only known them a short time, she was looking forward to seeing Isabelle, Salvatore and … Christoph again. There was something attractive about the German rep. She had tried calling the number he had given her, but on each occasion he was either out with a group or the voicemail kicked in.

Salvatore, predictably, had phoned three times. When the first call came, Didi had been cold, remembering their altercation at the bus but, since he made no reference to it, she softened in subsequent calls. Christoph, on the other hand, had not responded to either of the two messages she had left. Maybe he was away on the Aeolian Islands trip, or out on long cycling treks. Or perhaps – she tried to dismiss the thought – he just didn't want to call back. She was still a bit amazed by his silence, but when Salvatore rang the previous evening she hadn't dared to ask after Christoph, given that they were obviously in the midst of a feud over the good-looking sister.

Didi flipped through the Taormina pages in her guidebook, deciding what they should include for a relaxed-pace visit. Although nearby, public transport from their beachside hotel in Naxos seemed to encourage tourists to keep the taxi-drivers in pocket, but Didi wanted the challenge of planning the journey on local transport. Besides, a taxi would deliver them all too speedily. It could end up being a very long day.

Shortly after 10 o'clock, the packed local bus disgorged most of its teenage passengers at the Isola Bella beach stop – the one before theirs at Taormina-Mazzarò cable-car station.

'Are you comfortable?' Didi inserted her ticket into the automatic barrier. 'Have you been on one like this before?'

'Not in a built-up area.'

'It'll be fine. They make loads of journeys each day, up and down.'

The woman official released their barrier, as the descending white cab glided into the platform and the passengers left through the opposite gate.

'Though I *am* looking forward to taking things at our own pace.' Pauline sat in on a blue velour seat.

'Me too. Let's do the amphitheatre first, before it gets too hot.'

'Did you book a guided tour?'

'No need. Just the tickets. We'll take a couple of headsets – oh, look, there's a helipad. Isn't that where Donald wouldn't land during the G7 summit?'

'We've stopped. Why have we stopped?'

'To let the car coming down pass us. There's only a single cable on this bit.'

'Oh, he's putting on a bit of a spurt now.' Pauline clutched the grab rail, as the cab juddered and accelerated.

'There's no driver! They're controlled from the two stations.'

'Look at that beautiful villa with the pool. Though

wouldn't you hate to have this lot gawking in at you – how many times did you say a day?'

'Well, it runs from eight till very late – I guess maybe a hundred? Hey! We're right over a football pitch – and they're playing away oblivious.'

'That was quick – we're coming into the station!'

'Mind how you go when you jump off.'

There was a surprisingly long queue outside the gates of the Teatro Antico. Didi had assumed that once armed with tickets, they would sail in, but apparently the booking process served no other purpose but to control the numbers traipsing around a monument built in the year 3 B.C. They waited patiently.

'*Ach so!* You two also decide to come and visit Taormina!'

It was one of the solo Germans from their group – Heinrich or Helmut or somebody. Didi hoped he wouldn't attach himself to them for the day.

'Oh hello, Hans.' Pauline fiddled with the controls on her English-language version of the audio tour. 'Yes, that was a ridiculous choice last Saturday – visit the amphitheatre – *or* do the cathedral and churches of the big square. Most people wanted to see both. Silly guide!' She tried to pull her straw hat on over the headband, but it wouldn't stay.

'He's opening the gate now.' Didi linked her mother, in the hope that Hans would wander off on his own. The rest of their unguided group fanned out, as much as was possible whilst following the arrows of the recommended trail.

The visit culminated on the mid-level steps of the amphitheatre, the visitors looking down onto the stage area and the semi-intact ruins of the original 'theatre' building behind. Didi's camera clicked without interruption, as the mid-morning light allowed the clearest view out to the Bay of Naxos and the astonishing sight of Mount Etna, still puffing tentative smoke into the summer blue sky. It took some time for the group to clear the deep, uneven steps and join the main avenue back to the exit.

'So, what do you think of the beautiful Taormina? Very romantic, yes?' Hans was back.

'Oh absolutely!' Pauline handed her commentary gadget to the official as they went through the turnstile. 'I have never seen a view like it. That moment when you look across over the amphitheatre and see the bay and Mount Etna dominating everything – it's a once in a lifetime experience. It's a pity Jan didn't come, just to see that.'

'Jan is another friend who didn't visit Taormina?'

'Jan is my other daughter.'

'And she couldn't make the trip?'

'No. Well, she's just recently married and back from a long honeymoon.'

'He must come as well! Now, I wish you both *Wiedersehen*. There is lots to see.' Hans waved his sheets of paper and left.

'Coffee time?' Didi said.

'Oh, yes please, Deirdre. I could do with a sit-down.'

'If we go down the steps here, we'll find somewhere in the shade in Naumachie. Or so the book says.'

As they sat in the shade of the tiny alley, something Pauline had said was puzzling Didi. Why did her mother think it was a pity Jan missed out on the view from the amphitheatre?

'Was Jan considering Taormina for the honeymoon at some stage?'

Pauline shifted uncomfortably, but made as if she was just too hot, fanning herself with the street-plan she had picked up earlier.

'What? No, I never said she was coming here on honeymoon. I was just hoping they *would* come here one day. She would really have appreciated somewhere like Taormina.'

'Meaning?'

'Meaning nothing. Jan likes fine things – classy shops, designer labels. Look around you – they're all here. She would have had a ball.'

There it was again! Pauline was referring to the visit as if it were a missed opportunity, not a future project.

A waiter began dressing the adjacent tables with linen and cutlery for the lunch trade and pointedly put two menus on their table.

'I think we're being given a hint.' Didi glanced at the midday fare.

'Oh, not here. Somewhere more upmarket – with a view.' Pauline took out her purse to settle the coffees. 'Besides, it's too early.'

'Agreed. We'll head up Corso Umberto – the main drag – and see where that takes us.' Didi took the money and docket in to the cash desk and thought she would return to the subject of Jan and Taormina later.

She didn't have to wait too long. After visits to two churches, a cathedral and the library building in the principal square, they were ready for a protracted lunch. The iconic Wunderbar Caffè – with a peripatetic saxophonist providing musical accompaniment – made up in stunning views for what it lacked in culinary finesse.

Didi sat back in the rattan chair and sipped her Aperol spritz.

'Mom, you know when we were talking earlier about Taormina and how Jan would have enjoyed it, did you think at one stage she would come with us as well?'

'Yes. Something like that.'

'But you know she'd never leave that big lump of a husband of hers on his own for a whole month.'

'Deirdre, that's no way to talk about your brother-in-law.'

'Well, he is a big lazy good-for-nothing! Anyway, I don't think *I* would have come, had Jan been included in the invitation. We'd never manage to stay civil for an entire month.'

'This antipathy between you girls really disturbs me. Why can't you *try* and be more like your sister? You always have to do things the difficult way – all this independence and moving out of home, slumming it up in that squat on the South Circular Road with God knows whom —'

'*Mother*, do you mind? That's my home you're talking about, and if Jan had hitched up with either a doctor or a very sought-after professional musician, I don't think you'd be referring to *them* as "God knows whom"!'

'That's not what I mean. You're just *dossing down* there. It's not the same as having your own place.'

'At least I pay my way for the roof over my head.'

'Well, I'm sure Jan pays her share of the mortgage. No, you're missing my point entirely. I just want you to have a little home you can call your own, with some nice young man, as opposed to all this bohemian lifestyle, floating hither and thither at will. You're getting older and, believe me, men are best caught when they're young and know no better. Otherwise, they develop notions which are very difficult to break.'

Didi emitted a loud snort of derision. 'But I don't understand why you wanted to bring Jan along with us as well. Am I not company enough? Not to mention the cost. I know this trip must be very expensive. Could you have afforded the same again?'

'Well, no. It wouldn't have been double the price. It would have cost me the same.' Pauline made no eye contact, concentrating fiercely on the strawberry impaled on her swizzle stick.

'Now, I get it! You were going to bring Jan *instead* of me.

That's why it would have cost you "the same". How could I have been so stupid to think you really wanted to treat *me* for finishing my degree!'

'It wasn't like that. I asked Jan first. I didn't think you'd be bothered, stuck with me for such a long time. As you admit yourself, we don't exactly see eye to eye.'

'But she refused. So, you thought you'd move on to the B-team, since the A player wasn't available to turn out!'

Didi's voice had risen to a level sufficiently loud to compete with the saxophone meandering nearby. Several people at adjacent tables turned to stare, and one or two made a shushing noise.

Pauline looked sheepish. 'I didn't mean to hurt you, Deirdre, by asking you second. I really thought Jan would come with me. I was so surprised when she refused. Actually, it was *she* who suggested I bring you.'

'Oh, this gets better and better! Not only were you disappointed that Number One daughter declined your offer, but *you* didn't even come up with the idea of inviting your only other daughter. It had to be the *rejector* of the offer, who found the solution to this little problem of Mother wanting to go gad-about in Sicily for a month with no one to accompany her! You make me sick the way you can't see through that manipulative minx of a daughter of yours!'

'Deirdre, please! This is your sister you are talking about. You are both my flesh and blood. I raised you with the same chances and opportunities. How have you grown to be so different, to harbour such ill-feeling towards each other?'

'Ha, you admit it! She feels the same about me. And you were always making out that *I* was the one who had it in for her, when all the time she is no fonder of me than I am of her.'

'Well, she's not so openly hostile. Sometimes I think you're jealous of her.'

'*Jealous*? Of what, pray tell me, could *I* be jealous?'

'She's prettier than you for a start and has always had more success with men. While you're still thrashing around in all directions, she has married a fine young man and has a lovely home *and* managed to keep on her little job.'

'Are you deliberately trying to wind me up? On the looks score, yes, I agree. Jan did get the more conventional good looks and doesn't have to worry about her weight or her complexion like I do. But you know, Mother, for a woman of your age and experience, it never fails to amaze me how you cannot see deeper than a pretty, well-painted face, to the character that *should* lie beneath. Is Jan a decent person, beneath all her polish and designer labels? Or for that matter, is this wonderful marriage that she has all that it's cracked up to be?'

'Her marriage is fine. He's a good fellow, a little stubborn, but she'll soon sort that out.'

'*Mother*, listen to yourself! He's not a yearling to be broken! He's a man with his own thoughts and desires and, believe me, he has plenty of those.'

'What exactly do you mean by that? Substantiate that accusation, madam, or take it back.'

'Just what I said. He's a man of diverse passions, not a pet poodle that Jan can pull around on a short lead.'

'How dare you! If you have nothing more definite to reveal, well, I'd thank you to refrain from casting aspersions on other people. He is Jan's choice – and *she* has managed to get a fine husband.'

'Getting them is easy. Keeping them is the problem.'

'Smart words don't impress me, lady! It's time you lost that cynical tone, Deirdre, and maybe then some nice decent lad would be bothered with you.'

'Some "nice decent lad" like the one Jan's found? D'ya reckon? A nice decent lad who takes another woman off to a plush hotel, when his wife-to-be has to stay behind to attend a memorial service for her recently deceased father? Is that what you'd wish for me?'

'*What* are you talking about? When was this?'

'Last December. You *do* remember that Dad died last year?'

'There's no need for that. Not a day goes by when I don't think of Harry.'

'Well, then, you'll recall that your future son-in-law had some sort of voucher for a country-house hotel and he wanted to take Jan with him. But for once, you stood up to her. She roared and bawled and kicked furniture around the place, accusing you of jeopardising her future marriage, but you stood firm. Dad had been dead a month and you wanted both your daughters by your side at the Month's Mind. Jan stayed – reluctantly – but her beloved still felt compelled to use his voucher.'

'Where's all this leading? If you have something to say, spit it out, Deirdre. I've heard enough of your wild accusations to last me a lifetime.'

'Oh, patience, Mother, I'm getting there. He went, but not with Joe, as he told Jan. He was seen swanning down the avenue of the hotel in question, with an attractive blonde on his arm. So, unless Joe has taken to wearing women's clothes and sporting a blonde wig, I'd say it was safe to deduce that he wasn't anywhere near the place.'

'And how come you have such accurate information about a person's dealings in the far west of the country?'

'One of those fluke coincidences – Imelda. She was visiting her parents for the weekend and went to pick up her kid brother who works at the same hotel. She thought she recognised the guy on the avenue as Jan's boyfriend. They had met at rugby matches and most recently at the engagement party. But in case she might cause trouble unnecessarily, she asked her brother to check who he was. Donal confirmed the name and said the lady with him in the restaurant was also a resident. So that's your "nice decent lad" of a son-in-law.'

Pauline opened her mouth to deny it on Jan's behalf, but something in the detail of Didi's story made her hesitate. 'And if you had that knowledge, why didn't you tell your sister?'

'Given all that you have just accused me of feeling about her, how do *you* think she would have reacted? Do you think she would have listened to me? More likely she would have chanted the mantra of sibling jealousy, refusing to believe any of it, saying I invented the whole sordid story.'

'One last thing. Does anybody know who this blonde was?'

'No. But does it matter who she was? In fact, I didn't say anything about the whole episode because I thought it might have been a nostalgic once-off. Men often do things like that before they settle down. And anyway, I knew Jan would turn a blind eye, ankle-deep as she was in yards of tulle. I mean, what's a little issue like infidelity between a husband and wife, provided they have the legal documents signed, rings on their fingers and make a few star appearances as "Mr & Mrs"?'

'I don't like the way you talk, Deirdre. I never have, and I never will. I don't *ever* want to have this conversation again. You are a nasty, mean-spirited girl, and I feel sorry for you that you can't congratulate your only sister on her good fortune and move on. The past is the past. Whatever he may or may not have done, that's behind us now. Jan has no need to upset herself with this business.'

Didi was stunned by the coldness in her mother's voice and watched as she flung a €50 note onto the table, got up and weaved her way out into the Piazza, her firm little legs digging into the cobbles as she headed down Corso Umberto.

Despite everything, her mother was intent on 'not upsetting Jan'. At no cost must fragile little Jan be upset; never mind upsetting big robust Didi! Ah, sure, throw a few more insults at her while you're at it – Didi's well able to cope!

Right now, Didi didn't feel she could cope with anything. She waved at the waiter, with the intention of closing the tab, but changed her mind, and ordered another Aperol. She couldn't bear to face her mother. If Pauline thought she had only one daughter, well, let that daughter come to her assistance. Once this dreadful tour was over and they were back at the Panoramico, she'd look into getting an early flight home. She just couldn't spend another week in her mother's company, not after all the nasty things that had been said.

It was the end of the road for her Sicilian odyssey.

Chapter 24

Cefalù

The long gloomy street didn't look as if it housed anything other than private apartments. Isabelle checked the address: Via Gagini, 47. This was Via Gagini, and she had just passed Number 22. Dripping laundry splattered her from balconies overhead, as she made her way tentatively down the cobbled slope, her leather-soled sandals slipping on the centuries-worn stone. Several elderly ladies, dressed unseasonably in black, chatted outside their doorways or across the two metres which separated opposite palazzi. She tried the occasional '*Buonasera*' with the terrestrial women, who responded suspiciously.

Towards the end of the street, Isabelle noticed a fancy hand-painted sign, '*Daniela: Estetica*', its green lettering bordered by the silhouette of a woman's head. The tiled number declared it '47', so she was at the right place, but it surprised her that anyone in the image-business could operate out of such unimpressive premises.

The door triggered a set of windchimes, and a neatly proportioned, dark-skinned girl popped her head out from behind a pink-curtained cubicle.

'*Un attimo, signora. Ha un appuntamento?*'

'*Si.*' Isabelle checked her watch. '*Alle due e mezza.*'

Hearing the foreign accent, the girl reverted to English. 'I finish in two minutes,' nodding in the direction of the divider. 'There is coffee or some water.'

'*Grazie.*'

On a tiny table beside the counter, which served as reception, cash desk and evidently Daniela's canteen, an automatic water dispenser ejected conical-shaped cups on demand. Isabelle was glad of the cold drink, finding herself bathed in most unaesthetic perspiration.

It was the afternoon of the first performance of *Tosca*. As Rico's guest, Isabelle was sure to be in the limelight and, besides, she was overdue some professional attention to her appearance. She had booked a facial and a manicure and thought she might ask Daniela to do her make-up, since Italian women had a way of making more seem less. If the influx of weddings into the Panoramico had taught her anything, it had made her value the power of Sicilian beauticians.

She had spent the morning at the hairdresser's where Tonino had tried to tame her salt-ridden locks into something resembling a hairstyle. Newly cut layers enhanced by tawny highlights made the hairdresser proud that his work 'set off her beautiful face as an angel surrounded by 'is halo'. Much to Tonino's distress, Isabelle had laughed off his compliment, yet a glimpse of herself in Daniela's mirror confirmed that the shape, colour and movement of the new style *did* enhance her face. Certainly, the combination of suntan and the newly treated hair made her look fresher.

'*Signora, prego*? We start with the facial, and when you are relaxing, I do the nails. *Va bene*?'

'*Sì*. I was hoping you could do my make-up as well. I am going to the opera tonight, and I want to look my best.'

'*Certo*. After, we take a *pausa*, so the skin, it rest. I show you some products, OK?'

As Daniela worked her magic, destressing panpipes played in the background. Conversation was kept to a minimum – a combination of the therapist's limited linguistic ability and Isabelle's rapidly setting face pack. Happy to remain silent, Isabelle reflected on how her appearance had changed dramatically in the time she had been in Sicily.

There was nothing earth-shattering about this: people on holidays had time to spend out of doors, lolling in sunshine and enjoying sea-swimming. But in Isabelle's case, it was more than that. Allowing herself to experiment with an unknown hairdresser, be open to different colours and a dramatic style – this was all part of new Isabelle seeing off her past. She had reclaimed her body, taken charge of the way she wanted to look, and was re-presenting herself to the world, full of renewed confidence. Rico had played a part in the rejuvenation, but only a part. His praise, his touch, his appreciative looks had convinced her that she was a sensuous being in her own right, who did not need another's eyes to validate her sense of worth.

'*Eccoci*. Now, I take the colours for the nails. You like dark or French manicure?'

Isabelle pointed to a blood-red bottle, which met with Daniela's approval.

'Ah! *Che colore audace!* So, also, the make-up it will be strong.'

Con had always hated strong-coloured lipstick and nail polish. He said it made her look 'tarty'. Yet on the occasions when she had stumbled upon him draped around another woman at parties, the object of his passion invariably wore the boldest outfit and the most dramatic-looking make-up. It was the same when it came to clothes. If she dared to wear anything remotely sexy out into the wider world, he complained she was 'drawing attention to herself'.

As Daniela finished the last dramatic red nail, Isabelle felt relieved that she didn't have to care any longer what Con thought about her appearance. For the opera, she would dress in as imaginative and attractive a fashion as she saw fit, knowing that the man by her side would bask in the reflected glory of having his woman draw lots and lots of attention to herself.

As Isabelle entered the garden path to the villas, one of the waiters approached, carrying a room-service tray for Rico's.

'*Ciao, Isabella!* It *is* Isabella? Your hair, your face: all changed!'

Pleased at Davide's compliment, Isabelle pointed to the tray he was carrying. 'What's he eating at this time of day?' It wasn't yet five.

'*Zuppa di lenticchie.*'

Lentil soup? In the blistering heat?

The waiter rang the bell and Rico appeared in his shorts and a sleeveless white vest.

'*Grazie*, Davide.' He took the tray, and then seeing Isabelle over the waiter's shoulder, exclaimed. '*Come sei bella!*' Relieving himself of the tray, he hugged her, fluffing the new hair with his hands. 'You do all this for my special night? You are wonderful!'

'I wanted to do it anyway, but tonight *is* special – so I thought I'd make an effort.'

'*O cara*, I am so glad you are here.'

'Why? What's wrong?'

'Nothing. *Everything.*'

Isabelle glanced around *Stromboli*. Chaos reigned. Rico had pulled the table into the middle of the room and placed a white bath towel on the wooden surface, on which he was ironing his dress shirt. His orchestral score – open at a page he had obviously been revising – was discarded on the sofa. His tails and trousers were suspended on a hanger from the top of the bedroom door and the already-ironed white waistcoat hung on the back of a chair.

'Why don't you eat your food first, and then we'll see to

all this?' Isabelle stretched out her arm to indicate the ironing, the various bits of his dress suit.

'*Sì*, I really should eat something, or else I will have no energy to perform,' he said, sitting down and picking up the spoon. 'But, Isa, I am so nervous – you wouldn't believe how nervous I feel.'

She did. One look at the usually arrogant Signor Parisi convinced her that for some obscure reason this little run of *Tosca* was upsetting his equilibrium more than it should. She checked the temperature on the iron, upping it several notches and stretched the front panel of his shirt across the white towel.

'Look at you! Now you will think I am a typical, helpless Italian *mammone!* I always do my shirt myself.'

'What's a "mammone"?'

'A mammy's boy. A spoilt child-like man.'

'You are no *mammone*, Rico Parisi. This is only my practical attempt to help you before an important performance. I can't very well memorise your score, can I? So, I might as well free you up to do that, and iron the shirt while I am waiting.'

'*Grazie*. You are so sensible about things like this. You do not make ironing a shirt a feminist issue. You are doing what one friend would do for another. You are forgetting that you are a woman and I am a man.' Pausing mid-spoonful, Rico stared long and hard at her ironing figure. 'I don't know *how* I could have just said that, because when I look at you – so beautiful before my eyes – I *know* that you are a woman, the very best type of woman there is.'

There was something in Rico's tone that caused Isabelle to react. This was a declaration of love. She wondered if her feelings for him were quite as frivolous as she had previously maintained. But the whole thing was impossible: the travelling, the work, the wife.

In recent days, Monique appeared to be phoning less. Usually when they were out or in the hotel together, Isabelle would have to take a walk or excuse herself while Rico dealt with his wife's call. But over the past few days, there had been no interruptions. Initially, she had suspected that it was switched off, but then he had fielded a couple of calls from his mother and Stephen, when in her company.

She hadn't asked about Monique. It was their unspoken golden rule. She didn't want to hear about his wife. Neither would she listen to him criticise her, in her absence. But something was wrong with Rico this evening. She had never seen him look so vulnerable.

He stood, went into the bedroom and began rummaging in the wardrobe.

'What are you looking for?'

'My braces.'

'*Braces*? Why do you need braces?'

'Because when I sweat and lose weight during the performance – as I will – my trousers will slip and distract me. With the braces, they stay up, no matter how much weight I shed.'

'Let me look.'

Isabelle flicked through the primarily black clothes but could see no sign of braces.

'Are you sure they're here?'

'No. Try the drawers.'

Rico slipped the newly ironed shirt over his vest and stepped into his trousers. His bow tie lay flat on the table, and Isabelle noticed how his hands shook, as he picked it up. She was touched by this new nervous Rico.

'Let me.' She took the white silk bow tie and, standing behind him, both of them in front of the mirror, she began to do it up. 'Is that OK? Not too tight?'

'*Ti amo, Isabella.*'

Even Isabelle's Italian was up to that. In the heat of the moment, she replied in the only way she knew how.

'*Anch'io ti amo.*' I love you too.

Rico took her in his arms and they kissed, with a hunger that, had they had time, would certainly have been satiated. When they broke apart, Isabelle saw the elusive braces, hanging across the back of the sofa.

'There they are!' Isabelle draped the braces over Rico's shoulders, where he promptly seized them and attached them to his trousers. Then she helped him cover his waistband with a black silk cummerbund.

'When's Tommaso due?'

'Soon. About six fifteen.'

'Oh no! Look at me! I'm not even washed.'

'You are beautiful.'

'And you are biased! But I have to go and make myself

beautiful for the Beverlys of this world!'

'Don't leave me. I need you.'

'But do you need me dressed like a dizzy old frump in a summer's dress at an opening night? I don't think so. Fifteen minutes should do it, so don't let Tommaso go without me.'

'*Ti amo.*'

'Me too.'

In *Lipari*, Isabelle showered carefully, wrapping her newly styled hair and most of her face in a scarf. She had just stepped into her black-and-red silk outfit when her phone rang. It was Rico, practically hysterical.

'Isabella, I forget my cufflinks. I can't conduct in a dress shirt, without cufflinks. And Tommaso is here already! *What* am I going to do?'

'Don't worry. I'll get some.' Where was she going to get cufflinks at this hour? She'd phone Reception and hope Salvatore was on.

'*Pronto?*'

'Salvatore? Oh, thank God. It's Isabelle. Rico's in a panic. He's forgotten his cufflinks, and we have to leave any minute now for the performance at Gibilmanna. Can you help?'

'*Calmati!* I'll check with Signor Bruno. We might have some. Wait a minute.'

Isabelle retouched her hair, added a fresh layer of lipstick and sprayed two abundant blasts of Issey Miyake in her general direction, as she waited for Salvatore to come back.

'Isabelle? Yes, he has cufflinks for the silver-service wedding parties – the extra-waiters always forget their own, so he keeps a stock in the office. Can you come and collect them?'

'On my way.' Isabelle grabbed her hastily packed handbag, checked her face in the mirror and ran to the main hotel entrance. Salvatore greeted her with surprise as she was propelled through the revolving doors.

'*Wow! Isabelle, come sei bella!*'

'Thanks. So, where are the cufflinks? Do I have to go down to Signor Bruno's?'

'Afraid so. Half the joy is for him to see you like this!'

Isabelle sighed and hastened towards the banqueting office.

'*Signor Bruno, grazie mila.* I hear you have something for me.'

'*Allora! Che bellezza!* Obviously, Signor Parisi brings out the best in you.'

'Signor Bruno, the cufflinks*, per favore!*'

'*Eccoci!* But I hope you will thank me *personally* at a more opportune time.'

Isabelle took the small box and ran from the office. Rico, agitated, was standing between *Lipari* and *Stromboli*, in full regalia minus the bow tie which he had removed, an anxious Tommaso by his side.

'*Tesoro!* Where were you?'

'Got them! Here.'

Rico embraced her and all three got into the car.

Isabelle tapped the driver affectionately on the shoulder.

'Come on, Tommaso, put the boot down!'

'*Che?*'

'*Sbrigati, Tommaso, sbrigati!*'

Chapter 25

Gibilmanna

The orchestra was tuning up when Isabelle took her seat. She had stayed with Rico as long as she felt he wanted her to, redoing his bow tie and assuring him he was fine. Cast members came and went through the improvised Green Room in the monastery and all passed complimentary or friendly comments. Such a contrast from that dreadful, tense rehearsal when they had practically kicked her out!

Even though she hadn't known him that long, Isabelle eventually recognised in Rico's demeanour a desire to be alone. She kissed him and wished him luck with the Italian phrase '*in bocca al lupo*' – a superstitious way to avoid saying the unlucky 'Good Luck'.

She felt strangely proprietorial about the whole thing and, as she watched the public arrive from the viewing terrace, she was excited, but more than that: she was *nervous,* as if she were an intrinsic part of the production.

When the time came for the audience to take their seats, Isabelle had to clamber over the legs of seated dignitaries. She had been flattered to see that the ticket Rico had given her was in the VIP section. There was a certain irony in this, since in the course of her work at home, she was forever escorting her clients' guests to the best part of Dublin theatres.

The Gibilmanna setting was particularly idyllic. Not yet fully dark, the church was silhouetted against the fast-fading natural light of the petrol-blue sky. The superimposed set twinkled under the power of its own lighting and already the outline of a three-quarters full moon was visible to the right of the belltower.

A hush descended over the audience, followed by a lukewarm ripple of applause, as the northern Italian leader of the Orchestra della Madonie made his way onstage. Isabelle followed the spotlight in the direction of the masked entrance stage left. The diminutive figure of Rico appeared and, to a somewhat warmer welcome, he crossed in front of the orchestra and took his place on the podium. When he turned to acknowledge the reception, Isabelle felt a lump rise in her throat, proud when she realised how many pairs of eyes were trained on him in collective expectation. She had not appreciated how high an international profile he had, until she read his biography in the official programme. Although they had chatted casually about the various countries in which he had worked, it wasn't until she saw a stark, chronological list of the venues he had played, that she realised she was involved with a prominent name from the world of opera.

Entranced by Puccini's powerful music, Isabelle found it impossible to recognise anything of Beverly, Wolfgang and Paolo once in character. As she watched Rico conduct, she was struck by how every part of his body was involved. No wonder he had been so insistent about the braces! She had never imagined conducting could be quite so physical.

When the audience resumed their seats after the Act One intermission, the man to Isabelle's left spoke to her.

'Are you enjoying the performance?'

Isabelle was initially surprised at someone speaking English, but her neighbour turned out to be an American with connections to Filippo, the Festival organiser.

'Very much. It's really whizzing along. I thought it might drag in places.'

'That's down to the fabulous maestro. He really is allowing no slack speeds. Definitely one of Filippo's better finds. In fact, I am in the same business in New York and I am going to make this Rico Parisi an offer, if he has any availability over the next year or two.'

Year or *two*! Isabelle was surprised by how far in advance Rico might be booked up. No wonder his personal life was complicated, if he had to coordinate his schedule over such a long lead-time.

The tempestuous Act Two, which she had already seen in rehearsal, resumed and it wasn't long before it was shocking the audience with its brutal portrayal of a powerful man's abuse of position. Isabelle shivered when Wolfgang's Scarpia attempted to scare Beverly into submission. Reactions around her differed along gender lines, as Tosca plunged the knife repeatedly into his chest. The women were both relieved and triumphant, while the men, half-titillated by the violence that Scarpia planned to use, were subdued into shocked silence, as they watched the carmine stage-blood colour the white floorboards of the set.

Rico brought down his baton on Act Two and in a general movement of agitation as if restless to escape what they had just witnessed, the audience made to leave their seats. The second interval was shorter, so Isabelle decided to stay where she was, flicking through her programme and challenging herself to read some of the artist profiles.

She didn't know enough about opera to realise that the conductor takes a traditional bow at the top of the final act, acknowledging the audience's appreciation, and the playing of his orchestra. Therefore, when Rico resumed his place on the rostrum, Isabelle was filled with both awe and delight to hear a thunderous roar of approval accompany very hearty clapping. It was strangely satisfying to be sitting among hundreds of people, all focused on the public figure who just happened to be the private, personable man with whom she was intimate. She had an impulsive urge to elbow the lady to her right and say: 'See him? He's my boyfriend.' But that didn't sound correct It seemed a trifle juvenile to be calling a thirty-eight-year-old man a 'boy' friend. She would try again. 'See him? He's my lover.' That had a more artistic ring to it, but she feared she might get a cynical response in the form of: 'Oh yes? You and who else, dear?'

During the previous weeks, Isabelle hadn't experienced a desire to boast about Rico, but seeing him in this very public arena, she had an irrational compulsion to claim 'ownership' of his love. She knew she couldn't, principally because her feelings would be dismissed with a whole series of demeaning epithets. Her listeners would call it 'a holiday romance', 'a little fling' or make more cruel suggestions, ridiculing her gullibility and destroying the pleasure of the present by attributing lowly motives to Rico's actions. Isabelle had seen people react this way before: what was beyond the realm of their own experience was automatically denied existence, so they could perpetuate the myth that in their own pedestrian lives, they already had everything worth having.

Loud orchestral playing summoned her attention back to the drama. Tosca had arrived at the prison where her lover Cavaradossi was being held, and she was trying to convince him that he would not be executed. The soldiers were going to *pretend* to go through with it, since she had Scarpia's letter declaring Cavaradossi a free man. Isabelle had discussed this part of the plot with Rico many times. She couldn't fathom why Tosca had trusted Scarpia to honour his promise, since he had shown himself to be dishonourable in every other way. Rico had laughed, teasing her that she was expecting logic from opera-plots, something that was in short supply.

Despite the predictability of the climax, Isabelle found

tears involuntarily came, as she watched the heartbroken Tosca cry over her lover's dead body, before in turn throwing herself off the ramparts to her own death.

In the hiatus between the final bars of music and the outbreak of exuberant applause, Rico stood still, head bowed. The Sicilian audience went wild. Isabelle's VIP neighbours were extolling the merits of the singing, the strength of the production, the genius in the pit. The American gentleman was checking his programme for the director's name; he thought he could use him as well.

The cast took a company bow. The choirboys danced in, followed by the chorus, then the smaller solo roles. Finally, the major principals. Expecting the traditional booing and hissing, Wolfgang braved the audience, a sly grin spread across his face. Paolo made a slow, overdramatic entrance, waving a white handkerchief and scooping low in an exaggerated bow. Beverly walked slowly onstage and curtsied in one dignified movement. When the cast had taken two full calls, their Tosca left the line-up and made her way stage right. Her outstretched hand grasped Rico's and she welcomed him onto the platform.

Isabelle knew it wasn't wishful thinking on her part, as to who was the real star of the show, when she heard the applause increase several decibels. Rico acknowledged his gratitude repeatedly and, holding on tightly to Beverly and Paolo, he took the first full company bow. A moment of uncertainty ensued until the stage manager gave the thumbs-up from the wings and, leaving the line-up, Rico left his singers to collect Stephen.

The tall, awkward figure of the director joined his colleagues centre-stage, flushed with pleasure at the attention. The American agent beside Isabelle called out a couple of '*Bravos*' and scribbled something next to Stephen's name in his programme.

Isabelle fancied that Rico's eyes searched the VIP seats for her. Overcome by the moment, she couldn't restrain herself from blowing several kisses in his direction. It was hard to tell if he saw them – the footlights were on full – but he definitely looked her way. The collective high of the company was infectious and Isabelle was swept along by the emotion, even thinking favourably of Wolfgang and Beverly in all their contrariness.

As the audience filed out, Isabelle made her way backstage to the monastery Green Room. Beverly, still in costume, crossed her at the entrance.

'*Ciao*, Isabelle! Wasn't that something? He's some doll, your maestro!'

On her heels came Stephen.

'Hiya, Isabelle. Well, he should really be pleased with that one. It went splendidly. Are you two coming to supper?'

Although she hadn't heard anything of the arrangements, Isabelle was ravenous, and nodded assent. Tentatively, she tapped on Rico's dressing-room door.

'*Sì?*'

Isabelle pushed the door and entered.

'*Carissima!*'

Rico was standing there – a hot, sweaty figure, now

stripped to trousers and his sleeveless vest. Perspiration glided down his face, his neck; his hair was slick and damp.

'*Amore, scusami*. I must still have my shower, but first I need a hug.'

Wrapping her arms around him, Isabelle burrowed her nose in the delightful mixture of the healthy glow of three hours' hard work and Rico's usual smell of cigarettes and after-shave.

'You were terrific out there.'

'*Grazie*. You *really* thought it was good?'

'It was fantastic.'

'It was for my father. Do you think he would have liked it?'

'He would have been proud that his son has brought this wonderful music back home.'

This seemed to satisfy him. The anxious look passed, and he hugged Isabelle again.

'*Allora,* that makes me very happy. Now, I must wash, so we can have a lovely supper with the cast. Is that OK with you?'

'Of course. I'll wait outside the monastery.' Isabelle moved towards the exit. 'And Rico?'

'*Si?*'

'I think you might have stolen the show!'

'*Grazie!*'

Sitting on the steps, Isabelle watched the orchestra wander out in twos and threes. Wolfgang and Beverly left together – for once, not squabbling – and waved as they passed, enquiring if she and Rico would be joining them at the Gabbiano. Stephen and Gino came next, linking Ornella. The chorus, joking and flirting, headed off to their own party.

Isabelle thought she could get used to this. She had come to like these people, even in their artistic exaggeration. It was only a matter of acclimatising. Singers in other parts of the world could be no worse than cranky, hyped-up business people, with whom she had to deal on a daily basis in Ireland. If only Monique would disappear off into the sunset with some ballet-dancer.

'*Pronta, amore?*' Rico stood before her in his customary black shirt and grey flannels.

'*Si, pronta.*'

Hand in hand, they walked in silence towards the waiting Tommaso, the obligation of words no longer necessary.

Chapter 26

Cefalù

There was an unusual hush on Corso Ruggero when Didi came out of the Tourist office into the noonday sun. She squinted at her credit-card receipt: the two *Tosca* tickets had been pricey, for a small, local festival. When she booked, she would have been quite happy with one, but felt a bit mean not bringing Pauline. Now? Well, now she could think of nothing more unnerving than to have to spend a full evening in her mother's company.

It wasn't just the streets that were quiet – the restaurants were nearly empty, most holidaymakers opting to eat on the beach. She had a casual arrangement to have lunch with Isabelle, if they both happened to still be in town at one. Didi checked the time on her phone and messaged her.

With a very red face, Didi sat sipping a glass of white wine in Da Pippo, an overtly touristy trattoria on the corner of a small street leading down to the seafront. Despite the clichéd red-and-white-checked tablecloths and artificial flowers in wicker baskets, the owner was generous with his *amuse-bouches,* and bowls of olives and mini-bruschetta continued to arrive while she waited for Isabelle.

'*Wow*, you look hot!' Isabelle dropped a couple of red bags trailing shiny white ribbons onto the third chair. 'What have you been up to?'

'Decided to climb the Rocca. I hadn't been to the top before.'

'But in this heat?'

'It was OK on the lower stretches – you're mostly in the shade of buildings – but once you get onto the railed path, it's scorching. I can see *you've* been busy. What's in the bags?'

'Oh, a bit of indulgence.' Isabelle nudged her new purchases further under the tablecloth.

'*Signore?*' The waiter, eager to finally be doing something, was hovering with his order-pad.

'*Non ancora.*' Isabelle glanced down at the menu. 'Will I order a half carafe of white and some water to keep us going?'

'Do.'

'*Signore, un mezzo litro bianco e un'acqua naturale. Grazie.*'

'*Well,* the red bags?' persisted Didi.

'Oh, underwear. I bought myself some *broderie anglaise* stuff. Cotton work seems to be all the rage on the island. Do you fancy a pizza? We could share a large one.'

Didi had passed several shops displaying attractive embroidered cotton blouses outside, but underwear she would have had to seek out.

'Usually when a woman starts buying expensive underwear, it means there's a new man hovering in the background! Have you been busy, while I was chaperoning my mother round the back-alleys of Catania?'

Isabelle hesitated, not ready to disclose. The waiter arrived with the drinks and took the order for a large pizza to share. Isabelle seized the jug and topped up Didi's glass.

'*Grazie.*'

'*Cin cin.* It's a pity Pauline didn't join us. How's she been since the tour? I don't see much of you now that you're no longer in *Vulcano*. Where did they put you?'

'*Filicudi.*'

'What's it like?'

'Small. *Very* small, considering the tension between the two of us.'

'Finding the holiday too long?'

'Yeah. Not the holiday so much – my mother. I haven't lived with her for years, except in the few weeks following my dad's death, and then, I was in and out to college every day. This is all a bit intense.'

'You were brave to take it on! Though Pauline must think a lot of you to treat you to an expensive holiday like this.'

'That's just it. She didn't want *me* to come at all. That's what the falling-out is about. She let it slip that she'd asked my older sister first, but she'd declined.'

'Is this the perfect married one?'

'I only have one sister. Anyway, I don't know how she imagined Jan would abandon hubby for an entire month.'

'Still, is it such a huge issue to fall out over? Remember, I have no mother to fall out with anymore, and sometimes I long for a good old shouting match!'

'My mother can't understand why I'm so hurt at being second-best all the time. And there was other stuff said.'

'You can't let things continue like this.'

'I was trying to get an earlier flight home, but since it's the big August bank holiday, all flights heading north are full after the weekend.'

'Ah, just as well. *Talk* to her!'

The arrival of an enormous *pizza rustica* obviated the need for further conversation. It occupied the entire bistro table, a wall of viscous mozzarella and pert cherry tomatoes, two sharp cutters poised on either side.

Didi attacked the pizza first, lifting the messy slice to her mouth. After a couple of bites, she wiped the gooey cheese from her cheek. 'Isabelle, I bought two tickets for tonight's *Tosca* – for Pauline and myself – but the way things are, I don't think it's possible we could go together. I was wondering if you'd like to come instead.'

Isabelle looked long and hard into Didi's expectant face and knew she would have to come clean.

'Thanks for thinking of me, but ... I've already been. I was at opening night ... as Rico's guest. The thing is ... I ... we ... have been seeing each other.'

Didi set down her wineglass, having first taken a large gulp.

'*You* and Rico? Are you joking?'

'No. I have been seeing a lot of him over the last couple of weeks.'

'Well, that just goes to show how observant *I* am!'

'I'm sorry.'

'Why? What's Rico to me? Go for it, that's what I say!'

But Didi felt disturbed. The one consolatory aspect of the whole Rico Parisi embarrassment had been the hope that he was one of those self-contained musical geniuses, who despite their many opportunities, didn't need anyone. Isabelle's news had only reinforced that it was just she, Didi, he found unattractive.

There was a flatness in the ambience following Isabelle's disclosure. Didi wolfed down the remainder of her meal, while Isabelle pushed the heavy choice around the plate with no desire to linger at the table. The carafe long-since empty, the waiter gesticulated if he should bring another but, in sync, two heads shook, Isabelle doing the scribbling motion to request the bill.

In Piazza Colombo, from where the buses left, a few passengers waited in the shade of the little garden. Didi and Isabelle rounded the corner and as no one was at the stop, they knew the bus wasn't due for a while.

'Well, I'm off to Tony's for a blow-dry,' Isabelle pulled at her lank hair. 'It's impossible to do it yourself in this heat.'

'Oh. Right.'

'Enjoy *Tosca*. And invite Pauline – as an olive branch?'

'It's too early for olive branches.'

As Isabelle turned to leave, she was startled by the speedy swish of a purple-and-yellow-striped cyclist.

'*Hallo*, Didi! Signora Isabelle.'

Didi, although delighted by the coincidence of meeting, remembered all her unreturned messages and tried to appear cool. 'Hiya, Christoph! What's new?'

'A new group to meet very soon from the Costa Verde. Hey, Didi! You have taken a lot of sun! You are all *fleckles* on the nose.'

'You mean *freckles*! Oh, where's my phone! Am I that bad?'

'No. *Sehr hübsch*. Very pretty.'

'Marvellous! I'll be in competition with the big red lobster served for Scarpia's dinner tonight at *Tosca*!'

'*Ach so*, you are going to the opera?' Christoph's head swivelled between the two women. 'But of course! Your ... *friend* is the conductor, *nicht so*, Isabelle?'

Didi registered Christoph's insinuation. Had everyone in the hotel *except* her noticed this romance develop?

'Actually, I'm not going this evening. Rico will join me for a late supper afterwards.' Isabelle shifted off the pavement. 'I'll go again on the final night. Look, I'll have to split. Appointment. *Ciao*!'

'It is a pity I did not organise myself for *Tosca*.' Christoph dismounted the bike and locked it. 'Tonight is my only possibility. I have airport pick-up the last night.'

No longer cool, Didi saw an opportunity. 'Well, I have a spare ticket, if you'd like to come along with me.'

'I would!'

'Great! You might have to ditch the sporty image.'

'Do you think I am uncivilised?'

'Not at all. I am only teasing!'

'OK. At what time?'

'There's a shuttle bus at seven-thirty.'

'We'll drive. It's quicker.'

'All right. Meet you in Reception. Say eight-fifteen. Will that give us enough time?

'*Ja*, sure. Twenty – thirty minutes. So, see you later.' Christoph clumped off, his spiked shoes making a terrific racket as he went down the small aluminium steps to join his new cyclists.

Didi clapped so hard that the palms of her hands smarted.

'You enjoyed that!'

'Christoph, it was wonderful – much better than I had expected. Look, there's Rico taking his bow.'

The audience were on their feet, with cries of '*Bravo, maestro!*' and although Didi felt she couldn't possibly clap anymore, she managed another full minute of enthusiastic noise.

'We should go backstage and congratulate him. It really is an enormous achievement, to pull off something that wonderful in a difficult venue like this.'

Christoph was puzzled by Didi's excitement. 'Why is it difficult?'

'Outdoors, the breeze, everybody on different levels – that's much more problematic than inside in a more controlled environment. So, will we go backstage?'

'You go if you want. I do not know the man. I am sure he will be very busy.'

'Oh, don't be like that! Come with me. I always like to see somebody I know afterwards, if I've been involved in a performance.'

Christoph reluctantly nodded acquiescence, sliding a firm hand under Didi's linen top and rubbing the small of her back. 'Where do we go?'

'I'd imagine the actual monastery – I can't see them being allowed to use the church as dressing rooms!'

Several other people seemed to have had the same idea, because a counter-flow against the exiting patrons had established itself. Some of the orchestra, bow ties and jackets already off, hung in clusters in the courtyard, enjoying a cigarette. Didi noticed an informal line of people, programmes in hand, waiting in front of Beverly. Rico was nowhere to be seen. She was just about to ask one of the choristers where she might find his dressing room, when another group caught her eye. Two of the principals were shaking hands with a thin woman with long, dark, curly hair and Rico seemed to be carrying out introductions.

'*Ach so!* Here is your friend, with another beautiful woman. *Komm*, let's go and say hello.'

Now that they had come this far, Didi wasn't sure if they should barge over, when Rico seemed so occupied introducing this woman to everyone in such an important fashion. But Christoph insisted, his firm hand guiding Didi in the direction of the artists.

'Rico?'

'*Didi*! What a surprise! I didn't know you were coming tonight.'

'We enjoyed it very much, didn't we? Sorry, you know Christoph, don't you? He is the tour leader for the Aktiv holidays group.'

'Yes, I see you in the hotel. *Piacere*. These are my colleagues, Paolo and Wolfgang, invaluable members of my cast.'

The good-looking tenor, despite Christoph's oppressive proximity, took Didi's hand and kissed it. Wolfgang, in a more restrained fashion, offered his hand. On hearing the accent of a fellow countryman, Christoph began to chat to Wolfgang in German. The dark, curly-haired lady was transfixed by Didi, looking her up and down with what seemed like X-ray eyes, until Didi began to wonder if her underwear was visible through her clothes or something had come unbuttoned. With a pincer-like movement of the nearside arm, the strange woman latched onto Rico.

'*Chéri ? Tu vas pas me présenter?*'

Rico, looking uncomfortably from one woman to another, muttered their respective names.

'Didi, Monique – Monique, Didi.'

'*Enchantée.*' Turning to Rico, Monique hissed at him in French. '*C'est elle? Pas ton type habituel.*'

Christoph, already bored by his conversation with the pedestrian Wolfgang, was keen to have Didi all to himself, and decided to compete with Monique in who could out-cling their partner. Feeling unwelcome and aware of an atmosphere between this Monique and Rico, Didi reiterated her praise of the performance and, loosening Christoph's grip, left the monastery courtyard.

'Christoph, it's OK. You don't have to hold me quite so hard.'

'OK, I just thought you might prefer us to look like a couple in front of Rico.'

'*Whatever for?*'

'He is a Don Juan, and you, you were fascinated by him. Now he has another woman' – at this, Christoph chuckled – 'it would appear, another *two* women, so you don't want to be sad little Didi on her own.'

'I'm not one bit sad, thank you.' Still, Didi had to admit that she was glad of Christoph's presence when that volatile-looking Frenchwoman was giving her the once-over. At least that way, she wouldn't imagine Didi was Rico's girlfriend or anything.

Christoph was most attentive once they were alone again, opening the car-door, checking the seat was clean, asking her what type of music he should play. He suggested they head to Isnello for a nightcap, avoiding the long tailback down to Cefalù, by taking the higher road up the mountain.

'Gibilmanna is the place to watch the fireworks. From up here, you have a marvellous view.'

'What fireworks?'

'The big Ferragosto celebrations. Tomorrow is the fifteenth of August, the biggest holiday in the Italian calendar. There will be processions in town, and a fireworks display out over the sea, but you can see nothing from the seafront. It's better to watch from the hills. What are you doing?'

Didi sighed at the thought of enforced jollity back at the happy hotel, when she and her mother still hadn't exchanged a word since Tuesday.

'*Was ist los*? Some problem?'

'I've nothing organised. I'd forgotten how big a deal this Ferragosto is. The last time I was in Italy on the fifteenth of August, I was working in Rome. The place was deserted – most Romans gone to the beach or to their families somewhere.'

'There's a buffet-dinner and beach party at the Panoramico.'

'To be honest, I'd prefer to give that a miss. Anything else?'

'You could always come to eat at my house. I will have some friends, and we will look at the fireworks from the side of the hill. We have a good view out over the sea, and no trouble with lots of cars and parking chaos down in the town.'

This seemed like the answer to Didi's prayers. By joining Christoph and his friends, she had an ideal opportunity to escape the hotel and leave her mother to enjoy herself with the other guests, without all the nosey waiters pressurising them to sit together. Neither did she want to join Isabelle and Rico, after Isabelle's announcement earlier in the day. Anyway, if Rico was going to be stuck with that mad French friend tonight, Isabelle would probably want him all to herself tomorrow.

'Christoph, I'd love to come. Where do you live?'

'Very near the hotel. You could walk if it's still bright. It's just a little way up the Ferla road which is opposite the entrance to the hotel. I have a ground-floor studio in the last green building on the right-hand side.'

Didi recalled seeing a group of isolated houses ahead as she turned at the fork on her many photography walks. She remembered their plasterwork was painted an unpleasant shade of green.

'Fine. Give me your mobile number again, in case I get lost. What time?'

'Oh, come as early as you like – eight thirty? We'll eat later, and then can watch the fireworks around eleven.'

'Sounds good! Would you like me to bring anything?'

'No. Or maybe some fruit. A selection, you choose.'

Their drinks finished, Christoph offered to buy another, but Didi declined, suddenly exhausted from the long day climbing the Rocca and having had little rest before the turnaround for the opera.

'You look very tired, Didi. I think it is time I took you home safely to the lovely Panoramico and to your mother.'

'Thanks, Christoph. I'm fairly whacked all right.'

Christoph pulled in at the side of the road in front of Filicudi, gave Didi a chaste peck on the lips, got out of the car and went around to open her door.

'Thanks for a lovely evening. I look forward with pleasure to tomorrow. *Gute Nacht!* Sleep well.'

'Night, Christoph. See you tomorrow.'

Didi didn't wait to see him complete the tight U-turn in the narrow avenue, hastening instead to the comforting darkness of her little villa. Since it was nearly one, she thought it was reasonable to presume that Pauline was already asleep. As she closed the shutters on the front window, she noticed that Isabelle's veranda lights were still on.

Trying to clean her teeth as quietly as she could, Didi heard the reassuring noise of loud snoring emanate from the adjacent bedroom.

Chapter 27

Despite the closed shutters, *Lipari* was unbearably hot. Isabelle kicked off the sheet. Why was the apartment so bright? She *had* remembered to close the shutters, hadn't she? She reached for her phone on the bedside table. *9.10!* No wonder the place felt hot. Normally, she'd be heading to the beach by this time.

Then she remembered. This wasn't a normal morning. This was the morning after the night on which yet another man had let her down. Her eyes adjusted to the strong light and her head felt slightly fuzzy. She spotted the empty champagne bottle lolling at the foot of the sofa, a discarded glass curled up by its side, its pristine partner waiting – aloof – on the small console table. Oh no! She had drunk the entire bottle alone.

Slowly she remembered the increasing humiliation as she had sat and waited for Rico to return from his second performance. How she had waited and waited, but no ring came to the door. The many times she had checked her watch, rotated her phone for a better signal, even wiggled the connecting wire of the hotel line, in case it was loose. Nothing. How she had intermittently sat on the veranda (initially content with that first glass of champagne) and listened out for Tommaso's approaching car, waving at other guests as they finally made their way from the bar, watching for signs of life in *Stromboli*, in case he had slipped in unnoticed.

Shortly after midnight, she did something that in the few short weeks of knowing Rico she hadn't done before: she tried his mobile. Although he had given her the number early on, Isabelle had made a point of not calling him, given that he associated messages and that phone with Monique and hassle. When she succumbed, she found it powered off, and this only increased her anxiety.

There had to be a reasonable explanation. Some crisis with one of the cast – a crew member injured and needing hospitalisation. She should trust Rico, instead of automatically assuming that she was the reason he hadn't turned up. Two further glasses of champagne later, she had consoled herself that there was a perfectly logical reason for his non-appearance but then she heard the door of *Stromboli* shut.

Nervous but bolstered by the bubbly, Isabelle let herself out onto the back patio, clutching the remainder of the champagne bottle, and swung her leg over the lavender hedge. She was just about to tap gently on the glass door when she saw two figures inside. A small, wiry, dark-haired woman was enlacing Rico's neck with her arms. With a shocked intake of breath, Isabelle pressed her nose almost up against the window to convince herself that what she was seeing was real. Rico took the woman in his arms, smoothing the long, curly hair, and muttering words which Isabelle could not hear.

Her heart pounding in disbelief, she stumbled back over the lavender, tears already gushing. She had seen enough. That woman, who *was* she? The tiny figure, the long, dark curling locks – the dancer's physique. Deep down, Isabelle knew it had to be Monique.

If before she had thought the 'thing' with Rico was frivolous and empty, seeing him in the arms of another woman had clarified her position. She was jealous, enraged at the thought of someone else knowing him like she did. What troubled her most was that Monique was here – operating on *their* territory, in all the precious nooks and crannies of the Panoramico, where they had shared their intimacy.

Had Rico known she was coming to visit? Could he have been that cynical, not to mention it? Was Monique here for the duration? *Was that it?* Would she have to be neighbourly and '*buongiorno*' them over the hedge from now until she packed her suitcases to return to Ireland, without ever again sharing a private word with him? The thought was too upsetting to contemplate.

Her phone beeped – one of the mealtime reminders she had set on arrival. This was her ten-minute warning. Breakfast on the other side of the hotel was about to end.

Grabbing the easiest dress to hand, she pulled it over her head, splashed water on her face and donned a very necessary pair of sunglasses. Hesitantly, she opened the shutters and then the front door, dreading who she might encounter, but all was quiet apart from Mohammed the gardener, sweeping up geranium blossom and palm leaves, the windfall of the previous night's *scirocco*.

'*Salve, signora!*'

She had been seen. She had to come out now and make a dash for the breakfast terrace and hope they were still serving. '*Salve, Mohammed.*'

As she crossed the glaring, white flagstones, Isabelle began to shake in nervous agitation as she recognised who was directly in her path: Rico and the curly-headed doll had at least made it to breakfast.

'*Buongiorno, Isabella! Oh, this heat!*'

Shocked that he had addressed her and was showing every intention of stopping for a chat, Isabelle tapped her watch and kept moving, mumbling 'late'. Although she hadn't allowed him get to the point of introductions, Isabelle could hear the distinctive jabber of French, confirming that the retreating back was indeed Monique.

Still in a daze, Isabelle wandered over to the buffet in search of whatever remained, and caught the eye of Signor Giorgio as he knocked back his early morning espresso. The manager gave her an uncharacteristically disapproving smirk, which Isabelle read as satisfaction at her having got her comeuppance with the timely arrival of La Signora Parisi.

Neither did he seem all that displeased when the only thing she could find in the way of breakfast was a rather stale bread roll and treacle-black tea.

In the breakfast lull at Reception, Salvatore checked through the documents of those guests who had arrived the night before. His gaze lingered on the *carte d'identité* of one Monique Dutrout.

So, this was the famous Monique! Apparently, she had just turned up the previous night when Signor Giorgio was on duty. Rosario, the night porter, was full of it when Salvatore had taken over, since he, like everyone else in the hotel, was aware that Rico had teamed up with Isabelle. Salvatore was sorry he hadn't been on duty when she rocked up. He would have tried to warn Isabelle – phone her, or post a note under the door, but he could just imagine how that moral godfather Giorgio took great pleasure in the arrival of the wife. According to Rosario, she had stridently insisted that Giorgio let her into Rico's room, but the manager had explained politely that it was against hotel policy. He had offered to relieve her of her bag and show her into the restaurant. Monique had declined dinner but had offloaded the bag and asked him to call a taxi to the *Tosca* venue. Poor Isabelle! Salvatore hoped there hadn't been too much of a scene when Monique arrived at the opera.

One of Christoph's sporty Germans was looking for a

train timetable, just as Isabelle made her way across Reception, head down and wearing dark glasses.

'Isabelle! *Isabella, un attimo, prego!*'

'Hi, Salvatore. Did you want me for something?'

'*Sì*. I just wanted to know if you are all right. I couldn't help noticing that the famous Monique has arrived. It must be difficult for you.'

Isabelle was touched by Salvatore's thoughtfulness.

'It is. More than you can imagine.'

'Were you with him when she turned up at the opera?'

'No. I didn't go last night. I was expecting him back at *Lipari*, but he never showed up.'

'But he couldn't! Monique surprised him at Gibilmanna. She arrived here – oh, I don't know – Giorgio was still on duty, so it must have been about nine. Then she asked where the opera was and took a taxi. I don't think she was expected.'

'It doesn't make a whole lot of difference whether she was expected or not. He hasn't exactly sent her back, has he?'

'*Isabella!* How could he? Try not to think too much about them. What are you doing tonight?'

Isabelle groaned. 'I hadn't really thought about it, since Rico had something planned. Now, I guess we can take it that arrangement is cancelled.'

'Well, there's a special dinner here, followed by a beach party. Will you stay?'

'I don't know. I couldn't bear it if I had to watch Rico

ogle that – that emaciated *child* of a wife of his. I'm sorry. That wasn't really very nice, but that's the way I feel.'

'Don't apologise! But I think they are going to the procession, because Rico asked me what time it started. He also was trying to book a restaurant for afterwards. I told him they wouldn't take reservations for Ferragosto – everybody just turns up and queues.'

Isabelle was offended by the ease with which Rico could maintain his plans, substituting the company of one woman for another. His coolness in facing her earlier had recalled previous episodes with Con. The similarity scared her, particularly their ability to juggle two women.

'So, what time does the party kick off here?'

'The buffet starts at half past eight.'

'Oh, well, that'll be great fun – on my own!'

'What about Didi and Pauline? Couldn't you make up a table with them?'

'I don't think so. There's a bit of tension there and, besides, Didi mentioned she was going to dinner – up to that Christoph's place.'

'*Madonna!* Are you serious? Did she say she was going alone?'

'Haven't a clue. I think I'll just order room service tonight. I don't think I'm up to the "*da sola*" routine on the biggest holiday in the Italian calendar.'

'You *will* not be alone. *I* would be greatly honoured if you would join me for dinner. I have to be here, since I volunteered to let Rosario spend the night with his family, so I'm night-porter tonight. I might as well enjoy a nice meal and a little of the beach party before starting my shift.'

'Well, in that case, I would be delighted but I have to warn you – I'm not the best of company. This Rico thing has upset me.'

'*Cara Isabella*, I *too* am not in a party mood, since you tell me that Didi has chosen to go and eat with that Christoph person, but we will give each other support. *D'accordo?*'

'What is it with you and Christoph?'

'It's complicated. Perhaps I will tell you sometime, but please, Isabelle, if you have any influence over Didi, try and keep her away from him.'

'I'll do my best, but she has a mind of her own. So, where will I see you?'

'At the bar at eight?'

'Fine. And Salvatore, thanks for being so sensitive.'

'Remember, *you* are helping me too!'

'*A più tardi.*'

'*Si. Stasera alle otto.*'

Pauline sat on the terrace of the Bella Vista and ordered her third brandy. It seemed strange to be in town alone, when everyone around her was celebrating with their extended family groups. The waiter gave her a knowing look as he added the drink to the tab. Pauline felt sad. She wished this row with Deirdre would blow over. She had tried to resume normal relations, but Deirdre still seemed really offended by what had happened in Taormina. Since they had been back, the opportunity hadn't really arisen for Pauline to clarify what she'd meant. The longer it went on, the harder it became to put things right.

The rift had upset Pauline far more than she could have anticipated. When she thought about her two daughters dispassionately, she realised it was true that Jan was the one whose love and approval she sought most; she always expected that Deirdre would give *her* love unconditionally. And, over the past weeks, she had come to appreciate and enjoy her younger daughter. There was a freshness about her – an honesty that she often found lacking in Jan.

Deirdre gave her space to be herself. Jan would have frowned at all those downed brandies or glanced disapprovingly at the liberal amounts of cash thrown on the tiny glass-topped tables in the bar, when a hand of cards was suggested. Deirdre had left her to her own devices, for which Pauline was grateful. She would never have been able to enjoy Helen and Bobby's company, or dance the tarantella with Signor Bruno, had Jan been there. For a start, her elder daughter would have found the Manchester couple too common to be fraternised with and, as for Bruno, she would have given her a lecture on how these *maître'ds* were perpetually in search of frustrated rich widows with whom they could have their wicked way. She wouldn't have seen that she was just trying to have a bit of fun.

Yet here she was, on Ferragosto, alone. Where was

Deirdre? Pauline looked on enviously as inter-generational groups of Sicilians gathered, hugging each other warmly, as they prepared to assemble for the religious procession. She missed her daughter. This nonsense had gone on long enough. Shakily, she searched for her mobile in the big straw bag, and dialled Deirdre's number. It went to voicemail.

Slightly tipsy from the two early evening brandies, Pauline spoke: 'Deirdre, I don't know where you are, but this is your mother. I just wanted to let you know that I am really sorry for what happened in Taormina. What I said came out all wrong. I have enjoyed – *more than anything* – being on holiday with you, and I know now I have enjoyed your company far more than I could ever have enjoyed being with Jan. You and I are more alike than we admit. I don't know what you are up to this evening, but I hope you'll enjoy yourself. And Deirdre, I *do* love you, very much.'

The waiter hesitated before he placed the sad little lady's brandy in front of her. Wiping away a tear, Pauline thanked him, took her drink and asked for the bill.

'*Signora Pauline! Come sta?*'

Pauline looked up from the table, into the grinning face of Capitano Giacomo Sassi, the local guide with whom she had taken a tour a week ago. '*Oh Giacomo, ciao!*'

'What are you doing here, all alone, a lovely lady like you?'

'Giacomo, you know how it is ... my daughter – she's young – she has her own plans for this evening.'

'But, *Signora Pauline, scusi*, you cannot spend Ferragosto alone! You must come to the procession with me.'

'Maybe, but first I would like to go and have something to eat. I had very little lunch and I am hungry.'

'*Brava!* Let us go and have a very early dinner. After the procession, it will be impossible to get into a restaurant. If we eat now, we will not have a problem.'

Capitano Giacomo Sassi took Pauline's elbow and escorted her off the premises of the Bella Vista, supporting her slightly unsteady walk with a guiding arm. The waiter sighed as he picked up the money the signora had left, which included a very generous tip, as she hadn't waited for her change. He really would have to talk to Management again about that Giacomo; he was a liability, and not one a four-star establishment should encourage onto the premises.

Didi was surprised to find everything in the town closed. It was only just six, but the shops were shuttered and dark. The occasional stall was still operating, so she thought she'd run down to the Rotonda della Frutta near the bus stop, which usually kept good quality fruit and veg. She had decided to take some grapes along to Christoph's dinner party. As she made her way down the side streets, Didi passed groups of small children in white albs and the blue gowns of various religious sodalities, as they assembled in anticipation of the procession. Fussing grandmothers tweaked bows in their hair or roared up at an overhead apartment about where the much-coveted banner was and would somebody *please* bring it down now! Didi thought about the lack of excitement for such religious feast-days at home in Ireland. Here, it was a genuine community celebration, marrying religious and secular traditions with ease.

As she paid for the grapes, the vendor tried to press some red watermelon that he had reduced to clear on her. Didi wondered if she should throw in a couple of sections, to accompany the grapes. Waiting her turn to pay (the stall had become suddenly busy), she was convinced that she saw that old prowler guy linking arms with her *mother*, as they made for the lower sea road. Dithering over whether to drop the watermelon and run after them, or to complete her purchases in the hope that she would still be able to catch the slow-moving pair by chasing up the street they were taking, she opted to do the latter. Beads of perspiration dripped down her already hot face as she snatched her change, rammed the watermelon into the paper bag on top of the grapes and turned to run. Just at that moment, the little orange bus pulled into the square. A long line of people filed onto it, laden with parcels and large trays of pastries, their contribution to whatever party they were attending later on.

It was the last bus before the procession. If she went after Pauline and the old guy, she would have to walk the three kilometres to the hotel and the fruit would end up bruised and battered. The electronic thermometer in the shady Via Vazzana read 39 C. It was far too hot to walk.

Pauline would be fine. She was worldly-wise and wouldn't

be fooled by an old codger like that. Besides, Didi reasoned, she couldn't treat her mother like a child. That was always *her* complaint when Pauline gave unwanted advice or monitored Didi's movements. Let her enjoy her evening. They could both entertain themselves separately, and maybe the following morning it would be time to reopen the channels of communication.

Laden down with her beach things and the fruit bag, Didi managed to dig out the bus fare, but had left it too late to secure a seat. The orange bus lurched through the throngs of beachgoers who dodged and weaved in and out of the traffic on their way to nearby kiosks for ice creams or drinks, mingling with more formally clad visitors who had arrived early for the procession. Leaning her head against the cool aluminium pole, Didi thought of the evening ahead. It was satisfying to think that she had made so many new friends since coming to Sicily, that later she would spend the highlight of the Italian social calendar in the company of a party of people who a few weeks ago she didn't know. In Dublin, she always dreamed of meeting new people like this, but it never happened. The social circles were closed; it was hard to break into a new group. Here, everybody seemed to accept newcomers, and just include them around the table, no questions asked.

The traffic on the Via Roma was one long tailback. The bus driver chatted to the nearest passengers, commenting on the parking habits of some of the locals and talking about his plans for the evening. Didi was unperturbed by the lack of progress. After nearly a month in Sicily, she had slowed down, adopting the rhythms of those around her. There was something appealing about this slower way of life, which made her contemplate her imminent return to the more frenetic lifestyle of Dublin with a heavy heart. Maybe she should go back to night school and really work on her Italian. Then she could consider coming out next summer for the holidays! With that cheerful thought, she closed her eyes and ran through all the places she could try to find work. Going home in a few days didn't seem quite so bad now. She would be back. Of that, she was certain.

Chapter 28

The taxi stalled in the long queue heading towards the port.

'I stop here. OK, *signori*?'

'What do you think, Monique? There isn't much point sitting in the car. We can walk the rest of the way. *Si, va bene.*'

Rico paid the driver and held the door open as Monique climbed out. The police had set up a roadblock to the old town and were redirecting cars towards parking at the lower port level.

'I hope those shoes are comfortable. I imagine we'll do a lot of walking this evening.'

'I thought this was a quiet little town – *tranquille*. Look at all these people!'

'*Chérie,* nowhere is '*tranquille*' on the fifteenth.'

Monique was dressed in harmony with the nautical aspects of the day's celebrations, in a navy-and-white outfit, set off by a large sunhat and red accessories. Her high-heeled slingback shoes did not look as if they would stand up too well to the rigours of cobblestones and the sand-strewn promenade.

'Would you like to go to the port to see the skiffs escort the Madonna on her sea voyage?'

'Not particularly. You Catholics, you get so sentimental about these traditions. I'm sure we can see fine from up here.'

'*Va bene*. Come, I will show you the highlights of the old town. There is a beautiful Arab-Norman cathedral and some tasteful craft shops in the narrow streets.'

Monique showed more enthusiasm at the mention of shops, though no sooner had Rico said this than he realised that they were closed in preparation for the gathering procession.

'So, *mon cher Rico*, did you like your surprise?'

'What surprise?'

'*Moi*. My surprise visit.'

'Of course! I didn't think it was possible for you to visit, with your performances.'

'But, *chéri*, you know everything also stops in France on the fifteenth! Did you not think I would take advantage? Somebody has to make the effort, or else we would never see each other.'

Rico lit a cigarette. He wondered if now was the moment to discuss the amount of time – or lack of it – they had been sharing over the past twelve months. Their walking pace had slowed because as they reached the old walls of the town, the volume of bodies filing between the tall grey palazzi at

Porta Giudecca impeded progress.

'*Quel monde!* Are these all tourists?'

'No, I imagine most of them are locals or people from the surrounding villages here for the evening. Cefalù's fireworks display is particularly famous.'

'What a selection of lovely women for you, Rico! You really are spoilt in this town. Much better than at that hotel, where mostly they seem ugly.'

Rico sighed. He heard the customary suspicion leak into Monique's voice and recognised the twist the conversation would take. 'Yes. There *are* some rather eccentric clients at the Panoramico. Even Beverly, my Tosca, can be very odd.'

'And what about that big girl we met last night – Deedums. Would you call *her* eccentric?'

'You mean Didi? No, Didi is fine. She's a music student, here with her elderly mother. I feel sorry for her most of the time. I think she's a little bored.'

'And I am sure you make her less bored, *n'est-ce pas?*'

'Monique, what are you suggesting?'

'Nothing, *chéri*. I wouldn't have thought she was your type – not even for sex. Too big and awkward to handle.'

'Monique, *per favore*, stop! Do you know how wearing it is to have you suspect me of having an affair with every woman we meet?'

'Not with *every* woman. I'm sure you leave the ugly ones alone, but I know you, Rico Parisi – you have needs and they must be met, and in these last months you are certainly not satisfying your needs with me.'

'How could I? We have hardly seen each other since March.'

'And whose fault is that? You take work in New York – in Australia – places where we cannot meet for a weekend or a few days, if one of us were free.'

'They were fantastic contracts. I couldn't turn them down.'

'*Exactement*. But you could turn *me* down, abandoning me to the wolves on the dance circuit.'

'Not this again. You *know* I wanted you to come to both places, but you accepted that cover for the *Giselle* tour.'

'It *also* was a very important contract.'

'Monique, don't fool yourself. Henri never had any intention of letting you on. Arabella would have had to fall down and break *both* legs before you would replace her!'

'*Merci, chéri. You are too kind.* Any more insults you would like to make? Because if not, I am very hot and need to sit in the shade at this café and have a drink. Alone.'

Exasperated, Rico watched the wide-brimmed red hat sail through the crowd and make for a table at the water's edge. The surprise visit was proving to be tense. That morning, he had suggested the beach, but it was too hot; Monique suffered with prickly-heat rash. He thought she wanted to reconcile things in the bedroom, but when he made an overture she laughed in his face and told him to take his hands off her. Instead, they sat on the terrace of *Stromboli*, she in the shade reading, he taking the sun and intermittently doing the *Repubblica* crossword, like two elderly people in a retirement home between whom minimal social interaction was required, because they shared a patio.

On nearby Via Bordonaro, the traffic police were moving the last of the parked cars and mopeds, in expectation of the procession that would shortly wind its way towards the sea. Rico wondered if he should go and join Monique. It was so difficult to work out what she wanted. She was forever saying one thing, but expecting him to know that she meant exactly the opposite and then, if he didn't realise that, there was another row about why he didn't do what she had asked him *not* to do!

The decision, however, was taken out of his hands, as he saw the waiter engage her in conversation. Monique gesticulated in a dismissive manner and, haughtily grabbing her handbag, stomped out through the by now empty tables.

Rico was waiting at the rope cordon.

'*Qu'est-ce-qui se passe*? Anything wrong?'

'There is a *lot* wrong, Rico, but for the moment it is this ... *this primitive place!* They close all the bars and the restaurants for this procession. He would not serve me, out of *respect* for the passing parade. So, a woman can die of thirst, but he must respect his parade!'

'Don't worry. I'll get you some water in that little shop. Then we can choose a place to watch the procession.'

Monique raised her dark glasses as if to check that she was still in the company of the same man she had married two years previously. What was all this talk of religious processions? When had Rico ever been interested in these peasant manifestations of belief? Did he really expect her to stand for hours, hot and squashed beside dumpy Sicilian mammas, as row upon row of priests and altar boys filed past?

'Here, your water. I got two. I'll keep the other one in my pocket. *Naturale*, isn't it?'

'I prefer sparkling when I'm not eating. As you should know.'

'The man in the grocery shop said the top of Via Gagini is a good place to stand, because they pause at the little square in front of the Chiesa Santa Caterina, and you can hear the band quite clearly from there. *Andiam'*?'

Monique tested her dainty leather-soled slingbacks on the slippery, steep cobbles of Via Gagini, slugging from her water as she followed Rico uphill. The top of the street was a bottleneck with people standing eight deep. Strains of Chopin's funeral march announced the approaching bier, the appropriateness of which puzzled Rico, as he thought the fifteenth of August was supposed to be a happy feast-day. Perhaps the amateur brass-and-reed band had a limited repertoire and needed to make use of anything they already knew.

The elaborate casket, bearing the rose-bedecked statue of the Madonna, was placed on an ancient wooden frame and carried with evident difficulty by fifteen fit young men, who, according to Rico's neighbour, had been in training with just the wooden bier for the previous three weeks.

'Imagine! They volunteer specially and it's considered a great honour to be chosen.'

'*Imagine!*' Monique was feeling cold, the lack of sunlight in the narrow street rendering it chilly, her sleeveless dress now unsuitable.

'*Sal-ve Re-gi-na-a, ma-ter mis-e-ri-cor-di-ae!*'

The dignitaries, clergy and various sodalities of adults and children were singing as they followed the casket. At a suitable pause in the hymn, the crowd's concentration was broken by the repetitious sound of a butcher's hatchet dissecting a carcass on his wooden bench. The onlookers nearest the butcher's premises went to the door and asked him to stop the work. As prayers blared out over the loudspeaker, and the religious music reached its crescendo, the chopping was now punctuated with some contrapuntal whistling. This was the last straw for several women, who stormed the butcher's shop, enraged by his obvious lack of respect. A loud altercation ensued, far more distracting to celestial thoughts than the chopping and whistling routine.

Monique found the episode hilarious.

'*Oh là là! This is mad!* Better than a comedy. I cannot stay here. I want to laugh and laugh and the peasants will be offended. Come.' Pulling Rico by the hand, she turned down a side-street.

Although he allowed himself to be led away, Rico was angered by her attitude. Why did she have to sneer at everything? Calling the local people 'peasants'! After all, she was married to the son of one of these so-called peasants.

'Why do you always ridicule people?'

'*Chéri*, what people? Do we *know* those people? What are

they to you or me? Only a bunch of silly old women walking barefoot on cobblestones and some puffed-up officials in fancy uniforms. You cannot seriously be saying that you enjoyed that?'

'Maybe not, but it is not my place to sneer. It's their tradition, and since I am working in their town, I respect their customs.' Because she was irritating him so much, he added mischievously: 'Besides, *I* am the son of one of those peasants whom you deride. You should have shown more discernment in your choice of husband.'

'*Comment?* Don't be ridiculous! Your father sounded nothing like these people. I am bored. Where is this restaurant you promised me? I am cold and hungry and my feet hurt.'

'Let's go down to the promenade and sit and watch the sea. It will be warmer there, since the sun has been beaming down on the concrete all day.'

'And dinner?'

'Later, *chérie*. First, we need to talk.'

Religious music continued to waft towards the seafront. They sat down on a bench near the steps. Monique removed her red shoes and began to massage her feet.

'Monique, let's talk about our marriage. I have not been happy these past months – in fact, for longer than that. For more than a year now, I have been very *un*happy.'

Expecting such a conversation, Monique continued with the massage, unperturbed. 'Unhappy? And why would you be unhappy?'

'Because I am supposed to be married and have a wife to support and love me, yet I never see her. I don't get to spend any time with her, and yet I cannot behave like a single man, enjoying the company of women I meet, because I am unavailable.'

'*Pauvre Rico!* This is so sad. You say you cannot behave like a single man. But you are *not* a single man. Why do you wish to behave like one?'

'I'm only human. I need the company of someone who will listen to me, who will love me, with whom I can curl up at night. I don't think I can cope with this long-distance relationship any longer.'

'So, what would you propose we do? You are very welcome to travel with me. I can always do with some help. It won't be as interesting as being a famous international conductor, but the dance world isn't completely boring. I could always speak to Marie-Louise to see if they have any openings in the orchestra.'

'Monique, you are laughing at me!'

'No. I am thinking about a job for you, if you travel with the dance company.'

'I don't *want* to travel with the dance company! I want to continue doing my job, at which I am very good, but I want you to come *with me.*'

'*Eh le voilà!* You do not want to stop doing *your* job at

which you are very good, but you expect *me* to facilitate you, by stopping mine, at which I also happen to think *I* am very good!'

'Monique, if we are to survive as a couple, *some*thing – some*one* – has to give.'

'Well, that someone is not going to be me. And do you want to know why? Because I don't trust you. I don't trust that if I throw over my career and go on tour with you, you won't tire of me, and find yourself a glamorous singer or a sexy violinist, and where would I be then? I would no longer be a successful dancer. I would just be the dumped ex-wife of the famous conductor. *Non. Non merci. I won't risk that.*'

'Do you really think that little of me?'

'The evidence is all around me. When I phone, you are never there. You do not return my calls, or my messages.'

'Not true! I *do*, but not immediately probably because I don't get the message for several hours after you have sent it, since I'm in rehearsal with the phone turned off.'

'That is why I phone Reception and leave my messages there. That way, *they* know you have a wife and *I* know you get the messages.'

'But, Monique, the volume of those messages! The detail you leave. That is harassment, apart from being embarrassing.'

'So, tell me, *chéri*, why is it embarrassing for a man to receive some calls from his loving wife? Would it be because the husband is screwing Deedums or Beverly or maybe that attractive blonde we met on the terrace this morning – and the hotel staff are very embarrassed to have to talk to his wife?'

'This is getting us nowhere.'

'On the contrary, I think it brings us to the heart of the matter. So, who is she? *Who* is this woman who has provoked all these feelings of dissatisfaction in you?'

'No one in particular. It's me. I have been thinking about my past – about my father.'

'Your father, always your father! Can't you just accept he didn't like you, and be done with it? Why are you constantly seeking the approval of a dead man?'

'That is not very kind. I need to understand why my father rejected me, why he wouldn't accept me *as me,* why he wanted me to be somebody else.'

'Because maybe he saw you for what you are: a vain, egotistical man, and he wanted a different son.'

'Is that how *you* see me?'

'I have given up seeing you as anything! What we had six, seven years ago was fun. It was good. The mistake we made was in formalising it. My idea of what a husband is and does is very far from yours.'

'But I *want* to be a good husband, a good father —'

'*Oh non, non! Ça suffit!* I do not want to hear this mentioned again. I have told you my feelings. No babies! This is not going to happen. With the dancing and the touring, how could I have a child? Don't be ridiculous.'

'Well, we have a problem, because if this marriage is to continue, I want a child.'

'This is blackmail! You assert constantly *your* freedom. About how being married doesn't mean you *can't* have women friends – oh yes, you need Irena on the phone, and your other women friends for lunch and dinner. All just *friends, of course.* You tell me you don't need them for sex, but where I come from a man gives up his female friends when he takes a wife. His wife is everything to him – his best-friend, his lover, his confidante – *everything*. I *will not* allow you have all these women in your life. You have me! *I* am your wife. You have no need of any other woman.'

'Well, I'm sorry you think like that. I need my friends. You don't own me. If I choose to make friends with people who happen to be women, I will not bow to your jealousy and run away from them.'

'Then you will have no wife!'

'Already, I do not have a wife. I have a person who *calls* herself my wife but is more distant to me than some of my colleagues.'

'You have made yourself clear, Rico. There are men, *many men*, who find me very attractive, and who I find hard to resist. Don't worry. I will not bother to resist any more.'

'Are you talking about Henri?'

'What if I am? Is it any of your business?'

'I suppose not, but be careful with him. I don't want you to be hurt.'

'Do not be a hypocrite! You can't control me anymore. It is over between us. You make a scapegoat of this baby, so you can blame me when the marriage ends, but this is a ruse. Do you know why I came to visit? To prove to myself, *chéri*, that you and I don't care about each other anymore, and to seek out the eyes of the woman with whom you are sleeping. I have seen enough. When I go home, I will call my lawyer and we will start the papers for a divorce. That is what you want too but are afraid to say.'

'I'm sorry.'

'Don't be. Life with Henri will be a lot easier.'

The flagging conversation was interrupted by a booming noise out at sea. The organisers of the fireworks display were trialling a few test runs. People thronged the seafront, buying ice-creams or candyfloss from the casual stalls. The sight of food reminded Rico they hadn't yet made it to a restaurant.

'Do you still want to eat, or will we just stay and watch the fireworks?'

'We have had already enough fireworks. Besides, I am French, and my stomach needs satisfying. And what good is it having a husband, if you can't make him pay for dinner from time to time?'

Surprised by Monique's intention to see the evening through normally, Rico vacated their prime location bench, which was promptly pounced upon by some local teenagers.

'I thought we might try Da Nino on Via Bordonaro? I know the manager there, so we might have some chance of a table.'

'*Bien!* I will follow you.'

With no appetite, Rico led the way towards the restaurant, thinking for the umpteenth time what a strange woman Monique was.

Chapter 29

The Road to Ferla

The road to Ferla had no street lighting, but the magnificent sunset still cast sufficient daylight for Didi to see her way. Christoph had said it was the last green house on the right, and as she climbed the steep road she could hear family parties setting tables outside in the adjacent homes.

The ground-floor apartment in the last building had lots of lights on, but there was no sign of anybody outside. Didi opened the tiny spring-latched gate, made her way to the door and rang. Loud dramatic music was playing inside. Perhaps Christoph couldn't hear the bell with all the noise. She buzzed a second time. Through the glass-panelled interior door, she could distinguish his approaching figure.

'Hi, Didi! You are welcome!' Christoph swooped and gave her a kiss on the cheek. He was wearing a navy-and-white striped butcher's apron, looking very domesticated.

'My, you look the part!' Didi pointed to the apron, while

simultaneously offering up her bag of fruit. 'Towards the dessert bowl.'

'Thank you. So, you like my new look?'

'Very cool. Am I the first to arrive? I thought you said about nine.'

'Oh, it's no problem. They went into the procession in town – it's usually chaotic to get out afterwards. Can I offer you a drink?'

'Yes, please. A white wine would be nice.'

Didi settled herself on the sofa, observing the ambient candles perched on various shelves and surfaces in the living room. Despite the heat, the table on the pretty terrace was unset, its plastic chairs stacked in a corner. They must be going to eat indoors, which was unusual, but Christoph was German, so probably not as keen on eating *al fresco* as the Sicilians. Looking around, she noticed the dining table, which although dressed with a tablecloth, had no place settings. Some cutlery and several glasses sat casually to one side.

'Here we are: *un vino bianco per la signora.* Have you noticed how my Italian is improving?'

Didi was going to say it was about time, considering that he had been the Aktiv rep for the previous two years, but she nodded and took a sip of her wine.

'*Cin Cin! Buon Ferragosto!*' she said.

'*Salute!* Where did you pick up such a good accent?'

'In Rome. I worked in a bar there a couple of summers ago. Most of the Italian I know, I picked up on the hoof.'

'Rome, what a city! I would like to work there, instead of in this backward village, but my uncle is co-owner of the Panoramico, so he fixed it with Aktiv to take me as the rep. It's OK. If it were not for the weather – and the beautiful women, of course – I think I would have gone back to Germany a long time ago.'

'Do you not like it here?'

'I do, but the money is very bad. I will never be able to make anything of myself on what I earn here.'

'You seem to be doing fine. This is a very nice apartment – big for one person. The rent must be high, since it's in such a popular location.'

'Aktiv pay the rent. I don't even know how much it is.'

'Lucky you. I wish I could find a job that paid my rent. What are you cooking? I can smell something nice.'

'*Penne all'arrabbiata* – it's the sauce you smell.'

'And are you?'

'What?'

'*Arrabbiata* – angry – that's what the word means.'

Christoph snapped. 'Of course I know what the word '*arrabbiata*' means! But what would make me angry?'

'Christoph, relax! It was a joke.'

'Sorry. I will change the music. Wagner makes me short-tempered. Then I must see to my sauce.'

'Do you want any help?'

'*Nein, danke.*'

Didi checked her watch, a little anxious that no other guests seemed to be making an appearance. Christoph put on different music, which Didi recognised as *Tosca*. At least his taste in music was good, if his mood seemed a little off.

'I take it we are eating inside. Will I set the table?'

'Yes, too many mosquitoes outside. Being blond, I would be bitten. I imagine you too.'

'Yes, they like me as well. How many will I set for?'

'Just us. The others, if they come, may join us just for a drink later.'

'Oh.' Didi couldn't hide her reaction.

Christoph was on to it immediately. 'Is there a problem?'

'No. But I'm surprised. I thought you said a group of friends, that's all. I was looking forward to meeting some new people.'

'Am I not enough for you, Didi? Goodness, these Irish girls, what appetites!'

There was something in the way Christoph said this that unnerved Didi. She began to wish she hadn't come to this quiet apartment alone.

'Can you show me where the bathroom is, please?'

'Yes, after the bedroom on the right.'

Didi bolted the bathroom door and searched for her mobile. She felt uneasy. She'd have to ring somebody to come and get her, but who? The only local she could think of, whose number would be in the memory, was Salvatore. Sitting on the closed toilet seat, she nearly cried aloud when she saw her network showed no signal. Please God, let it only be in the bathroom, she prayed. She would sneak the phone out of her bag in the lounge and see would it work, but how could she call somebody with Christoph within earshot? Maybe she shouldn't go back to the living room at all. Was there a window in this bathroom?

'Didi? Are you OK? You are not sick or anything.'

'No, Christoph. I'm fine.'

'*Mach' schnell*, dinner is nearly ready.'

The bathroom window over the toilet was miniscule. Ideal for ventilation and keeping out unwanted visitors, but not conducive to allowing large 5' 8" Irish girls escape. She'd have to stop being hysterical and go back and face the music.

In her absence, the living room had changed completely. The main light had been switched off and, along with the incidental candles dotted here and there, Christoph had added a centrepiece arrangement to the dinner table. He had also drawn the blinds on the side windows, which overlooked the next house. Tosca and Scarpia were doing battle on the sound system.

'Signora, please be seated.' Christoph, now without his apron and in a fresh white short-sleeved shirt, was bowing.

Didi could see no option but to join him for the meal. Ever so politely, he served her pasta, poured more wine, and they began to eat.

'*Buon appetito*, Didi.'

'*Buon appetito*, Christoph.'

The clock on the wall chimed ten. How was she going to get through the meal and excuse herself gracefully? Didi began to think affectionately of the bad music and the old fogies down at the Panoramico. If only she could persuade

Christoph to accompany her to the beach party once they'd eaten, that might be the way to go. A sneaky look at her phone confirmed that the apartment was a network black spot.

It was clear nobody other than she had been invited. With a sickening feeling, realisation slowly dawned that no one even knew where she was.

They should have expected it would end up like this. With an influx of over 5,000 people and their respective cars, the town was packed to capacity and it was scarcely possible to walk around, let alone drive, on anything bigger than a moped. The taxi-drivers had sensibly turned off their signs and joined the festivities. Their meal concluded and the fireworks display over, Rico and Monique had no choice but to face the three-kilometre walk back to the Panoramico.

The uphill road to the hotel was slow and difficult, Monique was genuinely uncomfortable in her impractical shoes but, because it was dark, she couldn't risk walking barefoot. A sliver of glass or an overturned ankle would see her out of work for weeks.

Rico tried to make light conversation – small talk to pass the journey – but after several attempts he realised he was only creating more tension. An uneasy silence descended upon them.

When they finally reached the hotel, Monique collapsed into a chair on the veranda while Rico continued to

Reception for the cumbersome, wooden-tagged key. Salvatore was still on duty, which was strange since it was gone midnight.

'Good evening, Salvatore. The key, please? You are late tonight.'

'Yes, I am doing the night-shift for once. Did you have a good evening in town?'

'Oh, so so. We had to walk home – there were no taxis. Monique is very fed up.'

'I should have warned you. Last year it took me an hour and a half to drive home from here to my apartment. They had a one-way system in place – *Mad-on-na!*'

'Is the beach party still—'

Rico was cut off mid-sentence as the noisy roar of a motorbike drew up outside the hotel steps, causing them both to stare at whoever was arriving so inconsiderately at the late hour.

To their astonishment, it was Pauline, being helped from the pillion seat by the red-haired Prowler.

'I don't believe it!' Salvatore peered through the foyer window. 'What is *he* doing with Signora O'Rourke?'

'He seems a predatory type of man and, by the look of Pauline, he has been preying on the generosity of her purse this evening.'

Pauline swayed towards the desk as the motorbike roared away.

'*Buenas noches,* Salvatore. Deirdre isn't home yet. Is the key there by any chance?'

Rico, having been ignored by Pauline, said his goodbyes and left.

'Yes – *Filicudi* – it's here all right.'

Dropping her handbag, Pauline spilled the contents onto the floor. Salvatore came around the desk to help her pick them up. She'd *really* had a few drinks too many.

'It's very quiet here. Is the beach party over?'

'Yes, about half an hour ago. Some of the younger ones have gone to the disco at the Camping del Sole.'

'Oh, that must be where Deirdre is then.'

Salvatore weighed up whether or not he should say something. He had tried both Christoph and Didi's mobiles about an hour earlier: Christoph's was off, and Didi's went straight to voicemail. Salvatore had begun to feel on edge, as time ticked by and Didi failed to show up at either the beach party or the desk to reclaim the key. He wondered should he mention his anxiety to Pauline.

'Signora O'Rourke, Didi – Deirdre – didn't go to the beach party – she went for dinner to Christoph's apartment.'

'Christoph? I don't know any Christoph. Who is he?'

'You *do* know him. He's the German group leader.'

'Oh, that tall blondey fellow! Why are you telling me this? Deirdre would have told me herself, had she wanted me to know.'

'Because it's late and I'm worried about her. Christoph … Christoph sometimes takes advantage of situations.'

'So where does this Christoph live?'

'Not far from here. He has a studio up on the Ferla road

– the hill road just across from the hotel entrance.'

'Have you tried calling him?'

'Several times. He's not answering.'

'I'll try Deirdre's number.'

'Don't bother. It's not picking up either.'

'Should we call the police, do you think?'

'No, I don't think there's any need for that. It's only just after one.' Then, acutely aware of Pauline's anxious expression, Salvatore lightened his voice, adding, 'I'm sure she's fine.'

'*Mmm*. I hope so.'

Pauline took her key and walked back to *Filicudi*. The weather was on the turn – a wind had begun to blow, and the night was alternately brightly moonlit, or suddenly very dark, as clouds scurried rapidly across the sky, blotting out its light source.

She looked down at her swollen feet, the result of a long evening standing around, and thought that if she had more comfortable footwear, she might just walk up as far as that Christoph's place, to collect Deirdre.

In the absence of the veranda light, she had difficulty fitting her key into the lock, only opening the door on her third attempt. She put on her long, navy cardigan over her floral dress, slipped into her walking moccasins and went back out into the moonlight. Feeling slightly dizzy from the combination of drinks, Pauline battled against the swirling wind and walked down the hotel avenue. Salvatore had said the Ferla road began across the main road opposite the entrance.

She set off up the hill. Although the main road lighting ended about ten metres up the steep incline, Pauline decided it had to be the right way. It was little more than an access road with no footpaths. Still, if the moon came out again, she'd be well able to see her way. There were houses ahead on the right-hand side and they were giving off some light.

Had she been sober, this was not a walk Pauline would have undertaken, but her emotions were heightened by alcohol, and a gut instinct that her daughter might be in trouble made her determined. After all that had gone on between them during the past week, she had to prove to her younger daughter that she *did* care. Deirdre may have let her fend for herself in Taormina, but a mother could never abandon her child in her moment of need.

Scrunching up her eyes against the blowing dust, Pauline pulled the collar of her cardigan around her neck and plodded on up the dark road.

Chapter 30

Rico couldn't settle on the sofa bed. The mattress was thin and very uncomfortable. Its metal springs expanded and contracted noisily with every movement he made. When he had returned earlier with the key, Monique had marched into *Stromboli* ahead of him and gone straight to the bedroom. She threw out a couple of pillows and banged the door. Despite his discomfort, he was glad of the space.

Before turning in, he had closed the outside shutters, leaving their flaps open to let in air, as was his habit. Ferragosto had been suffocating; the hotel thermometer had hit 44 degrees Celsius. Two weeks of such extreme temperatures were about as much as anyone could take and local people were saying it had to break soon. Rico thought they could be right. There was a lot of cloud movement and few stars in the sky.

As he lay awake, one of the shutters began to bang. It

must have broken free of its catch. Rico knew he'd have to go out and either resecure it, or leave it pinned back open, which meant closing the full-length windows. Despite the ventilation, there was something strange about how hot the apartment felt. Maybe it was the *scirocco* again. He groped for the veranda light, flicked it on, but nothing happened. The bulb had really picked its moment to blow. But when the living-room light also failed, he suspected a power-cut. He would just have to depend on the erratic moonlight to deal with the shutter.

When he opened the front door, he was taken aback by a peculiar glow of light. A sudden gust of wind lifted a cloud of dust from the garden table. As Rico came closer, he saw that the table was covered with a dirty substance. *Ash!* The table was covered in wind-borne ash!

His immediate and irrational thought was that Mount Etna had erupted. But then logic intervened and he doubted even the great volcano could spew ash over a 90-kilometre radius. No, the problem was closer to home.

It was then he saw it: the strange orange sky haloing the hill of Ferla. Something was burning ferociously on the other side of the mountain. As Rico tried to figure out the topography, he had a sinking feeling that the part of the mountainside on fire was towards Gibilmanna.

Stumbling over furniture, he dialled Reception, but the line was dead. He needed to find out what was happening. Apart from Stephen and Gino's safety in the rented house, he was anxious that the church and their *Tosca* set might be threatened by the rampaging fires. Rico felt around on the floor for his discarded trousers, jumped into them and found his mobile in the pocket.

Once out on the avenue, he saw that he was not the only one disturbed. Salvatore and Signor Giorgio were talking to two Civil Defence men.

'Salvatore, this fire – where exactly is it?'

'Gibilmanna – the forested area surrounding it. We don't know if it's one or several outbreaks. These men are waiting to join a group of volunteer firefighters. Oh, Maestro, you must be worried about the Tosca set.'

'And my colleagues. I'll have to phone Stephen.'

'I don't think you'll be able to.' Salvatore nodded at the inert phone in Rico's hand. 'The helicopters – they interfere with the signal.'

'Are the hotel lines down?'

'Yes, but at least we should have electricity soon. We have a back-up generator.'

'And the phones?'

'No idea.'

Giorgio reacted impatiently to Rico's talk of phones and stomped off to join the recently arrived firefighters.

Rico took out a cigarette to light, and then thought better of it.

'You could always try one of the S.O.S. phones at the roadside.' Salvatore checked his two mobiles again. 'Still nothing. They connect directly to the emergency services. Try the forest rangers' station. They would have the most information.'

'I think I'll do that. I am too worried to wait. Where's the nearest one?'

'There's one near the level crossing, but it's quite a bit away.'

Giorgio, having waved off the firefighters, tuned back into their discussion. '*No, no.* Much nearer, just after the fork in the Ferla road. Up there!' He was pointing at the blacked-out hill.

'Yes, I know that road. I have been there before. I will go immediately.'

'Wait, Rico! Take a torch. You won't be able to see your way without one.'

'Even with this big fire in the sky?'

'You'll be in the shadow of the hill up there.' Salvatore handed over a square-lamped flashlight. 'Take this. Good luck. I hope everything is OK.'

'Thanks, Totò – see you later.' Rico switched on the torch and set off, nervous of what he might find out, but anxious to know the truth one way or the other.

When the orange lights on the main road below went out, it was the last straw for the already overwrought Didi. Her resolve not to show fear deserted her and she let her head fall forward into her hands and began to cry.

'Now, now, Didi, why the tears? Come over here to me and I will kiss them away.'

She couldn't even manage a response, hiccoughing

hysterically as she wondered what he was going to do next. The game of cat and mouse had been going on for the previous hour or more, ever since she had announced her intention to leave.

Dinner had passed peaceably enough. Despite her initial panic, Christoph had been chatty and polite. Didi had to force down the pasta, not because it wasn't good but because her stomach was so knotted with tension it made swallowing anything more substantial than a sip of water a major ordeal. Apart from a few lewd remarks and caressing the inside of her leg several times, Christoph's physical attentions hadn't been oppressive. She tried to drink her wine slowly, feeling she should keep her wits about her, but the soothing liquid made her feel less jumpy, so when Christoph opened a second bottle, she didn't protest. The recording of *Tosca* on a loop was now on its second airing.

It was when Christoph went to organise the fruit for dessert that his mood changed. He dropped the grapes and watermelon out of the greengrocer's paper bag onto a plate and stared at them. He looked across the counter-bar to the living area, glancing from the fruit platter to Didi.

'Do you find this funny?'

Didi looked back at him blankly.

'I suppose you and that cretin Salvatore had a little *laugh* about my dinner invitation. I bet he even suggested you bring *this* along!' With a swipe of his arm, Christoph cleared the plate and the fruit it contained off the counter, the white china shattering into several pieces as it hit the tiled floor.

'Christoph, what are you doing? What's wrong with bringing grapes? And it was you who told me to bring some fruit! What's Salvatore got to do with it? I didn't say anything to him about coming here for dinner.'

Suddenly, Christoph became contrite and walked slowly around the counter to retrieve the two bunches of grapes from the floor. Placing them in a bowl of water, he took a brush and long-handled pan and swept up the broken crockery, dumping the rather battered-looking watermelon into the bin.

'You are wrong, you know. About the grapes. I *love* grapes, but there is only one enjoyable way to eat them. *Komm!*'

Putting the bowl with the grapes on the coffee table, Christoph sat on the sofa and patted the adjacent cushion twice, authoritatively indicating he wanted Didi to join him. She did as asked, but when she left a gap between them, he mocked her, sliding up the sofa so close that she could feel his heat through the thin white shirt.

'That's better. Now for our grape-fest!' Dangling a cluster of grapes in his left hand, Christoph laced his other arm around her neck, pulling her head back, the grapes suspended over her mouth. 'Now, open big! You have to snatch one off the bunch.'

Didi thought it a silly out-of-season Hallowe'en game but decided to humour him. She seized a large black grape and bit into it, but immediately Christoph had his face right up against hers.

'Very good, but now I must take the seeds out for you.' With this, he closed his lips over hers, swirling his tongue inside to transfer the grape into his own mouth. Didi could hardly breathe. She pushed at him, but the grape, long since gone, had only been an excuse to initiate sucking and thrusting at her mouth. At a loss as to what to do to shake him off, she bit his lip, allowing her a couple of seconds to draw breath while he pulled back in pain.

'Oh, you little tiger! You like to bite, do you?'

'Christoph, stop! My hair! Let go!'

'No. I see you are enjoying this. A big strong girl like you likes it rough sometimes, *nicht so?*'

Didi was terrified. She was not dealing with a silly Hallowe'en game: the man was a maniac, and she was a fool to have ever entered his apartment. Making a production of checking her watch, she affected surprise when she realised it was nearly one o'clock.

'Look at the time! I haven't seen my mother all day. I think I should go over to the hotel and try and catch her at the end of the beach party.'

'Oh, I couldn't let you do that. It's far too dangerous to walk down that road in the dark.'

Although she didn't want him to accompany her, she thought that, if only she could lure him out of the apartment, at least there were other houses she could run to if he tried anything heavy.

'Why don't you walk me over? We might as well get a free drink out of the stingy management. Goodness knows, you deserve it, having to put up with their demanding guests!'

Even the flattery failed. Christoph was too smooth an

operator for a naïve ploy like that.

'No, Didi, I do not think you are going to any beach party tonight. In fact, I know you are going to stay and keep me company.'

She tried to make a run for it. Upending the grape bowl and its watery medium into Christoph's lap, she bolted towards the glass door, her hands trembling as she opened the latch. The mechanism released easily, but still the door did not open.

'I wouldn't waste too much time on that door. It only opens when it's not locked. Now, where *did* I put that key?'

'You've locked me in! Open this door immediately.'

'My passionate Irish redhead. I have locked *us* in, to keep us safe. This is a lonely road and, you never know, the Mafia might come calling.'

Didi would have issued their invitation herself, if it had meant that she could escape the clutches of this madman, but on the wrong side of a locked door with no phone contact to the outside world, her options were running out.

A cacophony of dogs barking distracted Christoph from his game. He looked out the terrace door and even pulled up the blind on the front window to see what was going on. Didi used the couple of minutes to calm herself and decide on a strategy. Her best tactic was probably to dissipate some of Christoph's anger. If that meant submitting to some of his advances, then it was probably wiser to suffer being pawed than strangled.

The dogs would not stop barking. Christoph searched in a

drawer, then walked towards the glass front door as if to open it. Didi watched as he undid the lower lock and, when he put his hand on the latch and pulled the door open a little, she hurled herself at the gap, trying to push him out of her way. She had forgotten his strength. He didn't cycle hundreds of kilometres a week without his fitness benefiting. Like a bug, he crushed her between his two arms, and flung her back inside.

'This town is full of crazy women tonight! Outside, a silly old one going for a walk and disturbing all the dogs in the district, and inside a foolish younger one who won't relax and enjoy herself. Didi, it is time to stop resisting me. You don't really want to escape. You came here because you *wanted* me. Now, you try to run away! I do not think this is very fair. Do you, *Liebchen*?'

Didi tried to look submissive. 'I'm sorry. After the lovely dinner you cooked and all the trouble you went to, I really should be nicer.'

'No matter. Come, we will get comfortable on the sofa. Let us forget all this nasty shouting.'

Reluctantly, Didi sat beside him and they kissed. He began muttering in German, none of which she could understand. Suddenly mid-aria, Scarpia was silenced, the lounge became dark apart from the dwindling flicker of the candles. The whole apartment, the house next door, the two villas across from the terrace, the entire hillside in fact, had been plunged into a pitch-black abyss.

Didi let her head fall forward and, for the second time, began to howl in anguish.

Rico was glad of Salvatore's flashlight. The moon, though nearly full, ducked and dived behind the clouds. Once he had passed the isolated houses on his right, the road curved dramatically left, inclining steeply for a couple of hundred metres. Nothing seemed familiar in the dark, even though he had been up this road before. Hot air was carried on an energetic burst of wind, from the distant fires.

Signor Giorgio's directions were perfect. A couple of metres from the fork stood the S.O.S. phone. The different service numbers were stuck on the inside of the box, and Rico, relieved to hear a buzzing electronic noise in place of the usual phone tone. He began to dial the Forest Rangers' number but stopped, startled by the roar of a car's engine as it took the bend erratically. He dialled again.

'*Pronto?* Which station do you need me to connect you to?'

'Gibilmanna.'

'No, it's not possible. There is no one there. All out at the fires.'

'Well, can you tell me the exact location of the fire? I am particularly worried about the Santuario and my company's opera set.'

'The church is fine. The fires are lower and the wind is coming from the south, so if they do spread, it will be in the opposite direction.'

'So, it's not in danger?'

'No. Eh, God looks after his own!'

'Is Pianetti nearby affected?'

'You have friends there?'

'Yes.'

'That's a good distance away, but, yes, they'd be in the line of the fire should it travel further. Don't worry. We will evacuate them in good time if it advances. OK? I must go – this line is very busy.'

'Sure. Thanks. Good night.'

With the mixed emotions of relief at the fact that *Tosca* was safe, and guilt that he was selfishly focusing on his own interests when local landowners were witnessing their land incinerate before their eyes, Rico retraced his steps downhill. His mobile still had no signal. Once it was live, he would call Stephen and check that the company members in the Pianetti house were fine.

As he rounded the sharp bend, he crossed the road to the side with the houses, finding it easier to see with their outline beside him, since the flashlight's batteries had all but had it. The moon was generous, showing her face for several uninterrupted minutes, during which something brightly coloured caught his eye in the ditch. It looked as if somebody's laundry had flown from a nearby balcony and was entangled in the roadside brambles. As he drew nearer, his knees began to tremble as he realised the bedclothes seemed to have legs. A woman was lying face down at the side of the road.

In panic, Rico tried the flashlight and attempted to lift

her. Then he remembered he shouldn't move an injured person, so he gently lowered the limp body back to the ground. The few short moments with the flashlight were sufficient to reveal that the person in the ditch was Pauline, who judging by the abrasions and a trickle of blood from her ear, had been knocked down.

'*Pauline! Pauline,* s*ta ferma!* Everything will be OK. It's Rico. I will get help.'

In desperation, he checked his mobile. Nothing. Would it be quicker to go back to the S.O.S. phone, or run to the hotel? The hotel was downhill. Besides, they needed to get Didi, and there were cars and maybe a doctor among the hotel guests. Although he hated leaving her, standing around dithering wasn't helpful. Rico removed his linen jacket and placed it over her chill body.

'Pauline, *brava. Coraggio.* I'll be back in a minute. *Sta calma!*'

He couldn't be certain, but the optimist in Rico thought he saw Pauline move her chin as if she had understood.

The electricity now restored at the hotel, Salvatore was lolling in front of the television, watching some reality show. He was having difficulty staying awake but, even if he did nod off, the phone or the noise of late clients arriving back would bring him around. One such client had evidently arrived. Noisy footsteps clattered up the steps and across the Reception area, the push-door banging behind.

'Salvatore! Totò! Where are you? Totò?'

'*Shhh*, Rico, you'll wake the entire hotel!'

'It's Pauline – Signora O'Rourke. There has been an accident. She's lying on the Ferla road. *Totò,* I think she is dying!'

'*Oh God! An ambulance!*' Salvatore ran behind the Reception desk. He checked the switchboard – the phone lines were still down.

From under the counter, he pulled out a box with a selection of mobile phones. Throwing two at Rico, he started to open the backs, looking for a particular SIM card.

'Quick! This one should work. When the signal is interrupted, this network still seems to take.' With the different card in his own phone, the display box lit up. 'Thank God!' He dialled.

Salvatore panted out the information to the emergency services as he and Rico half-jogged down the avenue to pick up his car. '*An ambulance, please! The road to Ferla – a woman is hurt – yes, it's serious – I don't know – yes, an accident!*'

As they skidded out onto the driveway, Rico was surprised Salvatore didn't stop at the villas.

'Salvatore! Didi? Shouldn't we get her? You've driven past *Filicudi*.'

'She's not here. She never came back tonight. She must still be up in Christoph's.'

'Where is that?'

'Very near. In fact, on the way to Ferla.'

A cold hand crept around Salvatore's heart when he

remembered he had told the already inebriate mother of her daughter's whereabouts. It was *his* fault that Pauline had been on that road in the first place.

'Here! Pauline's just beside that gateway.'

The headlights of Salvatore's car swept the road, taking in the sorry sight of a floral dress fluttering aimlessly in the wind. The ambulance lights flashed below on the port road – it would arrive in about two minutes.

Rico knelt at Pauline's side.

'*Cara,* we are here. It's Rico and Salvatore. You are going to be OK. The ambulance is coming and they will look after you.'

Salvatore was shocked. He had never been this close to death. No near relative of his had yet died, and although in the course of his work unfortunate clients met with accidents or had heart attacks, mainly it happened on the beach or in the privacy of their bedrooms. Tonight, he was being asked to witness this woman's life ebb away and he felt numb. He couldn't say or do anything that might make those final hearing moments better. He envied Rico his naturalness, the warm way in which he could keep up the comforting patter, knowing from the look on the ambulance men's faces, that all he was telling Pauline were lies.

As a series of strange noises issued from Pauline's half-turned mouth, one of the ambulance men put his hand on Rico's shoulder and slowly pulled him to his feet.

Salvatore and Rico stood in silence, while the paramedics spoke to the carabinieri. One of the policemen photographed Pauline's body and walked up and down the road, scanning with a powerful lamp for tyre tracks or skid-marks. Although the electricity was back, this stretch of road was still very dark, having no public lighting.

'Finished?' The senior paramedic moved in.

'Yes, you can take the body now. We have done what we need to on site. Next-of-kin? We will need an identification.'

This was the part Salvatore had been dreading: tracking down Didi and having to break the awful news.

'She is Pauline O'Rourke – a client at the Panoramico.. Her daughter is with her on holiday.'

'Can we find the daughter?'

'Yes, I think I know where she is.'

'Salvatore Nicolosi, isn't it, from Bagheria?'

'Yes, captain.'

'Well, you could probably do the identification, if you bring her passport with you to the morgue.'

Salvatore hesitated. If he followed the ambulance with the papers, that would leave Rico with the responsibility of finding and telling Didi, which, although he baulked at the thought, he felt he needed to take upon himself.

'Captain, this is Maestro Rico Parisi, another client and a friend of the deceased. If I give him the papers, could he identify her for you?'

The police chief shook hands with Rico. 'It's only a formality, since we all seem to know who the poor lady is.

And so, Nicolosi, you'll find the daughter for us?'

'Yes.'

But before they left, it occurred to Salvatore it would be wiser to have the back-up of the carabinieri, in calling to Christoph's.

'Captain, could you come with me? I'm sure she is in an apartment near here. It would be easier if I had your support.'

'Very well.'

'Rico, take my car.'

'OK. And Totò? When you bring Didi back, get Isabelle. She will need someone.'

When the ambulance and Rico had left, the two police officers and Salvatore made the short drive farther up the hill to the green houses. Salvatore pushed through the overgrown plants on the little path, and just as he was about to press the buzzer, a high-pitched scream ripped through the silent night air, penetrating even the loud operatic music that was playing. The carabinieri heard it as well, the younger officer automatically placing his hand on his revolver. A series of dull thuds as if furniture was being flung about and a woman's voice screaming were the carabinieris' signal to move. Telling Salvatore to stay back, the captain thumped loudly on the front door, while the second man went around to the patio to see if he could gain access through the back.

Defying the advice given to him, Salvatore joined the younger officer. Through the glass windows, both witnessed the distressing sight of Didi in her underwear, desperately trying to cling to her open blouse, its fastenings all ripped.

Christoph, dressed only in his shorts, was talking through the front door to the policeman, who was ordering him to open up immediately.

When Didi saw the two figures peering through the glass, she emitted a wail of relief and collapsed sobbing onto the sofa. Christoph, turning sharply to tell her to shut up, realised he was being observed through the back windows. Taking the key out of its hiding place, he undid the mortice lock and opened the front door.

'Capitano Paolo, excuse us! Eh, young love, you know, sometimes it can get very passionate.'

The police chief looked contemptuously at Christoph and ordered him to put on some clothes. Salvatore had rushed around from the terrace and pushed past to the sofa, where Didi, very embarrassed at being discovered half-naked by three men, was slowly ceasing to sob. The younger officer picked up her skirt from the floor and handed it to her, and Salvatore took off the khaki shirt he was wearing.

'*Eccoci*. Put these on and we will go home.'

'Oh, Salvatore, you warned me, but I was either too stubborn or too stupid to listen. You don't know what I've been through. He locked me in! I thought he would kill me, when he ... when he had finished with me. How did you know I was here?'

'Later. Never mind all that now.'

When Christoph emerged from his bedroom, he was elegantly dressed in a fresh white shirt and red chinos. The two policemen took him away, protesting. A second car had arrived to take Salvatore and Didi back to the hotel.

Capitano Paolo reappeared at the door and called Salvatore outside.

'We will do all the statements for this – this terrible business tomorrow, when she is calmer. Will you break the news about her mother on your own, or would you like some professional help?'

'Thank you. If you could have the doctor call? She has a good friend back at the hotel, another Irishwoman, and between the two of us we will do our best, but I think she should have a sedative and maybe –' he remembered Maria-Pia's predicament '– an examination, to support the case against Christoph.'

'Yes. I will phone Doctor Ferrara and have her call to the hotel within the hour. We will notify the coroner about the deceased. The hotel will need to inform the undertakers and the family to arrange repatriation of the body. The inquest will be carried out as soon as possible, in order to release the body. I'll call to see Giorgio and the management later in the day.'

'Thank you, Captain.'

'Don't mention it."

Salvatore handed Didi to the officer in the police car and got in beside her. Only the first part of her dreadful ordeal was over.

Still shaking, Didi rested her head against Salvatore's bare shoulder, almost elated by her rescue, but puzzled by the sombre mood of her companions as they drove back to the Panoramico.

Chapter 31

Hotel Panoramico

Isabelle was awoken by an insistent tapping on her window. She thought at first it was a disoriented magpie pecking at the linseed-perforated putty that surrounded the patio doors, but normally the birds waited till daybreak. It was still pitch-black outside. She sat up, turned on the light, a little nervous.

'Isabelle! Isa*bella! Sono Rico.*'

'What are you doing? It's the middle of the night!'

'*Scusa!* But it's urgent. Open up!'

Not having spoken to him since Monique's arrival, Isabelle wondered why he had slipped out of the marital bed to talk to her. She slid the door across and stood back.

'Oh Isabelle, something terrible has happened! I don't know how to tell you.'

Taking a closer look, she noted the blanched face, his dishevelled clothes, the dirty stains on his trousers and what looked like blood on his shirt. She beckoned to him to sit down.

Shaking, Rico asked if she had anything in the minibar.

'There's probably some brandy or whiskey. The gin is gone. I had it earlier.'

'Brandy, *per favore*. Is there a second for you? You might need it.'

'Rico! What's wrong? You really have me worried.'

She quickly handed him a miniature bottle of brandy.

Pulling the little cap off the bottle, Rico swallowed its contents in one gulp.

'It's Pauline. She ... she had an accident, out on the road. I found her. Lying in the ditch – very white, except for a long streak of blood —' At this, Rico swept his hand from his ear down the side of his neck. 'It was awful! *Oh Isabella*, Pauline ... is ... dead.'

This couldn't be happening, Isabelle thought. She was on holidays. There were friendly, happy people all around her. Only good things were supposed to happen. That poor canoeist drowning out at sea the first week had been traumatic enough, but she hadn't known him, or even addressed a 'hello' to him during the course of his stay. This was different.

Rico was slumped in her rattan chair – telling her that the fun-loving woman with whom she had shared meals and into whose ageing back she had rubbed sun cream – was dead.

She felt numb. Looking at him for confirmation of what she had just heard, she realised he was in shock. She went and took him in her arms, holding his head against her chest. Once there, his tears came.

'When I saw her on the road – her energy, her vitality all snuffed out – I began to think of my own parents, of their mortality – of *my* mortality and how fragile is a life when in the course of one day – you can be sitting playing bridge in a shady spot on the terrace, and then twelve hours later, lying cold on a mortuary slab. What's it all about, Isabelle, what's life about?'

Isabelle had no answer. All she had were questions, for which Rico wasn't yet suitably calm to consider.

'And Didi?'

'She doesn't know yet.'

'Oh Rico, no! How come?'

'Apparently she and her mother were arguing and went their separate ways for the evening. Didi had a dinner date with that Christoph, at his apartment. For some reason, Pauline was walking up the road to Ferla when she seems to have been hit by a car.'

'And where is Didi now?'

'Salvatore has gone to find her. We want you to be here when we tell her.'

'Oh.' Isabelle didn't know if she was ready to accept the responsibility that had been thrust upon her. No sooner had she registered this thought than she dismissed it as callous selfishness. 'Of course. I'll help any way I can. Poor Didi! I knew they weren't talking, but this? Often that sparking off each other is only a sign of affection.' She paused, remembering the back and forth with her late mother, but also picturing the long, peaceful goodbye she got to say to her. 'I'm sure Pauline thought the world of her.'

'*Purtroppo*, Didi will never know.'

A silence descended. Rico became calmer and they held each other for some time, until he once again became restless.

'Do you mind if we sit out on the veranda for a while? We could both do with a bit of air.'

Settling themselves on the white chairs, they talked in whispers.

'So, you see that I have a visitor.'

'If you mean your wife, yes.'

'Are you annoyed?'

'What right would I have to be annoyed?'

'That's not what I asked. I want to know if you felt anything when she arrived.'

'What do *you* think?'

'*Isabella*, you are tiresome the way you answer questions with questions! For once, could you give a direct answer?'

Isabelle didn't know how to react. She wasn't going to tell him how she felt and inflate his ego even more! What did he want? A pat on the back for springing his wife out of a hat like a sleek white rabbit?

'I ... I was disappointed when I realised she had turned up.'

'*Brava!* Maybe now we get the truth. Do you know something? So was I. Disappointed, when I saw her arrive at *Tosca*.'

'Don't! You shouldn't say that about your wife.'

'My soon to be *ex*-wife. We are going to divorce.'

If the circumstances hadn't been so sad, Isabelle would have laughed into Rico's face. How many times had she heard stories of married men in the throes of an affair make this announcement! They loved the *sound* of this particular line. It smacked of the adventurous, the daring, it made them seem proactive, but from what she had observed they loved the comfort of their marital status more. When the fancy declaration became a real possibility, they simply hadn't the energy to compile an inventory of which possessions belonged to whom, or to deal with an estate agent measuring up their jointly owned property.

Any sharp comment she was about to formulate was put on hold by the appearance of a vested Salvatore walking Didi back to *Filicudi*.

Dressed in the oddest combination of silk sarong and a masculine-looking khaki shirt, Didi didn't seem unduly unhappy.

Rico looked quizzically at Salvatore, as Isabelle whispered hello. A slow shake of Salvatore's head communicated that the difficult deed had yet to be done.

'Salvatore, Didi, why don't you come in?'

Isabelle looked curiously at Rico, since they had only recently fled the stifling apartment in search of fresh air. Now, he was suggesting they all pile back into the small stuffy space.

'He hasn't told her,' Rico whispered. 'We'll have to do it.'

Didi led the way, remarking aloud on the differences in layout between *Lipari* and her own rooms.

'Oh, it's the complete reverse of *Vulcano* – you have the patio off your bedroom. In the two-bedroom model, it's off the sitting room. Except, of course, in *Filicudi*, where it's immaterial *who* has the patio doors, since the patio itself is the size of a postage stamp.'

Without consulting anyone, Rico crossed to the mini-bar and pulled out all the remaining miniatures, mostly whiskey and vodka with unfamiliar labels. He handed Didi a plastic cup of neat whiskey.

As she began to protest, he said, 'Didi, I don't really know how to begin saying what I have – what *we* have to tell you. Tonight – during the power-cut – I was looking for a phone that would work, and I … I came across an accident … on the road to Ferla. Somebody – a woman – had been knocked down.' Rico paused, looking pleadingly at Isabelle and Salvatore for help.

With her head down, Didi was concentrating intensely on the golden liquid in her plastic cup, which she was swirling insistently.

'The thing is, Didi … the very sad thing is … that the lady who had the accident—'

'Was my mother.' Didi took the burden of the words out of Rico's mouth.

All four sat in silence – three focused on an emotionless Didi still mesmerised by her plastic cup.

'Is she dead?'

Isabelle got up and hunkered down beside Didi, covering the shaking hands with her own.

'Yes, Didi. I'm *so sorry*. It's awful. I don't know what to say.'

Didi's eyes were now fixed on some point on the floor and she didn't react.

Salvatore looked from Isabelle to Rico.

'Didi, would you like to go … to see her? I will take you, if you'd like.'

'To the morgue? No, thank you. I'll stay here, if it's all the same with you.'

The relative newness of their friendship heightened the feeling of helplessness in confronting the tragedy. Isabelle reflected on how at a certain level they could interact perfectly well, but with something this momentous, they were exposed as nothing more than four strangers cast up on the same island at the same time. They had no shared resources to draw upon, no experiences to sustain them, and really no deep knowledge of Didi and how she really felt about the death of her mother.

It was obvious from his demeanour that Salvatore wanted to do more, but he limited himself to practical solutions.

'Will I call your family in Ireland?' he asked.

'Not yet. Jan wouldn't like to be disturbed. It can wait until the morning. Anyway, I'd have to go and look up their number. I never call her at home. She turns off her mobile at night.'

Rico found everyone's reaction unnatural. Christ, the girl's mother had just been mown down, yet she was sitting immobile, her face showing no trace of emotion! She hadn't shouted or cried or knocked over the table in temper. He thought back to when the Stage Manager at Australian Opera had brought him the news that his own father was on his deathbed. He had cried like a baby, even though he had spent most of the previous twenty years hating him. *Why* were these people so cold?

Isabelle was also concerned. Didi's passivity wasn't normal. Obviously, it was shock, but she wondered if there weren't thoughts of guilt or regret buzzing around her head over the falling-out with Pauline.

Salvatore, dead on his feet, was hovering, ever attentive, trying to wrap Didi in a blanket of emotional support, to which she seemed oblivious.

'Isabelle.' Rico beckoned to her and led her aside. 'I am really sorry, but it's nearly six and I need to get some sleep. I have a performance tomorrow – tonight – and, on top of everything, a rehearsal with a new cast member, as Wolfgang has succumbed to a throat infection. I'll have to leave.'

'You do what you must, Rico. Be careful not to disturb Monique on your way in.'

'Isabelle, you have it all wrong.'

'Really?'

'*Si.*'

Rico walked back to Didi, hugged her hard, and told her to be brave and know that she was not alone. He then mouthed goodbye to Salvatore before leading Isabelle to the door.

'*Eccoci.* I will see you later, yes?'

'I don't really know, Rico.'

'Please, Isabelle, do not think badly of me.' With that, he kissed her on both cheeks, and released the catch on the door.

As Isabelle watched him go, the pre-dawn darkness was broken by the lights of a car parked outside *Stromboli* and the staccato sound of heels tapping on terracotta. Through the window, she saw Monique load her bags into the waiting taxi and exchange a few words with Rico, before getting in and slamming the door. Isabelle watched until the lights of the taxi disappeared.

On the sofa, Salvatore and Didi seemed to be getting close, so Isabelle wondered if she should go back to bed. Then a further knock on the door made her think Rico was back, but she opened it to a middle-aged woman.

'Signora O'Rourke?'

'No, Isabelle Ryan. I'm afraid … Signora O'Rourke …'

Salvatore, hearing the familiar voice, hopped up.

'Isabelle, it's Doctor Ferrara. She has come to check on Didi, to give her something to relax.'

'Oh, of course. Excuse me, Doctor. I – I thought —'

'I understand. You must forgive us Italians our formality. It is very sad about the mother, a terrible tragedy.'

Didi followed the doctor into Isabelle's room and they closed the door behind them.

'Who sent for the doctor, Salvatore?'

'Oh, I asked the carabinieri to contact her.'

'The carabinieri? Were they here?'

'They were up at the accident, when Rico found the body.'

'It must have been awful for him, stumbling upon Pauline like that.'

'Yes. But he was great with her. Oh, Isabelle, you should have seen how strong he was – how he comforted her as she lay dying before our eyes. I was no use at all.'

'Don't say that. I'm sure you helped.'

'No, I was completely useless. *Now*, maybe, I can be of use to Didi, but faced with death, I was scared. Rico wasn't. He put his own feelings second and thought of poor Pauline.'

Isabelle was surprised by Salvatore's disclosure. She hadn't any reason to believe that he would deliberately praise Rico to her, but she could see he was sincere. She had often questioned if Rico had space in his heart for others from whom he didn't stand to gain anything. Clearly, on the strength of Salvatore's evidence, she had been wrong. The door of the bedroom reopened.

'*Allora, va bene*. All done. I have given her some Valium to relax her, and I have done the other necessary examinations. Poor girl, she has been through more than someone so young should be expected to suffer.'

'*Grazie, dottore*.'

A little mystified by the doctor's parting words, Isabelle assumed that Didi had mentioned her father's recent death. Salvatore saw Dr Ferrara out and chatted with her for a while in the garden.

'Didi, try and sleep. I am just right by, if you want anything, or need to talk.'

'Thanks, Isabelle. I suddenly feel very tired. Maybe I should lie down.'

While Salvatore sprang to his feet to transform the sofa into a fully supine bed, Isabelle went into her room to look out something lightweight in which Didi could sleep. The first streaks of daylight were already sneaking across the bay below.

With Didi tucked up in the sofa bed, and a weary Salvatore insisting on keeping vigil in the uncomfortable armchair, Isabelle retired to her room.

She was emotionally drained but sleep just would not come. For the first time since she had been told the news, she was able to concentrate on how *she* felt about the sudden death. Selected images of Pauline flitted across the room: Pauline sunbathing, a minute mahogany-brown figure dressed in an elegant one-piece, stretched out in the best deckchair on the bathing platform. Pauline winning at bridge, her eyes scanning her friends' hands triumphantly as she placed her winning cards on the table. Pauline dancing around the pool, whooping exclamations at the band in Spanish or tangoing on the same occasion with the flirty maître d'. Pauline enjoying a gossipy drink on the terrace with Helen and Bobby.

Overcome by an unexpected sense of loss, Isabelle hugged her pillow close and wept.

Chapter 32

Following her tranquilliser, Didi slept for several hours. Eventually, the strong light streaming in through the slats of the shutters disturbed that sleep and she awoke to the unfamiliar surroundings of *Lipari*.

The first thing that came to mind was her terrifying ordeal with Christoph. She must have been so distressed that Salvatore had asked Isabelle if she could stay. Little by little, Christoph's odious menaces receded, and in their place came the frightening recollection of Rico's earnest face telling her Pauline was dead.

She lay on the uncomfortable bed, experiencing the worst kind of *déjà vu*. This was how she used to wake in the weeks following her father's death. She would open her eyes, snug and cosy with that early-morning sensation of contentment, until a dull, stabbing pain in the pit of her stomach would remind her that, in fact, she was very *un*happy, not at all experiencing feelings of cosy contentment. It was happening again. She had lost her second parent, and this time in far worse circumstances.

Didi tapped on Isabelle's bedroom door but, getting no response, opened it to an empty room. The strange assortment of clothes that she had discarded in the early hours of the morning lay on a chair. She felt like chucking the torn blouse Salvatore had insisted on carrying back into the wastepaper bin, but realised that was yet another thing she had to tackle: she needed to give a statement to the carabinieri about Christoph's assault. They would probably need the blouse as evidence. On the bed lay underwear and a T-shirt of Isabelle's which she must have thoughtfully left out for her.

Didi dressed, found her bag and walked the several hundred metres back to *Filicudi*. As she checked for the key, her phone was bleeping for a battery recharge. Then she remembered: she had no key. She had left it at Reception, assuming her mother would return first the night before.

When Didi came through the revolving doors, guests were milling around post-breakfast, clamouring for information. Many had heard of the sad accident and avoided her gaze. She was met by a grey-faced Signor Giorgio, who took both her hands in his.

'*Cara signorina, mi dispiace, tesoro. Mi dispiace tantissimo.* She was a wonderful woman, your mother. Come to the office and sit down. Do you need anything? A little breakfast? Something stronger? You just say what you need, and we will do it. All of us at the Panoramico, we are most saddened by this – this terrible accident.'

'I just came for – the key – to Filicudi. She … she must have had it with her, when, when …'

Somehow having to explain the situation to a disinterested person made her mother's accident a certainty. With Isabelle, Rico and Salvatore, Didi felt as if they were all in a play, in which she was acting the role of the bereaved daughter but, somehow, seeing Signor Giorgio look so sad, she became aware the play was over. Her mother really *was* dead.

The first tears came as she stood in Giorgio's office. He made her drink a caffè corretto and went to fetch the master key. A pale-faced Salvatore returned in his place.

'Didi, how are you feeling?'

'Terrible. It's only just hit me.'

'Come. Let me walk you back to *Filicudi*. You need to be away from all these strangers.'

Salvatore refrained from telling her he had a list that he needed to accomplish on her behalf, starting with the difficult task of phoning the family back home. They had checked the registration form, but the only contact Pauline had given was her own home address in Dublin.

'Didi, we have to tell your sister.'

'Oh, Salvatore, could you ring on behalf of the hotel? I'm such a coward. I don't think I could handle Jan today.'

'Well, it's becoming urgent, as the police have been in touch. They are trying to speed up the process, because Pauline isn't local. They hope if the *medico legale* – the coroner

– is satisfied, he will release the body – release your mother – to the funeral home soon. They want to know which undertakers you want to use. Didi, I am sorry to be talking about all this, but they need to know and I can't give them an answer.'

'It's OK. You have your job to do. Which funeral directors does the hotel … usually use?'

'We have a relationship with a small one in the town. But, you know, your sister should really fly out. It is too much to expect you to deal with this on your own.'

'You think Jan should come here?'

'Yes. I have checked the routings and they'll have to go via Rome. I am presuming the husband will come too? Since it's such a busy period, we could use our influence in the hotel to make the reservations.'

'Thanks. Come inside. I need to charge the phone for Jan's numbers.'

With trembling hands, Didi opened the door. The first thing she noticed was Pauline's big straw bag, obviously dropped as soon as she had returned from the beach the previous day, still fully packed, the damp towel rolled up between the handles.

As soon as life hit the phone, Didi searched for Jan's contact.

'Try her work number first – in case she has the mobile off.'

'*Grazie*. If she asks to speak to you—'

'Say I've had the doctor and I'm sleeping, which is half true.'

'*D'accordo.*'

'Thanks, Salvatore.'

'There is another matter. The carabinieri have questioned Christoph and still have him in custody but need your statement before they can press charges. Capitano Paolo has arranged to interview you this afternoon. Would that be OK? The doctor has emailed her report, so they're anxious to proceed with your formal complaint.'

'This all seems too much at the moment.'

'What do you mean?'

'Maybe I should just drop it. In a couple of days, I'll be back in Ireland, and I'll never have to see Christoph again.'

Salvatore cried out in dismay. 'Didi, I know you're distressed and, believe me, if we could avoid this, I'd arrange it, but this time we can get Christoph. We have all the evidence – police witnesses, medical report, and even me as an independent witness, in case he says the local police are setting him up. You *must* file the complaint.'

'You feel strongly about this, don't you?'

'If someone *you* cared about had been abused and humiliated like that, wouldn't you?'

'I suppose I'll do it then. Call me when the police arrive, and I'll try and gather my thoughts before then.'

'*Grazie*, Didi. You don't know what this means to me.' Salvatore hugged her, and armed with her sister's numbers, went off to make the difficult call.

Didi was relieved when Salvatore left. It wasn't as if she didn't appreciate everything he was trying to do. It was just that she had only begun to assimilate the fact that Pauline was dead, and she hadn't had an uninterrupted moment since it happened.

Filicudi was eerily quiet. She had been very unhappy about their post-tour apartment's meagre dimensions, particularly when she was forced to share it with a non-communicative Pauline. Now, silence reverberated around what seemed vast and airy rooms, and the place seemed desolate without her mother ironing on the table or singing some Frank Sinatra number as she washed her hair.

Now alone, Didi began to question *why* her mother was walking up a pitch-black road so late at night. Did Pauline know she was at Christoph's and sense she was in danger? Why else would her mother choose that lonely route for a walk, if she had no specific reason?

Suddenly Didi remembered the dogs barking and Christoph's annoyance at the commotion. He had even said there was an old woman outside! Instinctively, Didi knew the 'old woman' had to have been Pauline. She must have given up on finding Christoph's place and was wandering back towards the hotel when the car hit her.

Her recharged mobile beeped triumphantly, indicating activity. Expecting a WhatsApp, or a dubious meme from Tony, she was surprised to see the voicemail symbol: nobody left voice messages anymore. Didi pressed the appropriate digits to pick up. It was Pauline.

When she had listened to the message, Didi turned off the phone. Her dead mother's words quivered down the waves of the thin instrument, a haunting voice from some celestial world. Pauline had wanted to make peace with her, long before she knew it was going to be her last night alive. Didi wanted to listen over and over to the words she had spoken: her mother had loved her – maybe even more than she had loved Jan.

All Didi could think of was wasted time. Of the endless hours fighting and arguing over this dress or that friend. Had she identified sooner how alike in temperament they were, they could have shared a friendship. Instead, Didi had raised a protective barrier against her mother's approaches, lest she succumb to her life-view and end up turning into Jan. Too late did she realise that Pauline didn't want a second Jan; one in the family was quite enough.

A glance around *Filicudi*, reminded Didi that soon all visible traces of her mother would be sanitised away into the big check suitcase that Pauline had expertly packed and successfully steered through several airports and a variety of hotels. No doubt Didi's packing would be inadequate, but in the absence of anyone else to take charge, it would have to do.

A gentle tap on the door provided a welcome distraction from her sad introspection. Peeking out through the muslin, she was glad to see Isabelle, carrying a tray. For one awful moment, she had thought it was the carabinieri ahead of schedule.

'How are you doing? When I got back from breakfast, you were gone. Did you manage to get anything to eat?'

'To be honest, I didn't try. I – I had to go over for the key, because my mother ... well, she had it – and then Giorgio hijacked me and when I got upset fed me very alcoholic coffee. After that, food wasn't high on my list of priorities.'

'Here. Do you think you could manage something light?' Isabelle placed the tray on the table.

'Thanks. I was afraid you were the carabinieri.'

'Oh. I suppose there has to be an investigation into the accident.'

'Yes, but they're here to talk to me. Something else happened last night.' Taking the tea Isabelle had poured, Didi began. 'This isn't easy – but once I make my statement, the bush-telegraph will have it. Last night, when I went to Christoph's for dinner, things turned nasty. He expected – well, more than just company – and when I was reluctant to deliver – oh Isabelle, he lost it and tried to force the issue! He – *I am full sure* – he was going to rape me.'

'No! Didi! You poor thing! I always knew there was something weird about him.'

'Though some smooth operator! He tried to talk his way out of it to the police chief, saying it was "passionate young love, that had got out of hand"! And then, *then* when he was told to dress because they were taking him in for questioning, he appears as cool as anything, spruced up in a white shirt and trendy red pants, as if he were going to a wedding!'

'What happens now?'

'Well, they still have him in custody and hope to charge him. But they haven't taken my statement yet. So, the police visit later.'

'Would you like me to be here when the police come?'

'They said it'd be about four. So, yes, please, if you didn't mind. And your Italian is better than mine, if they get stuck in English. However, first I have the difficult trip to the morgue to get through. Salvatore is taking me.'

'I can come too, if it would help.'

'Thanks.'

The room phone buzzed.

'Hello? Oh, Salvatore. How did it go? Yeah, to be expected ... the cow! Sorry. Sorry, what am I saying, she's my sister after all ... *That* soon? How come? ... Are you sure you don't mind? ... No, you can't do both – Isabelle says she'll come with me ... He's not too busy? OK. See you later.' Didi replaced the receiver. 'My sister and her husband are going to try and make an earlier flight to Rome. Salvatore's going to Palermo to meet them this evening, which means he can't take the morning off as well.'

'We can get a taxi. It's not a problem.'

'No need. Signor Giorgio insists that he drive us. You have no idea how I'm dreading meeting Jan this evening. She's blaming me. I already feel so guilty about rowing with

Mom.' Didi stopped to blow her nose. 'Yesterday, when I saw her with that old codger in town, I decided I wanted to end this cold war. Only I thought I'd put it off until today. *How* do you think I feel now? Perhaps Jan would be right to blame me. My mother's death *is* my fault.'

'Now, Didi, that's nonsense. Everyone knows how well you looked out for Pauline during the holiday. *You* didn't cause the power-cut. *You* weren't driving the car that hit her. Poor Pauline died as the result of a combination of tragic circumstances and you cannot add the burden of guilt to the grief you already feel.'

'You're a good friend, Isabelle.'

'Now, finish your tea, and I'll call back for you at eleven. If you need me, ring.'

'Thanks. See you later.'

The bell in the local chapel rang seven times. Didi slumped in the uncomfortable terrace chair, and watched the sun disappear behind the west-facing Rocca. She felt drained.

As each unpleasant formality passed, she had begun to mentally tick off the items on her traumatic itinerary. The visit to the hospital mortuary had been every bit as harrowing as she had anticipated. She couldn't make up her mind if it was a good thing, that her dead mother seemed so like herself in life. There were no marks, no obvious injuries, nor any trace of the terror that must have crossed her mind in those last few seconds before the speeding car hit her. Pauline just looked like a younger version of herself, fast asleep after a long, hard day. Didi might have preferred some external sign that her mother was forever altered; it would have made it easier to believe she would never again open her eyes.

'Excuse me? I hope I'm not disturbing you, but I heard about your mother, honey, and I just wanted to offer my sympathy.'

Didi looked into the sunglass-protected eyes of Beverly. 'Thank you.'

'Such an appalling thing to happen on your holidays.'

'I don't imagine it's a particularly good thing to happen at any time.'

'Oh, *of course*. What am I saying!' Beverly began to babble, pushing the glasses up on to her head. 'I just meant being away from home and on your own, honey.'

Didi realised the woman was trying to be kind and regretted her sarcasm. 'I know what you're trying to say. Thank you for your concern.'

'When Rico told me at rehearsal, I was so shocked. It must be very difficult for him to give a performance tonight, with the memory of finding your poor dead mother so fresh in his mind.'

Isabelle, returning to the table with their drinks, saw the alarm on Didi's face, and plonked the glasses down noisily.

'Hi, Isabelle, I was just commiserating with this poor girl about her mother. Rico is very shaken by the whole thing.'

'Beverly, we appreciate your sympathy, but Didi has had a very difficult day. You might be kind enough to leave us to have a quiet drink.'

'Sure – I have to go anyway – final performance. Goodbye, honey.' Beverly replaced her sunglasses on her nose and left.

'Was she bothering you?'

'No, just making the usual empty noises people make at times like these. Thanks for rescuing me.' Didi took a sip of her wine.

'That wasn't too bad, the chat with the carabinieri.'

'No. I was dreading it, but they were very supportive. I got the impression they were glad to have something on slimy Christoph. I'd say he's good at slipping through the net.'

'Not this time.'

'Let's hope not.'

'You and Salvatore seem to be getting close these days. How do you feel about going home and leaving him behind?'

'Strange. I think I'll really miss him. I know all the plans have been made to transport us back, but I have no concept of having a life beyond this place. You know how that happens when you're away for longer than a usual package-tour fortnight? Your old life fades into insignificance, and your new environment becomes more vivid than what's *supposed* to be your "real life".'

'Yes, I know exactly what you mean.'

'And *before* the terrible, terrible conclusion to our holiday, I was thinking about returning to Italy – about looking for work here. That was one of the things Rico and I chatted about on that embarrassing night when I thought I was on a date with him.'

Both women grinned in complicity when they remembered their feelings about Rico's invitation.

'And what advice did he offer?'

'Ironically, he suggested that choosing a future career just to make Pauline happy was no basis for a choice. I might have to confront that now, since I can no longer use my mother as an excuse for indecision.'

'Take your time. With all this going on, it's not ideal to be making earth-shattering changes.'

'I disagree. I think when someone's life is brutally snatched, it teaches you the value of living each day as if it were your last. That's the thing I saw in Pauline. She hauled herself back from depression after Dad's death, and once she began to live again, she enjoyed simple things that I had never known her to like before. She had more fun over the past few months than she'd had for a long time.'

Isabelle thought about mature marital love, and how comforting it must be to roll over beside the same, uncritical body every night. The downside, of course, had to be the tedium of predictability: always knowing what the other was going to do, likely to say, want to eat at specified moments in your shared routine. Not for the first time did she question whether such security compensated for the lack of excitement.

'— so we got chatting to the Festival organiser, a man called Filippo di Gangi.'

Isabelle realised she hadn't been listening to a word Didi was saying.

'When was this?'

'I *told* you, that night Salvatore and I went out for a pizza. Anyway, this Filippo is looking for someone with a background in classical music, to travel around Italy doing the advance organisation for the festivals he runs. He gave me his card. I dismissed it as a nice but impractical idea, since I had to go back to do the teaching diploma in September, but now? After all that's happened, I'm not so sure that it was completely daft. I mean, Isabelle, I have no one to go home to Ireland for. Without Pauline …'

Didi's eyes filled up again, despite the temporary levity.

'That's not true. You have your sister and her husband at home.'

'*Puh!* She has no time for me and I don't really like her either. Without Pauline as intermediary, I can't see much future in that relationship.'

The adjacent terrace tables had changed occupants. The returning beach-people, all hot and sweaty in their sun-cream encrusted clothes, had given way to the early aperitif imbibers – generally well-dressed Germans of all ages and some elderly British people. No Italians were among their number, since it was alien to them, to consider eating at eight.

As yet another party arrived, Isabelle noticed the familiar form of Salvatore skipping down the steps behind them.

He had a couple in tow.

'Didi! I don't believe it! Salvatore's back already with your sister and brother-in-law.'

Didi spun around in her chair, shielding her eyes from the low setting rays, as all three made their way across the terrace. She jumped to her feet. The least she could do was welcome Jan properly.

Isabelle observed the approaching couple. Even silhouetted on the distant steps, there had been something familiar about them. There was no doubt that the woman was Pauline's daughter – small, dark-haired, fine-boned – and reminiscent of someone she knew or had seen somewhere before.

As the two bereaved sisters embraced, a glance at the tall, blond male bringing up the rear confirmed Isabelle's worst suspicions.

'*Con!*'

'*Izzie!*'

Chapter 33

Didi looked from Isabelle to her brother-in-law. 'Do you two *know* each other?'

Isabelle thought she'd let Con speak first.

'We ... we used to be friends – a good while ago,' he said.

About to amplify his answer, Isabelle opened her mouth, but Janice interrupted.

'Oh, come on, Conor, I don't think you're giving my sister an accurate picture of your relationship with Tizzie or Tilly or whatever her name is.'

Con and Didi chorused simultaneously: '*Isabelle!*'

'*Is*abelle. Why don't *you* tell us the true nature of your dealings with *Is*abelle?'

Salvatore, plunged into a sea of incomprehension, pivoted from one to the other, like a tennis fan following the ball.

Observing Didi's discomfort, Isabelle intervened.

'Come on! I don't think this is a very appropriate conversation under the circumstances. Con and I had a relationship for many years. Now he's *your* husband, Janice, and as such I take it is here to pay his last respects to Pauline, as are we all.'

'What's my mother's death got to do with the likes of *you*? Butt out and let her family deal with the matter. I don't even know *how* you come to be here!'

Didi had suffered Jan's bullying for far too many years to let it happen again. 'Please, Jan, don't cause a row. Isabelle stays, as my friend, as does Salvatore, to whom, I take it, you have no objections?'

Janice looked discontentedly from behind her Prada sunglasses and waved a conciliatory hand in Salvatore's direction. She deliberately turned her back on Isabelle and focused on the view out to sea.

Conor shifted from one lanky leg to the other. 'Can I get anyone a drink? A white wine and a gin and tonic, is it – Didi, Izzie – em, Isabelle? What would you like, Salvatore?'

'Orange juice, *grazie*.'

Janice pulled up an extra chair. 'How cosy this is – past and present all huddled around the table like one big family.'

'Vodka and lemon?' Conor waited.

She ignored him and he scampered up the steps in the direction of the bar.

'Aren't you upset about Mom, Jan? How can you find the energy to snipe at Conor and insult Isabelle like this? You should be too distraught to be picking fights.'

'*Me* picking fights? I am summoned – at an hour's notice – to come halfway across Europe and retrieve the dead body of my beloved mother, whom *you* couldn't manage to mind during your all-expenses-paid holiday, only to find you buddied-up with – *the slut* – that keeps my husband awake at night!'

Isabelle had had enough. Let them have their argument, but she was not going to sit and listen to this jumped-up social climber insult her! Unless Con was selling heroin to the clients at the health club, there was no way he could afford to fund the little madam's diamond earrings, Louis Vuitton accessories and clashing designer labels. At least when *she* had been with him, he was a real person.

'Isabelle, where are you going?'

'I'm sorry, Didi. I'll leave you to your family. You know where I am, if you need anything.' With that, Isabelle practically sprinted across the terrace.

'*Now* look what you've done!'

'Good riddance! What are you doing hanging around with an old saddo like her? What would you say she is – thirty-five – older? *Aah*, here's the expert back, let's ask him!'

Salvatore, horrified by Didi's sister, wondered could he bear to wait for his orange juice. What was *wrong* with the woman? He thought of his own family and the care and solidarity they would show, should, heavens forbid, anything happen to either of their parents. Even if he were as mad as hell with Maria-Pia, they would be united in grief and wouldn't have any energy for this sort of nastiness.

'Conor, darling, we are trying to work out Isabelle's age.'

'Where's she gone?' He set down the tray. 'I have a drink for her.'

'Oh, you'll just have to drink it, since you and she take the same poison. How cute is that! Anyway, you didn't answer my question: what age *is* dear old Isabelle?'

'Wiser than *you* anyway.'

'Come, come! That's not an answer. Thirty-six, thirty-eight?'

'Actually, thirty-*two* – a mere four years more than you!'

'Ah, yes, but *I* take care of myself. I have the body of a twenty-year-old.'

'Janice, you have the body of a twenty-year-old because you've never done a hard day's work in your life,' he said. 'You have been pampered and spoiled, first by your father, then by Pauline, and along the way by every half-idiot of a boyfriend who you sucked into your grandiose schemes. Yes, you're a twenty-year-old all right – an irresponsible, immature, twenty-year-old!' Lifting the two gins and the tonic bottles, Conor turned and went back to the bar.

Didi looked despairingly at Salvatore, hoping he wasn't going to desert her as well. Instead, he pulled a folder from the side of his chair and placed it on the table.

'Ladies, unpleasant as this is, I think we should agree the arrangements. The funeral directors sent this.' He selected a page from the folder and held it out.

Jan promptly snatched it. 'Oh, it's all in Italian. Well, that's not much use.'

'We *are in* Italy, Jan. What did you expect – Swahili?'

'Don't be smart. I thought it would be in English, since the deceased was English-speaking.'

'Unfortunately, Mom is no longer negotiating with them so it doesn't really matter what language she spoke. Here, give it to me. ... They're suggesting a prayer service in Santa Caterina around seven tomorrow evening, but with no remains? Have I understood that correctly?'

'Yes. Now, Didi, it's up to you – both. They'll transport the coffin to the church if you'd like, but as it'll be going to the airport later for departure on the eighteenth, they thought it better just to make one move.'

'Fine by me.'

Jan sloshed the bitter lemon into the vodka she had been ignoring. 'I don't see the point of a prayer service here at all. *And* without her coffin?'

'It was the hotel manager's suggestion, so Pauline's friends in the hotel and the community can pay their respects.'

'Yeah, Jan, so people who were fond of her can slip in quietly and say a prayer, without drawing attention to themselves.'

'Well, you two obviously have it all cooked up between you. I don't see the point in *me* offering an opinion.'

Salvatore was becoming increasingly impatient with Didi's sister. After two hours' sleep, he had done his shift, driven a three-hour round-trip to the airport, as well as liaising with the funeral directors, the carabinieri and the morgue in between, all on this family's behalf. For Didi, he would do it again, but the attitude of this arrogant woman was outrageous.

'I think I discussed the return journey already with Signora Jan. The itinerary is in your pigeonholes. You don't need to bother with that now.'

'Apart from the transport to the airport, I mean, *official* transport. No offence, Salvatore, but your car *is* very uncomfortable.'

Salvatore could no longer be bothered to appear civil.

'Would the signora like to book any particular make or model of car for the journey accompanying the hearse to the airport? I am sure the funeral directors can offer a range of cars comparable to any of the car-hire companies. What would you fancy? A GTI or say – an open-top Merc?'

'I suppose the convertible would be a bit unsuitable, but order something with decent air-conditioning.'

'Consider it *ordered*. Now, I need to check which room Giovanni has assigned you, so I'll leave you two in peace.'

Didi mouthed 'Sorry' as Salvatore pushed his chair back and left. 'I think I'll head inside too. I need to be on my own for a while.'

'Not just yet. Now all these "hangers-on" have gone, I need to talk to you. Didi, through your usual feckless way of living, *you* have killed our mother. Don't look at me all doe-eyed. If you hadn't been chasing anything in a pair of trousers all over the countryside, Mother would not have been wandering around in the dead of night looking for you.'

'Who told you that?'

'Your *friend* Salvatore was only too eager to fill us in on how it happened.'

'How was I to know she'd come looking for me? As far as I was aware, she didn't even know where I was.'

'Whatever. But let me make a couple of things clear. When we get back to Ireland, we'll go through the formal services of this funeral together, but after that forget about Sicily and anybody you met on this godforsaken island – and that includes Isabelle – *particularly* Isabelle. It's bad enough you both end up in the same hotel out here, without encouraging her friendship at home. I forbid it. You can keep your distance from my husband as well, because no doubt he'll use seeing *you* as an excuse to ask about your new best mate.'

'Listen to yourself – giving orders! Do you know something? I think you're scared – scared the pet poodle might slip his lead.'

'Don't you dare speak about my husband like that!'

'"*My husband, my husband*"! For heaven's sake, he has a name. Why can't you use it? He's a person, not an appendage. If you're so confident in your relationship, why issue an embargo on me keeping in contact with his ex?'

'I have my reasons. Show me where the reception in this hotel is, so I can get my key, since your friend Salvatore has evidently abandoned us. I need a shower before dinner.'

'Just follow the steps and you'll come to it. I won't be joining you for dinner. I have no appetite and need a bit of peace and quiet.'

'Fine by me.'

Finally free of Jan, Didi guiltily celebrated the fact that she was alone again. She felt *relieved*, which was strange, considering most people in similar circumstances would have welcomed the company of their only remaining blood relative, if they had been so tragically bereaved. Instead, Jan was an additional problem with which she had to cope, not a supportive older sister who would help lighten her load. Her behaviour towards Isabelle had been appalling. Didi wondered should she drop by *Lipari* and offer an apology.

In the shock of discovering that her new holiday friend and her brother-in-law were acquainted, Didi had failed to register that the long-term boyfriend who had caused Isabelle such grief could be none other than Conor. Her portrayal of him fitted perfectly with everything that Didi herself had suspected.

She couldn't help but recall the stories Isabelle had told her about the as then unknown Conor. Obviously, theirs was an important relationship, and the coincidence of stumbling upon each other on such an emotionally charged occasion must have been a shock.

Something from Conor's past persisted in niggling at her. Imelda had told that story of having seen him in Westport. It was the first weekend in December, she'd said. With a pretty blonde on his arm.

Isabelle was blonde. Isabelle had told her a tale about a wonderful, reconciliatory weekend in a posh country hotel with her former lover – a reconciliation that Isabelle had believed was sincere.

Meanwhile, on the same December Sunday in the front row of a south Dublin church, Janice had twisted her carefully selected solitaire, round and round her bony little finger, slightly bored with the religious ceremony that was her father's Month's Mind Mass.

Chapter 34

The sheet was bathed in perspiration and stuck to her, but she couldn't displace his weight to move to a drier patch. Her heart was pounding so loudly that it made her ears throb, and she knew she was about to enter that dizzy light-headed phase which, although disorienting, was wonderfully exciting. Probing fingers continued to extract every last sensation, even though he had long since entered her. His breathing was heavy and panting, and as the intervals between pants became shorter, she hoped he would hold off, until she was ready. Supporting himself on his arms, he arched his back and hovered over her, before exclaiming triumphantly, 'I'm coming, I'm coming, I'm *com-ing!*'

True to his word, he did. The satiated body sank exhausted on top of Isabelle. Rivulets of sweat trickled over her face and down her neck. The dead weight was impossible to move, and she wondered what the correct etiquette was when a lover collapsed exhausted from his exertions, leaving you on the brink of ... well, on the brink of what could transpire to be nothing at all.

Frustrated, Isabelle settled for giving him a hug. He responded with a couple of tentative snores, which worried her. He surely wasn't thinking of crashing out in this position – he'd suffocate her! Mouth-open, he snoozed for several minutes until, assisted by an encouraging jab of Isabelle's ring, he came to.

'Well, hon, that was hot! You certainly haven't lost your touch! Do you know what would seal the deal? A cold beer.'

'I'm surprised you can remember!'

'It hasn't been that long, has it?'

'Nine months – give or take.'

An awkward silence settled between them.

'So, where's that beer you promised me?'

'I didn't.'

'Self-service then.' Con clambered out of the bed and wandered into the sitting area, where he extracted two bottles of Moretti from the dingy brown minibar. He set about them with the bottle opener.

'Not for me.' Isabelle sat up in the bed, clutching the discarded sheet to her chest.

'Come here, Izzie, sit beside me.' He was patting her sofa, as if he owned the place, 'Now, we'll have to sort something out. You and me, hon – well, we're special. Christ, Isabelle, how I've missed you! Don't mind the thing with Janice. Sure, a bloke has to get married at some stage. But you! You're the love of my life – always have been, always will.'

Isabelle watched him, slouched comfortably, beer in hand, and listened as he delivered this nonsense.

'You see, the cool thing is, the guy who had my job before at Paces was from out of town, so they gave him the use of an apartment on the edge of the racecourse. When I took over, they chucked in the accommodation as part of the package. So, when I feel like a bit of space or have an awkward split-shift, I flit down there and watch the gee-gees being put through their paces on the track.'

Isabelle could imagine a few other fillies being put through their paces in the glorious bolthole apartment but refrained from mentioning it. 'Do you think, Con, we're really that well suited?'

'Babe, of course! We're the two halves of the whole – the bits of the sphere that your man Yeats was always going on about.'

'But *physically?* Do you think we're sexually compatible?'

'Don't you worry your head, Izzie. You're really good. I've no complaints, anyway!'

'Have you ever considered that *I* might have complaints?'

'Well now, love – I don't want to be nasty – but you haven't as much to compare with as my good self.'

Disadvantaged by her nakedness, Isabelle still had the self-confidence to realise that this was one great fool of a man. When he rocked up earlier, clutching two tepid G & Ts, what had she been thinking of, letting him in? It had taken this completely ridiculous episode to make her realise what a disaster he was.

'I think you need to get dressed and leave.'

'What? Sure, it's early yet.' Taking a thirsty slug of his beer, he grinned suggestively. 'Plenty of time for a quickie before I have to go.'

'No, actually I don't think so, because you have to go *now*.'

Sitting in all his ruddy nakedness, Conor appeared puzzled. His petulant bottom lip protruded – the vulnerable little-boy-lost expression he had spent the best part of ten years perfecting was on display. Isabelle was unmoved.

'Do you not love me anymore, hon, or are you worried about being mean to Janice? Is that what it is?'

'No on both accounts, Con. I'm not sure I *do* still love you. And as for Janice, she's not my responsibility. "Being mean" doesn't enter into it. Now, I think I'd like you to go.'

'You never used to be this cold.'

'Oh, I'm not cold, quite the opposite in fact. It's because I've discovered my real, passionate self, that I need a full-blooded relationship.'

'What you're saying, Izzie, is that our relationship isn't real.'

'Exactly. Maybe it was, but it blew itself out, and neither of us would accept that and kept prolonging the agony.'

'It wasn't – it *isn't* agony! I *love you,* Isabelle. I'll never forget how I felt when I saw you at the wedding! My world just came crashing down around me.'

'Really? Strange way to express earth-shattering love that, marrying someone else. I thought you weren't "into" marriage.'

'These things – sort of sneak up on you. One minute I was just seeing Janice, the next I was playing golf on Sundays with her old lad. And then – well, she was kind of tight-assed, so she wouldn't move in unless I kept promising more and more. Before I knew what was happening, I found myself in some fucking expensive jeweller's and she was looking at the top-price tray of rocks.'

Isabelle knew Con was telling the truth. She had seen and heard enough of Janice to know this had been her game plan. A tiny part of her felt sorry for him, though he seemed to have found ways around his predicament. Looking at it from the outside, both Janice and he seemed to have got what they wanted: she a good-looking husband and a flash lifestyle, he implicit permission to play away as long as it meant nothing and he trundled home eventually. As Isabelle clearly contravened the first clause in their agreement, this is what had stoked Janice's fire earlier.

He dressed quickly, realising she was not for turning. 'Can I ask you something? Why did you sleep with me if your feelings about us have changed?'

'Recreation? Exercise? Or maybe, because I knew I could.'

'That's not like you! You've changed, Izzie. Have you met someone else?'

'Yes, actually. I have. Myself. The *real* Isabelle has asserted her right to exist.'

'Ah fuck! I can't be doing with all that existential crap!'

'How eloquently expressed, Con! Now I need to shower,

if I'm going to make the restaurant before dinner finishes.'

'You're not thinking of going over for dinner? Janice has a table booked!'

'Why not? Even a bit of "extra-curricular" needs to eat. Just pull the door closed behind you.'

With that, Isabelle went into the bathroom, leaving Conor to prepare a face to meet his wife's suspicious questions. The power-shower played warm water on her back and shoulders, as the Issey Miyake gel coursed over her body, forming delicate little soap bubbles as it went. Under the massaging cool of the water, Isabelle began to giggle. An image hovered, of a nude Con sitting on the sofa sucking on his beer bottle as if it were a soother. This man – this overgrown boy – was *this* what all the fuss had been about?

Wrapping herself in a fluffy white towel, Isabelle thought of the other man that good fortune had thrown in her path and realised she needed to re-establish relations, before it was too late.

Decided, she dressed carefully. She *would* speak to Rico. After all, he had wanted to see her; it was she who hesitated.

It was the night of his final *Tosca*. She would wait up and watch out for him returning. They couldn't just leave things like this. Or, even if they *could,* she knew now that she didn't want to.

Chapter 35

Rico hugged Ornella and he made another attempt to climb into Tommaso's car.

'*Maestro, maestro!* My card. If you visit Napoli any time, don't hesitate. Or if you're looking for a sexy Cavaradossi anywhere interesting, you know where to find me!' Paolo embraced Rico.

Stephen stood next in line in the orderly queue that had begun to form, as company members waited to say their goodbyes. 'Will I see you at the airport tomorrow, by any chance?'

'No, I leave the day after. I'm having a day to myself before returning to Rome.'

'Well, you deserve it, after all the time you've given everyone else. Thank you, Rico, for making my first opera so memorable.'

'*Figurati*, I was only doing my job. And you, my friend,

made it easy. You are a fine opera director, Stephen. *Un abbraccio.*' This time, Rico initiated the embrace. 'Stay in contact, won't you?'

'*Sì.*'

The final remaining cast members shook hands or kissed as appropriate, and eventually Rico got to leave. The last-night *Tosca* party had been a loud and convivial affair in Stephen's rented house in Pianetti, where, with the nearest neighbours a good kilometre down the hillside, people had let their hair down, without worrying about noise or disrupting other diners, as they would have if it had been in a restaurant.

Rico had stayed far later than intended. It was nearly two when they left. Tommaso chatted idly as they drove, pointing out the various smouldering fields from the previous night's fires. Although saddened by such widespread devastation, Rico was in a world of his own.

He recognised the feeling: it was the usual anti-climax, each time a curtain went down on a run in which he was involved. Notwithstanding the squabbles or the difficulties inherent in any piece, once the show was over, nostalgia mixed with a sense of purposelessness, and he was sad to say goodbye to cast and crew. Sometimes he thought it was the loss of the micro-world into which he escaped every day, away from the concerns of his real life, and where the only things that mattered were Cavaradossi's tessitura or Tosca's high Cs.

He had hoped to arrive back at the Panoramico nearer to one o'clock, on the off-chance that Isabelle might still be around, but he had stayed too late. It was unlikely she would still be awake.

The following day would be their last in Sicily. She would return to her life in Dublin, resume work, and in time (but not before her lovely golden suntan had faded), probably look up that Conman, whom Rico suspected was not completely out of her life. He would fly back to Rome, do his laundry and repack his suitcase for the imminent departure to Berlin. He might also stop by the solicitor's office to brief him on the state of affairs with Monique. It was all so clear-cut, so organised: flights to be taken, schedules to be met, his itinerary forever propelling him forward on some perpetually spinning wheel.

Yet, two days previously, Pauline thought she would fly home from her holidays this weekend – and look what had happened to that great plan. Rico sighed when he thought of the sad arrangements Didi must have to make, and if for no other reason than to find out what was happening, he needed to make contact with Isabelle.

'Maestro! You are very quiet. The silence of nostalgia? You are sad to leave beautiful Sicilia, no?'

'Yes, Tommaso. Nostalgia.' Then, suddenly, Rico had a thought. 'Tommaso, tomorrow, are you busy?'

'Not particularly. The airport? I thought you fly the next day?'

'Yes, I do. No, tomorrow – take me to Polizzi again, for one last look.'

'OK. What time will I pick you up?'

'The morning, but not too early, say about eleven?'

'OK. Here we are – the Panoramico! Till tomorrow!'

'Good night, Tommaso.

'Good night, maestro.'

As he expected, there were no lights on in *Lipari*. Isabelle had probably long since gone to bed. When he pushed the door inwards, a folded piece of paper caught his eye. Good! Maybe she had written him a letter. Rico unfolded the page expectantly, only to see the letterhead of the hotel's stationery. It was a note from Signor Giorgio, apologising that his departure date had been recorded erroneously and, as a consequence, the reservations' staff had thought *Stromboli* was free from the following morning. If he would be so kind as to oblige them, the best sea-view room was at his disposal for the final night without charge. The staff would move his belongings for him.

Although he hadn't anticipated having to pack for another day, it had to be done sometime, so he might as well accommodate Signor Giorgio. Apart from his scores, there really was little in the way of clothes: he had long since perfected the art of travelling light. He would assemble his bags first thing the following morning. Then, it was off to Polizzi with Tommaso.

Rico had no firm idea what made him want to return to his father's birthplace. He wondered should he invite Isabelle to join him? It would be a way of spending some time together and talking over a few things. Of course, there was Didi to be considered. Perhaps Isabelle wouldn't want to abandon her. He would call in to *Lipari* in the morning and see what she thought.

He had also come to another decision. When he returned to Rome, he would organise his things for Berlin but, once ready, he would put them aside and take the car out of the lock-up and drive north to Viareggio, where he would spend a few days with his mother and brother. Ernest could notify Berlin that due to unforeseen circumstances he was compelled to arrive two days late. After all, if he had been prepared to delay to try and sort things with Monique, surely his mother deserved at least the same effort? Besides, the resolution of any problems he had with his own family was eminently more achievable than a last-ditch aspiration to rescue his rickety marriage.

Monique's precipitate dawn departure was the first honest thing she had done in years. Neither of them wanted to spend a minute more in each other's company and she had taken her chances with an earlier stand-by flight. He found a long 'things-to-do' list that she had left behind, mostly concerned with legal and property matters. Rico had given it a cursory glance, but it wasn't his style to battle over unimportant possessions, when his happiness was at stake. He would still have his apartment in Rome, and she hers in Montpellier, neither of which formed part of their marital possessions. The only thing they jointly owned – and that had to be decided upon how to divide or if to divide – was the summerhouse in Fréjus.

But these were matters for another day. Exhausted, Rico rolled over to sleep, conscious of all the unfinished things he had to do, before he could leave Sicily behind.

Chapter 36

Although Salvatore had feared the management's reaction, the ultimatum still came as a shock. It was one thing to know that you wanted to leave a job in search of something more interesting; it was a different thing altogether to have your employer 'request' your departure. Their fancy words obfuscated the actual demand, but the subtext was clear enough: either Salvatore must retract his witness statement about Christoph's alleged sexual assault of Didi or the Panoramico would retract its contract of employment with Salvatore.

This all became clear when Salvatore cornered Signor Giorgio, to remind him he had swapped his day off and wouldn't be working Monday. Giorgio, despite many faults, was a humane man, and understood Didi would need a friend to see her through trips to the funeral directors and the prayer service later in the evening. In principle, Giorgio didn't have a problem with the arrangement but when he and Salvatore were alone, he took the opportunity to share the current feeling of the hotel directors.

'Totò, you are a great worker, and much appreciated in the hotel. *I* know all the work you do. However, a problem has come to my attention.'

'Oh, tell me, Signor Giorgio. What problem?'

'The problem concerns the same unfortunate young lady who has just lost her mother – your friend Signorina O'Rourke.'

'Yes?'

'Well, apparently, she had a dinner date with Christoph Kraus, and it – well, it became a little heated. The young lady has lodged a complaint with the carabinieri, that Christoph sexually assaulted her.'

'That's right. He did. Having first locked her in and making her suffer for several hours.'

'Perhaps, but we have a problem. You *do know* who Christoph is?'

'I know *what* Christoph is, but when you ask if I know *who* he is, yes, I do: he is the nephew of Signor Franz, a shareholder in the hotel.'

'Exactly. Now, you understand why your statement to the carabinieri causes us an embarrassment.'

'I don't see why. It wasn't Signor Franz who attempted to rape Didi.'

'*Shhh!* You mustn't say these things, Totò! Listen, you are like a son to me. I do not want to see you in trouble. Please, retract your statement.'

'Or what? If I refuse to, what will happen?'

'Salvatore, they'll fire you! Signor Franz will see to that. Say you can't be sure – maybe they were playing games.'

'You want me to lie, to save my dead-end job in this place! Signor Giorgio, have you forgotten that Christoph is systematically preying on vulnerable Panoramico guests? Do you want to be the manager of a hotel who would endorse that?'

'Of course not! But he is popular with the groups. I suppose I could ban him from the hotel in future, apart from Aktiv meetings and guest enquiries.'

'Fine words, but won't Signor Franz have something to say about *your* job, if you do that?'

'Probably. Please, Salvatore, I am trying to help.'

'I know. But, Signor Giorgio, *you* have two daughters. What if Christoph seduced one of them, and subjected them to the same … indignities that Didi and others have had to endure. How would you feel then?'

'I would break his bones with my bare hands.'

'Eh, exactly. I will *not* be retracting my statement. Nor will I wait until they dismiss me. You will have my letter of resignation in the morning. I will work my three weeks' notice, which I will gladly do if you make my resignation public, *very public* tomorrow, before the Board has a chance to dismiss me.'

'I'm sorry, my friend, I'm so sorry. Your references, I will prepare now – before any trouble starts. OK?'

'Thanks, Signor Giorgio. You have been a good boss to

me. Will I see you at Signora O'Rourke's prayer service later?'

'Sure. *Alle sette?*'

'Yes.'

Salvatore left Giorgio's office shaken, yet excited that he had confronted such an ultimatum and done the right thing. It was only a matter of time before he would have left the Panoramico anyway. No better way to resign, he thought, than on a matter of principle.

With the free day now official, his first port of call was *Filicudi* and the second trip to the funeral directors with Didi. The snooty sister and her husband had already left in a taxi, practically ignoring him in Reception as they sat waiting for the car. The husband didn't seem too bad. He tried to make conversation when Salvatore was writing down the Funeral Home address, but the bossy little wife summoned him back to her side, where he went like a lamb. Salvatore couldn't help thinking what would happen if a Sicilian woman had humiliated her husband similarly in public.

All the shutters of Filicudi were open, a good sign, Salvatore thought. Didi was at least up and moving around.

'*Ciao, sono io!* Where are you?'

'On the patio, hanging some clothes to dry. I had run out of decent-looking things. I'll need something for this evening. You're very casual – not working?'

'Day off. We've a lot to do.'

'What time are we expected at the funeral directors?'

'He said any time after ten-thirty.'

'OK. I've been choosing some music and a couple of readings. I'll just go get my iPad. It's really helping me to organise things for the service. I thought I might play some of my mother's favourite pieces on the church organ, if that's all right?'

'Oh, you play the organ! Excellent! Well, it's unusual, but I'm sure if we call by the Santa Caterina, the sacristan will be there.'

'I suppose we'd better take Jan and Conor with us.'

'Gone already. In a very comfortable taxi.'

Didi laughed but reined it in immediately.

'Don't feel guilty, Didi. Pauline would want you to laugh. When I think of her, all I can see is her smiling and enjoying herself around the place. She wasn't a miserable woman. Neither should you be.'

'You're beginning to really know me, Salvatore.'

'Maybe I am *getting* to know you better. But do you know me? There are lots of things I have kept from you.'

'Whatever for? I thought we were friends. Don't you trust me with your secrets?'

'Oh, they're not secrets particularly. Just things about which I don't wish to worry you.'

'After all that I'm dumping on you! Come on, out with it, whatever's bothering you.'

'Well, I've just resigned.'

'I knew you were thinking of leaving – but why so suddenly?'

'It's over my witness statement about Christoph.'

'So, it's over *me* really! Oh, Salvatore, I don't want to cause you any trouble. What happened?'

'Christoph is the nephew of Signor Franz, a big shareholder in the hotel. Giorgio tactfully told me that either I retract my statement or I have no future at the Panoramico.'

'Change your statement. Hold on to your job! I'm sure we've enough on that creep without it. Don't be foolhardy on my account.'

'It's not *only* on your account. Do you remember meeting my sister Maria-Pia, the day you were going on the Island tour?'

'Yes, I remember her. She snatched Christoph's phone number out of my hand.'

'The reason she went so crazy was not out of jealousy, but in an effort to protect you. Christoph spent most of last July trailing her, and finally, when he won her confidence, he pounced.'

'*That's* why you punched him at the cinema!'

'Yes. Because she wasn't as lucky as you. She lacked the experience to judge the situation and play Christoph along. She protested and wouldn't let him do anything, which, of course, his warped mind found exciting. He raped her, Didi.'

'*Oh, no!* The poor girl! And afterwards, what happened?'

'Nothing. She told no one. She kept it to herself for over a year, until her behaviour become so strange that my mother thought she was having a breakdown. Finally, she opened up to me, but refused to make a complaint. She thought nobody would believe her, compared to well-thought-of, well-resourced Christoph.' Salvatore paused. 'After this morning's *communiqué*, I can understand why.'

'But that's appalling! Can't she add her complaint to mine? I'm sure it would be taken seriously, with the police as witnesses this time.'

'Maybe. I'll talk to her. *Now* you see why I was horrified when you were thinking of dropping it.'

'Of course. Why didn't you tell me then?'

'Because you had just lost your mother. Because you had been sexually assaulted. You had enough to cope with.'

Didi looked into Salvatore's serious face, the cheeks slightly flushed. His tightly cut hair was sharp – attractive. For the first time since she had known him, she saw him as a fanciable man.

'Come here, you!' She reached out and hugged him, no longer in the asexual way which she was used to, but instead allowing her face to linger in front of Salvatore's until, finally, he read the signal that she wanted to kiss him. Their two sets of lips sought each other out and having found a rhythm, set about kissing more confidently.

'*Allora*. At last. I've been longing to do that for some time.'

'Have you now?'

Salvatore grinned. '*Senti*, I don't want to kill the mood, but we need to leave for the funeral home.'

'I'll just fetch a shirt to throw over this dress. Air-Con.'

Salvatore continued chatting through the open bedroom door. 'I don't know how you'll feel about this, but someone has turned himself in for causing your mother's death. A young driver, who says he wasn't travelling fast, but could see very little in the blackout – well, that's his story. When he heard the thud, he thought he had hit a dog – all those isolated villas on that hill have Alsatians. He was afraid the owners would prosecute, so he panicked and drove off. It was only when he heard the news the following day that he realised what he had done. He walked into the police station and confessed.'

'That's something, I suppose.' Didi joined Salvatore in the living room, passing Pauline's packed suitcases, tucked in against the wall. 'Though I don't envy the driver, having to live with the guilt of her death – accident or no accident. Will we go?'

'*Andiam*. Shutters open or closed?'

It was an old-fashioned thing she knew, but Didi couldn't help remembering her mother's insistence that they close the blinds in the house out of respect for her poor dead father, not so many months before.

'Closed, please.'

As they walked towards the staff car park, Salvatore and Didi met a very flustered Isabelle. Not having seen her since the encounter with Jan the previous evening, Didi was first in with an apology.

'Think nothing of it, Didi. It's not your fault that your sister is every bit as nasty as you painted her. How are *you* bearing up?'

'Better. We're on our way to the funeral home and the church. I'm hoping to play some music later.'

'That's a good idea. The more involvement you have, the better you'll feel afterwards. I remember.' Isabelle hesitated. 'I don't suppose anyone has seen Rico? I swung by *Stromboli*, but the chambermaids insist he has left. They kept repeating '*partito, partito*', enunciating louder with each reprise. That couldn't be, Salvatore? He's not due to leave until tomorrow.'

'I've no idea. I'm off-duty today. Would you like me to go and ask?'

'No, you're on your way out. Those silly girls must have got it wrong.'

'We'll have to go, Isabelle.'

'Sure. He's bound to be lurking somewhere. See you later.'

But Isabelle didn't feel as confident as she sounded. *Stromboli* had looked decidedly abandoned and, although Rico had a sparse collection of belongings, there was a difference between an apartment that was minimally bestrewn, and one that was cleared out.

She watched as what she now perceived as a new couple drove away in the little white Fiat. Happy as she was that Didi and Salvatore's relationship was blossoming, it only made her more determined to find Rico. What if he had decided to leave a day early? Preferring instead to be positive, Isabelle thought about his usual routines and decided to take a stroll towards the port, where frequently Rico rambled to the lone bar in search of his beloved *Repubblica* and his even more beloved morning coffee. Yes, that was where he would be, ensconced in some interesting article, watching the yachts come and go and probably on his second espresso by now.

Rico and Giovanni carried the suitcases, music scores and various bits and pieces to the new room in the hotel's main building. As hotel bedrooms went, it was spacious, but its pièce de résistance had to be the magnificent view across the bay, which although the same aspect as *Stromboli*, benefited advantageously from the elevated site that the third-floor room enjoyed.

'Thank you, Giovanni. I'm going down to the bar for a coffee. Will you join me?'

'No, thank you, Signor Parisi. I must hurry back to Reception. Signor Giorgio is in a very black mood today. If he caught me ….'

'I understand. Thanks for your help.'

'You're welcome!'

Breakfast was over in the restaurant, so Rico had to choose between a dejected-looking pain au chocolat and a toasted cheese sandwich which had made their way into the bar. Rejuvenated by the coffee, he broke the miserable-looking pastry into several pieces, marvelling at how its deflated appearance mimicked his own humour. He recognised the post-performance blues, but he couldn't help thinking that the low mood had also a lot to do with his reluctance to leave beautiful, seductive Sicily. In particular, the thought of saying goodbye to Isabelle bothered him. He hoped he wouldn't behave as he sometimes did when he found himself becoming fond of someone on tour – by avoiding the goodbyes completely. Still, it wasn't yet time for goodbye. He had told Tommaso eleven, so if he wanted to catch Isabelle, he'd better call by *Lipari* soon.

Leaving money on the bar counter, Rico crossed the terrace towards the villas.

But he had lingered too long over his soggy pain au chocolat. She had evidently gone out for the day. The shutters were closed, but their green slats had been left open. Through the gaps, Rico could distinguish scattered belongings and several dresses hanging from the curtain pole, signs, perhaps, of preliminary packing? Furious with himself for being so casual about planning their last day, he turned down the path to be greeted by the sound of Tommaso's car-horn outside *Stromboli*.

'*Morning, maestro! Ready to go?*'

'One minute, Tommaso. I have to collect some things from my room – my new room in the hotel. I don't live here anymore.'

He'd forgotten his phone, and he needed it to capture some flavour of Polizzi to show his mother, when he would visit Viareggio later in the week. Perhaps it was better he had missed Isabelle. Some things needed to be done alone.

Her walk to the port had been invigorating but not fruitful. Isabelle had ordered a *spremuta,* bought the local newspaper and chatted with the barman. No, he hadn't seen the maestro. He had been on since eight that morning and would have noticed him. Besides, he would have enjoyed dissecting with him the review of *Tosca* which was in *La Sicilia.* The barman turned to the appropriate page and tapped his finger insistently on the column. Isabelle opened her own copy and, as she struggled with the language, she could feel herself becoming emotional each time she read Rico's name. How had she let herself get to this point? The final day of her reinvigorating, obliterate-the-past holiday was about to conclude on a note of dissatisfaction. She had this overwhelming sense of incompletion. Misunderstandings needed clarification, but she had missed her opportunity to explain how she felt. Rico had obviously nothing further to say to her and had decided the most prudent course of action was to disappear ahead of schedule.

As she battled the strong easterly sea breeze on the trek up from the port, she reflected on how life's relationships were cyclical. It wasn't so much that the same relationships repeated themselves – although that happened too – but each partner in a new relationship often repeated the same behaviours, even though the twosome involved was different. Her relationship with Rico had reawakened feelings of frustration that she had experienced many times with Con. Yet her principal motivation in coming away to Sicily had been to steel herself against susceptibility to fickle emotions and, although the trip had succeeded in restoring her self-confidence, in the process she had allowed someone new in, thus rendering herself vulnerable all over again.

Was that the choice? Become cold, calculating and inaccessible to avoid hurt (and thereby cut yourself off from the enrichment that an honest exchange of feelings brings) or be open and trusting and let game-players take advantage and ruthlessly exploit this perceived naivety?

Then there was the serendipitous and unfortunate coincidence of Con's new in-laws turning up in the same hotel. Isabelle thought about Janice, and the attraction someone like her held for men. She could acknowledge Janice's very obvious charms, but she wondered why the men in her life couldn't see the manipulation. Didi recognised it. Isabelle had sensed it, even in those few short moments outside the church on their wedding day. As Didi had opened up more, she had reported that Pauline had even begun to recognise this side of her elder daughter's character which, despite tacitly supporting it as a strategy for 'getting your man', didn't make her like Janice any more for employing the tactic.

When Con had come knocking the previous evening, Isabelle had felt the old excitement flood back. She had been flattered by his compliments and, if she were brutally honest, the thought of wiping the smug expression from Janice's perky face was terribly appealing. She even believed him when he said he still loved her. She imagined that what he had with Janice was the accepted, external expression of a conventional relationship – in this case a marriage – but, because Con had failed to acknowledge that he craved a deeper engagement with someone than Janice could ever give him, he had created this *impasse* for himself. Where he had lost her sympathy was in the assumption that she would willingly supply the deep, meaningful emotions while he conformed to the status quo and continued to present his designer-wrapped marriage to the world.

Out of breath from the uphill walk, Isabelle turned into the hotel avenue under the unrelenting lunchtime sun. A sideways glance at Filicudi revealed the O'Rourke family – Con and Salvatore included – arranging lunch platters on the table of the shady front terrace. Now was not the time to seek out Didi; that would have to wait.

She pushed through the bougainvillea archway that led to the other villas, and was shocked to see two young blond boys cavorting about in swimsuits on the front veranda of *Stromboli*, as their mother, a tall Germanic-looking woman wearing a baseball cap backwards to protect her neck, was busy hanging out wet beach towels.

'*Hallo!*' The woman smiled.

'Eh, *hello.*'

With a very shaky hand, Isabelle turned the key in the door and escaped into the dim light of *Lipari*. It was all over. She had really done it now. Rico was gone.

Chapter 37

When they arrived in Polizzi, Tommaso had left him, claiming business with a distant relative in Gangi, a nearby town. Maybe it was because the pressures of *Tosca* were over, or some sort of a solution to his domestic difficulties had been agreed, but Rico felt more happily predisposed to explore the town this time round. He had brought with him the names and phone numbers of fellow Parisis in Polizzi that he had researched after his first visit, and thought he might ask the locals for help.

The Bar dello Sport in the central piazza looked a likely starting point, so he pushed through the multi-coloured beaded curtain into its inner sanctum. He was heartened by the age-profile of the drinkers. A group of elderly men sat around shot glasses of *grappa*, playing cards. The younger generation, a couple of sprightly sixty-year-olds, were rattling the table-football in a corner.

The barman acknowledged him.

'Good morning! What can I get you?'

Not wishing to mark himself out from the locals, Rico ordered a *grappa*, although it was very early.

'Tourist?'

'Sort of. My father was born and lived here until he was a teenager.'

'Ah! Welcome back, then! What was your dad's name?'

'Parisi. Giuseppe Mauro Parisi.'

'From which comune?'

'That's the thing. I don't know. But I have a list of all the other Parisis in the area.'

The barman took the page and frowned.

'This one is my cousin – she is from Gela originally, moved here about five years ago. *He* is an engineer, a northerner who came from Pistoia, outside Firenze. I'm sorry, the others I do not know. You should ask Antonino.' The barman pointed to a low-sized man with a cap. 'His family has lived here for three generations. He knows everyone.'

'Would you …?' Rico gestured to offer Antonino a drink, in the hope that he might make the introductions. As the barman filled his glass, Rico pulled out his wallet to pay, and thought of the family photos he carried permanently behind his identity card.

'Antonino says it's OK to chat with him,' said the barman. 'Go on – he's very nice.'

Rico introduced himself to the group of old men, and a

chair was dusted down and pushed in his direction.

'Thank you.'

Speaking slowly in Italian, Rico explained his quest, conscious that men that age probably only spoke *siciliano*. As he finished his tale, he placed the black-and-white wedding photograph of his mother and father on the worn wooden table.

The elderly group huddled around the picture, pointing, laughing and exchanging jokes in dialect, none of which Rico could follow.

Finally, one of the sixty-year-olds offered an explanation.

'They knew your father. He was in school with Fernando.' At this, the interpreter waved a hand in the direction of a grey-haired man with a curling moustache, who, acknowledging the introduction, raised his glass in Rico's direction.

'*To Peppe Trombettista!*'

'*Peppe Trombettista!*'

'*A toast!*'

To a man, the lunchtime drinkers in Bar dello Sport joined in the toast.

'*To Peppe!*'

Before the Italian-speaker deserted him, Rico had to ask one thing.

'*Excuse me*, but why on earth was my father called *Peppe Trombettista*?'

'Because he was always playing that infernal trumpet!'

'*What?* My father played the trumpet?'

The interpreter relayed Rico's ignorance to the group, who went off into more peals of laughter.

'Your father and his trumpet were famous. He won it eventually in a game of cards, right in this very bar, from the son of the house where he used to work shoeing horses up in Nociazzi.'

At this, Antonino shuffled forward and pulled up a chair nearer Rico. Muttering something at the interpreter, he became agitated.

'He wants to tell you the story.'

Thus, alternating between Antonino's Sicilian dialect version and the Italian translation, Rico listened to how his father had acquired his nickname.

'The young Peppe began working in the stables when he was ten. At first, he didn't earn any money but the signora used to give him food – vegetables, fruit – for which his mother was grateful. The master's son was a spoilt, only boy of the same age, who was forever receiving unwanted gifts or lessons to improve his skills at this or that. One day, the music master was sent for from Petralia, to teach the son the trumpet. Despite the teacher's best efforts, all the son could manage was a series of burping and whining noises, which sent the horses in the nearby stables into a frenzy. Peppe, not understanding what was making the strange noises, went to the house and tapped tentatively on the living-room window, where the lesson was taking place. The frustrated music teacher, in an attempt to humiliate his pupil, invited the boy to prove that even a stable-hand could get the hang of this instrument. Your father took the shiny new trumpet in his hands and, following the teacher's instructions, pursed his lips and blew gently, producing a pure and exquisite note on the first attempt. The teacher was so impressed, as was the young master, that every afternoon when the music lessons were taking place, Peppe was sneaked into the living-room and taught alongside the master's son.'

Rico was stunned. His father had learnt to play a musical instrument and never let anyone know about it! He was sure that not even his mother knew that her husband of forty-five years had been an accomplished trumpeter.

'And how did he end up owning the trumpet?'

The interpreter put the question to Antonino, who began to shake his head, with all sorts of negative implications in the shaking.

'This is when the story takes a bad turn. Peppe used to keep the trumpet in the stables to practise, presenting it on the day the teacher came. The young master had absolutely no interest in music, but because the mistress could hear wonderful sounds emanating from her drawing room, she insisted that he continue. Seeing no way out of his weekly torture, the son, by now fifteen, came to a monetary arrangement with Peppe whereby he would turn up and take the lessons, and once the signora could hear the sounds of joyous trumpet music, she believed her son was diligently studying away. Instead, the young tearaway was riding around the countryside, getting into bad company, betting and card-playing for money.'

At this, Antonino paused and indicated he needed a refill. The barman brought the bottle and waved away the note Rico offered him.

Enlivened by a gulp of *grappa*, Antonino continued.

'They were discovered. The young master went back to his lessons alone. Your father lost his job, much to the annoyance of his parents, who cursed him for learning anything as frivolous as a musical instrument. Somehow, all of Polizzi believed it was Peppe who had thought up the trickery to extract money from the gullible young master. Your grandfather arranged to move the family to the North, to escape the shame brought on them by his musician son. On the night before they left for Firenze, Peppe met the young master here, in this bar. The spoilt son, guilty that he had brought trouble upon his friend, placed the trumpet on the table between them, and shuffled a deck of cards. It shouldn't have been a contest, since the wild tearaway spent far too much time gambling, but your father won the trumpet on only the second hand. The following day, the Parisis left Polizzi forever, and no one who saw them go could confirm whether or not Peppe was carrying a trumpet-case.'

Antonino, tired from the storytelling, nodded at Rico, shook his hand, and resumed his place among his friends. Rico took a note from his wallet to tip the gentleman who had bridged the linguistic gulf between *siciliano* and Italian. Reclaiming his parents' wedding photograph from the table, he shook hands with all present and placed the half-empty grappa bottle between them.

'Salute!'
'To the son of Peppe Trombettista, salute!'

Back in Cefalù, in Room 405 with the superb sea view, Rico made a knot in his tie. Shortly, he would join his new friends in the Chiesa Santa Caterina at the memorial service for the dearly loved Pauline. He pursed his lips into a trumpet embouchure and studied his reflection in the mirror.

'Son of *Peppe Trombettista!*'

He had never had any inclination towards brass or woodwind. Once in Siena, a music teacher was convinced he had the lips of an excellent flautist. This afternoon's revelation suggested that some of his musical ability may have been inherited from his father, the father who he had hitherto perceived as an ill-educated labourer and conservative pen-pusher. Giuseppe's resentment of Rico's musical career began to make sense.

As he waited in Reception for a car to the church, Rico signed the card of condolence that he had bought earlier. Signor Giorgio, looking resplendent in a black suit, snow-white shirt and broad black tie, escorted the grieving daughter and her tall husband into his highly polished Alfa Romeo. On first glance, Didi's sister was so like their mother that it made Rico shudder. He thought of Pauline's mangled body on the roadside, of her cold limbs, elongated on the marble slab in the hospital morgue. When he looked a little closer, the neat little features of the older daughter were sharp, and her smile lacked the sincerity that Pauline's would have had.

'Let's go?' Federico, the beach man, was beckoning him towards a dusty-looking Fiat Punto.

Isabelle walked up Via Roma carrying a large spray of lilies. She proceeded slowly, as she did not want to arrive bathed in perspiration, since the only formal outfit she had was a long-sleeved black jacket.

Outside Santa Caterina, familiar faces from the hotel and beach stood in twos and threes, reluctant to enter. Some nodded a greeting, but nobody with whom Isabelle was particularly friendly had yet arrived. She knew it was strange bringing flowers to a church with no coffin, but she couldn't bear to think of Pauline's funeral casket taking the lonely motorway journey to the airport the following day without some floral adornment. Didi's mother had been a woman of excess – a lover of plenty, and although Isabelle had never been to her home, she imagined its tall vases overflowing with many varieties of flowers of a similar colour.

On the pedestrianised Corso Ruggero, Signor Giorgio had requested the on-duty policewoman to lower the bollards to allow his convoy of cars through. Isabelle was alerted to the arrival of the chief mourners by the scattering of shoppers farther up the street, as they ducked into doorways to allow them pass.

Feeling slightly frumpy in the badly cut jacket, Isabelle stood out like a beacon, her large contrasting white lilies in relief against the sombre outfit.

Con and Janice climbed out of Signor Giorgio's car, Giorgio fussing the waiting guests and staff out of their way. Janice had evidently had her hair freshly blow-dried and it bobbed around her shoulders in all its glossy splendour. Dressed immaculately in a short black skirt-suit, she adopted the Sicilian funeral tradition and did not dispense with her sunglasses, even as she entered the church. Con hovered, ill at ease, in beige chinos and a crumpled navy blazer which seemed uncharacteristically too large for him.

Once Giorgio gave the signal, guests and chambermaids, waiters and barmen, Mohammed the gardener and Vincenzo the driver – all the ancillary staff with whom Pauline would have had contact during her stay, filed into the church. Isabelle followed the slow-moving mourners and stopped halfway up the aisle, choosing a seat on the right-hand side.

Santa Caterina church was a curious mixture of baroque ornamentation and plainer taste from a different era. Looking around, Isabelle saw a lot of familiar local faces: some of the politicians who frequently drank on the hotel terrace, the chief of police with a uniformed officer. That awful old man with the trainers and the dyed-red hair, whom Rico called the Prowler. Even the man who drove the local bus had joined a couple of the chambermaids in a nearby seat.

Janice and Con were sitting in the front row. A clergyman had come to sympathise with them. Out of the side vestry, Salvatore emerged and Con signalled to him to join them. Still no Didi.

Cutting through the tense silence of the church, the stops of the large gallery organ wheezed into action and the confident playing of *'Jesu, Joy of Man's Desiring'* filled the air. Isabelle turned in her seat, to see Didi's long red locks undulate to the rhythm of the music. She's playing at her own mother's funeral – how brave! The prayers began, and the readings, some in English, delivered by Salvatore, Janice and a tour rep, and others in Italian read by Signor Giorgio and Luigi the barman, were punctuated by Didi's poignant playing.

Isabelle was no musical expert, but she thought Didi's pieces were more joyful than the standard funeral repertoire. In their execution, she never faltered. There were no missed notes or stumbled passages; this was a daughter's final performance in honour of her mother.

The short service over, the mourners began to shuffle out into the twilight. Isabelle brought her flowers to the funeral directors and explained she wanted them to travel with the hearse to the airport, to keep Pauline company on her last Sicilian journey.

Feeling subdued and very alone, she waited at the back of the church for Didi to come down from the organ loft.

As Janice and Con approached, she overcame the embarrassment she was feeling by complimenting them on the lovely service. Con looked awkward and, Isabelle thought, a little dishevelled, but offered her his hand and shook it warmly. Janice, sunglasses now doubling as a hairband, stared at Isabelle coldly.

'Yes, well, I suppose it's necessary to allow acquaintances pay their respects. Mother's *real* ceremony in Dublin will be a private affair, only for close family.'

Con interjected. 'Yes, but I'm sure if Isabelle is back home by then, she would like to come along – for Didi's sake, if nothing else.'

'I think Isabelle probably knows her place in all this, don't you think, Conor?' With that, the grief-stricken daughter left the church, her high-heeled shoes resounding on the tiled floor.

'Izzie. Sorry about that. Are you OK? You were very hard on me yesterday!'

'I'm fine. And I wasn't hard – just honest.'

Confused, Con leaned in to give her a peck on the cheek, just as a low-sized, dark-haired man materialised behind her.

'*Ciao, cara!* Here you are.'

Spinning out of Con's kiss, Isabelle threw her arms around Rico. 'Oh, Rico, thank God you're still here! I thought you'd left. I was so upset.'

'*Shhh! Calmati.* Do you think I'd go without saying goodbye? What sort of man do you think I am?'

Isabelle looked at Con's retreating back and thought: that sort of man.

'I couldn't find you anywhere. Then new people moved into *Stromboli*. Oh, Rico, I thought I had lost you – forever. No Rome address, no home numbers, no nothing.'

'Come! I think we should continue this conversation somewhere else.'

'I was just hoping for a few words with Didi.'

'She has already left. She is fine. I was up in the organ loft with her. Didn't she play well?'

'Yes. She was great.'

'Come on. Let's go back to the hotel, have something to eat. Besides, I have a surprise for you.'

'A pleasant one, I hope.'

'Of course. I think we could all do with cheering up.'

Isabelle linked her arm though Rico's and walked up the Corso in the direction of a taxi. As they reached Piazza Duomo, a familiar green Alfa Romeo passed them, a blond-haired Irishman peering incredulously through its back window.

Isabelle snuggled into Rico. The night was bright and everything in the room was clearly visible, even with only two small candles lit. The top-floor room allowed the privacy of curtainless panoramic windows. Below, early trawlers pushed out into the bay, the twinkling mast lamps tracking their movement like mini lighthouses. The terrace spotlights illuminated the late-night drinkers below, throwing distorted shadows onto the hotel's wall and silhouetting the many spectacular plants in a strange green glow.

'I feel *guilty* about all this self-indulgence. First the wonderful dinner and the champagne and now – *well*, making love like this. It's only a couple of hours since we were at a funeral service.'

'Don't. It's the most natural instinct in the world. Confronted with death, our immediate need is to reaffirm life. No human experience comes as close to both life and death as sexual intercourse. One minute you are pulsating, vibrant and alive – and the next, you are incapable of moving a muscle. The French do not call it *la petite mort* for nothing!'

'Please! Nothing French tonight. I don't want to ruin the wonderful ambience.'

'Sorry! I didn't think.'

'I'm only teasing. We can't ban all things Gallic because of Monique. Think of all the wines we'd have to forego – the cheese, the quiche —'

'I never had much time for quiche. Think of the music! Could I live without Debussy or Bizet or Gounod?'

'Probably not, but maybe concentrate on the Italians? Put *Tosca* back on.'

Rico got up from the bed and walked over to the room's sound system, hitting 'play' but skipping to a particular track.

'*È lucevan le stelle*,' the tenor sang.

In a giddy moment, Rico pulled a flower from the vase and, waving it as a baton, conducted himself as he sang

Cavaradossi's big aria, prancing naked around the candlelit suite. '*And the stars shone brightly,*' he translated, as he waved his arm at the music player. '*Isabella, sono inammorato di te!* You are my Tosca, my Mimi, my Juliet, my Beatrice! All the great loves of music and literature rolled into one!'

'And you, dear crazy Rico, are a foolish romantic without a bone of realism in your body!'

'This *is real*. What we have here and now, *is* real. And it will remain real, even when we are apart, because it's sincere. Neither time nor place can negate what we feel. What does it matter that you'll go back to Dublin and me to Rome? So what? Do you not bring me with you? When I go on to Viareggio, do you imagine I will not think of you, as I look out on the cruel sea that swallowed up that other great romantic of English poetry? Do you believe I am as fickle in my affections as the Conman?'

'Rico, I can't possibly answer that. I feel I have known you forever, and yet the truth is I know very little about you. Maybe the Conman – as you call him – started out like this as well. Most passionate love begins believing itself to be invincible.'

'What are you saying? That you do not believe I am in love with you? Notice, I deliberately say *"I am in love with you"*, not that *"I love you"*. Speakers of English debase this great emotion, by using the same verb to describe love of another, as to express feelings about – oh, I don't know, about football! "*I love football*", "*I love chips*", oh, and by the way, *"I love Isabelle"*.'

Propped on her elbow, Isabelle smiled at Rico's committed performance. 'I *do love* you, Rico, more than football, or chips, or anything. *And* I am quite in love with you and expect I will be for a very long time. Just don't place the burden of expectation on our feelings, because logistics are all against us. That doesn't mean that when I leave tomorrow, I will leave you behind. I couldn't, even if I tried. A part of you is now me, as I hope I am a part of you.'

Finally hearing what he wanted, Rico abandoned his floral-baton, and jumped back onto the bed, taking Isabelle in his arms. 'Every last minute is precious. Tomorrow, when we leave for the airport, we leave *together*.'

'Are you sure? Your flight's much later.'

'So? I go stand-by for an earlier one. I drink a lot of coffee. Once I have seen you away safely, what does it matter? What a practical little worrier you are, *amore!* Tommaso can take us both. I only have to call him to change the pick-up time. When do you need to be at Punta Raisi?'

'My flight is at two. I suppose about midday. If we leave here at ten-thirty, I should be fine.'

'Or even a little before. I'll ask him to come at ten fifteen.'

'It's a pity I'm flying home direct – otherwise, we could have shared the Rome journey.'

'Don't worry, *tesoro*, there will be many journeys in the future.'

Coming out of any other mouth, Isabelle would have scoffed at the promise. Yet when Rico pronounced it so authoritatively, his voice rich and sincere, she believed every syllable. As they settled to sleep on their last night in Sicily, she knew she would see him again. Where and when, she couldn't predict, but some things were too important to cast aside.

Chapter 38

Isabelle's packed suitcases stood to attention like soldiers on parade. She would be sad to leave *Lipari,* despite its idiosyncrasies. It had taken her the first week to realise that if she switched on the air-conditioning, the television *and* the bathroom light at the same time, the fuse would blow. Then there was the funny slope on the bathroom floor, that supplied the lucky guest with their own indoor pool, if the showerhead were pointing in a particular direction.

Newly arrived, tense and irritated by life in general, these things had infuriated her. But as she relaxed, she grew to understand that if she adapted her behaviour, the problems went away. Understanding *Lipari* became a metaphor for understanding life. You could continue to create problems for yourself by wanting everything 'just so', or you could modify your expectations and avoid the problem, by being less demanding.

The only problem she envisaged this departure morning was the difficulty she would have settling back into life at home and work at the agency. Dublin would seem dull after endless days of sunshine and drama in the land of the prickly pear. It had been a long stay – over a month in which she had achieved most of the aspirations she came to Sicily to fulfil. Her emotional growth was exponential and disproportionate to the time she had been away. It sounded clichéd, but a different Isabelle would fly into Dublin this evening.

Her choice of accommodation had contributed to this. A random selection from a hotel App had seen her pitch up at the Panoramico. It was a strange place – not just a hotel, more like a family, a community. Once you were sucked in, it was very hard to let go. Nowhere had this been more in evidence than at Pauline's memorial service. Isabelle was amazed by the cross-section of personnel who had turned up. Of course, there were those who – just like in Ireland – were present because they felt obliged to be. But the sight of the chambermaids, still in their pink uniforms and unflattering runners after a long day, made Isabelle feel theirs was a genuine expression of sympathy at the loss of a lovely lady. The elderly bus driver in a side pew, his blue shirt stained with the sweat of shuttling tourists back and forth from hotel to town all day long, had touched her. No one even knew the man's name, and yet for a month they had hopped on and off his bus, making small talk about the weather, the forest fires and anything else that was happening. He had come, because Pauline had been his passenger and her accident had happened on his route. Isabelle knew she would miss this sense of a small, close-knit community, back in the impersonal city.

She had arranged to meet Didi for breakfast, since the previous evening had been hijacked by Rico's romancing. She hoped Con and his awful wife were having room service. She really wasn't up to another run-in with Janice in front of her sister. The funeral party were booked on the late flight from Palermo, so Isabelle reckoned the airport was safe enough.

'Morning.' Isabelle, carrying her breakfast tray, approached Didi from behind. 'Sorry I'm late. Last-minute check that I'd cleared everything from the room.'

'Oh, hiya! Back to dear old Dublin then.'

'Hard to imagine, when you look out at this.' The two women stared silently at the vast expanse of blue. 'Still, I suppose we have sea at home as well.'

'The sea isn't everything.'

'You're thinking about Salvatore? Hard to leave him behind.'

'Yes. I'm thinking about Salvatore and my life. About the fact that I'm returning home – with no Pauline to shepherd or cajole through the journey. I don't even know what I'm going back to.'

'Have you definitely ruled out the teaching diploma?'

'Yes. I could defer by pleading emotional trauma, but I don't think I want their place, neither this year nor in the future.'

'What *do* you want to do?'

'Come back to Italy. You remember that guy, the festival organiser for *Tosca*? Well, I rang him and he's willing to see me in Rome, whenever I'm back.'

'Goodness! Things *are* moving fast.'

'Since Salvatore has resigned, he's going to Rome to find work. It would be nice to know that if I'm offered a job, I won't be alone without at least one good friend.'

'*What*? Salvatore has resigned?'

'Yes, over the Christoph thing. Apparently, Christoph's uncle is some big-wig on the board – shall we say – pressure was applied.'

'On Salvatore?'

'Yes. Jump or be dropped from a height. He took the autonomous route.'

'Well, I'm sorry to hear that. I'm disappointed in the hotel management.'

'That's the way things are here. It wasn't Giorgio's fault. He's been decent about references and everything, but he's also a paid employee. Otherwise, how are things with you? Your absence was noted last night – by *Conor* – of all people. He kept asking about a dark stranger, who I *knew* just had to be Rico. It nearly drove Jan berserk.'

'Well, following a distressing day in which I thought he was "gone" gone, he shimmied down from the organ loft where you had been keeping him captive – page-turning – I'm told? He treated me to a lovely last evening.'

'You were happy, so?'

'Happy doesn't do it justice!'

'Stop! TMI! Good luck to you. Whatever happens.'

'Didi, time is getting on and I want to see Salvatore and some of the staff. We're leaving from out front about ten fifteen, if you want to wave us off?'

'Oh, the royal plural all of a sudden?'

'Rico is travelling to Palermo with me.'

'He's smitten.'

'He's just catching his plane – a little early.'

'Oh, yeah?'

'See you later?'

'Sure.'

When Isabelle arrived at Reception to say goodbye to Salvatore, Rico was there, settling his bill.

'*Buongiorno. Tutt'a posto?*'

'Yes. And how is Signor Parisi this morning?'

'*Stupendo.*'

'Salvatore, Didi told me your news. I hope things go well in Rome. She has my Dublin address, so keep in touch, both of you. If you're over, I'd love to meet up.'

'*Certo*. And when I get settled in Rome, I'll message you.'

'Totò, *grazie mille*. Rico shook Salvatore's hand. 'It has been a wonderful stay, and I hope the Panoramico realises the gem they are losing.'

'Thanks, Maestro, but it was my decision. Sometimes,

you just have to move on.'

'*Capito.* I understand this very well.' Rico carried his smaller luggage through the revolving doors and came back for that controversial large trolley-bag. 'Are you good to go, Isabelle? Tommaso is always early. We should bring your things up from *Lipari*.'

'OK.'

Out front of *Stromboli*, the German lady and her sons laden down with goggles, flippers and all sorts of seafaring craft, were heading for the beach. She greeted Rico and Isabelle as they crossed on the path.

'*Eccoci. Arrivederci, Lipari!*'

'Don't. I'll cry.'

'*What?* You'll cry about leaving this poky apartment?'

'Yes. I get attached to places.'

'And what about to people?'

'Stop fishing.'

Taking her bags and hand luggage, Isabelle said goodbye to *Lipari* and followed Rico to the car park where Tommaso was waiting. The driver packed as much luggage as would fit into the boot and put the excess onto the passenger seat, strapped in.

'*Pronti? Andiamo?*'

'Nearly. I thought Didi was coming to see us off.'

'*Eccola!* And here's Salvatore – and, oh, your favourite person, the sister and her husband.'

Rico wasn't mistaken. Obviously waiting for a taxi, Con and Janice hovered at the top of the steps.

Didi ran to the car and embraced Isabelle.

'Rico, look after this one, get her safely on that plane back to Ireland.'

'Didi, take care of yourself. Maybe we'll see you in Rome?'

'Perhaps.'

Rico sat into the back of the car and Isabelle climbed in after him. She thought a civilised wave at Con and Janice wouldn't be out of place. She raised her hand, only to be startled by the sight of Con bounding down the marble steps, two at a time.

'Izzie, mind yourself! Safe home.' Leaning in through the open car door, he hugged her awkwardly, grasping her hand in an over-enthusiastic squeeze. Finally, relinquishing his grip, he pulled back and waved them off.

Tommaso reversed and the Peugeot disappeared down the hotel avenue.

'*Madonna! He* is a lot less cold than his little painted wife!'

'Who? Oh, Con, yes.'

'Are *all the men* in Ireland called Con?'

'No. Just a certain type.'

Rico, leaning back against the leather headrest, stretched out his arm and took Isabelle's near hand, caressing each individual finger lovingly. Reciprocating the affection, Isabelle leaned into his body, her right hand clenched tensely.

As the Peugeot joined the queue of cars at the entrance to the toll booth, the elderly driver engaged Rico in conversation. Isabelle, taking advantage of the distraction, opened her hand to reveal the object Con had placed in it.

The distinctive logo of *Paces Health Club* smiled up at her, with Con's name and title – *Personal Trainer* – embossed in silver beneath. There was a club number and a new mobile, but the whole thing felt too substantial for a business card. Turning it over, Isabelle realised why. Taped to the back, below a scribbled address, was a key. The handwritten message read: *'In case you change your mind.'*

Shoving the card into her pocket, Isabelle mused at how Con never really gave up. Despite everything she had said, he still held out hope of winning her round. *Never* would she give in to such unadulterated egotism.

'All right, *gioia*?' Rico gave her forehead a quick kiss.

'Yes, Rico, fine.' Smiling, she caressed Rico's arm with her free hand.

As Tommaso's car made a sudden acceleration to overtake a slow-moving coach, Isabelle closed her fingers firmly around the shiny key in her pocket.

After all, never was a very long time.

THE END

Printed in Great Britain
by Amazon